THE MASKED RIDER ARCHIVES
VOLUME 3

MASKED RIDER

ARCHIVES VOLUME 3

FEATURING

OUTLAWS OF THE MOCCASINS

AND

BRAND OF THE QUANAHY CLAN

BY GEORGE A. STARBIRD

PLUS

THE DEVIL'S HENCHMEN

BY WILLIAM H. STUEBER
& LINCOLN HOFFMAN

WITH AN INTRODUCTION BY
JAMES REASONER

ILLUSTRATIONS BY
MONROE EISENBERG

ALTUS PRESS • 2021

PUBLISHING HISTORY

"Introduction" copyright 2021 James Reasoner. All rights reserved.

"Outlaws of the Moccasins" originally appeared in the February 1936 issue of *The Masked Rider Western Magazine* (Volume 2, Number 3).

"Brand of the Quanahy Clan" originally appeared in the March 1936 issue of *The Masked Rider Western Magazine* (Volume 2, Number 4).

"The Devil's Henchmen" originally appeared in the April 1936 issue of *The Masked Rider Western Magazine* (Volume 3, Number 1).

TABLE OF

CONTENTS

JAMES REASONER

WHO WAS THAT masked man?
No, not that one. I'm talking about the other masked rider of the plains who starred in his own pulp magazine for 19 years (more or less), had a new lease on life with a series of paperback reprints in the Sixties and Seventies, and is still in print today with this series of volumes from Altus Press/Steeger Books reprinting his earliest, rarest adventures. I'm talking about the Masked Rider, of course.

Given the huge success of the Lone Ranger radio program that debuted in 1933, it's not surprising some enterprising pulp publisher, in this case Lincoln Hoffman of Ranger Publications, would try to cash in on that success by creating a similar character. When *The Masked Rider Western Magazine* published its first issue, cover dated April 1934, it featured a lead novel entitled "The Black Caballero" by Oscar Schisgall. The star of this novel is the Masked Rider, an outlaw who wears a black cloak and hood that completely conceals his identity as he roams about the West, battling villains and righting wrongs. You see, while the law may consider him an owlhoot (the "Robin Hood of Texas", he's called sometimes), he's actually a hero. With the help of his Indian companion Blue Hawk, he rides to the rescue of folks who are the victims of all sorts of criminals, never expects any rewards for his dangerous efforts, and when the job is over, the Masked Rider and Blue Hawk ride away to seek excitement somewhere else, answering the siren call of the frontier.

Given all that, it's certainly easy to see why the Masked Rider is considered to be an imitation of that other masked man. But there are some differences that make the Masked Rider a very interesting character in his own right. The Masked Rider has no origin story, although there are hints as to his beginnings in some of the stories, and while the other masked man occasionally uses a disguise of some sort, the Masked Rider spends a significant part of the time in most novels playing the role of drifting cowboy Wayne Morgan. "Playing the role" is important here. Oscar Schisgall strongly implies in the very first novel that there is no real cowpuncher named Wayne Morgan. That identity is as much a disguise as the cloak and hood. This is reminiscent of how, as The Shadow, Kent Allard sometimes adopted the identity of Lamont Cranston, a wealthy clubman/adventurer who actually existed in that fictional world. Wayne Morgan, though, is completely fictional (we assume) and exists only to hide the Masked Rider's true identity, which we never learn.

"The Black Caballero" is Schisgall's only Masked Rider novel. In the past, there's been speculation that it was published as a stand-alone Western novel before the pulp was even thought of. It appears that this isn't the case, since no copies of such a novel have ever surfaced, and the story's length, just under 30,000 words, would seem to indicate that it wasn't published separately. My feeling is that Lincoln Hoffman asked Schisgall to write the story for the first issue of Hoffman's new pulp magazine.

Following Schisgall, several other authors alternated

in penning the exploits of the Masked Rider, and each of them added more details to the character's background. William H. Stueber, who wrote the second and third novels, hints that, as a young man, the Masked Rider and/or his family suffered some sort of injustice at the hands of powerful criminals. Stueber implies that this is the reason the Masked Rider sets out on the quest to deliver justice to settlers across the frontier, even if he has to do so in ways that put him at odds with the established law.

Jay J. Kalez, author of the fourth novel, states that the Masked Rider was born somewhere in the wild country along the Texas-Mexico border. George A. Starbird, the next author in the rotation, specifies that the bounty on the Masked Rider's head is $15,000. Before that, we knew he was wanted by the law but didn't know what the amount of the reward was.

Lincoln Hoffman, the magazine's publisher, took a turn himself at writing the Masked Rider's adventures, using the name Orrin Hollmer (a name previously used by Stueber on one of his novels), and it's Hoffman who informs us for the first time that Blue Hawk is a Yaqui Indian. Before that, he was referred to vaguely as a "Mexican Indian." Hoffman also says that the bounty on the Masked Rider is $15,000 in *Texas*. There are other rewards for him in other states. It's pretty clear that the Masked Rider is regarded as quite a desperado.

The magazine was published on a very erratic schedule, indicating that it suffered chronic financial and distribution problems. The title was changed between the third and fourth issues, dropping *"The"* and becoming simply *Masked Rider Western Magazine*. Teetering on the brink of oblivion it may have been, but it clung stubbornly to existence. Conceived as an imitation of that other masked man, the Masked Rider in these early novels developed into an interesting character, sometimes coming across as an Old West version of The Shadow, displaying influences from Robin Hood and Zorro, as well, and starring in tales that often have a bizarre element and sometimes have the Masked Rider battling not only villains but also the sort of existential angst and emotional torment that you don't run across that often in Western pulps.

So who was that masked man?

That's perhaps the most intriguing thing about him. In the end, we just don't know.

THIS VOLUME LEADS off with "Outlaws of the Moccasins", George A. Starbird's second novel starring the Masked Rider, from the February 1936 issue of the magazine. Starbird previously wrote "Bad Men of the Cuyahogas", which appeared a year earlier in the February 1935 issue.

Starbird was born in San Jose, California, and graduated from Stanford University in 1932. With his sights set on a writing career, he had more help than most aspiring authors do. Bestselling novelist and newspaper columnist Kathleen Norris lived in the area and perhaps was a family friend. She bankrolled Starbird's move to New York, where he would be in the center of the pulp publishing business, and within a short time he began selling to various detective magazines, as well as a couple of short stories to *Boy's Life*. He sold a short story to *Masked Rider Western Magazine*, as well, and Lincoln Hoffman must have liked it, because he tapped Starbird to write some of the magazine's lead novels.

"Outlaws of the Moccasins" centers around the efforts by competing groups of villains to locate a fabulously valuable gold deposit. Starbird involves a pair of feuding families, a Romeo-and-Juliet romance, a sinister preacher who may or may not be a genuine man of the cloth, a lynch mob, and the Masked Rider and Blue Hawk, of course, who once again risk mortal danger to make sure the villains' plans are thwarted and deserving innocents are not only protected but also reap their rightful reward.

Starbird mentions the background that William Stueber established, the mystery of the Masked Rider's origins and the idea that he and/or his family were victimized by powerful criminals when he was a young man. It's a fast-moving tale with plenty of action. The Masked Rider appears only briefly in his Wayne Morgan identity in this one. Most of the time he's in his usual cloak and hood.

Starbird's third and final Masked Rider novel, "Brand of the Quanahy Clan", appeared the next month in the March 1936 issue of the magazine under Starbird's Val Masterson pseudonym. The reason for the pseudonym is unknown, but Starbird is one of only two authors to have Masked Rider novels appear back-to-back during the Ranger Publications run, William Stueber being the other.

"Brand of the Quanahy Clan" opens with an eerie, atmospheric scene which finds a horse wandering around in the night with a dead man on its back. The Masked Rider and Blue Hawk are drawn into this adventure when Blue Hawk is robbed and framed for a crime he didn't commit. In their efforts to clear the Yaqui's name, our intrepid pair are drawn into a plot with some similarities to the previous tale, including feuding families and a seemingly doomed romance. There's also a hunt for hidden loot and finally an epic, hand-to-hand battle between the Masked Rider and one of the villains, something of a rarity since most of the conflicts in this series involve gunplay.

This was Starbird's last appearance in *Masked Rider*

Western Magazine. Within a year, after another handful of stories in various Western and detective pulps, his writing career seems to have come to a close after not quite four years in the business. He returned to San Jose and went into the insurance business. He also became a civic leader and served as San Jose's mayor during the 1950s, building up such a reputation that when he passed away in 1994, he was remembered as one of the town's leading and most respected citizens.

William H. Stueber returned in the next issue with his final Masked Rider novel, and it was his last tale for a very good reason: he died while writing it. In an editorial in the March 1936 issue, either publisher Lincoln Hoffman or editor Maurice J. Philips wrote that Stueber's body was found in the cabin where he worked, with page 126 of the manuscript of his current novel still in the typewriter. That novel was "The Devil's Henchmen", completed by Lincoln Hoffman and published in the April 1936 issue. Hoffman's notes about Stueber in the March and April issues indicate that he suffered from health problems, but I don't know what they were, only that he died at the young age of 37.

The Masked Rider has a personal stake in this tale, as two of his old friends are murdered and a girl who once helped him escape from a posse is in danger. Stueber delves deeper into the Masked Rider's past in this tale than any of the previous novels have done and gives the reader more hints of an actual origin story for the character, without ever filling in all the details. The Masked Rider is also faced by as formidable a trio of villains as he's encountered so far and takes on one of them in another epic fistfight. All the showdowns in this novel are very good.

With their gloomy, Gothic overtones and brooding, angst-ridden hero, these early Masked Rider tales are

unlike anything you'll find in the other Western character pulps. They weave an eerie, immersive spell around the
reader, while still providing plenty of traditional Western
thrills. Give them a try, and you'll see what I mean.

OUTLAWS OF THE MOCCASINS

BY GEORGE A STARBIRD

CHAPTER I

THE CUFF

"**P**OR DIOS, SENOR,*" said the rider of the sorrel. "I do not think this *mulo* ahead will go far at this pace."

The noon-sun of the higher mountains was blistering hot. Its white rays cast a deep shadow on the face beneath the towering dark sombrero of the speaker. But that shadow did not obscure high cheekbones, a somber, bronze face—a Mexican's. A Mexican's—yet his upright seat, the quick meaningful flash of his black eyes, the heavily carved saddle and *tapaderos* that reached nearly to the ground would add words to that definition. His voice was guttural from a lifetime lived south of the border. In it not only Mexican, but Yaqui blood spoke in the accents of proud Aztec forbears. Such was Blue Hawk, true son of the southern border.

Behind him, a rider on a black stallion nodded, bent over and examined the spoor Blue Hawk had been watching.

The canyon in which the two riders rode was nearly a mile and a quarter wide, a huge gaping chasm gashed out of the green, tree-blanketed mountains about them.

In it the vegetation was sparse, the terrain sandy and rock-strewn. For the last ten minutes the two riders' trail had led along the edge of what, in ages past, had been a wide shallow river. Water had not run over the blistered

flat rocks and jagged culverts of the river bottom for time beyond man's advent.

Protected by the towering cliffs on either side, the gully was silent, sun-scorched, stifling. And now, to the man on the black stallion, the empty silence of the desert-like arroyo hung over it like an ominous and threatening cloud.

In the delineations of this rider and his mount, more than one man had read for himself quick alarm, even terror. Matching the stallion, the rider was dressed entirely in black. Boots, sombrero and saddle. From the saddle upward, a huge, all-enfolding cape covered his shoulders and torso completely. Above that, a black hood, marked

only by the twin slits of eye holes, disappeared beneath a cowman's black hat.

For some moments the two had followed the tracks of a burro and a man. Curiosity and a certain uneasiness had led them onward. The burro's tracks were deep and unevenly placed. Yet in them haste and precaution read as plainly as if the words were written in the sand bordering the trail.

Time and time again, that walking man had stopped, pulled his burro behind a jutting rock and paused, evidently examining the trail behind him. Then moved out into the open again, where the staggering burro had stumbled and fought its way onward.

For the first time in several minutes the man in the black cape spoke.

"He wasn't out of water, Hawk, because there's plenty up in the mountains," the hooded one said. "There's only one of two explanations left. He's either trying to get away from someone to save his belongings, or else he's got something on that burro he wants no one to find out about."

The Mexican shrugged and urged his sorrel forward. "*Si, senor.* If he is trying to get away, he would not use a burro that can scarcely walk. *Senor,* he went along here but a short time ago—maybe twenty minutes. And that burro, he is carrying—"

"Wait." The word was clipped out, cold with warning.

Blue Hawk's head flipped up and followed the outstretched arm of the masked man.

A brief exclamation burst from his lips.

To their right, a quarter of a mile away, the wall of the canyon rose a sheer thousand feet. On its lip a fringe of trees were limned against the sky. But what had caught the masked man's eye was a movement at the base of the cliff.

Two miniature figures, that of a man and a burro, were beginning to work their way up a shelf-like trail that wound up the cliff. As they watched, the man paused, pulled his burro out of sight behind a rock. For a moment, the man's head appeared and paused, examining the trail up which he had passed.

"*Senor,*" exclaimed the Mexican, "then he is not hurt as you first feared—"

A terse word from the other brought Blue Hawk's sentence to an end.

Another exclamation, filled with warning this time, broke from the Mexican's lips.

"*Amigo*, he does not see the other."

As he spoke the man and the burro left their place of hiding and began once more the laborious climb upward. Below, evidently hidden from the climber by the outcroppings of rock about the cliff's base, two more figures were visible. One was a bay pony and the other, silhouetted against the white rocks, a man with a rifle. Momentarily, the sun glinted on the barrel of the weapon as it was lifted and braced against the rocks behind which the man stood.

The man in the black cape drew in his breath with a quick inhalation. His hand jerked down and swept out one of the forty-fives hidden under the borders of his black cape.

"*Senor*, you can't shoot—"

"It'll warn him—give him time to get to cover," snapped the masked man.

The Mexican's hand flipped out in urgent warning. "No, *senor*, no! There is only one man we can see. There may be others here in the gully. Remember, the price on your head may be many times the value of that burro's pack!"

The eyes behind the hood were cold, glinting; the finger that had begun to tighten on the trigger paused. For a second, frozen to statue-stillness, the masked man and Blue Hawk watched and waited for the puff of smoke, the ominous explosion that would mean the end of the man climbing the cliff.

It did not come, for the ambusher brought down his rifle and slid out of sight. In another second he reappeared, leading the horse, heading for the base of the cliff and the trail there.

Unsuspecting, the man leading the burro continued upward.

"It's only a matter of minutes now," snapped the man in the hood. "He'll be able to shoot again and we haven't a chance of stopping that rifle shot riding up from behind. There's another trail going up the cliff behind us. We'll take that—"

Cat-like the great stallion wheeled.

"*Senor,* if there are others, they will shoot—"

The masked man did not answer.

THE BURRO PUFFED up the last remaining feet of the trail, past the few whitened boulders that graced the rim of the precipitous bluff. Behind it, the rock-ledge trail led, steeply angled, down the thousand foot sheer drop to the flat below.

The animal had gone perhaps a hundred paces from the lip of the bluff before the man plodding along before it grunted. With a half muffled snort the small animal halted, its bellow-like sides making the single rust-colored and battered kyack roll awkwardly, top-heavily. It was glad to rest.

Not so the man leading. He wore the tall, battered hat of a cowman. But his other clothing and the straw-colored beard that straggled across his shirt front and rose over his cheekbones in a thin blanket of curly hair were rather those of a prospector.

Nor did he wear the high-heeled boots and tight dungarees of a range rider. His shoes were hobnailed, heavy. A pair of worn bib overalls bagged sloppily down over the tops.

About the trail the heavy boles of tamarack pines lifted massive columns out of the brush and low growing manzanita. Through their hulks the man's dark, small eyes, half hidden in the overgrown brush of his beard and eyebrows, flitted nervously. Anxiety and alarm shot through them when nearby manzanita limbs moved sluggishly under a breath of midday breeze.

But in the passing seconds when no human or beast was visible through the trees, the man's shoulders relaxed and he walked quickly back towards the burro.

"Thought sure'n Hades someone would be up on the top here when we come up. Guess that movement we seen wasn't nothin' t' get surprised over." He slapped the burro a resounding thump on the rump. "Wall, Leana," he said, a little louder now, "we got it. Got plumb near a fortune in that there kyack and no one's the wiser yet. They'll go a plumb long ways afore they ketch Johnny R asleep. Come on, *Sue-e-e*, let's be travelin'."

In response to another loud whack on the hind-quarters, the burro did not move a hoof.

Johnny R—for that was the name he was known by in the cattle country—laughed shortly, hoarsely. He let the burro idle hip-shot while he fumbled in the bib pocket of his overalls and produced a small object. For a second he looked at it. When he put it back in its traveling place he grunted and slapped the burro once more.

"Every time," he said, half-wonderingly. "She'll pull 'er off north, by gosh!" He shook his head as the burro grunted and moved off with her load. "Every time." He was nodding his head now.

"Off north, by gosh!"

A HUNDRED YARDS away, beyond the point at which the up-rising trail slid up over the bluff lip and into tall trees, a man suddenly rose from brush and slid quickly forward. A dark sombrero was pulled well down over his forehead, yet it did not conceal, beneath its rim, the blue bandanna tied securely about the lower part of his face. His body was heavy-shouldered, bulky; about it a mottled cowhide vest fitted tight.

In spite of his high-heeled boots, he ran forward quietly, easily. As he did, the polished barrel of a revolver now held in his hand, glinted light. By the time he reached the meeting of the trail and the trees, Johnny R and his burro were no more than seventy-five yards away.

Then, with a grunt, the blue-masked man dropped to one knee. The revolver came up, cuddled momentarily in the crook of his left elbow. Above the sights suddenly appeared Johnny R's wavering, moving back. The kneeler pulled the trigger.

For a passing second the echo of the revolver's explosion rattled through surrounding woods, only to be absorbed by the thick brush. The burro snorted and shied off the trail, out of the way of Johnny R's dropping body.

By that time the masked man was running on pumping legs towards the fallen man. But he did not run fast enough to frighten the burro. The load on its back was far more important to him than the body in the trail.

He covered the seventy-five yards from the bluff lip to the burro, then slid to a stop, kneeled. His revolver moved downward. Abruptly, a noise, an alarming fearsome noise from the trees beyond the animal, stopped him. It was the quick hammer of hoofs, the high squeak of strained saddle leather.

The man in the blue bandanna flipped up his head, gave a startled, fearful curse. In another second he leaped to his feet, his gun rising instinctively. But it stopped. Surprise laid paralyzing fingers on him.

"The Masked Rider!"

He should have shot. Coming toward him, the black apparition and its hulking mount were a target as large as the pines around him. Yet he did not shoot. Before he had collected his senses, or his finger finished tightening about the trigger of his ready gun, the stallion was barely yards away—lunging to a stop on forelegs like great steel braces.

The black's reins were hooked over its saddle horn. Above two upright ears, the round ugly muzzles of twin .45s centered on the man standing in the trail. His own gun was still at hip height, its muzzle deflected. The ambusher swallowed clumsily. It was too late.

When the upright figure on the stallion spoke, the man before him lowered the gun.

"Drop it—in the trail," ordered a cold, metallic voice from within the unrevealing, flowing cloak.

The gun clanked against the hard-trod earth. From the twin slits in the hood, two hard, green lights moved now into the bandanna-covered face and told the owner of the face that he had acted wisely.

The stallion shied a little, side-stepped. Johnny R had stirred, then sat upright with a quick jerk. From beneath his bushy eyebrows a pair of bloodshot round eyes took in the cloaked form, the stallion, then the bandannaed face of the man above him. The eyes grew rounder. Fright and alarm wrote an instant message in them.

"Th'— Th' Rider!" he stammered through trembling lips. "Why—"

In another second Johnny R was on his feet. For seconds his frantic eyes stared at the cold mask beneath the black sombrero. The hidden face smiled with grim hard lips.

"Then he didn't get you," The Masked Rider said tersely.

Johnny R seemed to wake from his daze. Anger, suspicion shot into his eyes. A curse jerked out of him. With a quick move he wheeled on the man nearby whose face still was hidden in the blue bandanna.

"No, he didn't," Johnny R's hoarse, high-pitched voice snarled. "I was a-waitin', playing possum fer this rat. I was ready for most anything. So when he shot and missed, I dropped. If—"

Before the other could move, Johnny R's hand swept up, yanked at the blue cloth covering the other's features. The man jerked backward—but too late.

"Sam—*you!*" Johnny R's voice was strained, not human. "My God—after all I done for you, you try this!"

The Masked Rider surveyed the cruel, loose-lipped features no longer hidden. With quick movements he slid from the saddle, stooped, and flung the man's revolver into the brush.

Johnny R seemed to take new notice of him, for he wheeled again. His bearded face was frightened, lined with tight white markings.

"What d'you want?" he asked in his high strained voice. Backing away now, he moved closer to the burro, glanced reassuringly at the battered kyack on its back. Then he wheeled.

"You don't want me, Mister—Mister Masked Rider," he stammered. "I ain't got nuthin' here either. This sidewinder—after all I done fer him—wuz—" He stopped. "But he wuzn't huntin' fer anythin', mister. Jest let me go—"

ALL THIS TIME he had been backing away from the two men, grappling at the burro, jerking its head about in the trail.

"You don't want me—I'll keep away from you, mister. I won't tell anyone yer around here."

The man in the mask looked into the loose-lipped face near him. It was sullen; the brooding eyes watching his every move.

The cloaked figure shrugged. The voice that came from it was a drawl—a cowman's drawl.

"I don't want anything you have," said The Masked Rider. "Fact is, I figured for a minute he had killed you—maybe for whatever's in that kyack. Helpin' you out, that's all."

The figure near the Masked Rider spoke up.

"He's lyin'," he snapped angrily. "There's gold in that kyack—I know!"

"No there ain't—! I didn't steal it either!"

Johnny R was moving rapidly now, pulling the slouching burro back-trail towards the rim of the bluff and its whitened granite slabs.

"You keep away from me. Keep away, Sam!"

The man in the black cloak did not move. When Johnny R was fifteen yards from where the trail angled abruptly and dropped away into the steep descent, a cry behind him cut through him like a knife.

A long crying wail, the call of a mountain cat, sliced the air. It emanated from a point set back in the trail. Johnny R wheeled, let out a startled, incredulous oath. Suddenly, much nearer than the point he was focusing the manzanita brush parted. Through it appeared a white marked head, the walking form of the sorrel.

It was hidden by trees from the two other men. When the face of the rider appeared, Johnny R let out a yell of anguish. He brought his open palm down with thunderous force on the burro's haunches.

With that he wheeled, grabbed at its halter and bolted. In another second, too, the man in the mask had plunged forward. A cry of warning shot from his lips. Blue Hawk on the sorrel moved. But it was too late.

In wheeling, Johnny R misjudged the downward trail and his nearness to it. The burro, under the impact of the sudden blow, had lunged blindly forward. With a frightened whinny, the animal disappeared from sight over the edge. And as it did its shoulder caught Johnny R, shoving him before it.

The Masked Rider had left the ambusher behind in the trail. Silently the man spun his heavy body about and without casting another glance behind him plunged headlong into the sheltering cover of brush and manzanita. In a second it had covered him as completely as though a blanket had been pulled across his trail.

Now only two men remained where four had been.

THE MAN IN the mask pulled up at the edge of the chasm. Blue Hawk, who ran in moccasins, reached it nearly as quickly as he did.

There was a rattle and roar of stones below them. Nearby thunder shook the earth about them. A cloud of dust hid the sheer, almost perpendicular wall of the shelf and the moving bodies they knew should be within it.

The man in the mask wheeled. He knew that in leaving

his prisoner he stood a chance to lose him. But he had to risk that, now.

Far below them, rattling in fright and pain, they made out the voice of the bearded man.

"I can't hang on! I'm stuck here, but I'm a-slippin'!"

With a lightning-like move, Blue Hawk slid over the edge of the cliff, only to be stopped by the grip on his arm.

"Listen!" the man in the mask said.

The voice broke through the dust cloud again. "I'm a-goin'! You, up there! I stole that gold. Part of it belongs to th' Weldons—th' Weldons, y'hear? Tell 'em—! Not Sam—"

But they did not hear the rest. A puff of wind cleared the dust cloud nearest to them. Through it they made out the form of the burro caught in a jutting crevice of rock. It had fallen head first and with terrific force, then rolled outward and dangled, its fore-quarters jammed tightly in the niche. No second look was needed to see that its neck had been broken.

There, after plunging into space with the animal, Johnny R had evidently clung for fleeting seconds—and let loose.

The ancient kyack had broken open. And from it a small glittering stream, a yellow sparkling shower of sunbeams, spattered dully against the whitened rocks. Slowly, the nuggets dribbled one by one out of sight among the serrated seams of rock.

Beyond them another dust cloud shifted and opened, showing a sight that brought a curse from the masked man. It was a dark form tumbling, sliding, rolling limply down the rock face. The bearded man's body continued its descent, pausing now and then when it caught against the hard outjuttings.

For a long time—hours for the men on the lip of the cliff—the body flopped, caught on shelves, seemed to shiver and drop again into sun-lit distance.

Finally, far below them, but still outlined by the rocks, they saw the body stop falling and roll, twisted and awry, on the last stone at the bottom of the shelf.

As it did, from the trees that dotted the small, flat valley below, two figures disengaged themselves. Both were men on ponies and quickly they made their way across the dry-grass flat between the trees towards the distorted shape.

When the newcomers reached it, The Masked Rider turned to Blue Hawk.

"The other man," the Indian said slowly. "He is far away, far down trail by now."

The figure in the mask nodded his head slowly.

Blue Hawk turned, placed one foot in the sorrel's stirrup. "And this other—he had gold, *senor. Mucho.* Who was the man—"

Briefly, yet shrilly, the masked one whistled before he answered. The great black stallion downtrail shook its bridle irons and came forward at a slow lope.

"I don't know," said The Masked Rider slowly, "but as for the gold, you're right. Was it the *Weldons* he said?"

Blue Hawk nodded. *"Si, senor."*

The masked man shook his head. "That other—Sam couldn't be a Weldon."

Blue Hawk shook his head. "No. When this man fell, he cried that it did not belong to this Sam."

The two hooded eyes turned on the Indian, cold, meaningful. "If the gold was the Weldons', he'd stolen it. And this other *hombre* was after it. Our job is to tell the Weldons."

THE INDIAN TURNED, watched the masked figure mount.

"But, *senor*, who are they? Today we should travel far south—into Nevada, perhaps, too. If we do not go, *senor*, I think perhaps our fine sheriff friends in Montana will send word on by mountain eagle to stop you," he laughed briefly. "But no, *senor*. Many false crimes have been blamed against you—it is justice that false law cannot catch you. May it always be so. But still, we cannot wait to tell these—Weldons."

The man in the mask was silent. When the Indian spoke again, doubt was once more in his tones.

"There are many miles before us. We ride?"

The cloaked head shifted. "Over the mountain there is a town called Wild Vein. We'd better drop in, leave word with the sheriff there. We'll stop off first, Blue Hawk—but not for long."

"The sheriff, *senor*. Even without the mask he might recognize you. A short note dropped—"

But The Masked Rider did not seem to hear the cautious suggestion. As many times before, a duty had risen in the path of his ceaseless wanderings. A duty that for some might not demand performance, but for him, in spite of whatever dangers might lurk in recognition or capture, it remained—a duty. Tell the Weldons he must. It did not matter if word from Montana was flying on grapevine wings along his trail, offering a reward for him for a crime and still more crimes, none of which he had committed. There was a code—his code—a man had died with a request on his lips. To The Masked Rider a dying man's plea was a command—transcending death and danger.

CHAPTER II

DAN WELDON

THE SUN WAS well above the fringe of the mountain ridges the next morning as Dan Weldon mounted the last rise in the Moccasins and descended the rugged, winding trail in the direction of Wild Vein. Occasionally a high-pitched squeak off in the thick underbrush beside the trail told him that chipmunks and other early risers of the forest had begun their explorations of the cooler shadows.

Dew, however, still lay thick on the mountain grass and flipped from overhanging branches into his eyes. The steady *clump—clump* of his gray's hoofs, the rasp of his saddle gear resounded hollowly in the silent jack-pines as he rode. But neither of these sounds, nor the delicate fresh odor of yellow arnica flowers, lupin, and cedar made an impression on his senses.

He rode quietly, thoughtfully. Once he stopped, alighted to tighten the *cincha* of the gray in the manner of a man in a dream. When he mounted again and moved onward, his jaw was tight, his thin lips pressed hard together.

There was nothing particularly good-looking about Dan Weldon. Weather had stained his face the color of ripe walnuts. Yet youth and clean living had kept it without lines. His nose was pudgy, almost stubborn, which trait was counterbalanced by the easy, indulgent crinkles at the corners of his mouth.

He rode relaxed, laxily, in the manner of one born to the saddle. In his rawhide gloves his hands were knotted and calloused from the stinging friction of many a whale line, the tiring steely grip needed to keep an axe under control.

That's what he had been most of his life, he thought, a worker! And for that he was cursing himself at this moment. A worker and not a fighter. The hell!

Riding along, Dan Weldon skinned the sharp needles off a drooping jack pine limb, let them trickle slowly through his gloved knuckles.

Before Weldon, across a shallow valley, the roofs of Wild Vein made their appearance. When he saw them, he pulled the gray to a halt to survey the approaches to the town.

The light cowman's hat was shoved back from his forehead, revealing a mop of unruly blonde hair. As he looked, Weldon pressed his lips tighter together, reached for the battered, ancient .45 riding on his right hip. He gave the cylinder a quick roll with his thumb, made sure that there was a bullet in each of the chambers. When the revolver slipped back into its holster, he fumbled in the breast pocket of his hickory shirt, brought forth a grimy bit of paper. This he opened.

It was addressed to him and read:

Time does iron out plenty of rough spots in people's lives. For instance, the Rands and Weldons. It's about time we patch up—to my way of thinking. If you're ready to shake and be friends, so am I.

Abe Rand.

P.S. Drop in and see me tomorrow. There's certain business I'd like to talk over with you. Very important.

A.R.

Weldon returned the slip of paper to his breast pocket. A rider—a Rand man from Wild Vein—had dropped it off at the Open A.

A half-bitter curse crept up to Dan's lips. Hell, the message had come only last night and here he was, first thing in the morning, riding over to settle up. Why'd he come—so *pronto*, anyhow? If the Rands thought he was skittish—

But they wouldn't think he was afraid when he got through with them. In that past night Dan Weldon had lain long, thinking the thing out. Yes, he was a responsible man now. For over a dozen years the blood feud that had harassed and anguished the lives of the Rands and the Weldons had lain dormant. For all those years, stubble-bearded old Joey Ridder, who was practically his foster father, had argued, pleaded with him not to start the war going again. Refused to let him have a revolver when other young men wore them steadily on the trail. Taught him the law of the Good Book. That to turn the other cheek—

Rats! It was nonsense. For years Dan Weldon had been too soft. Joey Ridder had been a father to him. But there was a time when you came to know that life was hard, when you began to recognize duty before you.

The time had come to settle old debts. Abe Rand had led the riders the night of the last battle of the feud, had left behind him a trail of silent bloody shapes. Dan's mother, father and brothers. Only Rand blood could pay off. All through the night, Dan had battled with himself—unable to decide to go peacefully and meekly to see old Rand. Now he was on his way—with a .45 warm from handling. What the note meant or why Abe Rand had decided that quits should be called interested Dan Weldon not at all. He was sure Rand intended some deceit.

ONLY ONE MAIN street straggled through Wild Vein. Along its irregular sides a board walk fronted several of the buildings. Three saloons, a grocery store, a general merchandise establishment, a bank and the sheriff's office made up the busiest block. A harness shop, hotel and numerous straggling frame houses completed the town proper.

Dan Weldon's gray plopped into town and stirred up little spirals in the main lane. Dan rode up its length as far as the grocery store and walked the pony back. Only an occasional Indian squaw and a lolling puncher here and there inhabited the street. No one he knew.

A sign caught Weldon's eyes. He pulled up the pony. The sign read RAND GENERAL MERCHANDISE STORE, and the second story of the building was not a false-front as were those next to it, but had rooms for rent. Inside the store, beyond the half-darkened windows, Weldon watched a figure move and step out of the door. Weldon turned his pony's head and walked it for the hitch rack in front of the store.

Middle age showed little in the posture of the man who came out on the board walk facing Weldon. Hess Rand, son of old Abe Rand, held himself erect. His black beard was stiff, virile. Nor were his eyes true records of the years they had gazed with acrid humor on the world. They were black, snapping. At the age of forty-five, Hess Rand was as clean-limbed and clear-eyed as he had been at eighteen.

He did not smile or give any indication that he had recognized Weldon, but eyed the other steadily. Finally, he said:

"So you came in early. My daughter, Lorie, said you'd be here on the dot. Didn't figure she was right."

At the mention of the girl's name, Weldon's lips tightened.

He said: "I come to see your father."

"Shore," the other replied, "but this morning I'll do th' talking for him, Weldon. Come inside."

Weldon shook his head. "We'll do our confabbing outside, Rand. Right here is good enough."

There was a cold tone in the other voice that warned Rand of a tougher job before him than he had suspected. He smiled, grimly.

"This talk we're gonna have won't do out in the open." He glanced along the street. "Let's try the livery stable," he added tersely and stepped off down the walk.

Weldon followed the other towards the building labelled Callaghan's Livery Stable, tied his gray in a corral further down the street and walked back toward the high arched door of the place Rand had entered.

As Hess Rand walked towards the rear of the stable a mixed odor of paints, new hay, harnesses and horses assailed his nostrils. He sniffed thoughtfully.

For many hours the previous night he and his father had considered calling young Weldon to see them. Even now, he wondered at the ease with which they had evidently been willing to let bygones remain such.

The previous morning Abe had delivered into his hands the means, the sure clue to a fortune—in gold. A fortune that they knew should, by all rights be at least shared with the Weldon clan.

After consideration, Abe had sent a galloping messenger to the Weldon Open A. When they'd met Weldon, the course of future action should be determined. Either the feud would be forgotten and the fortune divided or the last remaining traces of the Weldon family would be wiped from the land. On the latter possibility Hess's mind was dwelling as he stepped into the interior gloom of the livery stable.

It was a hay-strewn, smelly interior, yet the odors to Rand were as familiar and enjoyable as the clean sweet scent of pine needles. A long lane of stalls lay before him. In them occasional horses' hind quarters moved, or a tail swished at non-existent flies.

Farther beyond, hay had been piled, a mounting shadowy stack in the corner of the barn. Beyond that the back door opened into a sort of shed in which various rigs and wagons were stored awaiting hiring or sale. At one time that shed had been a separate building; later it was joined to the livery stable. Its main and front door opened on a side street at right angles to the stable entrance, for it was a corner plot of ground.

Hess Rand passed down the line of stalls, passed the sweet-smelling mixed hay and stepped through the small door at the rear of the place into the wagon shed.

A header bed had been dismantled. The various parts and wheels hung or lay stacked around the walls. Two buck-boards completed the furnishings.

In the center of this disjointed setting Hess Rand turned and watched Weldon enter.

CHAPTER III

DEATH DRAWS A HAND

HE SAW A steady jaw, stubborn nose and light steely eyes that returned his gaze undauntedly. The Weldon's elbows were close to his side. The ugly butt of a .45 showed just below the right one. There was no doubt about it, the youngster was not being drawn blindly into a trap.

Rand swallowed. His first inclinations—to call the Weldon and force the issue—disappeared. He began walking towards the other, his hand coming up, a wide smile moving his bearded lips. If he was going to be straight-forward about calling quits, why not make a good job of it?

"I'll shake hands with you and get on," he said. "Abe's still in bed. Figger you probably'll want to be dustin' back to the Open A."

Weldon nodded, looked at the hand Rand extended and made no move.

Hess Rand flushed, lowered it. In another second his face was smiling once more.

"Wall, mebbe I can't expect you to take me literal first thing—on this letting bygones be bygones, Weldon. Don't blame you much, as a matter of fact. Wait, lemme talk for a minute," he shook off Weldon's interruption.

"It's been a long time since th' last of our troubles. That's one reason why we're willing—no—anxious to call off the whole affair. But that ain't the only reason. We're going into a partnership!"

For a second Dan Weldon let his eyes wander across the face of the man before him. Memories, half-forgotten pictures of Abe, the elder Rand, kept streaming across his mind. But the man standing before him, Hess Rand, did not resemble those pictures. There was something about his infectious and proud smile that dulled the sharpness of determination in Weldon. Still he did not relax.

"Meaning how?" he asked slowly.

Rand's voice rose. "Weldon, there ain't a reason in the

world why we shouldn't shake hands. We're rich. There's gold on your land—"

Hess paused momentarily, regarding the frown that passed over Weldon's face.

"You doubt it," he said quickly, "and I don't blame you. Look here. There used to be a ranch cook on the QR, the Ludlow spread, by the name of Johnny R. Queer sort, but always had plenty of money. Sometimes lots of it. No one could figger out where he got it. Couldn't have saved it up. I knew him well."

Rand looked up, studied Weldon's features carefully.

"Last night a rider brought Johnny R in. Fallen off a cliff and all but killed himself. Well, he had, in fact. By the time the rider got here, he was practically dead, unconscious. But he came to before he died. Asked for you, called out by name: 'Dan Weldon, come here!' Others tried to get him to tell them the message, but, no sir, he shoved them away. Wouldn't talk. Abe saw he was a-going to die any second so he waved everyone out of the room, even me. Then he said to Johnny R, 'I'm Dan Weldon, what can I do for you?' Johnny was so far gone by then he didn't know the difference. Abe found out where the money's been coming from—gold! In the Moccasins, on your land! Oh, I guess it got Johnny in the end, stealing off of you—and he wanted to confess. We're rich, boy! There's a fortune up in them hills and all we have to do is go after it!"

Weldon's cold blue eyes did not cease to study Rand's moving face.

"But Johnny didn't say exactly where it was," Rand continued. "Just gave Abe the clue and told him to go get it. Another thing, the Masked Rider's in the country. Johnny'd had a scrape with him. Gone over the cliff with his burro. But he never got as far as explaining any more. All of a sudden—Pop!—and he was gone."

Hess Rand slapped his thigh with a resounding crack. "I've got that clue all right. We're sticking with you Weldons on this deal, and you'll have to stick with us. You admit if Abe hadn't been there to take Johnny's message, you'd never heard anything. That's why our claim for a half-interest's legal—by God. From now on, no more feud. We're partners!"

Dan Weldon looked at the outstretched hand. His lips straightened in a tight line.

"There used to be six Rands," he said slowly, "and five Weldons. That was before the range war ended. I don't know whether you remember that last battle, Hess Rand, but your paw led your family over the mountains and into Open A land. No warning neither, Rand. And when you got through there was only me, my baby brother and Joey Ridder left. Joey took us south with him after that, for three years. When we come back, there wasn't no Open A left—cattle gone, fences down and our house burned. You remember that?"

For all his control Hess Rand could not help but wince inwardly at the bitter words. Truth it was, and painful.

"We came back," said Weldon, "to nothing. What we got out there now, didn't take a day or a year to grow and build. It took a hell of a lot of years, Rand, remember that. Not only that, there was always a chance, Hess Rand, that you'd come back. From what your paw'd said before this, I figured the feud ain't dead at all. That's why I'm back here. If this is the time to settle up, I'm willing. But you're talking about settling up because you ain't got a leg to stand on with your claim of half that gold, Hess Rand, and you're thicker'n I thought, if you figgered I'd fall for the story!"

Weldon took a step backward, steely eyes pinned to the other's face. His elbows were tight against his sides again, waiting.

RAND TIGHTENED HIS jaw. "Maybe you won't," he snapped. "Lissen to me, Weldon, we're ready to play square and back up our words. Man, we could have had all the Open A land we wanted when you left. Did we take it? No! Maybe you're too young to recall what the war started over. Abe Rand, my father, made a gold strike on your land years and years ago. That's what started the war—but the strike never turned out to be worth a cent, though the hard feeling did. Now we know the gold is there for sure—only we're going to you first, Weldon, and showing you the proposition. We don't want your Open A land. We got all the land and cattle we ever wanted—"

"By robbing and killing," said the other without hesitation.

Hess Rand's eyes bristled. For a second it seemed as though his temper would get the better of him. For this impudent young whippersnapper Weldon to talk back to him, to insult him openly was enough to— But he checked himself and took another, more potent tack.

"Your paw used to have plenty of money, didn't he? He used to buy guns and cattle and fancy dresses for your mother. And he never sold mor'n hundred head a year. Where'd he git all the money, do you know?"

Weldon's eyes did not relax, he made no move.

"From the bank," Rand snapped. "From the Wild Vein bank across the street there. And he owed an $8,000 first mortgage to that bank when he was killed. Well, eight years ago the Rands bought that bank and they've never said a thing about that mortgage. Don't worry, it's still good and binding, we took care of that. But did we want the Open A on foreclosure? Rats! The land itself wasn't worth a damn. But it is now, Weldon. *It is now!*"

Momentarily Dan Weldon's determination was shaken. It was true his father had always had plenty of money. And perfectly possible that he had mortgaged the Open A, borrowed from the bank. Besides, Rand had little reason to lie; he, Weldon, could call for the mortgage any time he wanted. But—

Hess Rand broke into his thoughts again. "We could foreclose right now, Weldon, and get all this gold land I been talking about, without spending a red dime on lawyers' fees. Only we ain't gonna do it—we want to end the feud. This is our way of helping it along!"

There was a moment of silence. The hard lines in Weldon's face slowly relaxed, he spoke easily, quickly.

"I have a kid brother. No reason he should ever get mixed up in this feud. Lord, he doesn't even remember it. If that mortgage is legal, I'm willing to talk turkey with you, Rand. Only—"

Hess Rand raised his eyes. Weldon's mouth was suddenly bitter once more.

"Only what?"

Dan Weldon spoke out. There was a terse note in his voice, a note that seldom sounded there.

"Let's see that sure-fire clue, Rand."

For a passing second their eyes met, clashed. Over the even lines of Hess Rand's face a dull flush rose, spread. His hand came up, rubbed along one darkly stubbled cheek.

The sound of Weldon's voice caught his thoughts up

short. It was true that he had to show the meager evidence in his pocket to complete the partnership deal. An inner voice cautioned him to slow up, proceed with care.

Entire honesty and straightforwardness had never been part of Hess Rand's make-up—nor his father's.

He slapped his hand to his pant's pocket, let a look of amazement break across his features. "By God," he stammered into Weldon's face, "when I come down here I forgot to put it in my pocket. Left it up in the house when I dressed. Holy Smoke—"

He looked up at Dan Weldon's stubborn face. A curious struggle seemed to be going on there. The eyes were hard set, the mouth tightening.

Hess Rand grunted. "We'll go on up to th' house. Sorry, boy, I missed bringing it down. Anyhow—"

He broke off short. At the last moment his decision to open his hand to the Weldon had been blanketed by wariness. What if the Weldon saw the evidence, called his hand, shot him down and galloped off with it? Nothing in the world would save the gold then. Old Abe's and his entire claim rested on his possession of the clue to the caché. Without it, or dividing the knowledge with another, left them unarmed. And with a Weldon, that might well be committing a form of suicide.

SO HESS RAND stalled. If he got Weldon up to the house, he would be backed by Abe. Then Weldon wouldn't dare—

In Dan Weldon wonderment at the queer antics of the bearded man before him was turned to alert distrust. Hess Rand was stalling. His first words had carried the implication that the clue to the gold was on his person. Now, in an about-face, Hess Rand denied that fact. It looked like a trap. The more he thought about it, the surer Weldon was.

Weldon's hand drifted down to the .45 he had holstered. He moved back towards a buckboard. Determination shown in his blue eyes, in the straight line of his lean lips.

"Rand," he grated, "you're a damn liar. This caché story is part of a trap—what kind, I don't know. You're a fast thinker and a slick skin by reputation, Rand. Mebbe holding you up done blocked your trap. Remember this, I come here in a fairly open mind to end the feud. Indian talk don't do that. I'm not a damn fool enough to call your hand now, with a hundred of your men around here. I'm dusting. But the next time we meet, it'll be a hell of a lot different!"

Weldon stepped around Rand, walked straight toward the tall, barred doors of the shed, never for a moment considering the hand that Hess Rand was easing towards his gun.

At the doors, Weldon paused, laid his weight behind one arm and swung up the heavy, six-foot iron bar that held it. The big frame moved open, allowing a full view of one of Wild Vein's back streets. Weldon strode out into the street, let the big door swing shut of its own accord.

He did not look behind as he passed several men moving in the street, but went straight towards the corral where the gray was lolling hip-shot under a willow tree. He slid into the battered hull and left the corral.

If no one in the street paid more than passing attention to Weldon, there was one person elsewhere whose eyes were pinned on him as he left the stable.

She stood behind the windows of the Rand Merchandise store, erect, lithe, youthful. When she saw Weldon mount his pony, her dark eyes clouded, a slight flush suffusing the tanned smoothness of her cheeks.

Lorie Rand, daughter of Hess Rand, knew by Weldon's

lone appearance that for some reason the talk between the two had not borne fruit. But that situation alone would not have caused her to flush....

The Rands and Weldons had fought for many years. But during a hiatus in which she had grown to womanhood, the feud had lain dormant. In spite of this, she had heard her father and grandfather discuss the Weldons many times, often in violent and angry terms.

It was under these circumstances that she became aware of the existence of the last of the Weldons, Dan and Bucky.

She knew her grandfather had led that blood-stained group of Rands away from the Open A after the last great battle of the feud. On his hands and on those of her father, too, were the life blood of Weldon's father, mother and brothers. How different had his youth been from hers— no father, no mother, no one to love him—and only the Rands responsible for it.

Yet never, as long as she could remember, had word come to her that Dan Weldon was ready and seeking to avenge their deaths. Tuned to the hard-bitten environment about her, she did not need to be told the part that vengeance played in the emotions of the men of the range, even in her father's and grandfather's.

Curiously, then, admiration had attracted her toward Weldon. Though he was not aware of her, she watched him closely, listened to him speak when he traded in Wild Vein or rode in to range parties with the rest of the countryside.

In this way she found he was hard-fisted and hard-bitten as any of the riders of the range. But withal he never spoke of hate for the Rands. Yet somewhere underneath, buried deep, she realized the raw wounds must lay unhealed. It was not human nature to forget them entirely. But Dan Weldon had done what none of those about him could have done—conquered the desire to kill, to avenge. Thereby, in her eyes, he had strengthened his courage a thousandfold.

It was thus that though unconscious of this admiration, she grew to watch for Dan Weldon's infrequent visits to Wild Vein, and when he did appear she followed his actions closely, studied behind the stern outer shell with which he faced the world, the facets of his nature that drew her towards him.

Now, as Weldon's straight square shoulders jogged out of sight of the Rand Store, a tinge of regret touched her inwardly. Affection and admiration grew to life within her. Weldon was riding away, which meant that for some reason, her father's decision to call off the feud had not materialized.

Under the circumstances, she might now never be able to speak to Weldon, to laugh with him, or to call him by name. As she turned away from the window, Lorie Rand's eyes were more clouded than ever....

BACK IN THE wagon shed, Hess Rand watched Weldon's frame disappear through the big door. He gave a slight shrug, an oath that might have meant anything.

For a second he stared at the double shafts of sunlight streaming past the panel to the musty, feather-scattered dirt on the shed floor. Then he reached into his pocket, brought out an object, regarded it in his open palm.

It was a piece of rock an inch square. A curiosity it might have been in geological circles. But to Hess, it was only that—a chunk of stone. For a second he examined the strange black sheen of its surface, the regular glittering strands of either mica or iron shot through it.

In a sense he had misled Weldon. This piece of stone

was only a clue to Johnny R's caché. No word as to how it should be used had been given Abe. And only the statement of a dying prospector who might well have been crazy claimed that it led to a fortune. Yes, Johnny R had told Abe that: "a fortune...."

Hess Rand shrugged his shoulders, pocketed the rock. Maybe he had been right in holding off the final evidence from Weldon. In any case, he'd talk to his father about it, get his reactions.

He stepped towards the smaller door that led into the livery stable proper.

As he did, a figure who had been listening to the conversation disengaged itself from the tall stack of hay in one rear corner not eight feet from him. On plunging silent legs it rushed at the appearing form of Hess Rand. Five feet away the figure leaped, raised its arms. In its hand a jagged, broken collar-hame whistled through the air, descending with a bone-crushing blow alongside Hess Rand's head.

Without a word, without even a murmur of agony, Rand dropped heavily in his tracks, slid awkwardly, limply back into the wagon shed.

The figure followed him, bounded animal-like towards the object in Rand's hand that the man believed led to a fortune.

A second later, the figure rose, started towards the door leading into the deserted livery stable. The man paused, stared puzzled at the rock he now held. Suddenly, then, it dawned on him that without explanation, the rock might mean little.

The figure wheeled as though a shot had been fired behind him. On the floor of the shed, Hess Rand rolled over heavily, opened his eyes. A muffled, painful grunt of astonishment burst from his bearded lips. His elbows moved, he struggled to rise.

In another second the figure was on him. Rand's murmur had meant but one thing—recognition. In the figure's hand a long-bladed hunting knife glinted the morning rays seeping past the tall door. With a tremendous heaving blow, the man brought the knife down and sank it hilt deep, square into the broad chest of the still half-dazed Rand.

Hess Rand dropped back, dead.

CHAPTER IV

JUDGE LYNCH

BEFORE HE HAD reached the end of town, the sign of The Dollar Bill caught Weldon's eye, stopped him. Momentarily his mind played with the idea that Hess Rand might, in a fit of rage, gather his henchmen and lead them out after him. But he let that thought pass. Hess Rand was not so crude a worker as that. One thing could be attributed to him. He did not deal in hired murder or robbery. If he had troubles, they were usually settled by either himself or Abe, his father, alone.

With a shrug, Weldon turned the gray in to The Dollar Bill hitch rack and alighted. In this morning's happenings, a new responsibility seemed to have been thrust upon him. The blood feud had again been taken up. From now on there would be regular practice with the battered .45. Eventually—

In the manner of his hard-bitten environment, Weldon's method of celebrating the coming of a new responsibility, was in taking a drink.

He flipped his pony's reins over its head, let them drag in the dust before the saloon. With a quick, easy step and without glancing behind him, Dan Weldon entered the flapping doors of The Dollar Bill. Inside, the first morning idlers inspected him disinterestedly.

Weldon ordered, snapped off a pony of whiskey. He eyed the sloppy, fat shape of Bill Tolman in charge of The Dollar Bill. Inwardly, Weldon felt the glow that whiskey imparted to expectations of battle. The Weldon-Rand feud had once more come to a head. The long years of suspense, of nervous waiting, were over. Weldon ordered another drink.

Now he was aware of a rumble of voices growing in the street outside, the rumble of running feet. He passed them off as the morning noises of the town coming to life.

When a full dozen boot heels crashed suddenly on the board walk before The Dollar Bill, Weldon wheeled about. Tolman, the bartender, faced the door, too. In another second, the flapping panels burst open under the impact of a massed group of eight or nine bodies. A man with a stubbled beard, a glittering Colt .45 in either hand preceded them. Weldon saw, too, that the men behind him were armed. Something in their faces—

More men swarmed in through the doors then, shouting, gesticulating, pointing at something near the bar of The Dollar Bill. By then he realized that the men meant him, and that they were coming for him....

Too late Weldon snapped for his gun. A red-headed, bucktoothed cowboy pressed a revolver like a ram-rod into Dan Weldon's breast bone. Two others were holding his elbows, gripping his wrists behind him. The battered .45

on his thigh was yanked from its holster. He was pushed, pulled, tossed outside.

On the board walk in front of the saloon, Weldon had a chance to scan the faces about him. They were silent, grim-lipped. Somebody was uncoiling a rope.

A chill runner of alarm shot up Weldon's backbone, though not more than twenty men were in the crowd that jostled before The Dollar Bill.

Someone yelled, "Dead Man's Tree!"

That was all. Like a wave the men in front of Weldon parted. He was pushed through them, across the street, down past the jail and beyond the few houses that fringed Wild Vein.

"What th' hell you after?" he snapped at the bucktoothed cowhand before him. He knew the question was foolish, but he sparred only for time to collect his wits. The surprise attack had scattered them.

A hoarse, mirthless laugh from the puncher greeted him; it was reechoed by other men nearby. Someone had produced a small bit of whale line and was rapidly and effectively binding Weldon's wrists.

There was a stir among the grim-jawed men. They parted to allow the entrance of a tall man whose day's growth of beard bristled in the morning light. The gorge of young Weldon rose.

Sam Ludlow was bull-necked, gross-bodied. His eyes were cold, protruding. Bad living was written large on him. But in spite of his dissipation, he was still one to fear, for he was a dead shot and had no scruples about taking human life. Most men, even in this hard country, would walk a long way around Ludlow rather than risk an ugly mood in him.

He strode forward, a pair of rock-like fists gripped at his sides as big as small hams.

"There's Ludlow, he'll do the talking," someone snapped.

"Okay, Sam," the redhead said and stepped aside.

Ludlow stopped before the youth, spread his legs apart. "Hess Rand usually did his work himself, but I figger he'd want us to carry on for him now. Who's got the line?"

"Here," boomed a voice at Dan's left.

A LOOP SWISHED out of the crowd and settled in a cold and merciless circle about Weldon's neck.

Dan's voice, for minutes powerless to move, suddenly stirred. It popped off his lips almost involuntarily.

"Listen, Sam, what're you in on this for? You damn fool—you got the wrong man—for somethin' I don't know about!"

"Shut up," snapped Ludlow. "What're we doin'? It won't take long to sink in!" He wheeled, pointed toward the trees. "Y'see that fir tree, boys? That's Dead Man's tree. I say if you've got an unpleasant duty to do, best thing is get it over with. Bring him this way."

"Wait—you empty-headed jackasses! Who's makin' fools of you?" Weldon shouted. He yanked back on the arms that began to pull him, dug his heels into the ground and stopped them. As he did, the noose about his neck tightened. The men yanking at him stopped, waited for an order from Ludlow.

For a second Weldon was silent. The faces banked in the woods around him were like a sea of cold masks. Occasional angry murmurs ran through them like waves and died away. Above the dark bobbing heads one or two fists rose; shouts of hoarse anger impinged against Weldon's whirling senses.

"What're you aiming to do?" he shot at Ludlow.

The loose-lipped one nodded. "Lynch you. Right from that limb over there. When the law don't act the way we like it around here, we people take it in our hands. Wait for a jury to haggle over you for three months? Hell, no! For killers like you there's only one answer!" He moved closer, thrust a stubbled, lined face mere inches from Weldon's. "Lynching!"

Prodding, angry bodies pressed against Weldon. The faces about him swam in a mottled blaze of colors. The buildings beyond the trees seemed to weave unsteadily. He tried to press back against the bodies, stop them, but they were inexorable, unheeding. Weldon turned his face from Ludlow to the others.

"You men are damn cock-sure you're right?" he shouted. "Have you got a couple minutes to spare to listen to me? Maybe it ain't right to hang a man like this; have you stopped to think about that? I've a right to say something. I've a right to know why you're doing this, ain't I?"

Ludlow wheeled, an oath on his lips. Again the moving, shoving bodies about Weldon paused.

"Listen to you?" he snarled. "Did you listen to Hess Rand before you killed him? No, you didn't!"

Weldon suddenly became conscious that there was a girl elbowing her way to Ludlow's shoulder. How she had gotten so near, without his seeing her before, he could not understand. Something about her face should have caught his eyes.

She was not tall, her head coming only to the height of Ludlow's heavy shoulders. Her long hair, for she wore no hat, was raven black and moving in the wind. She was dressed in a full riding skirt that accentuated her lithe slimness. But it was her face that magnetized Weldon's eyes. It was high-cheeked, with skin of clear olive smoothness. Dark pools of eyes gazed full into Weldon's features, never wavering, never displaying the slightest hint that the man on whom she gazed was about to die.

It was Hess Rand's daughter. How old she might be he had never wondered. Now she stood before him, about to watch him die, her gaze cold, unimpassioned.

"I didn't kill anyone," he said, talking to her suddenly. "They're sayin' Hess Rand is dead—but I didn't know anything about it till right now. I—"

The eyes continued their steady gaze. Ludlow thrust his rugged shape forward, cutting off Weldon's words.

"Don't talk to her. Even a murdering rat like you ought to know better. I'll tell you why we're doing this. You killed Hess Rand. If we don't hang you for it, old Abe Rand will never wait for a jury to do it. He'll shoot you himself. But side-winders like you don't deserve even that. You hang!"

Weldon's mouth opened. He had started to appeal to the girl again. Grasping for straws, he hoped that from her, time, time to tell his story, to get the frenzied minds about him to listen, could be gained. But the expression in her face remained the same. The eyes continued to stare at him, yet seemed not to see him....

Rough hands began to push him again, hurry him forward.

There was another disturbance in the ranks of faces. Like parting waters they moved and from them materialized a lanky, raw-boned shape that came in long strides towards Sam Ludlow. Within Weldon a spark began to glow. On the breast of the lanky man glittered a five pointed sheriff's star.

Weldon had seen Mark Broderick, the sheriff, before; knew him to speak to. With his every step the glow of relief within Dan Weldon grew stronger. His eyes burned on the sheriff.

"Being sheriff in these parts, Ludlow," Broderick said, "I come to claim this prisoner. You going to hand him over without trouble?"

Ludlow's big body moved forward, placed itself between the sheriff and Weldon.

"No, Broderick, we ain't," he said slowly. "The law ain't quick enough to satisfy Wild Vein. And when it ain't, it's time we wake up. He's gotta die—right away."

"Ask him why," Weldon's voice cut in, "why he worked these men up to this. It's personal." The youth's voice rose. "Trouble we've been having on the Open A that he's getting even for!"

Ludlow wheeled as though he'd been hit. "Sheriff, that's a damn lie!"

Broderick looked at the faces about him, then at Weldon. His duty was plain and he was willing to go any reasonable length to perform it. But in the angry glances, the determined faces that surrounded him, there was little hope of assistance. He hesitated perceptibly. The spark of light in Weldon went out.

"Sheriff, you haven't got the right to let them do this to me. It ain't the law in any language. Why are they lynching me? They ain't proved a thing!"

Broderick rubbed his lean jaw, silent. Ludlow wheeled, shoved his face close to Weldon's.

"Why? You killed Hess Rand. But worse than that, you

knocked him out, then killed him, before he even got a chanct to draw his gun. How do we know it? You were the last man seen with him. He went into Callaghan's Livery Stable this morning. A little later *you* come out the back alone. Leaving Rand behind with a knife in him. Is that enough reason to lynch him?"

The last was addressed to the men pressed in close to Ludlow. An angry roar that had only one meaning answered him. Weldon gulped, strained vainly at his bonds.

"But I couldn't have," he blurted in a high-pitched voice. "It wouldn't stand to reason. If I killed him, why wouldn't I try to run away? Did I? No, because when I left him, he was alive. I swear it!"

Broderick moved closer to him, "The prisoner is entitled to legal defense. That's the law. And I'm here to uphold it. Ludlow, surrender this prisoner!"

A hoarse undertone of voices greeted this. Weldon saw hands beginning to move down to ready six-shooters, saw men's bodies begin to crowd in closer to the sheriff, surrounding him, shouldering him back into the street, away from Weldon and Ludlow.

Again, as before, the faces swam before the youth. Through them the calm, erect head of the Rand girl seemed to move apart.

Little white seams appeared on Broderick's weathered visage. He gritted his jaw, eyed the angry features near him. That he was fighting a losing battle was evident. Indeed, it was too late for resistance. They already had Weldon. They were determined to hang the man now, to go to any extreme.

And he was aware of another thing, that if he did get the prisoner away from the mob, his chances of keeping him safe in the nearby rickety jail of Wild Vein were slim. Sooner or later, Weldon would die. The manner of his going, its importance to the sheriff's sense of duty, were his reasons for trying to stop the lynching. That Weldon had killed Rand seemed pretty evident.

Broderick allowed the shoving, intruding bodies to shoulder him away from the prisoner, almost to the outskirts of the throng. From there he watched with squinting angry eyes while other men grappled at Weldon's shape, hurried it towards the fir Ludlow had indicated. It stood on a knoll somewhat apart from other trees.

The sheriff began to drift with the men towards it. They paid little attention to him. By the time he shouldered his way to the tree, the long length of whale line had been tossed over the limb.

A rider had half-hitched its other end around his saddlehorn. His pony stirred, drawing the noose tight about Weldon's throat. Just enough to cut off the youth's breath.

Beads of perspiration broke out on Dan Weldon's forehead. He clenched his fists, stopped his breath from sucking in too rapidly after the noose slackened. All the sure youth within him protested against his fate. It couldn't be true. There must be some way out. Men did not kill another human on as slim a pretext.... Never again would he look on the round, shining face of Bucky. Nor watch Joey Ridder swinging out of the barn and approaching the house, his long white walrus-mustaches moving in the wind. No, no! There was some way....

Ludlow turned from a low voiced conversation with other men and moved closer to him.

"Mebbe," his blood-shot, bulging eyes were glinting

half-triumphantly, "mebbe, Weldon, you'd like to confess now."

Dan Weldon shook his head, kept back burning, useless words that might reveal the state of his emotions to Ludlow.

He said softly, "There's nothing to confess."

Ludlow shifted his body. "All right, Rouse, pull her tight!"

Dan Weldon braced his body as best he could. Before him the sea of angry red faces merged in a blurred haze. The noose around his neck moved tight.

CHAPTER V

SAM LUDLOW

A ROAR FROM twenty throats swelled up, clamored in Weldon's ears. A length of riata that had been passed over the limb above him suddenly looped down loose in his face.

Ludlow, who had stepped back, came forward now on striding, angry legs.

"Stop!" he shouted. "What th' hell now?"

He wheeled on the men who had turned away from Weldon. At the edge of the small crowd nearest Wild Vein a Mexican Indian in a peaked sombrero was standing, his arm thrust out, pointing accusingly at someone in the crowd.

When Weldon could see him better, the native seemed to be weaving on his feet, seemingly on the verge of lurching forward on his face. His high-cheeked, bronzed features were contorted with passion, his angry eyes glared at the object at whom he pointed. With what appeared to be drunken abandon, he raised his voice so that everyone near could hear.

"Robber, thief, *ladron! Attencion, senors!* Dees—dees man steal from me!"

He patted his hip pocket drunkenly, "I work t'ree weeks for dees money in my pocket. Dees man see me come here and he steal it! *Ladron!*"

Without warning the Indian lunged forward at the object of his rage. Someone stepped forward and stopped his drunken, staggering approach. The man at whom he had pointed, a buck-toothed, lanky puncher, flushed angrily and snarled back:

"No stewed greaser is going to call me a thief. I never seen him before!"

The man bent, yanked out his revolver and would have pulled the trigger had not the man who halted the Indian roared out to put the gun away.

Ludlow cursed and wheeled on Weldon.

As he did, the brush beyond the trees was split open by a charging black shape that burst into their midst with the pent-up fury of a runaway locomotive.

Ludlow lunged back, a muffled shout rose and was cut off short.

The big black stallion came to a jolting stop directly in back of Weldon. In its saddle a lean, hooded shape who wore a great black sombrero sat, twin .45s peeping from the lower edge of the inky cloak. Through the eye-slits of the hood, greenish sparkling lights took in every man of the crowd, held him motionless.

Intent on the drunken Indian's accusations, no one of them was prepared for the sudden attack.

Sam Ludlow's face paled. He opened his mouth to speak, only to be interrupted by the masked man.

"Turn around, all of you. Face the other way."

Though more than twenty guns were in the crowd before The Masked Rider, not one of their owners made a move for his. There was a hushed murmur, then slowly the men near Weldon turned their backs, facing the roofs of Wild Vein less than a hundred yards below them.

"I don't need to say what will happen to the first gent that goes after his gun," snapped the figure in black. "But just to stop any ideas of trouble, start unloading, one after the other. You first there, in the red shirt."

The puncher in a dirt-stained crimson garment at the left fringe of the mob pulled out his gun and dropped it in the dust behind him. One after the other guns came out of holsters and waist bands.

Standing no more than five feet from The Masked Rider, Weldon felt a perceptible thrill trace up his spine. So this was the end— Momentarily he wondered if the masked man intended to take him away, or to allow him to escape. He looked up at the sound of the voice again.

"You in the red shirt. Take it off and drop it behind you."

The owner of the garment grumbled, but pulled off the article of dress and dropped it behind him.

The man in the hood said: "When the law can't manage something, it's time right thinking citizens support it so it will manage in the future. Who's sheriff in these parts?"

Broderick, who had been in the midst of the crowd, turned and stalked forward facing the masked man.

"Cut the rope."

WITHOUT A WORD, Broderick whipped out a jack knife, sliced the bonds that tied Weldon's wrists and yanked the noose from his neck.

Broderick was an old cowman. In other days he had been uptrail to Jackson Hole, the Simpson River country. For a full twenty-five years he had choused slick-ears through the *brosada* from the line north. Because he knew miners and their habits he had been elected sheriff by the respectable citizens of Wild Vein—including the Rands. A hard-bitten, tough *hombre*, Broderick, one who would stick a cold trail out to get his man.

Now he looked with half-admiring, indulgent eyes on the hooded man who had stepped between Weldon and death, but waiting his move, watching for an opening.

Ludlow wheeled. He spoke to the crowd behind him, unheeding the stranger with the drawn gun, "Folks, we come up here to do an unpleasant job. This rat killed Hess Rand. Are we going to let him get away now?"

When the answering roar died away, the voice of the hooded man spoke out.

He said: "Just now, I've got you between the frying pan and the fire, Ludlow. You better add that the first rash move they make, you're going to meet your Maker, whether He wants you or not—and I reckon He does *not!*"

"Atta boy," said Broderick. He pulled Weldon backward until both of them were against the big fir. Safe, at least, for a few moments.

LUDLOW WATCHED THIS move with narrowed eyes.

"He killed Hess Rand," Ludlow snarled. "A hell of a way to act! What does he mean to you?"

"Not strange," said The Masked Rider quietly. "Listen

to me, Ludlow,"—he raised his voice—"and you, too, all around here." Then he turned back to Sam Ludlow. "Why'd this boy kill Rand?"

The hulking one shrugged. "What difference does it make?"

He was interrupted by a voice at his elbow. The Rand girl stood at his shoulder, straight, slim, her dark eyes glittering first on the masked man, then on Weldon.

"I'll tell you," she said tersely. "He killed him for one thing—gold! Last night Grandfather told us—me and my father—he was going to call Weldon and settle the feud. Why? The night Johnny R died he gave Grandfather the clue to a fortune in gold cachéd up in the Moccasins. On Weldon's Open A land. He made him promise he'd share it with the Weldons. Oh, Abe showed it to us. But Father took the clue that would lead us to the caché; he took it into the stable this morning. That's why he was killed!"

Momentary silence gripped the throng.

The hooded man's voice said, "What was it?"

The girl looked first from Broderick to Ludlow before she answered. Then she said: "A piece of rock. Black rock with little markings in it—either of silver, mica, or iron, Grandfather said. When we found my father this morning, that piece of rock wasn't on him!"

Unheard by the others, Ludlow said softly to himself, "Rock?" His face was questioning, curious.

Then Ludlow wheeled. The masked man was speaking once more. Now to the girl.

"Then it should be on Weldon, if he took it."

"I saw your father," Weldon said to the girl, "but he was killed after I left. I haven't the rock you're talking about. When I saw him last, he swore it was still at the house."

"He's lyin'," grated the voice of Ludlow. "Rand probably showed it to him. Then he took it."

Broderick stooped quickly, ran his hands expertly over the clothing of Weldon.

"Ain't anywhere on him," he told them.

The rider turned towards the girl. "Do you want this man lynched now?" he asked quietly. "Even after you've heard this? The reason I'm asking you," he explained, "is this crowd will disperse at your say-so. The man was standing quietly at The Dollar Bill bar. He made no attempt to save himself when the crowd came after him. The thing he might have killed your father for isn't in his possession. Not a very clear case, to me. Is it to you?"

Dan Weldon's eyes were glued to her face. He saw the dark flashing lights in her eyes disappear. As before her high-cheeked face took on that unimpassioned, detached stare; the lips immobile, inexpressive.

Inwardly, Lorie Rand's heart bled a river of sadness. The whole substance of her dreams lay in shattered fragments before her eyes. This man, this light-haired stubborn-chinned man before her had betrayed her instincts. She had counted on him, had found in him a yardstick by which she could judge the stature and honesty of other people. Now there was no guiding light. She floated on a dark and turbulent sea of her emotions, racked by inner tides.

Her father was gone. Killed by this man on whom she had counted. Whom she had grown to respect because, head and shoulders above the rest, he did not deal in blood and violent passions.

Yet in spite of this inner turmoil, she stood there looking squarely into his eyes, silent, motionless. Then suddenly the long-lashed lids dropped. That was her answer to the man in the mask.

"In that ease," he snapped, "the prisoner's coming with me! Sheriff, get those guns into that shirt and tie them up."

Broderick moved forward. He knew the man behind him had him covered, that no move on his part would escape the other's eyes. He bent, stacked the guns inside the shirt, then tied them in a loose bundle.

As the sheriff finished, a tall figure who had been in the crowd turned and faced the masked man. He opened his mouth as if to speak.

"Make it fast," snapped The Masked Rider. "This isn't a time for fooling."

"Few men," said the figure, "have ever had reason to believe Reverend Slick Furbish spoke in jest—and Mister Masked Rider, there was a time when such talk as your'n would have goaded me to violence and bloodshed!"

A sound as of sneering laughter ran through the crowd.

Furbish was tall, at least four inches over six feet and lean to a point of grotesqueness. At the end of a long, gangling neck, his round small head moved with rapid jerking movements as he suddenly chuckled. A day's stubble of reddish beard bristled his chin and accentuated the unwholesome condition of his blackened and snagged teeth. His eyes were large. The black irises sat like shiny beads in their whites.

To complete the weird character of his person, he was dressed entirely in black, in the long frock coat of an itinerant preacher. His uncut collar was dirty. Dressed so, he had all the characteristics of some loose-hung bird of prey that abruptly began stalking back and forth across Weldon's path.

The chuckles that shook his frame stopped. "Th' Lord," he said in his high hoarse voice, "has descended to deliver a sinner to his sins. Time was when Slick Furbish was a sinner. I done treated life with disdain—spilled blood, too! But, erring Brother, I have seen the Light even as you will. I have bade you stop before these hosts, to show them a living illustration of the depths to which greed and hate will go. Bless ye, Brother, fer all yer sins!"

BRODERICK GRUNTED ANGRILY. He knew Furbish from the sky-pilot's previous visits to Wild Vein. With characteristic disbelief in the sincerity of the man, the sheriff regarded Furbish as no less than a windy exhorter and cheap evangelist.

Weldon eyed the crowd about him. The expression of hatred in their faces struck him with vehement, chilling import. He felt himself returning that hatred. Loathing for the speed, the injustice of their accusations stirred him. Thank God, he had escaped them.

Slick Furbish raised a long, lean arm to stop the murmur in the crowd. And as he did the report of a rifle snapped through the momentary stillness. A small puff of smoke popped out from the upper story of Callaghan's livery stable a hundred yards below, set back from the street.

Broderick cursed, made a vain lunge at Weldon's form. The youth slumped forward. Blood was already spewing down his face, soiling his light hair by the time he hit the ground with a heavy thump, reddening the dust.

The big black stallion had turned completely around, startled by the shot. In the saddle the masked man turned, facing the throng. He saw Weldon's body hit. Saw too that Sam Ludlow had suddenly wheeled and dodged in back of Slick Furbish and was running bent over in the direction of a shallow tree sheltered gully not more than twenty yards from the crowd.

At the same second too, he had spotted the glint of light on a rifle barrel down the street of Wild Vein, in the upper window of the livery stable.

He made his decision with lightning speed, whipped up one of the forty-fives and pulled the trigger. The shot roared hollowly in the trees and was followed by a breath-taking moment of silence. In that silence the upper window of the livery stable came to life. A glittering shape appeared and clattered noisily two stories below on the hardened earth before the building. It was a rifle.

In another second The Masked Rider's eyes were pinned on the crowd before him. He forgot momentarily about Sam Ludlow. Although his purpose was not to let the man get away from him, circumstances had forced it. Moreover, the victim that lay bleeding in the dust before him took his instant attention.

"He's not dead," the rider snapped. "But he needs a doctor right away. Sheriff, get him aboard that pony."

The horse that had been meant to hoist Weldon at the end of the lynching riata was still standing wild-eyed at the fringe of nearby trees. Without a word Broderick stalked to it, led it forward and hoisted Weldon across the saddle. He mounted.

"This lynching mob's all through," snapped the hooded man, "besides their guns are in that shirt. By the time they get that open, you'll be out of sight and riding. Get him to a doctor in a hurry."

Grimly Broderick nodded. In the next second the big black stallion had wheeled and crashed into the wall of brush from which it had come. There was a moment of silence. Then somewhere off in the brush came the high long wail of a lonesome mountain cat. Farther away, somewhere beyond the barrier of jack pines on the other side of Wild Vein, the cry was repeated—once.

The Masked Rider had left Dan Weldon behind. Now he followed the man who had bolted from the crowd when Weldon was shot. He knew Sam Ludlow had more to gain than justice from the death of Weldon. For Sam Ludlow had been the man who attempted to murder and rob Johnny R on the cliffs of the Moccasin.

As the masked man disappeared, the rear door of the livery stable was burst open, giving light to a figure that scuttled out and ran along the wall out of sight of the main street of Wild Vein.

He was short, squat, almost deformed. His shoulders were brawny, all out of proportion to his height. His face was covered by a dark stubble. Matted black hair grew long on his sloping forehead and a ridged scar of an old bullet wound pulled down a corner of his small squinting eyes in a perpetual look of disdain.

Blizzard Kemp did not seek to retrieve the rifle he had dropped in the street before Callaghan's Livery Stable. He had felt once already the stinging slash of the Masked Rider's bullet.

The hooded man had shot at the only portion of Kemp's body visible. To the distance that separated the livery stable and those efficient .45s, Kemp owed his life. For along the side of his neck a painful searing slice had been cut—the mark of the Masked Rider.

Without looking behind, Kemp dodged around a corner of the barn and disappeared. He was satisfied that he was alive, and that it was likely that the identity of the man who had fired the shot was unknown.

CHAPTER VI

JAILED

IT HAD TAKEN only a matter of a moment for Sheriff Broderick to kick his pony away from the throng under the tree and out of sight. He took a sheltered trail and arrived in Wild Vein proper through the trees behind the jail. Momentarily, he pulled up his pony and examined the figure hung over the saddle before him.

Weldon's face was pale, but he breathed steadily. As Broderick paused Weldon gave vent to a deep-seated groan.

That was Broderick's answer. Whether Weldon died or not was, indeed, small moment to him. The fact remained that he, Broderick, was the credited marshal of the town, sworn to keep the peace and protect the community. In this case, he decided, it meant getting Weldon into jail as fast as possible. After that he'd get the doctor.

That those had not been The Masked Rider's plans or that Weldon might die disturbed Broderick little. The murmur of the approaching throng from the knoll behind town brought Broderick to life.

He climbed down from the pony, pulled Weldon to the ground and with a few practiced motions unsaddled the beast. With a resounding thump on its rear, Broderick spooked it back into the woods from which he had come.

Then he turned, hoisted Weldon over his shoulder, gathered up the saddle and the bridle and disappeared into the shadows of the Wild Vein bastille.

What bothered Broderick most was the jail itself. The outer walls were rickety and worm-eaten. Before another maddened mob his chances of holding his prisoner safe were decidedly poor. A little liquor might do many things. The lynching, just avoided, had been started in the morning without benefit of spirits. Given a haranguing and a drink, any of the men behind him would again be potential mob material.

Secondly, a great deal depended on Abe Rand's reaction to the prisoner. In Wild Vein, a Rand's word was law. If old Abe chose to shoot it out with the prisoner, little could be done to stop him. So Broderick decided the best thing was to get Weldon out of sight as soon as possible.

Inside, after some fumbling, Broderick got the heavy door behind him closed, clicked the grating lock and heaved Weldon off into the further reaches of the building. By the time he got a cell opened and the wounded man on the cot inside, the sheriff was breathing heavily.

When he straightened up over the rude cot, a feeling of satisfaction passed through him. Weldon's lips had parted and let forth another weak groan. His fingers twitched. Then suddenly his eyes opened, focused on the seamed wind-tanned features above him.

"Coupla fingers of White Mule," said Broderick, laconically. "That'll do you."

A few moments' fumbling in another part of the jail and Broderick reappeared. The drink of raw liquor he brought back was poured without ceremony down Weldon's throat.

The prisoner blinked his eyes, rose to a sitting position on the cot. He looked vacantly at the handcuffs Broderick had brought back with the liquor and with which he was now in the process of manacling him.

"Jest knocked out," grunted Broderick coolly. "You come to in time to get what's coming yer way."

Weldon looked at the sheriff quizzically, then examined his cell. It was not large, nor designed for comfort. The door was of seasoned oak. One hole in it, two-foot square and barred served as a food entrance. Beyond the hole was blank wall.

A single stool and the cot with a few brown pine needles strewn on it were all that proclaimed its former occupancy. The musty walls were of tough pine lumber, tightly nailed together. All in all the cell was built by someone who meant to discourage escape. It was impregnable as a stone dungeon—against one man's escape.

One single window high up on one of the walls allowed the entrance of scattered beams of light past two steel bars. Beyond that, he realized from the assorted noises without, was the main street of Wild Vein.

Weldon brought his mind back to the man before him.

"In time for what's coming my way?"

"Well, son," said the sheriff, "seems Abe Rand's mighty apt to be polishing up his .45, waiting till you get yerself, together enough to stand up and shoot. He'll be coming over this way, I figger 'fore long to find out if I done really spooked out of town with you or holed up. Jest th' same, you better run a loop around yer nerves, git yerself sorta buttoned up and ready for trouble."

"Because he thinks I killed—" Weldon, jerked himself up on one elbow, felt dizziness pour over him like a cold shower. He fell back. "Who shot me?" he asked. "I remember hearing a rifle go off somewhere—"

"Didn't see him," Broderick said. "Yer pal in the black hood shore did though. Here, lemme see what happened to you."

The bullet had come within a half inch of taking Weldon's life. Skimming the scalp, it had cut an angry gash over his ear that left a slow ooze of gore running down the side of his cheek.

BRODERICK GOT UP, left the cell and returned with cotton and liniment. He patched up the wound, then washed away the clotted blood. By the time he had finished, Weldon had a firm grip on himself.

"If you're wise," Broderick was saying, "you'll keep yore mouth shut tight and stay outta sight. Plenty of time later to tell people what you might not have done. I got my duty and that means protecting you, not arguing yer case. Far as anyone in Wild Vein's concerned, you an' me are on our way down to Morbank and a doctor's. I'll hide out until sundown, then mosey out the front door of my house, if I ken get there without being seen."

Weldon kept bitter silence. The injustice of it! An hour ago, he had ridden the trail into Wild Vein a free man, coming to settle a personal debt. Without making a single criminal move, he had been reduced to the estate of a felon, a murderer. For a moment then, freedom had been within reach. A turn of the wheel and he was back where he'd started.

Still, he considered, if he had to meet Abe Rand, far better to die that way than at the end of a whale-line. At least that was a man's way of going.

But more than anything else, the picture of the Rand girl stayed in his mind. It did not seem possible that this girl, so slim, so indelibly stamped with femininity, could be of the blood that had shot his father and brothers down. No, she could not share the fiery hate that flowed in Rand veins. She was—she had to be different. As for Abe Rand—

"When Rand comes," Weldon said slowly, meaningfully, "you tell him I'm plumb ready for him and been waiting some time."

Broderick grunted automatically.

"Showin' fire, eh?" he returned. "Well, he might and might not come." Unconsciously, he pulled forth a segment of Star tobacco, jerked off a wad.

"If he does," he added half to himself, "danged if I ken see how I'm gonna stop him from coming right in here. Yes sir, when Abe does git riled up—" he shook his head. "Well, maybe it'll be a good pay-off fer a brimstone-chawing young buck at that!"

"You heard what I said to tell him," was Weldon's answer.

Broderick rose and went to the one window of the cell. By hoisting himself on the stool, he could observe a greater part of the main street, see a portion of his cottage on a small rise behind the jail, see the store and several saloons.

The street was all but empty. It was already the siesta hour, and the better part of the town had retired behind closed doors in spite of the recent excitement. No sign of the angry gesticulating mob that had gathered on the hillside was visible.

Broderick shrugged his shoulders and climbed down. "Siest'in," said the sheriff, "but jest hibernatin' and storin' up trouble enough to raise holy hell when I come outta hiding tonight."

He looked for a long time at the recumbent puncher. Then he said: "Yes sir, this Masked Rider done complicated a simple problem no end. Irregardless though, he's gonna shore be up in th' air when he finds out you ain't no where in the country-side getting plastered up by a doc. For th' time being son, yer jest non compis nowhere as far as him and Wild Vein are concerned. By gosh, anyway, there won't be a lynching around here tonight if I ken help it.

"We'll lie low a couple of days," he went on, "and take you down to Morbank some night—" Broderick stopped, looked again closely into the face of his prisoner. "Now why th' hell did that Masked Rider want you?" he asked suspiciously. "Yes sir, he done said he was gonna take you away with him. You ain't in with that Masked Rider, are you? 'Cause if you are, I shore pity yer hide!"

Weldon met his gaze with serious, cold blue eyes. "Maybe," he said succinctly, "he knows I'm innocent. I heard rumors that the Rider's liable to take a hand where he thinks someone's getting a raw deal. You might think that over, Broderick, when my trial comes up."

Broderick nodded.

AT THAT MOMENT in another part of Wild Vein, the self-styled cleric, Slick Furbish, stalked loosely out of the house where he had taken temporary lodgings. He walked rapidly up past the Rand Store and entered the high trees and brush that bordered close to the house behind.

His small round face was red, angry; his eyes flashing with unconcealed rage. Like a tall, ungainly bird, he made his way through the jack pines and manzanita until the town behind him was no longer in sight.

Then he stopped, waist deep in the brush and examined the forest about him.

In a high croaking voice he called: "Kemp— Oh, Kemp!"

As his voice died away, not far from him a figure rose from a disguising barrier of leaves and limbs. It was the squat man who had earlier in the day sent the bullet at young Weldon. With an oath, he walked towards the preacher.

CHAPTER VII

THE LUDLOWS STRIKE

THE BLACK STALLION crossed the flat, mounted quickly into the jack-pines and manzanita that studded the opposite slope. The Masked Rider had noted the disappearing Ludlow's direction well. In spite of that, by the time he reached the opposite side of the flat, the gray the other rode had vanished.

Once more the thin tight lips clenched. The hooded man rode steadily for some minutes, then pulled the stallion up in a woody dell crossed by a cattle trail leading down-slope to the flat behind him.

There the lands rose again. Through the trees there floated the wailing, long cry of the mountain cat. He waited moments after that, silent, an upright, broad shouldered figure on the beautiful horse.

A faint crashing through the mesquite that hid the borders of the dell was followed by the appearance of Blue Hawk's white marked sorrel.

The Indian was smiling as he approached, yet no greeting passed between them.

He said, "*Senor,* again you acted one second before death. Now—

Before the soft, guttural voice of the Indian could continue, the masked man interrupted.

"Hawk," he said quietly, "a man rode across the flat a moment ago out this way. You saw him?"

The Indian nodded.

For a second the cold gray eyes of the rider moved across the proud, bronzed features.

"And you recognized him?"

"*Si, senor.*"

"We must find him."

"I understand, *senor.* He rode rapidly up the trail we are on. Then backtracked farther on. From high up," Blue Hawk pointed behind him, "I was watching him well. But a moment, *senor.*"

The masked man turned. The features behind the hood broke a smile.

"Do you want to know what a good job you did of acting the drunk man?" he said laughing briefly. "I don't need to tell you—it worked, didn't it?"

The bronzed face of the Indian flushed, broke into a smile, then sobered.

"No, *amigo,* never do I need be told I have done what you requested. It is this, *senor,* this sheriff did not ride out of town. I see him from high on the mountain. He delivered Mister Weldon to the jail, then scare away his horse and carry Weldon inside."

There was a brief silence, broken only by a sibilant whistle.

"He's going to hide him there," the masked man said slowly. "That means Weldon isn't going to die, at least." He turned abruptly to the other.

"Ludlow wanted that gold in the kyaks. When he missed it, he wanted the clue to finding where it came from. That's one reason for his being so anxious to capture Weldon redhanded. The other is if he got rid of Weldon, the second partner in the gold caché would be dead. With Weldon, Hess Rand and Johnny R dead, Abe Rand would be his only competition."

The Indian nodded. "For this *Senor* Ludlow there is yet another reason, no?"

The Masked Rider chuckled low, humorously. "You're right, Hawk. He may have a very personal reason for wanting to get rid of Hess Rand's suspected murderer."

For a moment they were silent; then the Indian nodded again. "All this is well, *senor,* but we are hours behind on our trail. Many days of hard riding stretch before us if we are to reach—" he shrugged slowly at the interrupting hand the other raised, "Yes, I understand, *senor.* We have heard the request of a dying man. That must be answered. If we do not succeed—" he looked into the half concealed eyes, smiled, shrugged, surrendered. "I have ridden many trails with you, I know you well. I think, *senor,* we will stay here to help him—perhaps first to release young Weldon from the *carcel?*"

When he answered, the cloaked rider's voice was soft, rising in the low guttural tongue of the Yaquis: "You have spoken well, trailer of many men. You have seen how my thoughts lie, why the lonesome trail we ride is brightened only by our vengeance against the lawless—for it was the lawless who put us—me—outside the law. The stout one who has ridden before us can give many words of interest. So we shall seek him out, to hear him speak."

The Masked Rider seldom used the tongue of the Indian. It was only when some deeper emotion stirred him with the desire to impress his sincerity on the other. Without a word Blue Hawk wheeled his sorrel, let his dark eyes flash across the surface of the cow-tracked trail. Then he pressed the sorrel's flanks and moved off at a slow trot.

SAM LUDLOW HAD pressed his horse as hard as possible up from the flat and into the mountains. Only with effort did he repress the angry curses that welled up within him. But haste seemed to calm his impatient anger. For, after moments of hard riding, he pulled up suddenly.

In this time, the man in the mask and Blue Hawk had closed up the distance between them and Ludlow. When they spotted him, astride his motionless gray in the trail some distance beyond, they turned out of the trail, began to shift higher up the nearby hillslope, well hidden by trees.

The trail in which Ludlow's pony now stood was well travelled. It led from the higher Moccasins straight down into Wild Vein. In spite of that, manzanita and toyon bushes grew in close to it. From their tops lifted the shooting spires of tall jackpines.

Ludlow moved abruptly. Ahead of him, coming down trail, he heard the quick patter of trotting hoofs. He turned off the trail, waiting for the riders' approach. When they appeared, his head shot up and a low ejaculation slipped from his lips.

The dun pony and the sorrel that had trotted into sight around a bend carried well equipped riders. Both had rifles slung in scabbards before them. Across the shoulder of one hung a bandolier of rifle ammunition.

"Hullo, Sam," that man snapped out, pulling up his pony.

Ludlow eyed the riders suspiciously. One, his brother, Art Ludlow, had features resembling his own—without the puffy rolls of mottled skin that hung around Sam Ludlow's jowls.

Art Ludlow's eyes were squinting, moving hard and curious across his brother's face. The second rider, a puncher by the name of Hansen, lolled now across his saddle bows, a loose wad of Star bulging his cheeks. Two Colts on either of his hips gave him an atmosphere of readiness, too.

"Where yuh comin' from?" queried Hansen. "Thought Luke was with yuh."

Sam Ludlow grunted. "He's back in Wild Vein. What're you after, Art?"

The other Ludlow moved uneasily in his saddle.

"Better ride offen the trail, if you don't want to get over-seen by someone comin' along it," he croaked. "Galoop."

Art jabbed a pair of cruel star-rowels into his dun's flanks, bounded off to the right of the trail through the high growing toyon brush.

Sam Ludlow and the puncher, Hansen, followed.

Blue Hawk, farther up the side of the mountain, climbed into the saddle of the sorrel at The Masked Rider's command and waited.

Below them now, at the base of the small, brush-marked embankment on the lip of which they stood, the two Ludlows and Hansen had pulled up their ponies.

A whisper rose to Blue Hawk from the crouching, black-cloaked form stooping a few feet from the sorrel's nose.

"I'm going down the other side—nearer to them," the man in the mask said. "I'll lay money Dan Weldon's mentioned. If Sam Ludlow expected this brother of his and his pal—it may be a lot worse. You stay up here, mounted. Come down if I give the call."

"Senor," whispered the Indian, "if they see you—"

But by that time The Masked Rider had crept out of his sight into the heavy growth of manzanita. With heavy anxiety pressing him, Blue Hawk turned the sorrel's head, walked it slowly back from the small bluff lip and out of sight.

Like a moving tenuous shadow, The Masked Rider crept through the brush towards the three horsemen below. He moved as a forest animal, silently, keeping down wind from the horses for fear they might smell him and whinny, until he was within hearing distance of the three men. Then, disguised by the welcome blanket of down timber and low growing brush, he paused.

What he risked coming near the three men he did not consider. Certainly, attired as he was in the garb of the most hunted outlaw in the West, he was, in a sense, dooming himself. But long exposure to such threats had given him what some men might call callousness and others, courage.

"—Johnny R seen yuh!" Art Ludlow was blurting in a tensed, high pitched voice, though the only emotion shown by his face were two white-lined streaks down the tanned cheeks. "Yuh shore played them cards purty, Sam!"

Sam Ludlow's eyes sparkled, the faint traces of a sneer twisted his loose lips up away from his ugly darkened teeth.

"Actin' like a spanked two-year-old again!" he snapped. "Sometimes, Art, you ain't got a two-year-old's sense. If we gotta act fast now, keep yore mouth shut and listen."

Art Ludlow's head shot up. His eyes hardened, cold gray lights cast suddenly through them.

"It was yore idee, Sam," he snarled. "Following Johnny R. And now you hung it up proper. I gotta right to squawk— an' damned if I don't. If Johnny's burro went over the cliff, some gold went with it. What happened to that?"

Sam Ludlow's mouth suddenly tightened. "I went back that same afternoon, quite a bit later. Let myself down over the edge, clear to the burro. There wasn't a speck of gold near it—anywhere! Every bit gone!"

Art Ludlow swore. "And you were gonna foller and draw down on Johnny when you located his gold caché. You located it all right—but now its gone. Shore! A sweet mess of tripe—"

Sam listened to the outburst from the angry lips of his brother. With an ugly curse he snapped Art up short.

"Try it yourself, if you want. The whole valley's up an' watchin' every bad move anyone makes. By this time at least ten men know that gold's disappeared. Whereto? You tell me!"

"Wall," retorted the other stubbornly. "You just quit going off half cocked. I heard before Johnny R died he give this here caché of his to the Rands—providin' they'd share it with Dan Weldon. When I heard that it made me plumb sore. A Weldon! I slung on a gun, got Hansen, and come a-runnin'. I'd jest as soon draw down on Weldon as anyone else. Maybe Hess Rand himself. By God, if you can't handle this thing—mebbe a little not so cross-eyed shooting will!"

Sam Ludlow let his lips twist in a bitter and sarcastic sneer. "I had ideas like that on Weldon about fifteen minutes ago. Me going off half cocked! You long-eared jackass—Hess Rand's dead!"

For a second a curious silence gripped the two men before Sam Ludlow. Art Ludlow snapped his half open mouth shut with the clip of a steel trap.

"Hess Rand!" his hand dropped down to the revolver at his side. "Daid! Yer hidin' something now, Sam, by God—!"

But he did not finish his sentence nor did his pony move forward at the pressure of his knees against its flanks.

Instead, it shied sideways, its eyes wide open, bulging. On them suddenly had burst the rapid, thunderous hammer of a pony at full gallop.

"Look out," Sam Ludlow's voice ripped through the tensed air. "If that's someone from Wild Vein, I figger they better not see you *hombres* when yer supposed to be on the QR. Get over there, outta sight."

HANSEN, THE PUNCHER, wheeled his pony, pointed its nose in the direction of the group of stunted pines behind which The Masked Rider had crouched. Art Ludlow spurred off to their right, towards the rising bank of the brush-lined cliff.

But before either of them could move their horses more than a few feet, the hard riding horseman burst into sight. His pony was dripping lather; they could hear the whistle of his quirt, hear its hard slap on the heaving haunches.

Sam Ludlow's voice rang through the clearing. "Hang on, Art. It's only Luke!" Both the other riders pulled up their ponies with a jerk, half turned in their saddles.

At that second the oncoming horseman spotted them in the clearing and yanked his pony in their direction. He pulled it back on its haunches with a hand of steel not yards from Sam Ludlow's horse.

"Sam!" he was blurting, "Broderick done got away from me—"

Over Sam Ludlow's face a grim expression appeared. He cursed in a soft, sibilant voice.

And as he did a warning gasp from Hansen clamped their attention. To a man, they gyrated towards the puncher, saw his pony shying away from something in a toyon bush towards which it had stretched an eager nose to graze. They saw too that Hansen, with lightning movements, was grappling at his gun—saw it coming upward.

"Th' Rider!" his exclamation sliced through the air.

Like an apparition, a black wraith materialized from the shadows of the waist-high brush. At the lower fringe of the long flowing cloak that hid its head and shoulders completely, the sunlight glinted truculently on the bared barrels of two ugly .45s. The spiteful crack of a gun sliced the air of the clearing. Then another. The last shot came from Hansen's rising Colt.

By that time the masked figure was backing away, turning towards the three other men.

The pony Hansen rode seemed terror-stricken to statue-like immobility. They could see Hansen's back strain, stiffen to ram-rod tension. Then abruptly the sorrel he rode reared. Hansen swayed drunkenly and toppled, a falling tree, from the saddle.

But in the seconds they had seen this, none of the three Ludlows had been motionless. The startling suddenness of the masked man's appearance had, in a sense, stunned them. Then they went into action.

Sam Ludlow's gun spoke first, sending a noisy messenger of death past his pony's nose. Art had wheeled in his saddle, hand whipping downward, then upward. His bullet followed Sam's.

But neither of them took toll of the figure in the brush. After Hansen's shot, the black cloak had lunged backward, out of sight of the three riders. Their bullets sped through empty limbs and leaves.

In another second, like the rush of three juggernauts, they slammed their ponies towards the thin barrier that separated them from the cloaked gunman.

Art's dun went head first like a battering ram through the manzanita limbs, leaving a swath for the others to follow. After him came Sam and his brother Luke. Their guns were up, their lips tight and white. In the hands of each a weapon was ready to send destruction before them.

For twenty yards, Art Ludlow's pony tore down and trampled a wide opening through the brush and stunted pines. He pulled it up, its forefeet pawing at empty air.

A startled, incredulous oath was on his lips. His head whipped first to right, then left—staring into the waving limbs and branches for a sign of a moving figure. By that time, too, Sam and Luke had yanked their mounts to a halt.

For a second all three sat there, strained, waiting.

"He's in the brush," hissed Sam. "For cripe's sake, get hid! If he shoots again—"

"Where'd he go?" Luke asked in a tight, strained voice.

"You damn fool!" snapped Art.

He dropped from the saddle, slipped in under his pony's neck and appeared between his pony and Sam's. In another moment all three of them were dismounted, hidden by the bodies of their horses, waiting, heads only showing over the saddles.

The precaution seemed useless. Though they strained their ears, burned the brush with intent, squinting eyes, no movement, no sudden wafting of a limb that would show anything more than its being stirred by the winds, claimed their attention. The cloaked one had vanished.

After a long time, Art finally moved, pulled himself into the saddle with an angry grunt.

"He's around here somewhere," he said in a low voice. "By golly, that was him all right—The Masked Rider. Sam,

I couldn't believe it at first. If he was a-listenin', what'd he hear?"

He turned to his brother, saw the tight, angry lips of Sam Ludlow pulled back in an ugly snarl.

"Follow me—!"

CHAPTER VIII

MEETING IN THE HILLS

WHEN THE BLACK stallion and the sorrel finally put the pine-dotted ridge of Koll Mountain between them and the Ludlows, they right-angled off the trail and downward. The black stallion led swiftly through the thick trees and brush covering the slope. A moment later it splashed into the water of a small stream at the hill's base. They sloshed upstream for some time. Moments later the stallion heaved itself out of the creek and into a little clearing.

The masked man slid out of the saddle and studied the outlying country for a few moments. Behind his hood his face was sober, tight-lipped.

"If we try to capture Weldon, there's no telling what might happen. A fight with Sheriff Broderick certainly— he may be killed. I'm not ready for that. With Weldon hidden in the *carcel,* he's safe for the time being. In the meantime I still want to talk to Sam Ludlow, alone. I want you to go back into town and check up on everything we have missed concerning Hess Rand."

The Indian's face was enigmatic. *"Si, senor."*

He watched the other, his every sense on the alert for strange sound.

"If Weldon will keep quiet and out of sight," said The Masked Rider, "it will give us time to work. We need answers to two questions. Who killed Hess Rand and where is the gold? Two pretty tough orders, *amigo*—but once they are answered, we ride south again."

Blue Hawk's face was sober. Inwardly, he feared for the welfare of The Masked Rider. In a hostile country where rewards lent constant temptation, anything might happen. Further south, perhaps, there would be less danger. But when the masked one said he must stay on, Blue Hawk's loyalty would keep him at his friend's side.

He nodded. But as he did, he tensed and spoke with quick intake of breath.

"A rider, *amigo*, coming through the brush. You hear?"

The masked man paused, eyes searching the trees on the hillside about them.

"There is," he snapped. Then he turned, pulled the stallion out of the clearing and into the shelter of nearby brush.

He said softly, "You ride back to town, Hawk."

Blue Hawk's face was etched in anxious lines as he wheeled the sorrel and disappeared in a direction opposite to the oncoming horseman's.

The masked man did not have to wait long. Before a moment had passed, the brush on the farther side of the clearing opened and a pony stepped into sight. There was only one rider. She, Lorie Rand, nudged her pony to a trot.

With a bound the masked man pushed his way through the limbs and into the path of the girl's mount.

With a startled exclamation she yanked the horse up sharply, her face paling.

"You—What—?"

The Masked Rider walked forward, took the pony's

bridle and looked up at the girl. Dismay and anxiety were written large in her gaze, but not fear.

He said: "Sorry to startle you. Don't worry about my actions. As long as I'm still interested in Dan Weldon's case, I'd like to know why you're up in this part of the hills. This isn't the way to Moccasin Cut."

For a second the girl stared at him, color returning to her face.

"I know that," she said abruptly. "I—I've been to the Open A."

If her answer surprised the masked man, he did not let it show in his voice.

He said: "Why?"

There was an expression now in the girl's face of definite uneasiness, as if she wished to tell something yet was not entirely convinced it would be safe. Then as though she made her decision abruptly, she said:

"I don't know why you're interested in helping Dan Weldon. But I guess he needs as many in his favor as he can get. I'll tell you why I went up to the Open A. To see the ranch cook—Mr. Ridder. Coming back there seemed to be a group of riders on the trail ahead of me, so I cut off and came down this way. I'm—well, I was in a hurry."

"Why did you want Ridder?"

There was a short silence. The girl seemed to be considering something again.

Then: "You remember there was a knife left behind by the murderer?"

The hooded man nodded.

"Then when Weldon was wounded, you returned the shot and a rifle fell out of the upper window of the livery stable. You must recall that too. Well, both the rifle and the knife were taken into my father's—" she flushed, bit her lips—"into the Rand Store. I was looking at them. There were letters, words stamped into the knife blade. Jones and Landers, Boise, Idaho. I wondered about that and looked the rifle over. I understood better when I found the same name in the rifle's stock. Both of them were sold in Boise, Idaho!"

The eyes half-hidden by the slits of the hood were glittering, expectant.

"They weren't the makers of the weapons either," went on the girl hurriedly. "There was a book at the store with lists of outfitters. Jones and Landers of Boise were listed. Oh, I didn't say anything then, but I suspected there was some relation between the two weapons. They *must* have belonged to the same man. I—well, what mattered then was whether Dan Weldon had ever been to Boise. Above anything else, I don't want an innocent man hung for my father's death—there's been too much innocent blood shed already."

THE SINCERITY IN the girl's voice brought up the masked man's eyes with a jerk. He looked at her searchingly, then said:

"What did you find?"

"I—didn't tell Mr. Ridder why I wanted to know. After all I'm a Rand and he was anything but cordial. Besides, I wanted him to tell me the truth. You see, he hadn't heard a thing about Dan yet. He said—Dan Weldon had never been in Idaho in his life. Not only that, but Dan wasn't carrying a rifle nor a knife when he left this morning. I—" her face flushed painfully but she went straight on into the next sentence—"I didn't stop to tell him about Dan then. Oh, I could never forgive myself if anything happens to

Dan Weldon if he's innocent. I want to find out where he is right away, see if he's badly hurt. I—"

As if she suddenly realized that these were not the words a Rand should speak, the girl paused, gazed hard at the man before her.

For a moment the masked man said nothing. When he spoke it was quickly and meaningfully. "No court would accept either that evidence or Ridder's in a hundred years. There's only one chance in a million that these two, the knife and the rifle, could have been brought all the way from Boise by different people. That's evidence enough for me—for you too, I guess. But I wouldn't tell anyone—until we can collect more evidence, until we have an indisputable set of facts."

With a motion he loosed the mount's reins and stepped aside. That seemed to be the gesture that the girl was free to go. She frowned, pressed her pony's ribs. As it started off the masked man spoke.

"You'll be able to see Dan," he said enigmatically, "in town."

For a second the girl continued moving away, then she stopped the pony and wheeled, a quick question on her lips. But by that time, the man in the mask had moved through the heavy brush and disappeared.

A moment later he mounted the black stallion and circled the clearing. As he did, sounds up the hillside told him that a party of horsemen was coming slowly along the trail to Wild Vein. Recollections of the Ludlows who had been searching for him a short while before, turned his attention that way. With a move of the reins, he guided the black stallion up the brush-spotted hillside.

CHAPTER XI

BUCKY

O LD, WHITE-MUSTACHED JOEY RIDDER did the cooking at the Open A. Also the milking of the three Jerseys. One of young Bucky Weldon's jobs, when he'd finished lunch, was to round up the "milk-critters," bring them back to the corral early so that they wouldn't eat too much alfalfa grass in the south meadow and get bloated.

He usually finished this chore at two-thirty, idled his horse for a while, then set out for his rabbit or chipmunk traps to see his past night's catch.

But on this day, immediately after the corral bars swung shut on the Jerseys, Bucky cast one long look at the ranch house. No sign of life about the kitchen meant that Joey had retired for the afternoon siesta. The two Open A pounchers were in the weather-beaten bunk house talking.

Bucky cast another look in their direction, then wheeled his pony, headed for the ranch house. For a long time he busied himself in a room apart from that in which Joey snored. When he had accomplished his purpose, Bucky sneaked out the back door, mounted the little dun Dan had given him.

Minutes later he was spurring up the trail in the direction of the Moccasins, secure in the belief that neither Ridder nor the Open A punchers had noticed his departure. He closed his lips and applied the spurs more freely to the little dun's flanks.

That his big brother, Dan, had gone to Wild Vein was for Bucky a foregone conclusion. Although Dan would have sworn that Bucky knew nothing of the Weldon-Rand ancient blood feud, he knew about everything there was to know. Occasional words passed from the lips of careless, come-and go punchers, conversations of school-mates down at the Morbank school, had given him a fairly complete knowledge of the state of affairs.

He knew the rider who had dropped Hess Rand's note at the Open A was from Wild Vein and the Rands. Adding Dan's hurried departure to his strange non-appearance for breakfast, Bucky concluded that Wild Vein was the answer. And if it were Wild Vein, it meant only one thing—the feud.

Joey Ridder would have denied that to his last breath. But not Bucky.

Riding up-trail, Bucky put the facts of the case through his mind. Dan was no doubt in Wild Vein. If he were, he might need help. That help should come from a Weldon. It was Bucky's job to carry on. Had he waited only minutes longer, he would have seen Lorie Rand on her visit. But he left too early for that.

An hour and a half later he watered his pony in a small stream flowing along the base of Koll Mountain. When the pony climbed out of the creek and into the trail, Bucky looked up to find that his way had been blocked by three horsemen. The sight of them sent a quick finger of chill tracing down his backbone. In their faces he read annoy-ance and surprise. This suddenly seemed to be erased by jeering amusement. Sam Ludlow, one of the riders, spread his mouth in a wide, derogatory grin.

With quick, nervous glances, Bucky examined the other faces, found them also to belong to Ludlows. But before he could wheel the little dun, Sam Ludlow had pushed his towering gray forward, grappled at Bucky's mount.

Many and hateful deeds had been attributed to the Ludlows—by the Open A, no less than by other cowmen in the mountains.

For that reason Bucky shrank a little within himself but managed to blurt out: "Let my pony go, you Ludlow. I ain't doin' anything."

When the sound issued from the figure on the pony, Sam Ludlow broke out in a hoarse, rattling laugh. His bulging eyes glinted, blinked. Cold rage clamped on Bucky's soul.

The Ludlows saw before them a small figure, all but tented in an enormous brown sombrero. From beneath the brim, which hung suspended on a pair of over-sized ears and half covered the eyes, a ruddy small chin stuck out at them in defiance. It never occurred to Bucky that Dan's best sombrero might not fit him. His own had been hopelessly battered and dirty. On so momentous an occasion only the best should be used.

Hardly less ludicrous than the hat was the remainder of his equipment. Into the waistband of his trousers he had tucked a bulky, bone handled .45 that had once belonged to his father and had been given up by Dan when it shot neither straight nor consistently. Outlined against his thick small chest, the gun had mammoth proportions. Then, too, there was the matter of boots.

Around the ranch Bucky's footwear was a pair of prosaic and dirty hobnailed shoes. When he spotted the ones under his brother's cot, overwhelming desires had gripped him.

Thus, out of a pair of high-topped, embroidered "high-heels" rose two pipe-stem legs clamped firmly around his little dun's fat barrel.

When Sam Ludlow finished his siege of spiteful laughter, his eyes changed, sobered. He grated:

"Where you goin', younker?"

The "younker" raised further desires in Bucky to rid himself of his unwanted company. His teeth clamped tight on his tongue.

"Don't bother talkin'," Ludlow snapped. "I know yer headin' fer Wild Vein. Gonna find yer big brother an' back him up with that eighteen pounder there?"

But the small hunching figure before him did not open its lips. Its eyes flitted beyond their faces, searched for avenues of escape that did not show in the heavy and low-growing brush.

ART LUDLOW SPOKE up then: "Goin' intuh Wild Vein?" he sneered. "Shore grow their tadpoles young an' frisky— th' Open A. Eh, Luke? Seems tuh me said tadpole's gonna get a sure enough surprise, too."

Luke, the other brother, deposited an over-chewed wad of Star into nearby-brush before he answered. He was leaner, lanker than his brothers. His face was long, hatchet-shaped, seemed to slope forward at an incline from the top of his low forehead forward to the tip of his sharp long nose. His eyes were small, beady. When he spoke, he drawled through loose, cruel lips words that congealed Bucky Weldon inwardly with unnamed premonitions.

"Surprise?" Luke drawled acidly. "Hell, that ain't no word fer it! By God, long as they didn't get Dan Weldon strung up, mebbe next best thing is to carry on down the line. I vote a return back to town. Now that we done got Hansen outta the way an' shore enough can't find hide nor hair o' this Masked Rider."

It was a long speech for Luke Ludlow, and though his

brothers regarded him as the thicker-skulled member of the family, they listened carefully. When Luke finished, Sam grunted in acknowledgment.

"Might be a lynchin' bee after all," he grunted. "You take him, Art, an' le's turn back."

The other Ludlow pushed his pony forward, grabbed the bridle of the little dun with rough, sure hands. Bucky's pony backed up, only to be yanked forward.

"Let my hoss go," snapped its rider. But before he could help himself Bucky was jerked back against the cantle and moved rapidly forward.

The two other Ludlows lined out in the trail behind them at a quick trot. His reins surrendered, Bucky was hard put to stay in the saddle. His oversized boots didn't help that situation either.

But he scarcely noted this physical discomfort. The implication that had lain in Luke Ludlow's words ate at him like slow-working acid. Something about a lynching that Bucky didn't understand. But the idea, the thought that something might happen to his big brother, Dan, filled him with vague worries. Dan could lick his weight in over-sized wildcats—which also signified that he could lick about anyone in the world. Dan was all right and would probably be waiting for him in Wild Vein—

Then, too, the Ludlows had mentioned The Masked Rider. Bucky had heard that name many times—in fact he couldn't remember when he'd first heard of the outlaw whose name was mixed in an adventurous and exciting aura of crime and good deeds. In Bucky's imagination he had grown to legendary proportions. He rode the night winds on a great black horse whose speed was that of wings.

Bucky Weldon's attention was abruptly taken to other

things. The little dun clambered around a corner of the trail after Art Ludlow's big gray. In doing so, he had placed trees between Bucky and the following riders.

With a quick move of his small body, Bucky jerked his right foot out of the stirrup, pulled it over the horn of his saddle and jumped. He landed with a crash in the close growing brush, lunged headlong into it.

Somewhat higher now up the hillside, well hidden from the trail by a barrier of manzanita, The Masked Rider crouched. In coming around the bend in the trail, Art Ludlow had exposed himself in full view so that the masked man was unexpectedly the witness of the surprising act of the strangely attired figure following Ludlow.

When he saw the figure leap from its saddle and dodge into the nearby growth, a low whistle escaped him.

Art Ludlow had caught Bucky's movement with the corner of his eye. No sooner had the youngster dropped from the saddle than Art pulled up his pony, whipped out his revolver.

Simultaneously Sam and Luke appeared around the bend. They seemed to recognize the trouble immediately for both were out of their saddles before Bucky entirely disappeared.

Using it like a wedge, Sam threw his body into the brush.

"All right, Luke, he'll get th' shaver," Art shouted.

Luke pulled up and spat resoundingly. "Shoulda kept an eye on him, b'gosh," he commented lazily.

The two did not wait long. More crashing in the brush heralded the approach of Sam. He appeared, a kicking, swearing, big hatted form tucked under one of his massive arms. He brought his burden up into the trail, set it roughly upright between himself and his brother Luke.

When he released his hold, a small fist whipped upward and connected with a sullen thud on the point of Sam Ludlow's bulbous nose. Ludlow let out a curse, grabbed at the kicking, scratching shape that again attempted to escape.

By the time Sam got Bucky's arms stopped, his face was purple, his eyes bloodshot, glinting. This did not seem to affect the boy at all. He stood with drooping head, face concealed by the over-sized sombrero.

"Try that again," snapped Sam Ludlow, "and you'll get th' whaling of yer life, Weldon. Hear?"

But the small shape did not deign to answer. With a sweeping motion, Ludlow heaved, deposited the young-ster on the dun's hull. Then he turned, strode towards his own pony.

He had not gone eight paces before Bucky Weldon wheeled in the saddle and threw. The rock he had concealed in his hand was the size of a hen's egg and was propelled by all the force of a well-developed throwing arm. It connected against the back of Sam Ludlow's head with a loud "Crack!"

Ludlow stumbled forward, caught his balance, then straightened. Slowly he turned. As he did a curious, strained silence lay over the three riders. Ludlow came forward at a half run, his arm upraised, his face contorted in cruel, violent and, for the wide-eyed lad on the dun, terrifying lines.

THE MASKED RIDER swooped up from the brush through which he had crept until he was mere yards from the four horses. When Sam Ludlow started to run towards Bucky, a .45 slipped up into the cloaked figure's hand and bored a second on the charging, bull-like figure. The gun exploded with a vituperative snarl.

Sam Ludlow's body went headlong, landed face down in the well trodden trailway with a crash.

Now another pistol appeared in The Masked Rider's other hand and centered on the open-mouthed, wheeling horsemen.

"Reach," a cool, steely voice fell against their ears.

Both Art and Luke Ludlow swallowed and began to curse. But their hands came up, crawled past their shoulders and stopped.

"Now drop that gun," the masked figure told Art Ludlow.

A .45 clanked noisily in the gravel.

Bucky Weldon had not moved. He sat with wide eyes and stared at the flowing black cloak, the hood and the big black sombrero jutting above the low-growth brush on the hillside. A small sound grew in his throat.

"Holy catfish! The Masked Rider!"

Sam Ludlow, face down on the ground, stirred, began to move. Before he'd raised his face out of the dirt, the cloaked figure's voice had cut through the air, stiffened him again to inanimation.

"Stay where you are, Ludlow."

Sam Ludlow stayed.

The figure half turned to Bucky Weldon. "Ride up until you're beside me," he ordered.

Bucky, in a half daze, retrieved the reins that hung over his dun's small head, turned the pony in the trail, pushed it up the hillside, being careful not to place himself between the masked man and the Ludlows.

That The Masked Rider had saved him from an almost

certain ghastly fate was just beginning to percolate through his mind. The action had been so surprising, so completely astounding for him that no fear of the meaning in the cloaked figure's words attacked him. He simply did as he was ordered.

When the little dun had crashed through brush to The Masked Rider's side, Bucky grinned.

"All right," said the cloaked figure, "keep going up hill. You, Ludlow,"—his voice was cool knife thrusts against the ears of the men—"you three and I have got plenty *palabra* to make soon. Little inconvenient just now. But be expecting me. Better stay where you are, faced the other way for at least a full minute. I'll be able to watch you considerable distance through the trees. *Adios.*"

The little dun struggled bravely up the nearly 45-degree climb.

In less than a minute they had mounted a hillside, crossed the small ridge at its top. There, like an ebony statue, Bucky saw the horse of his dreams. A magnificent, towering stallion who bowed its head, came forward at a slow trot.

Without a word the hooded man swung himself into the saddle. "Follow me," was all he said.

They rode for some time down the opposite side of the hill at a quick trot. Reaching a trail there they loped along it, then turned abruptly into the trees and off the beaten path.

A moment later the masked man pulled up.

By then the full import of his position had dawned on Bucky Weldon. Beside him, in full legendary regalia, rode The Masked Rider. Bucky took in his long disguising cloak, the lithe, sure seat with which he rode the stallion. The awe that lay in the adolescent's mind left him somewhat speechless.

"You're a Weldon," the masked figure said slowly. "I'd almost swear to it—even wearing that hat."

Bucky swallowed, paid no attention to the indulgent tone of voice. Curiosity had gotten the better of him. He said: "You're Th' Masked Rider, ain't you, mister?"

The figure said, "Some people call me that."

"Some? Everyone, tuh my way uh thinkin'. Holy Gee, what'd you do to Sam Ludlow, anyway? I thought surer'n Hades he wuz a goner—"

"Twisted his ankle. Shot the heel off his shoe and he tripped up. It worked better than I'd even hoped it would. Landing on his face left him stunned enough for me to hold up his brothers."

"Boy!" exploded the youth.

The green eyes in the slit hood twinkled, then became meaningful.

"Too bad, too, because I wanted to make talk with him."

"Why?"

But the masked figure did not answer. He turned the black's head, said, "You stay here, wait for me, before going on into Wild Vein."

The mention of the town drew other thoughts to Bucky Weldon's mind. His face, half hidden by the sombrero, whitened and tensed.

"Mister," he said in a high, strained voice. "If you know me, you must know my big brother, Dan. Mebbe you heard. Nothin' ain't happened to him, has it?"

"What, for instance?"

"Well—" Bucky stuttered. "Well, they said—"

The hooded figure nodded abruptly. "You'll find him I expect," he said, cautiously. "Eventually—if he isn't in Wild Vein now. He'll be all right."

But that didn't satisfy the youngster. Beneath his hood the masked man gritted his teeth. He wanted to tell the boy Dan was in jail and safe for the time being. But what if he went into Wild Vein, let the word slip out? No, that certainly wouldn't do. The hidden thin lips tightened.

"That's all the more reason for taking him into town," he said to himself, thinking of Broderick. The sheriff would keep the boy until it was safe to let him see his brother.

"You wait for me," the masked man repeated.

He wheeled the black stallion, pushed it at a rapid trot across the grass-blanketed clearing and out of sight. The black made its way carefully through the brush until nearly a quarter mile had been covered.

When it stopped, the hooded man's hands rose. From them, as before, issued the lone, long wailing cry of the lonesome mountain cat.

Then The Masked Rider wheeled his mount, trotted back in the direction of Bucky Weldon. In Wild Vein Blue Hawk would hear the cry and return. As The Masked Rider, he most certainly could not be seen in Wild Vein. Blue Hawk could take the boy into town, leave him with Broderick. In the meantime—the danger of Dan's brother being alone in Wild Vein would be avoided.

Coming into the clearing the black stallion was abruptly pulled up. Across the grass, near the trees it had left, no dun stood, no big hatted, hunched shape appeared. Bucky Weldon had vanished. Horse and all—as completely as if he had been waved out of sight by a magician.

CHAPTER XII

QUIEN SABE?

A MINUTE'S EXAMINATION of the dun's tracks told the hooded man that the younger Weldon had disappeared alone towards the well tracked trail near the clearing. Lost in the welter of prints there, the masked man shook his head slowly, turned the black again towards the higher vantage point from which he had sent the cry.

There he slid out of the saddle, awaited the coming of the Indian. Twice he repeated the lone wailing signal before a brush dimmed movement on the slope below him advertised the approach of Blue Hawk.

When the sorrel clambered up the slope and into the group of trees, the Indian's face was somber, questioning.

"I think I have heard the call the first time, *senor,* but with the distance I am not sure. The second time I was in the street of Wild Vein and came. It is well. I have found out many things."

The masked figure nodded tersely, described his meeting with Lorie Rand, the coming and disappearance of the younger Weldon. The smile which had been growing on the face of the Indian disappeared when it was finished.

"There are no *Mexicanos* in this town, *senor.* Only after long and uninteresting talk did I find a man to tell much of what I wish."

The hooded figure bowed its head, spoke slowly. "Old *Senor Lobo* himself, *amigo,* couldn't smell out more vermin nests than you, Hawk, I know."

A trace of a smile touched the corners of the Indian's

eyes. He went on quietly: "That night when this Johnny R. died, he said one thing someone did not mention before. He said to *Senor* Rand, 'I am give this all to you, but you must divide it half with the Weldons.' We know that. But before that he was delirious for long time from his wound. He would say over and over again, this *Senor* Jackson who sweeps out the Rand Store told me—'It'll pull her off north.' Just that. 'It'll pull her off north.'"

"And that means what?"

"*Senor,* you shall guess as well as myself."

Under the hood the hard lips invisible to the Indian were tight set, determined.

"It had some bearing on where the caché of gold might be?"

"I know from your tone," said the Indian, "that you think that true. I also do."

"What else?"

"This black dressed preacher man who stopped the sheriff and Weldon when they appeared in town."

"Furbish—Reverend Slick Furbish," said the man in the mask.

"He wishes to pass himself as such."

"What about him?"

"I rode a round-about way into town, *senor.* At one place, two men who are in the brush talking, look up and see me. One of them, this preacher man becomes red in the face, angry. The other turns about, walks in the other direction and out of sight. Then I ride on into town."

The masked figure wheeled suddenly.

"One man, I say, *senor,* was the preacher," went on Blue Hawk. "The other is very thick, very broad. He looked, shall we say, *senor,* like a monkey man? With one very bad eye. In town I find that this man is he who shot at *Senor* Weldon. A man had let him hide in his house for a while. Then lent him a pony to get out of town. They think then he had done a good thing—killed Weldon. I have heard that that man is still near Wild Vein—but avoiding the sheriff."

"Hiding now outside Wild Vein?"

"*Si.*"

"Meeting on the sly with the dressed up critter that stopped us."

"*Si.*"

A low musing whistle escaped from under the black cloak. For some moments the two men were silent.

Then the hooded man said: "Do you think the girl knows what Johnny R said when he was delirious?"

Blue Hawk shrugged. "*Quien sabe?*"

The black hooded head turned. "Maybe when she hears that about pulling off north she'll be able to tell us more about the caché."

"But *senor,*" the Indian's voice was questioning. "She is a Rand. Her family—"

The masked one stopped him. "I don't think, Hawk, the feud will mean much to her—for long."

THE MORNING DEW had long been dry on the sill of the little barred window in Dan Weldon's cell when Sheriff Broderick appeared.

A night in jail had not improved his prisoner's temper much nor had the growing emptiness in a stomach raised on breakfasting before complete daylight. The injustice of his position had grated more on the youth with each passing moment of the morning. Even doomed men must eat, he told himself, and eyed the blinking, well-fed face of the sheriff with jaundiced angry eyes.

When the cell door opened, Weldon's manner changed. On a tray before him lay two golden, glistening fried eggs, fried potatoes, biscuits, and a cup of steaming coffee. He grunted, blinked.

"Hell of a way to treat prisoners," sniffed the sheriff unsmiling. "If it weren't so damn uncomfortable sleeping in a cell, danged if I wouldn't move in here. Providing, course, that Ma kep' on feedin' th' prisoners. Plumb onprofitable too—with only thirty cents *per persona* per day allowed by th' city of Wild Vein for feeding prisoners!"

But Weldon did not answer. He busied himself with Broderick's burden, oblivious of external environs. This the sheriff watched with faint amusement.

"You feed plumb hearty fer a all but condemned man," he commented slowly. "Figger as how you ain't supposed to be here, kinda go slow on thet gobblin' noise emanating from sech feedin'—"

Weldon grinned, wiped his mouth with a sleeve and attacked the coffee. When he had finished that, he looked up at Broderick and began the makings of a cigarette. His first drag he took deep and satisfyingly. When the twin streams of smoke came pouring from his nostrils, a sort of heavy sigh escaped from his lips.

"My compliments to th' missus, Broderick," he said. "Now I expect we come down to brass tacks on business."

Broderick nodded. "Shore. First thing, son, is you and me begin thinkin' up ways tuh get you outta this town, sight unseen. No one seen me last night, ner this morning yet. Like as not though a coupla ornery-minded critters 'round this town'll be rarin' up on their hind laigs wantin' to know what in hell I did. Wall, last night I figgered all that out."

"How?"

"Well," started the Sheriff, but got no further.

There was a sound of heavy boots stomping in the other part of the jail. A voice, loud and demanding, thundered through the building.

"Broderick! Hey, Sheriff Broderick—where th' hell—?"

The sheriff slid up to his feet, his lips tightening, his eyes suddenly serious.

"Son of a gun," he said hurriedly. "Abe Rand." His voice rose. "All right, Abe, I'm a-comin'."

Broderick rose, closed the cell door behind him. His brown battered sombrero disappeared.

Weldon could hear him saying, "Hullo, Abe. What ken I do for you?"

Then their voices dropped away to a mere murmur, dimmed by the wall that separated Dan's straining ears and the sheriff's office.

But Weldon did not pin his ears to the cell door for long. He heard other steps approaching from the rear of the jail, looked up and found a dark feminine face looking quietly through the foot-square opening in his door, examining him calmly, searchingly.

Weldon jerked erect, subconscious questions arising to his lips.

"Hello," said Lorie Band softly. "Don't talk too loud. I don't want Grandfather to hear me in here—Broderick either for that matter."

Weldon nodded, scanned the girl's high-cheeked olive features before he spoke.

Then he said: "How did you know I was here?"

A half-smile seemed to flash across the girl's dark eyes, then disappear. Her face was serious, quiet.

"I saw Broderick coming down from his house this morning—sneaking through the bushes with a big tray of food and two cups of coffee. I happened to ask Mrs. Broderick a little later if there were any prisoners in jail. She said only Leo Fast Pony."

Weldon frowned. "Yes, he's over in another cell—keeping quiet. Pretty smart of you, though."

The girl did not smile at this, but looked squarely into Weldon's eyes. The young man flushed.

"Well, why are you here?" he said angrily and for the first time then it was the Weldon blood that spoke.

The dark eyes flipped upward, shadowed. A flush spread up Lorie's cheeks, suffused her forehead and disappeared in the raven black hair pulled back from her face in a sweeping hawk's wing. Weldon grinned abruptly.

"Don't mind me," he started.

"I meant nothing coming here," the girl broke out. "I thought I'd find if you were really here and not out of town. I've found out. Good-bye."

She turned and would have left, though she did not want to. But Weldon jammed his body tight against the cell door, his smile gone, his face serious.

"No—please don't go yet. Tell me, you came inside here for some reason Miss—Lorie!"

The girl wheeled, her dark eyes no longer flashing but now almost pleading.

"You had no reason to speak that way. Besides—it's not really like you. You know I don't want trouble—I want justice—not more blood on Rand hands."

She paused, torn with indecision. She had but meager

proof that this was not the man who killed her father. But combined with that was the voice of her instinct that had told her Weldon was not of the stripe of a murderer from the first.

Now as she looked at him, heard him speak to her, call her name, it came over her with overwhelming import that more than admiration of Weldon's actions had driven her to him, to fight for him.

She turned, looked deep into his eyes, and said abruptly, "If Grandfather finds you are here, he will insist that you and he shoot it out on the spot. I—I can't bear the thought of either of you doing that. I—"

A tremor of electricity sped up Weldon's spine.

"Lorie," he said; reaching out of the narrow window and taking the small hand that had poised fleetingly on the bars before him. "Lorie, you came because you don't think I killed your father. I know that—I'm sure of it now. If I know that you believe in me, it'll help me convince the others I'm innocent. Please, tell me you have faith in me."

She looked up at him slowly. Then she told him what she had discovered concerning the knife and the rifle. When she finished she added, "They hunted yesterday afternoon until after dark in the livery stable and The Dollar Bill for the piece of rock Father had. They didn't find it. But if they do, that will prove everything to them—"

Weldon gritted his teeth. "But they won't find it! I tell you I didn't have it. You believe me. You have to!"

The dark eyes rose, looked full and long into Weldon's. "Yes," the girl said softly. "Yes, I really do—I must go."

The hand vanished and with it the high-cheeked, dark face that had suddenly brought happiness and meaning into Weldon's existence. The youth turned back to his shad-

owed cell, a high, brimming river of contentment and courage suddenly running through his soul.

He had not been in this mood for ten minutes when a
commotion in the street claimed his attention. He grabbed
the low stool, clambered up on it and stared cautiously out
into the glaring light of morning.

He did not know what he would see, but he did know
that it would be something not for his own good. Life was
like that. A ray of hope and promise of beauty that sent his
blood tingling hot—and the next moment—

CHAPTER XIII

DAN!

PRIDE BEFORE WORLDLY possessions was a maxim
firmly stamped into Bucky Weldon's mind at the
Morbank school. But, in the manner of most platitudes,
the saying should be colored by expediency. And this latter
fact Bucky Weldon was almost too willing to accept that
morning. Pride should not come, for instance, before grub.

When The Masked Rider had left Bucky to ride up the
hillside, the younger Weldon had taken quick summary of
his position. Discretion got the better part of valor. If he
stayed with The Masked Rider, he would perhaps go on
indefinitely scourging the range country, bringing death
and destruction to evil-doers, perhaps robbing an occasional gold train to liven and smooth the way of their living.
In the meantime, however, his search for his brother would
go unattended. Perhaps at that very moment Dan might
be wishing for him, calling for his help.

So Bucky had left his new-found mentor, ridden rapidly in the direction of Wild Vein.

By the time he had arrived there—in a round-about way to avoid further meeting with the Ludlows—darkness had already set in. The sight of a booming small city like Wild Vein in full evening regalia awed him. Bright lights repulsed rather than attracted him. For some time he lurked in far shadows watching the goings-on in the main street. His brother Dan was nowhere to be seen.

About that time, too, his unattended stomach began to call his attention. Without money, there would be no food, he thought suddenly. And in his hurried departure from the Open A, that small matter had missed his attention.

When he finally found a barn at the farther edge of the town and sneaked into it to sleep, the emptiness in his stomach was an absorbing and disquieting condition. However, sleep did come, and after sleep came the morning.

When he awoke, his hunger had grown to proportions all out of keeping with his previous consideration of the importance of food. He climbed out of the hay rubbing his eyes at the already risen sun. People were moving in the street of Wild Vein—for his previous day's exertion had made his sleep somewhat longer than usual.

When he stepped into the street, Bucky's legs weaved under him. Two people up near the Rand General Merchandise Store suddenly seemed to leap sideways a full eight feet, then a tenth of a second later, appeared where they had been before. Distinct and unexplainable dark spots swooped for a moment across the horizon and disappeared.

However, in the daylight, Bucky Weldon, in spite of the

state of his stomach, had a sure conviction that today he would find Dan. His big brother had always been exactly where he wanted him when he wanted him. All he would really have to do was call out, "Dan— Oh, Dan!" and Dan would appear.

But such unmanly action as calling his brother, Bucky immediately repressed. No, Dan was in town; he knew it, was sure of it.

Bucky walked out into the middle of the street towards the Rand Store farther up the block. As he did, he passed the jail, stopped and looked at it curiously.

A man appeared around the corner of The Dollar Bill saloon. He saw Bucky and halted in his tracks. A peculiar look seemed to run across his face and break immediately into a wide, unhandsome grin.

"Hullo there, rannyhan," the man coughed. But there was no cordiality in his voice. Bucky stared at the jail again.

When the voice broke out once more, Bucky turned and examined the speaker. Curious sounds were emanating from the man's face, his eyes blinked owlishly.

"Purty toney, you cow dudes," croaked the other. "Hey, Jake!" he called in a louder voice. "You been tuh Mexico an' seen Gila monsters an' such strange an' ferocious critters. But you ain't seen this hyar b'fore."

A face appeared through the flapping panels of The Dollar Bill. Bucky regarded it with cool stare. A smile writhed, moved across the man's face, became an open "O."

"Jumpin' mountain-snakes! Is it standin' thar—er am I seein' it?" queried the red headed, buck toothed cow-puncher leaning out the door.

The first man, who was tall and gangling, began to hunch toward Bucky, his eyes squinting.

"In town fer a coupla days, I take it, stranger," he began almost cordially now. "When yuh got yer stock all cut out, branded, an' counted, a little rec'ration comes in right handy. Ain't no place like in town tuh take it—Wine, women, an' hard liquor didn't never hurt no man—that is, I say, in judicious quantities. Only one thing, mister, do go careful-like with that there now buffler gun yer carryin'. Sheriff Broderick ain't partial tuh broken winders an' such. Savee?"

Bucky shoved the sombrero on the back of his head, nodded slowly, understandingly. He had not figured on such amicable reception in Wild Vein. Town people were just like range people after all. The fact that he had not just completed the branding of the Open A herd was a mistake on the man's part that Bucky wrote off to quiet, bourgeoisie life. Branding on the range would not start for at least five weeks.

BUT SUCH CONSIDERATE regards on the part of the other made Bucky wish more than ever that he had gone further into the subject of food the previous night. Just now he was too busy to take care of the detail.

"Thanks for th' advice, mister," he said slowly. "Mebbe you ken help me out a bit. I'm a-lookin' fer Mister Daniel Weldon." He pronounced the name slowly. "He's in town here somewhere and I figgered you might've seen him. I'm his brother."

The red-headed puncher, Abe Macom, coughed abruptly, swore and came striding all the way out of the saloon doors and into the street. The lanky, friendly man looked closer at Bucky's small chinned face, the big .45 in his belt, then examined Dan's rodeo boots carefully.

"Dan Weldon?" he asked with a soft whistle. "Yeh, I do

believe now I heard uh him." He turned once more, yelled: "Chammy! Jim! Come on out here a minute."

More faces appeared and Bucky found himself surrounded by a curious and long-limbed group of range men. Grins came, widened, then went when the first man passed around the word that Bucky was Dan Weldon's brother, that he was in Wild Vein to find him.

The faces grew in number. More grins, more subdued talk and then more staring as though he were some strange and outlandish animal. Bucky's gorge began to rise.

The first man disappeared into the background, his place being taken by the men he had called Chammy and Jake. They moved closer.

"Figger like as not Sheriff Broderick oughtta hear bout this," Chammy Rogers said.

But Jake Macom shook his head slowly, his face grim-lipped, almost angry.

"What th' hell? If th' kid don't know where his brother is, how's he gonna tell Broderick? Figger that? Blood's thicker'n water. Side-winders come young same as they come full size."

At this insult, Bucky's jaw clenched, but he held his tongue. The group suddenly opened and gave shape to a gaunt figure in black. Its small face was red; anger emphasized its grotesque lines. With a hoarse rumble Furbish swept up his arms, stopped the growing murmur that had greeted Jake Macom's words.

"What have we here, my boy?"

Bucky regarded the intruder angrily and looked the other way. He examined the nearby shape of The Dollar Bill, turned his head to take in the side wall of the jail.

"Shame! Shame!" exhorted Furbish, "that the baiting of innercent children should be yore sport. Who are you, boy?"

That was enough for Jake Macon. He stepped towards the preacher. "What d'yuh mean, buttin' in this way?" he snarled. "We ain't doin' anything wrong. It ain't to yer advantage either—actin' like holy awmighty, you long-legged ole raccoon."

Furbish's face went pale, then turned three different shades of red in rapid succession.

But he had not taken his eyes off the small face before him. He saw Bucky's eyes, now pointed towards the jail, expand like eggs broken on a hot griddle. The youngster's mouth opened and from it burst an explosion that was heard by every ear in the crowd.

"Dan!"

Up at the jail window, Dan Weldon had watched the coming of his younger brother to Wild Vein, the goings-on in the street. He saw his brother's eyes flick in his direction, his mouth open. Dan Weldon let go the bars of the window as if they were red-hot.

But the crowd in the street had heard Bucky. Slick Furbish wheeled as though he had been struck. Myriad voices rose in the crowd, questions, burning questions.

"Yelled his brother's name jest then."

"He was lookin' at the jail, Jake. Ask him what he saw!"

"I bet Weldon's in town. Right inside there!"

And in the middle of the crowd Bucky Weldon held his eyes pinioned to his toe-tops. Sure, that had been Dan. Why, he'd seen him right up in that barred window there! But for some reason Dan had ditched when he yelled. There was some reason he didn't want anyone to know he was in Wild Vein, or to let Bucky recognize him.

Through the younger Weldon's mind a curious train of thoughts ran. But most incomprehensible was that he had seen Dan and that in some strange way he had done something Dan didn't like. With queer inner sinkings, he clamped his mouth tight shut, refused to answer the hundred questions that the crowd popped at him.

Slick Furbish had strode forward, gripped the young Weldon by his shoulder. "You yelled fer yore brother. Where is he? Did you see him?"

Bucky shook his head.

Another voice cut in. "Shore he did! By golly, he wuz lookin' at the jail jest then. I bet—"

"Hyar," a voice was roaring in the street. "Whut's a-go-in'on?"

It was Sheriff Broderick's voice. When he heard it, Dan Weldon slipped up, cocked his head sideways so that only one eye examined the scene in the street before him.

Broderick was standing in the dusty road, regarding the shape of his brother. Furbish's long black arm was waving. "Where yuh-all been, Sheriff Broderick? As a man of th' Cloth, I have a right to know why—in a time like this—you shouldn't be cogni—cognizant of sech gatherings in yore streets."

Broderick's eyes hadn't moved from the younger Weldon who now stood, weak inside from the manifold premonitions that dogged him.

Furbish made a grandiose gesture. "He's seen Dan Weldon!"

But Broderick didn't pay any attention. He said: "Shore, I heard some noise up in th' Rand General Store—was a-talking to Abe Rand. But I didn't figger anything was wrong till I come out an' see you a-millin' in th' street. Who are you, son?"

The figure before him with bent head did not reply.

"Young Weldon," said Jake Macom.

Broderick grunted as though he had been hit. He went forward, hard lines in his face casting it in a white, tight expression. When he spoke his voice was hoarse with pent-up rage.

"Young Weldon! Then you-all been baitin' him here in th' street. By golly, if I don't tan someone's hide—"

He went to the small figure, put a hand on its shoulder.

"Wait," snapped Furbish. His eyes were flashing, a wide grin spread across his face. "I'd like to find out one thing. Me and a coupla people here jest heard this lad yell out his brother's name. Like he'd all of a sudden seen him—f'r instance, over in th' jail. You got anyone in there?"

Broderick looked at the round, ruddy face before him, examined the grinning questioning smile.

"Sure!" he snapped angrily. "That drunk Injun, Leo Fast Pony. If he was attractin' attention out here that means someone's been sneaking red-eye into the jail again. Goldarn it!"

"Didn't sound to me like he seen no Injun," Furbish said suspiciously.

"Well, that's all he coulda," returned the sheriff. "An' if I see anyone sneakin' in there to look at that Injun, I'll larrup his ears down. Meddling with my prisoner—!" Broderick snorted and moved the slouching shape on pipe-stem legs towards the house on the little rise behind the jail. "If he seen anyone it was Leo—an' th' way you ring-tail baboons been carryin' on, wonder he didn't see General Grant his-self in there!"

That seemed to quiet the angry murmurs in the crowd. They began to disperse, leaving Slick Furbish alone and cogitating in the middle of the street. Occasionally he glanced at the jail, a suspicious light growing in his eyes.

He seemed to make up his mind, for he wheeled on his heels, strode rapidly up the street, past the Rand General Store and out of sight.

A lithe, broad shouldered shape stepped around a sheltering corner of a barn about a block below the jail. It was Wayne Morgan. With squinting, dangerous eyes, he watched the preacher disappear.

He said softly to himself: "Reverend Slick Furbish."

Morgan had arrived in Wild Vein just in time to hear the sounds of the cat-calls in the street. From behind the corner of the barn, he watched the crowd carefully, saw Bucky glance around and shout the one word that had set the mob on edge.

He had watched the sheriff dodging the crowd's questions. Morgan stamped out the quirley he had been smoking and turned to disappear from sight of Wild Vein's main street.

Dan Weldon, he realized now, had to be gotten out of jail in a hurry. If he guessed rightly, there would be a mob at the jail before long. Furbish had heard Bucky shout and had guessed that the youngster's eyes had not deceived him. And a mob—stirred up by the grinning preacher-*hombre*— would want Dan Weldon's life.

CHAPTER XIV

FURBISH ACTS

W AYNE MORGAN AND Blue Hawk took a position near the summit of one of the higher hills surrounding Wild Vein. Below them the street of the town and the front door of the jail were clearly visible. The Indian sat, silent, motionless beneath a towering fir as the time passed. But not so the long limbed form of Morgan. Nervously, he paced between the trees, seldom relaxing his gaze on the tiny village below them.

For the present he had decided to delay his visit as Wayne Morgan. That would require explanations which might hamper his determination to strike hard and fast when a crowd appeared before the jail.

FOR A LONG time Furbish stayed in the rough little room he rented while in Wild Vein, seated on his blanketed bed, deep in thought.

Around three o'clock in the afternoon, when the town began to come to life, Furbish stood up, examined himself carefully in a mirror and strode out the door. Where questions and hard problems had been in his mind before, determination now lay.

He made his way rapidly through town, into the woods some distance behind the Rand General Merchandise Store. Before long he pushed his way through low branches and stopped.

When he called softly, "Kemp—Kemp!" the squat, wine-tun shape moved out of the shelter of nearby trees and approached him.

Kemp's stubbled beard did not disguise the hard line of his lips, nor the angry glints of his small beady eyes.

"Wall?" he questioned sullenly.

Furbish grinned, a short chuckle came up into his throat and died. "Kemp," he grunted, "you shore look like the last of the Philistines. You recall how the Lord told them—"

Kemp swore. "Lay off your damn fake Holy-rollerin' around me, Furbish. I don't like it and never did. What d'you want?"

Furbish's grin disappeared. His eyes puckered, stared at the stubbled features.

"You remember," he said in a cool voice, "I was askin' you a question yesterday when we were interrupted by that damn Indian. You didn't answer me. Now, what I want to know is, *why did you shoot Weldon?*"

"You know damn well!" Kemp snapped. "He killed Hess Rand. It would've been a damn good thing to get rid of th' rat. I had a chance, and took it!"

For a second their gazes met and clashed. In Furbish's eyes, bright suspicion sat. "Well," he said succinctly, "I'm a-mighty suspicious, Kemp. If it's really somethin' unlawful, remember all crimes meets th' final and inexorable punishment of the damned! For yore own good—"

Kemp swore, cut the preacher's words off short. He wheeled on his heel, started stalking rapidly through the brush. But before Furbish could move or call, Kemp turned and came back.

"I wanted to see you too, Furbish. That gold that went over th' cliff with Johnny R's been stolen. You got any of it?"

Furbish's red eyebrows lifted. "No."

"Well, I'd wring your filthy neck if I didn't believe you couldn't of got over the cliff," snapped the squat-one.

"Lissen, mornin' b'fore last you an' me come riding towards Wild Vein. You recall how and where we found Johnny R after he fell over th' cliff. He was delirious-like, talkin' to himself. Well, he kept saying sorta, 'She'll a-pull her off north' every few minutes, then: 'You ain't gonna get one single dollar, Sam.' Something liken to that. It was the only name I heard mentioned: Sam. Who'd he mean? Sam who?"

Lights seemed suddenly to break into Furbish's eyes. "Sam?" he repeated wonderingly. Then his voice changed. "Strange, weren't it? The first time we'd met in fifteen years out in that canyon, we run plunk into that pore critter all done in." He cocked his head on one side like a big bird of the crane family. "Sam?" he mused. "Unless it mightta been—of course," he exclaimed, "Johnny R used to live out there. It was Sam—!

His mouth clamped shut with a noise like a closing trap before the next syllable came out. Suspicions flicked into his gaze. "What d'you want to—"

But with a snarl Kemp was on him grappling at his arms, his big steely fingers crushing muscles and bone. Furbish grimaced.

"Who was it?" snarled Kemp thrusting his face into Furbish's. "You know, you damned old rat!"

Furbish had in reality suspected who the "Sam" was when he first heard it on Johnny's lips. He yanked his arm out of Kemp's grasp. For the past few days he had wondered many times how Sam Ludlow was connected with the poor creature they had found not three minutes after he and Kemp, whom he had known fifteen years before when he was traveling under a far different brand, had met in the gully. For his own subtle purposes he wished

Kemp to know who the "Sam" was, yet did not believe it best to tell him outright. His foil had raised Kemp to a fever heat.

Furbish pulled his arm out of Kemp's grasp.

"Wall," he drawled slowly, "if you done overpowered yerself with curiosity and want to act like a spoiled two-year-old, I'll tell you. It was Sam Ludlow, probably."

"How d'you know?" snapped the other.

Furbish shrugged his shoulders. "You asked me what I think. That's what I think—"

Kemp did not speak. He grunted, started to move away, only to be stopped by Furbish's hand on his shoulder.

"There's a fortune in gold up in them hills, Kemp. What you think is that if you trail this man, find out what that man knows, you'll get a lead before anyone else does. Plus a little luck, you might find this caché. If you do, Kemp, you're going to steal it!"

Kemp's eyes widened, his full lips twisted sarcastically. "And what would you do, Reverend Slick Furbish?"

The small round face before Kemp flushed slowly. Furbish's massive adam's apple twisted, rose and fell. He blinked slowly. "Wall," he said softly, "fer a consideration," he pronounced the word carefully—"fer a consideration, I'll tell you something. Now, I'm not shore of it, but you ken do what you will with the idea. I only ask that I get my share of whatever you—er—" he scowled searching for a word, "er—gross."

Kemp nodded slowly.

"It's this," Furbish's voice lowered a full tone. "I figger Broderick done still got Dan Weldon—" at that point his voice dropped, became an almost inaudible whisper.

Kemp listened carefully, his beady eyes two gleaming slits of suspicion and avarice. Finally he nodded.

CHAPTER XV

A STORM BREAKS

S HADOWS WERE ALREADY beginning to lengthen across the main street of Wild Vein when Blizzard Kemp mounted the board steps in front of The Dollar Bill and entered. Once inside the low ceilinged, smoke-filled room, he paused at the door, ran his eyes through the small crowd, the several cowmen playing five card at the green table in the far corner of the room.

He went over to Tolman behind the bar and, leaning forward, spoke a few words in the fat barkeep's ear. Tolman grunted and pointed.

"Shore, that's him," said Tolman. "Sam Ludlow, his brother Art too."

Kemp nodded, said, "Thanks," and turned in their direction.

Sam and Art were hunched over whiskey ponies in a far and darker corner of the room, talking softly, confidentially.

"Hullo," said Kemp. "Understand yer Sam Ludlow."

Ludlow looked up, eyed the newcomer quizzically. Kemp pulled up a chair, placed it closer to the two Ludlows' table.

Ludlow's eyes widened. "Yer Kemp, ain't yuh? Thought you ditched outta town after you plugged young Weldon. What happened, law let you go?"

Kemp flushed a little, looked steadily into Ludlow's eyes.

"Long as I didn't shoot straight ain't no reason I can't come back into town, is there?"

Ludlow grinned humorlessly. "Jest th' same th' sheriff ain't seen you, I'll lay to that. Murderous intent's still a crime 'round these parts."

Kemp looked the Ludlow straight in the eye. "If it was, you wouldn't be sitting here yerself," he said to the would-be lyncher.

But Ludlow didn't smile now. His eyes began to squint, watch the face of the other questioningly.

"What's he mean, Sam?" asked Art Ludlow quickly.

"Lynchin'," Sam snapped. "What's on yer mind, Kemp?"

The stocky, thick-shouldered one hitched his chair closer, looked about him to see that no strangers lay within earshot. His voice was low, hissing, when it hit against the Ludlows' ears.

"Been looking around town most of th' afternoon fer you. Heard you wuz in town and also that there wuz three of you. Where's yer other brother?"

Sam Ludlow eyed Kemp warily, then shrugged his shoulders. "Why?"

"Has a bearin' on what I'm gonna tell you," snapped Kemp.

"Go on, tell him," Art Ludlow cut in, "What's wrong with it?" He turned to Kemp. "Luke's up in th' Moccasins looking fer that there gold caché we been hearing about and the gold that went over the cliff. He couldn't wait tuh get his fingers intuh it—which don't mean nothing at all. 'Bout fifty people up there I figger now, an' one chanct in eight billion uh findin' it."

"That's what I wanted to know," argued Kemp. "No, he won't find it. But we might!"

Sam Ludlow pinioned the speaker with translucent, bulging eyes. "If it's so good, why you cutting us in on it?" he snapped suspiciously.

"Lissen," hissed Kemp. "I'll tell you. *Weldon's still in jail!*"

For a passing second curious silence lay over the men. Then Sam Ludlow spoke. "How yuh gonna prove it?"

"I will," said Kemp. "If he's in jail there's one way of finding out."

"What?" asked Art.

"What?" Kemp wheeled. "Use yore brain, ranny," he bent forward. "A little talk," he snapped. "A little moving around th' crowd here and there. First thing you know we'll have a hundred men rarin' tuh go."

Sam Ludlow nodded. He rose, looked down at his brother and Kemp. His face was grim-jawed now, the small beady eyes flashing angry, cold flames. "I get yer right," he snapped, "and it won't take ten minutes. Come on, Art. You too, Kemp. Hey, Tolman!" his voice raised above the murmur of voices, "A drink for everyone!"

SHERIFF BRODERICK SAW the mob forming in front of The Dollar Bill from the Rand Store. He had been in to see Abe Rand again, found him talking excitedly though subduedly to Sam Ludlow. He hadn't butted in, but had gone outside again. There the crowd's noise attracted him. In it he saw Art Ludlow's nodding head, gesticulating arms.

In the moving dark bodies down the street from him he read instant warning. Without a word he ducked his head, moved at a run across the open street towards the jail. Once in his office he buckled on his Colts, grabbed a rifle off of the rack above his desk and swung in through another part of the jail, locking doors. He intended to stop at Weldon's cell but the racket outside made him give that up.

Voices, the hard trample of many feet sounded in the street outside. Broderick turned in the half dark of the jail's interior and went towards the open door. He stepped out onto the small wooden walk, just in time to stop the form of Art Ludlow from stalking up the steps and into the place.

In the semi-dark area before the jail there was a sight that set Broderick's lips grim and determined. Half a hundred people clamored there. The speed with which they had assembled was surprising.

Immediately behind Art Ludlow was the form of Kemp.

Broderick raised his voice, bellowed in a tone that stopped the murmurs and half shouts arising from the small sea of faces.

"What you folks after, Art?"

Before Art Ludlow or Kemp could answer a big form came pushing its way through the crowd.

"There's Sam Ludlow," called someone. "He'll tell you, Broderick!"

A second later Broderick fronted the oldest Ludlow. Sam's face was grim-lipped, his battered sombrero pushed back from his head.

"We want justice, Broderick," Ludlow shouted in a voice that carried far back into the crowd and raised a shout of approval. "We demand to know who you got in that jail!"

Broderick's lips twisted in a wry smile. "And who do you think?" he returned. "Leo Fast Pony, folks," he called out. "But you ain't gonna have him. By God, I'll shoot down the first *hombre* that comes a step closer, bar nothing!"

"We don't want him," voices came from the road. "Tell him, Ludlow. We want Weldon!"

A cool chill finger traced its way up the sheriff's spine. He saw the crowd part again and give place to the shape of his friend, old Abe Rand.

Lorie Rand's grandfather was slender, long-limbed. A dark store suit, the trousers of which were tucked in high embroidered boots made him stand out in bold relief against the crowd. High cheek bones set off the angry dark pools of his eyes, the grim straight line of his lips, his virile white goatee.

"Sheriff Broderick," he said in a carrying voice, "I understand you're supposed to have young Weldon still in jail. People around here claim they seen someone inside there today—that didn't look like any Indian. As justice of the peace of this town, Broderick, I order you to divulge said information to the town immediately!"

Broderick looked down into the handsome old face of Abe Rand. He did not believe that Rand would allow the lynching of young Weldon. Abe Rand's code was sharply and honestly defined. If Weldon were inside, old Abe would take him, shoot the matter out without a moment's waste.

For a passing second Broderick wondered if that wouldn't be the easiest way around a difficult problem. But he made up his mind, clenched his teeth.

"Sorry, Abe," he said. "Even if Weldon wuz in here, I couldn't let you have him anyway."

Ludlow broke in. "Folks," he called out. "Yuh see? He ain't answered a straight-forward question yet." He turned. "If Weldon ain't in there Broderick, why ain't you away watching him?"

The sheriff's face colored but he didn't answer Sam Ludlow's question.

"In the name of the law," he called out, "I ask you folks to disperse immediately."

"Disperse?" roared a mocking, bull-like voice. "Hear that, folks? If he won't give him up, by God we gotta get him."

Broderick had not seen two small shapes who had ducked in through the crowd, moved in close to the wall. One of them, young Rod Tolman, bent, hoisted a smaller, lighter shape on his shoulders. That figure's creeping fingers gripped at the wall, then clutched grimy small hands on the two short bars of the single high window.

The sheriff wheeled as though he had been struck. "Get down from thar!"

But it was too late. A high piping voice cut through the air. "He's inside! I jest seen him—over in the corner of the cell—moving! He's in there."

Like a flash the two small shapes had disengaged themselves from the wall and bounded out of sight into the crowd. Broderick stooped, his eyes flashing, the rifle held ready at his hip.

Roars of approval cut the air. Then roars of violence and rage.

"We want Weldon!"

"Broderick's a-lyin'!"

"Come on, Abe, let's hang th' yellow rat!"

The crowd in the street was moving now. The mottled haze of faces swirled before the sheriff's eyes; a thousand voices seemed to roar in his ears. But he stood his ground, waiting for the two threatening forms of Abe Rand and Ludlow to move.

At that second Broderick felt a hand come out of the

dark behind him and touch his shoulder. He knew the touch and paled. His wife, Ma Broderick, had had a key to the back door of the jail for years. For some reason she had left the house, entered by the rear door and now stood at his side.

"What is it?" he mumbled.

She was sobbing and frightened, he could tell by the low shake in her voice.

He felt her leaning forward, talking to him. And as she did, his trail-seamed features tensed perceptibly.

A second later he snapped in a low voice, "Tell the lad."

THE MASKED RIDER moved back into the shelter of low-growing brush behind the jail when he saw the door open. He made out the figure of Ma Broderick closing the door and running slowly towards the house on the knoll. As she passed, the sob that caught in her throat was plainly audible.

But for the second that did not take the masked man's attention. His trained ears, keyed to the sound of the closing jail door, told him that that door had not latched shut. It was a signal that wrote demands for instant action within him.

Like a tenuous shadow he moved out of the brush and a second later slid inside the rear entrance of the place. In the darkness ahead he could hear the heavy-breathing of Weldon sounding above the muffled roar of the crowd outside.

"Weldon." It was more of a brief command than a signal.

"Yes," came from the farther shadows. "Who is it?"

In another second the masked man was standing before

Weldon's cell. He could see the face of the other, illumi-nated by the meager light from the high window. It was drawn in hard, fighting lines.

"It's you," snapped Weldon. "You're back. Listen, you helped me once. Now for God's sake, do it again. Ma Brod-erick just came in. My brother, Bucky, was eating up at the sheriff's place. Someone broke in the window, got him before he could yell. By the time Ma Broderick got into the kitchen Bucky and the kidnaper were gone. Gone!"

It was the cry of a tortured animal that racked the masked man's ears.

"Did she see him?" he snapped.

"Broderick told her to tell me this. She—she thinks it's Kemp!"

"Kemp? Then he's—"

"Sure he is," burst in the other. "He kidnaped Bucky so he'd be able to find the way up to Moccasin cut and out again. Somehow he found out where the gold is. It's plain as day. If he doesn't get the gold, someone else will and Kemp will hold Bucky for ransom. If he finds the gold, God knows what will happen to the kid. Go after him, you can get him. He hasn't had much start. I don't give a damn what happens to me."

Something seemed to click within the masked man's mind. Outside the shouts of the mob were growing stron-ger. He knew that Broderick could hold them only a matter of minutes now. Besides—

"Listen to me," he shot at the pallid face behind the bars. "I brought an extra pony for you in case I could get you away from this lynching mob. It's behind the jail. Go left and into the brush. My black is near it. You know the way to go. Now get out of my way!"

Out in front Broderick's ear drums were nearly split by the thunderous roar that filled the small, thick-walled jail. He recognized in that sound the escape of his prisoner, the wrecking of the cell's lock. But that did not shake him.

"That's Weldon getting out," roared a voice in the crowd. *"Come on!"*

"Come on?" Broderick roared. "Th' first one that tries is gonna get a slug in the stomach. I'm sheriff in these parts and I won't stand by an'—"

But he didn't finish his sentence. An object spun over the heads of the crowd. An object that sped a true and violent course straight for Broderick's head. He did not see it coming. The rock struck with shattering force square against his right temple. With a grunt the sheriff dropped from sight.

For a second the mob poised in startled silence. Then, with a roar, surged forward, pushing the line of men at the front towards the jail door.

Sam Ludlow reached the door of the jail first, he plunged for the darkened entrance, yanking at the gun in his right holster.

He stepped over the prostrate form of the sheriff. But as he did, something that had all the force of a battering ram came out of the dark at him. It caught him on the chin, sent him crashing backward against the pressing bodies. The force of his falling slowed the rush momentarily. Just long enough for a shape to materialize out of the darkness of the jail's interior.

Outside meager light outlined it. For a second the men in the first ranks stared open mouthed. In the dull light, a dark sombrero, a hooded head and shoulders stood in hazy delineation against the shades. Through the twin slits of the hood, cold glinting eyes reflected the feeble rays from the street. Dully apparent to them too were the ugly snouts of two forty-fives peeping from the rim of the low-hanging cloak.

"Th' Masked Rider!"

The cry rose, billowed through the crowd in growing, overwhelming roars.

Jake Macom, who had joined the crowd early and now stood on the right of Art Ludlow, came to life first. In the half-darkness, his hand whipped downward.

Two revolver shots that sounded almost simultaneously split the silence. Macom's bullet plugged the door frame near the masked man's head. But the pellet of lead that followed the flare of the gun at the fringe of the black cloak went true to its mark. Macom plunged forward, slid to his face on the wooden steps.

Pandemonium then broke like a bolt of lightning over the mob. Guns were flipped out, triggers pulled. But before any of those shots were fired, the masked figure had leaped out of the revealing background of the doorway. The jail's heavy door swung shut with a thunderous clap. All of ten bullets slugged into the heavy oak as a bar dropped on the other side.

The cloaked form wheeled, raced down the short hallway towards the rear door of the jail, leaped outside.

A figure, doubled up, appeared around the corner of the jail, lunged towards him. The man did not see the masked form. When he did, he pulled up with a grunted oath mere feet away.

Like a boxer, the cloaked shape wheeled. One gun came up, descended with crushing force on the forehead of the man before it. He dropped like a sodden sack.

When the figure hit the ground, The Masked Rider bent, slid into the shades. Before him a soft voice was whispering.

"Here, *senor.* We must hurry. He got the extra pony."

In another second, the black was wheeling, following the disappearing shape of Blue Hawk's sorrel. On his back the cloaked form dodged the low hanging limbs behind the jail and disappeared into the gloom.

A handful of running cursing men dodged around the jail corner, stumbled over the limp shape there and made for the wide swinging door that now opened on the interior. One of them, Sam Ludlow, cursed, leaped in.

MOMENTS LATER THE black stallion was pulled up in the shade of jack pines a quarter of a mile outside of Wild Vein. For the first time then did Blue Hawk speak.

"*Senor,* was there no time to get the boy?"

The cloaked figure shook its head.

A soft murmur sped from the Indian's lips, "*Si, Senor.* What then?"

"Kemp has kidnapped the boy."

There was a long moment of silence then. From far behind them dim shouts above the subdued roar of voices came distinctly. Finally the Indian spoke.

"If he has gone into the mountains, *senor,* there is a way to find him."

"How?"

"Patience," said the other, "waiting. Blue Hawk has eyes that will see many things—sometimes far away. In two days, *senor,* I think I will be able to seek him out, though he hides well."

The hooded figure sat in silence, then said: "Two days is

a long time, Hawk. A lot of things can happen. But before we can go further now, we have to get the girl."

"The girl?"

But the masked man did not continue. The Indian seemed to understand his meaning. Without a word he wheeled the sorrel, moved it through the low hanging branches. In another moment he passed out of sight-on a trail he knew would tax even his alert, finely trained trailing instincts.

HOURS LATER, RIDING along a moonlit trail in the Moccasins, the Indian pulled the sorrel up. Ahead of him, the quick noisy beat of a hard pressed pony's hoofs had caught his trained ears. Though the oncoming rider was still some distance ahead of him, the Indian turned his pony off the trail, into the thick brush and awaited the approach. Before many minutes the rider appeared, leaning over his pony's neck, pushing it as rapidly as possible in the direction of Wild Vein.

In a fleeting bit of moonlight, Blue Hawk saw his face as he passed. It was Luke Ludlow. When the rider vanished, Blue Hawk appeared. There was a questioning frown on his bronzed features. But without further thought the Indian pressed his sorrel rapidly up-trail.

Nearly a mile down-trail from where he had passed Blue Hawk, Ludlow rounded a bend in the narrow, tree-bordered path and drew his pony to a jerking halt. Before him, square across his path stood a horse. Its rider was half hidden in the shadows of the trees, but not enough to conceal his hulking thick shape, the massive contours of his heavy shoulders. Luke Ludlow grunted, his hand instinctively drifting downward towards his gun.

Kemp had taken his time, leaving Wild Vein. And at

that moment, Bucky Weldon, well tied, was vainly writhing some distance off the trail.

Kemp said, "Hullo, mister. Do you mind if I ask yore name? I'm huntin' a party called Luke Ludlow an' figgered yo're maybe him."

Luke Ludlow grunted, eyed the half concealed shape before him. Then he said: "I might be."

With that the massive man on the pony across the trail moved his mount forward until his and Ludlow's ponies stood shoulder to shoulder in the moonlight. Ludlow saw then that a half smile was spread across the stranger's face.

The man was saying, "M' name's Kemp. Bliz Kemp. Yer brother Sam Ludlow said you'd be up in th' Moccasins and that if you were coming down into town, you'd told him you'd be riding this trail."

"That's so," nodded the other Ludlow. "But I got purty urgent—" he stopped.

There was a moment of silence. "Wall," said Kemp, "to get down to business right off, you don't need to be backward with me. Sam, Art and me jest found out that Weldon wuz in jail in Wild Vein."

"Huh?" blurted the lanky Ludlow.

"Shore, he wuz in jail, but he ain't now. They finally made Broderick confess he'd holed him up. I wuz sent along to meet you, tell you to dust down-trail and meet Sam and Art outta Wild Vein. Sam said you'd know which trail to take. He's doin' a coupla things around Wild Vein and needs you."

"Then he's still in town," snapped Luke.

"Might be," Kemp admitted. There was something in the Ludlow's manner that sent a shadow of suspicion into

Kemp's mind. He watched the other's moonlit face with squinting, intent eyes.

"Well, if he is," said Ludlow abruptly, "I might stop him in time."

Kemp did his best to make his voice sound unsuspicious. "What for?"

Luke Ludlow leaned forward in the saddle. "I wuz up in the Moccasins," he said in a low voice, "long as you and Sam are sorta in this thing together, I might say, I done located something in th' river valley shore got me figgerin'."

Kemp grunted. Inner light struck him. Luke was stupid.

Luke Ludlow's voice cracked in a long laugh. "Maybe it's what they were talking about in town and mebbe not. Yes sir, up in th' river valley, what do you think I done found next to a great big rock jest like it? This!"

The Ludlow's face was wreathed in a quizzical grimace. He fumbled in his pocket, produced an object that lay for a second in his hand, revealed by the soft glow of the moon.

It was a black piece of rock, obsidian perhaps, with a spider web of shiny little veins running through it. Thread-like veins which for a passing second reflected the silver radiance that bathed the trail.

Ludlow's pony jumped back, reared. Kemp's mount snorted in terror at the deafening explosion that thundered above its ears, wheeled, only to be thrown back on its haunches by the powerful hand on its reins.

Luke Ludlow's lanky, loose jointed frame bent in the middle, plunged awkwardly from its saddle and plopped in the trail. When he fell, he landed spread eagle, face up to the moonlight. A darkened, round hole in his forehead seemed to move, then run in a black river over his contorted face and to the ground....

In another second, Kemp, the smoking pistol still in his hand, had clambered down from his pony and was bending over Ludlow, grappling at the object clutched tightly in the closing fingers....

AS HAD HAPPENED many times in his life, The Masked Rider had reacted to an inner message, a divination based on his understanding of human nature.

When he turned the black stallion's head, it was in the direction of the Moccasins; and before many moments, he had left the deep murmurs of the street of Wild Vein well behind. Then pushing the stallion up a steep embankment, he entered the main trail that mounted into the dark silent reaches of the wooded range.

Not long after that, he pushed off the trail and waited, hidden by the underbrush.

After some moments his trained ears told him his waiting had not been in vain. Clear sounds of a pony coming rapidly uptrail broke the forest stillness. The hoof-beats grew in volume, became a muffled trip-hammer approaching him.

In another moment a rider, mounted on a struggling, bulging-eyed horse, burst into sight around a corner in the trail. The pound of hoofs, the high squeak of strained saddle leather filled the air.

Before the approaching pony was seventy-five feet away, a muffled word escaped from the dark hood. With a single quick motion, the stallion went forward and bounded square across the trailway, poising there.

The oncoming rider pulled its mount back on its haunches, let it rear and come back to earth with a solid thump. The pony snorted, then backed fearfully away from the other horse.

Before The Masked Rider, and now fully revealed in the random rays of moonlight that illuminated the trail, was a woman. She wore a hat whose brim cast heavy shadows over her-face, obscuring it. A split khaki riding skirt descended from lithe, small hips and drifted down to the tops of trim riding boots.

"You following Dan Weldon?"

The girl stiffened. "In a way—but—"

The drawling voice under the hood interrupted her. "Where are you headed for?"

There was a pause. "The Open A."

"How did you know he was there?"

"I didn't. I—I knew he'd escaped, and that Bucky had disappeared. I thought the Open A might be the best bet before too many people left town hunting for him. They're trying to make up a posse, you know. I—well—"

Indecision shook the girl's voice. "Oh, you know as well as I do that we Rands have no real claim to that gold. Besides, Dan Weldon needs money. But he needs something more than that. He needs help, and men to back him." There came a new tone. "Yes, men to back him up. Men like you, perhaps. Can't you do something. Can't you—"

"You're right," broke in the hooded man. "But you haven't answered me. What are you doing up here, why are you on his trail? What can you do?"

A pair of anguished, dark eyes turned into his. "I—I don't know. I did the only thing I could think of—I came as fast as I could, hunting for him. If I find him, then—then—"

It was a cry in the night that to the masked man became the voice of eternal Woman, calling, searching for the one she loved. Hastening to protect, to lend her meager strength against the indomitable crushing forces of a hostile world.

"You're going up-trail," she said. "Please—please let me ride with you."

For a moment The Masked Rider turned her words over in his mind. It was true that riding with him placed her in a dangerous position. But her peril was still greater if she rode alone. So without a word he turned the big stallion into the trailway.

The girl seemed to take that for her answer, for she pressed her pony's ribs, followed the masked man off into the indistinct shades, her heart beating with trip-hammer blows that seemed to shake her whole body.

Before, she had been uncertain of her course, had struggled too much between conflicting emotions and interests. Now, her mind made up, she followed with complete faith the path her heart and mind indicated.

CHAPTER XVI

ARROYO AMBUSH

WHILE THE SUN was erecting a halo of shimmering spun-gold over the bare spiny ridges of the farther hogs-backs, The Masked Rider pulled his black off the trail, motioned the rider following to do likewise.

The place where they stopped was overrun with wild and splendid beauty. The trail behind had risen in the Moccasins, mounted a ridge and now, as if poised for a leap into space, projected to the edge of a sheer dizzying embankment.

Before them lay Moccasin Cut.

"Better let your animal graze a bit," the masked figure said. "That's a tough pull up here."

Lorrie Rand dismounted. As she did, both she and the hooded man were jerked to alert attention. Without a sound, the man on the stallion slid out of the saddle and leading his mount, strode towards the girl.

"Out of sight—in a hurry," he snapped.

It took no more than a second to pull the girl's mount well out of the trailway and into nearby brush. Her face paled as she watched him pull the big black after him.

"Who could it be?"

The hooded man gave no answer. Below them and out of sight over the lip of the cliff came the sounds of a rapidly climbing pony. As the sounds grew, it became increasingly obvious that the rider was in great haste, sparing his pony little in its rapid progress up the nearly perpendicular trail.

The heavy thumps came closer. As they did, one of the .45s hidden beneath the black cloak came out and centered on the place where the trail led up on to the flat.

At that second a sorrel's head appeared, bobbing frantically. Its rider came abruptly into view. A quirt whistled and slapped the pony's haunches. The animal recoiled, then bounded the last few feet up-trail. With a snort it gathered its muscles and leaped out across the open space.

With a low shout, the masked man bounded out of the bushes and into full view.

The rider of the sorrel let out a frightened squeak and pulled his pony up.

"Holy smoke!" blurted the big-hatted figure on the sorrel's back. "The Masked Rider!"

The hooded man walked towards the sorrel.

Bucky Weldon let out another subdued exclamation as Lorie Rand stepped out of the bushes also and approached.

"What—what d'you want?" he questioned nervously.

"Just an explanation," said the hooded man stopping. "Where'd you come from. Where's Kemp—and your brother?"

Bucky's face relaxed at the friendly tone. For a second he eyed the girl questioningly, then turned to The Masked Rider.

"Kemp? That's what Dan and me'd like to know. Dan, he's down in there," the younger Weldon turned and pointed below.

He paused, then seeing a fuller explanation was necessary, he said: "I wuz eatin' dinner an' this fellow Kemp reached in and pulled me outta th' window. He brought me up here, on the saddle in front of him. It was after midnight when we got up here, so Kemp built a fire in a ravine. Dan, he seen it from th' top here and come down. There wasn't much after that, 'cause we—" he accented the 'we'—"done give Kemp what was coming to him. Only he got away. But," Bucky added, "we got this pony of Kemp's."

The hooded man nodded. "Why are you up here?"

"Well, Dan allowed as how he'd like to stay down in the gully and keep after that gold. He said Kemp'd probably hide around down there too, but Dan wasn't gonna leave for no crooked, thievin' hoss-thief, no-how. He says, 'You git th'—'" Bucky paused, glanced at the girl and flushed. "He said, 'Git outta this ravine as fast as I could and keep on going to th' Open A.' He wuz gonna meet me there later."

"And he stayed below there," mused the hooded man.

He glanced at the girl's face. It was pale. For a second her eyes searched his,' questioning.

The Masked Rider said abruptly. "If I shoot three times, that means that it's safe to come down. If I don't shoot, wait up here until the middle of the morning then go on down to the Open A. If anyone starts up the cliff, keep hidden until he's well out of sight."

Bucky Weldon's mouth snapped open. "If you're goin' down, me too!"

When the others turned, Bucky colored. "Well," he stated lamely, "Dan might need me if there's a battle."

A look that Bucky saw plainly passed between Lorie Rand and the hooded man. She looked up.

"But who will take care of me?" she asked.

Bucky flushed a bandana-red from his shirt collar to the roots of his tangled, blonde thatch. He hitched at the cannon-like weapon still in his belt. That the khaki-clad vision whom embarrassment would normally keep him from speaking to had abruptly called upon him for aid and uncompromisingly bestowed upon him the estate of manhood, he was profoundly aware. For a second he was unable to speak.

"Well," he stumbled finally. "Well, I guess I *could* stay."

The girl smiled. And with that smile transferred herself to a permanently worshipped niche in Bucky's heart.

The masked figure was walking towards the black, mounting it and turning towards them.

"Remember," he said. "If I shoot three times together, come down. You might stay near the edge where I can see you from below. You'll be safe up here for the time being. There'll be a lot of gold-crazy bad men around here. Take care. *Adios!*"

He waved, wheeled the stallion and started for the cliff's lip where the trail slipped past whitened boulders and out of sight.

BUCKY, STILL FLUSHING with the importance of the duty that lay before him, walked towards the edge, watched the hooded figure and the towering stallion pick their way slowly down the rock-ledged ribbon clinging to the face of the bare granite wall.

Once at the base of the cliff, the man in the hood was traveling on strange ground. For that reason he kept to the shelter of trees, avoided the open trailway that wound across the flat base of the valley and into the woods on the other side.

Once he looked back, saw the two dotlike figures high above him watching his movements.

The Masked Rider had calculated Johnny R's caché was somewhere in this valley. The fact that Lorie Rand could recognize the probable position of the caché was information he would have to use later.

On the other side of the valley the terrain changed much. The ground was sandy, boulder-strewn. A glacial river had once wound through it, cutting deep arroyos in the valley bed, leaving the earth barren and dry. Occasional clumps of cactus in the dry river bottom bespoke the fact that no moisture and great constant heat had killed off much of the other vegetation.

Through these deep gullies the black stallion wound. Nearly half an hour after he had left the base of the cliff, the hooded man pulled the horse to a slow walk, moved carefully through the scrub oak dotting a sandy *barranca* side. His lips were tight, the gray eyes burning through the twin slits in the hood were intent, watchful. Every sense was trained on the trail ahead. Any moment, he knew, one of the Ludlows, Kemp, perhaps even Dan Weldon, might appear in the gully-channelled valley bottom.

The black heard the sounds first, stopped, its head and ears rising, its eyes exploring the dark barrier of stunted oaks through which they were passing. Without a sound, the masked man slid from the saddle, moved at a slower pace.

He could hear the sounds plainer now. Ahead of them a pony was walking slowly on hard rock or boulders. Click, click, then a brief rumble when its shod hoofs hit a loose footing of boulders.

The hooded figure's jaw tightened. With swift, sure motions he pulled the stallion's reins over its head, let them flop free on the ground. Then he bent, moved silently into the shades of nearby low-growing parched trees.

He had not gone a hundred paces before a low whistle escaped from his lips and he slid into the disguising cover of a mesquite bush. Slowly his hands crept downward, gripped with fingers of steel about the hard butt of one of the .45s half-hidden by the flowing cape.

He was on the lip of a narrow, winding gully. A hundred yards away he could see the source of the sounds. A sorrel pony, heavily laden, was making its way down the gully. Flung over the saddle and lashed together were two bulging gunny sacks. As he watched, the pony slithered on its imperfect footing.

But the back of the man leading it, when its outlines showed, brought a lower, more intent whistle from the hooded man. It was Dan Weldon.

The Masked Rider moved, pushed aside the bushes

that separated him from the edge of the gully. With lightning-like speed he dropped face down on the earth, inert.

A movement, the barest flashing glimpse of a colored object nearer him than the laden horse had caught his eye.

For a second The Masked Rider lay as he had fallen. He saw the movement again, recognized it as a human figure partially hidden by the rim of a boulder in the base of the gully. He saw its back come farther into view when it eased out of the hiding place Weldon had just passed.

The man was low, squat in stature. His wide shoulders jutted out from his bull-like neck. A dark shirt made the delineations of them hard to see against the rocks. But nonetheless The Masked Rider did see a gun barrel. It glittered blue rays of the sun rising over the rock, and it pointed for the moving pony and Dan Weldon's back!

Kemp had been in the gully, had seen Weldon and his pony coming, and hidden himself. Now that they were past him, he braced himself, prepared to shoot.

A revolver exploded with hollow thunder against the walls of the narrow gully. In reality two guns went off simultaneously, their roars blending. But Dan Weldon heard only one.

What felt like a red-hot knife sliced into his shoulder, spinning him around and knocking him with violent force to the earth. But his mind reacted with speed equal to the bullet's. In falling he twisted, dropped behind a nearby boulder, cutting him off from another shot from the gully.

Pain sent a hazy film across his eyes, blurring sight of the rearing pony. But in spite of it, he grappled for his gun with his good hand, hoisted himself to his feet and lunged out from his shelter.

A second shot was never fired. On plunging legs Weldon

rounded a corner in the gully bottom, heaved himself up the treacherous, gravelly side and into the low-growing mesquite and scrub oaks dotting its rim.

In acting so, he missed seeing what occurred in the gully. Once hidden by the trees, Weldon gripped his teeth against the driving pain in his right side, moved noiselessly up the gully lip....

Following the shots, a curious scene had been enacted in the gully bottom.

A squat hulking shape erected itself from behind a boulder. It lunged in the direction of Weldon's snorting pony, sliding, scrambling in the loose rocks, striving to keep its balance with frantic haste.

THE FIRST SHOT had been from the hooded man. In the last instant he had seen Kemp's gun move. The one clear target was the dark blue-black shape of Kemp's gun. The hooded man shot at that.

Fortunately his bullet had connected with Kemp's gun just as the thick-set man was pulling the trigger. Kemp's shot hit high. Then a force like a giant hand seemed to grab him by the wrist, jerk him out of the shelter of his boulder.

By that time the hooded figure was already moving. He leaped clear, felt himself suspended momentarily in nothingness, then landing with a solid jolt. Crouching, he ran forward, lunging for the stumbling scurrying shape down the gully.

Kemp heard him coming. He was near Weldon's pony and slid to a stop, turning. His loose-lipped mouth dropped agape. Stuttering words slipped from him when he saw the hooded apparition.

"Th'—*Th' Rider!*"

The masked man came to a stop. "No less," he gritted. "Reach, Kemp."

Kemp's hulking arms arose while he tried to collect his scattered senses. In another second his stubbled features were sullen, the scar that pulled down the corner of his eye a pale streak against them.

But he could not keep his eyes on the masked face. Irresistibly they were drawn to the pony that now stood eyeing them, ears erect. There was something suspicious about the bulges of the gunny sacks slung across its saddle. They were hard bulges, as though the bags contained rock of some sort. But they were heavy for the pony, too heavy perhaps to be only stones, for the animal shifted on its legs unsteadily.

"I found it," blurted Kemp. "He was a-stealin' out of a caché of mine, robbing a claim I made up th' gully. If I shot him it serves him right!"

The figure in the hood smiled grimly, moved flashing eyes across Kemp's face and to Weldon's pony. It showed a brand that was definitely not an Open A.

What he should do with his prisoner, he had not yet decided. Weldon was still up on the gully lip somewhere and might appear any moment. If he saw The Masked Rider—

The muscles of the hooded man tensed. Why the hell hadn't he thought of that before? Weldon wouldn't know he wasn't trying to steal his treasure, only trying to save it for him. Besides, if the masked man did shout at Weldon, make peace, Kemp could use that for potent and damaging evidence once he got the ear to listen to him. A Weldon linked with The Masked Rider!

"If he was stealing it," drawled the hooded man, "maybe

we better go up and see what he left behind at your claim. You can just lead me uptrail—"

There was no doubt that he had punctured the feeble lie Kemp had offered, for the man's face was suddenly blank before he covered the expression with a snarl of refusal.

CHAPTER XVII

A STALL

SOME WAY BACK from the gully rim, Weldon crouched in the brush. Before him, clearly defined now, he could see two figures in the gully bottom. A shadow of a curse sped from him. The Masked Rider! Shore, it was. He'd been kidding himself all the time. It was The Rider who had shot him, The Rider who had freed him at Wild Vein. And for one reason. The gold—

Angry fires burned within Weldon. Here he'd thought all the time the hooded man was trying to help. Another film of pain flashed before Weldon's eyes. He was badly hit, strength wouldn't be in him long, he knew. The hickory shirt he wore was already sopped with the gore that oozed steadily from the bullet wound in his shoulder. He braced himself against the dizzying waves that seemed to engulf him. The Masked Rider had freed him, only to trail him to gold, then murder him!

Slowly he lifted his revolver, pulled the bead on the black-cloaked shape in the gully bottom. Who the hell was that other rat, he wondered. He let that question pass, and pulled the trigger. A reverberant roar beat against his ears.

When the smoke cleared, Weldon gazed unsteadily into the gully. No longer were there two shapes there. But for some reason his instincts told him that with his unsure aim he had hit neither, that they had dodged for cover. In a matter of seconds they would seek him out, shoot him down like a bogged steer.

Laboriously, painfully, Weldon pulled himself to his feet, staggered uphill through the stunted pin oaks. As he went, the path before him became dimmer. Black dots, watery films now seemed to obscure his vision and make him bump into occasional trunks....

THE MASKED RIDER had fallen backward, pulled Kemp with him when Weldon's shot screamed over his head. In spite of this, the forty-five jabbed into Kemp's ribs had not eased up.

The hooded shape crawled into the shelter of a boulder, motioned with the .45 that Kemp do likewise.

"Now get up," he snapped at Kemp.

When the cloaked figure rose, Kemp imitated it.

"What're you gonna do?"

The hooded shape shrugged. "Tie you—until I can get hold of the lad up there. Long as this's out of his caché, I'm gonna give it to him."

Kemp grunted, stared at the masked face. That he did not believe those words was written plainly in his expression. He sneered.

"Like hell!"

The Masked Rider said nothing. A short bit of whale line was coiled over the saddle horn of Weldon's pony. The hooded figure glanced at the gully rim, strode out into the open and got the rope.

At his terse order, Kemp turned and gritted his teeth

while his wrists were being firmly and conclusively lashed behind his back.

The hooded man muttered, stepped backward towards the shelter of a nearby boulder. A black hat suddenly took shape over a boulder further down the gully. It moved jerkily, seemed to advance. A second later a head was added beneath the hat, then a body mounted on a straggly-tailed roman-nosed iron-gray.

A low whistle escaped like steam from Kemp's lips. The man who now appeared in full view riding towards them was Slick Furbish.

But from the masked man no sound, no indications of the warning chill that shot up his backbone, came. Perhaps it was intuition, perhaps his acute sixth sense that sent a warning message shooting into his brain. His eyes flipped upward beyond the gully lips and narrowed. The shock of what he saw, reverberated like the explosion of a gun against his senses!

The iron-gray Furbish rode was moth-eaten, anemic. It clambered painfully up the bouldered bottom, approached the hooded figure, Kemp and Weldon's pony. When it was fifteen feet away from them, the self-termed man of the Cloth pulled up.

"Greetings," he began in a hoarse voice. "And may God be with you." As he said the last, a mocking smile lighted up the narrow slits of his beady eyes. "I trust, Brother, you'll treat a pious minion of the Word with due respect. Figgerin' as how I know you by reputation, you'll admit it took some courage of convictions to approach you open-handed and friendly. After all, son, it was fer yer own good."

Furbish's expression suddenly became solemn, serious.

The hooded figure gritted his teeth. Damn hypocrite,

he was saying to himself, try to gloss it over will you. You have a reason here, out with it!

But he said aloud: "It'd be a pretty low outlaw that'd take advantage of your position—even though its a damned fake. Taking you up on your peaceful words, I'm telling you to unload whatever's bulging your right hip pocket under that coat."

Furbish grunted, examined the ugly snout of the .45 that peeped at him from beneath the flowing black cape.

"Don't mind at all," he stated. "I come unguarded to make *palabra*. You recall me. M'name's Furbish, Reverend Slick Furbish."

With elaborate casualness, Furbish lifted his long-tailed black coat, removed a battered Colt from his rear pocket. This he let drop with a clank to the gravel.

"Only keep it fer wild animals, an' sech—" he started.

The words that came from beneath the black cloak had a cool metallic ring that made him clip his words off short.

"What did you do with the girl and boy?"

Doubts flashed across Furbish's mind. He had expected to approach this subject slowly, to expose his carefully planned bomb before the other when it would explode with maximum effect.

He opened his mouth, started to talk. He had been forced to act abruptly as it was. At present he knew he possessed knowledge of vital and consuming importance to The Masked Rider. Yes, he had seen the three riders stop on the rim of the bluff, realized that for some reason, the Rand girl and young Weldon were now in the company of the most wanted outlaw in the West.

When he had first seen the three, his instinct had been to run for help, to aid and abet in the capture of The

Masked Rider and collect a fair portion of the reward. But subsequent events, the shot in the gully, had attracted his attention....

It would be a tough proposition he told himself. Though he prided himself on being a quick and lucid thinker in tight places, he recognized now that the man before him was his equal, if not more than his match. He thought rapidly, decided to lay his cards on the table.

"Mister Rider," he said, "ain't no use obscurin' th' situation no more'n possible. Yer standin' right beside a person as means considerable to me—fer sentimental reasons. An old friend. I wouldn't like him to come to no harm, irregardless."

He ran his eye over the squat ugly shape of Kemp who regarded his self-elected savior with sullen and suspicious eyes.

"Not only that," said Furbish, "without lookin', I figger there's a plumb handsome bit of cash on thet pony which I'd appreciate to carry away. Jest now, both these seem to be in yore possession, guarded. What ken we do about it?"

The question was purely oratorical. He himself had to answer it.

THE HOODED MAN recognized that and was silent. He stepped back nearer to the wall of the arroyo, slouched lazily against it. But beneath his cloak his muscles were tensed, ready, his eyes never moving from the small ruddy face of Furbish.

That he faced an oily-smooth, unscrupulous customer he did not discount. Furbish knew he was holding the upper hand, had planned on it. It seemed obvious that Lorie and Bucky were in Furbish's clutches. To get them out of the mess without endangering them would take quick and sure action.

"Yer part in this little play is easy," Furbish was saying. "In th' first place I got two men that'll come a-running if you lift that gun er pull the trigger. Afore I fall offen this horse, th' girl and the kid'll be dead!"

Furbish's tone had changed. His pudgy face reddened, he bent forward in the saddle menacingly.

The hooded shape shrugged. "Where are they?"

Furbish jerked a thumb over his shoulder. "Upp'n th' other gully—where no one'll ever find them—if you make us kill them."

"And what do you want me to do?"

Furbish swallowed. It looked as though his plan would go through quicker than he'd thought. He considered a second, said tersely:

"Leave Kemp down here. Ride up to the top of th' bluff and turn around. You'll see me wave, which means th' girl and th' kid'll be left free to beat it. By that time me'n Kemp'll have this horse an' its load safe. I wouldn't ask you to promise not to come back—but if you know whut's good fer your skin, you wouldn't."

For a long time The Masked Rider seemed to be considering Furbish's words. Occasionally the gray eyes turned to the black-frocked man's face, studied the expression there. The growing tightness of his position rang a danger bell in his mind. He'd have to forget Dan Weldon for the time being. Yes, Dan was wounded, but probably not badly. He'd gotten away. Lorie and Bucky were in real danger. He had himself to blame for their plight. Now if Furbish were lying, even in part....

"Don't worry," snapped Furbish as if recognizing his thoughts, "they're up there. Safe, too—unless—"

"I'll believe that part," the hooded man said softly. "Who are they with?"

"Art and Sam Ludlow."

The Masked Rider swore softly. One of these men had tried to butcher Johnny R and lynch Weldon. Yes, both Ludlows are equal to anything. Human lives—

"One thing," The Masked Rider drawled. "Gold and money don't mean a thing to me. Neither does Kemp. But I'd hate to be cold-decked. I'll let you have the pony, I'll give you Kemp. But how am I to know you really have young Weldon and the girl?"

"My word," snapped Furbish.

The cloaked one nodded. "And what else?"

Furbish hitched uneasily in the saddle. That there was a thorn in what seemed a smooth path, he was suddenly, painfully aware. The upper hand he'd held, began to slip. He made a desperate grab for it.

"I'm a man of the Cloth," he snapped. "Seems to me—"

"Nope," said the other. "Better than that."

Furbish swallowed. His palms felt suddenly sticky, wet. He could not call to the Ludlows, tell them to bring the girl and boy into sight and prove his point. He could not go to them, formulate a plan to get Kemp and the gold some other way.

In fact his whole plan depended entirely on quick action, on sudden acceptance of his demands by the hooded figure. He was between two fires.

This the hooded man sensed when Furbish hesitated. A floating straw seemed to come into range and The Masked Rider grasped at it.

"I'll give the pony and Kemp up on one condition, Furbish. That I see the girl and young Weldon released safely. Nothing less, nothing more."

A sort of chill breeze seemed to whip Furbish's backbone. That move involved untold dangers for him. However, the events of the past minute made quick, effectual steps necessary.

"I'll go get them," he said, "bring them back—"

The Masked Rider shook his head. "Nope. We'll go together."

Furbish floundered for words. In the hooded figure's voice a form of retribution seemed to come.

"Back track, Furbish. *Pronto.* I want to see this thing through."

The so-called cleric grunted, turned his moth-eaten pony. He walked it slowly back the way he had come. Behind him trudged Kemp. The Masked Rider brought up the rear, stalking long-legged and ruthlessly behind them, leading Weldon's pony.

The hooded man kept an anxious eye on the sparse brush and occasional cactus that dotted the arroyo lips. But no sign of Dan Weldon appeared. In a few moments they were far enough down the arroyo to be fairly safe.

The gully widened suddenly. A hundred yards below them a wide band obscured the terrain beyond. Ponderous granite boulders marked a corner.

Furbish swore, yanked his pony up short. Over the rim of one of those boulders beneath them a hat, then a face appeared. In another second a pony stepped out from behind the rock coming up the gully. Other horses' heads showed. The man riding jerked up his head and swore. It was Art Ludlow and on the pony behind him The Masked Rider made out the head and shoulders of Lorie Rand.

CHAPTER XVIII

THE RIDER
STRIKES BACK

THE ACTION THAT marked the appearance of Art Ludlow and Lorie Rand was instantaneous. A scarce hundred yards away and half hidden by the boulders at the corner, Art Ludlow offered no target at all for the hooded man. Besides that there was instant danger that a chance shot might reach Lorie Rand.

Kemp and Furbish grunted in astonishment. In the next second the black-coated rider had leaped from his saddle and unmindful of attack from behind, plunged headlong for the right side of the gully and the shelter of the rock there. Kemp too, sensing the impending battle, ran after him. Scarcely three seconds after the appearance of Art Ludlow, both of The Masked Rider's prisoners had taken cover in the tall boulders on the right side of the gully.

The hooded shape behind them had sworn softly, jerked himself towards the opposite wall of the ravine with twice the speed of Furbish's retreat. That the preacher had been attempting to double-cross him all along, that he had no connection with the Ludlows' holding Lorie Rand and Bucky, was an instant and positive conclusion. Furbish's fright and escape proved that. The Ludlows had taken Lorie Rand and Bucky. Furbish had seen it, and gone on.

Before Art Ludlow could recover from the surprise of

the meeting or go for the gun in his holster, all three of the figures up the arroyo from him had disappeared.

With a snapped-out oath he wheeled his mount and pulled Lorie Rand's into the shelter of the ravine corner. Behind them Sam Ludlow grated a question, but Art did not have time to answer. On the little dun behind Lorie Rand's horse, Bucky stared wide-eyed at the quick effectual motions Art Ludlow was making to get them hidden.

The Masked Rider had let his prisoners go without a struggle. No sooner had he gained the protection of the left wall of the arroyo than he threw his body behind adjacent boulders and scrambled swiftly up the fifty yard wall and into the sheltering, though sparse brush on its rim. Gaining this, he bent, unholstered the second .45 under the black cloak and moved forward.

Somewhere below him now, Art and Sam Ludlow had taken shelter. The hooded man snaked swiftly across the hundred yards that had separated the two parties in the gully, then lowered himself and slid on his stomach towards the rim below which he knew the Ludlows should be.

A soft curse grated from within the *serape* when he reached that point.

The white glare of the arroyo's sandy bottom fifty yards below outlined some figures there. But they were those of only four horses, including the little dun Bucky had ridden. Of their four riders nothing could be seen.

The Masked Rider squinted his eyes, examined every protruding bulge of the gray boulders for signs of movement.

Art and Sam Ludlow had chosen their shelter well. An outjutting of the arroyo wall protected the boulders behind which they squatted. Two of the larger ones, before and behind them, prevented attack from either up or down the gully. Through an inch-wide niche between two larger rocks, Art Ludlow crouched, examining the rim of the *barranca*.

The Masked Rider could see the slight movements of Art's dark hat. No sign of Lorie or Bucky showed, nor of Sam Ludlow. The hooded man concluded that Sam was watching from another more completely hidden portion of their fortress.

Sheltered thus, the Ludlows could wait for an attack, have every advantage of concealment and pick approaches off at will. They knew that sooner or later The Masked Rider would have to show his hand, knew that, with the girl and Bucky as hostages, they held a terrific advantage. That was the reason they had picked them up on the cliff, brought them down into the valley.

Up on the arroyo lip The Masked Rider came to a quick and definite decision. Half-hidden by a mesquite bush, he propped himself up on an elbow, squinted along the blued, long barrel of his .45. The weapon went off with a sullen roar.

The target, a fleeting glimpse of the top of Art Ludlow's battered sombrero, disappeared instantly. In the next second the hooded man dropped flat on his face. The returning bullet that spurted from between the boulders hit the gully lip and screamed off on a tangent.

But The Masked Rider's purpose had been established. He had drawn the Ludlows' fire, announced to them where he was and that there would be no quarter.

HE SLID SWIFTLY back from the rim, right angled off down trail. A minute later he was maneuvering up to the rim a hundred yards beyond the Ludlows, picking out points of shelter on the rocky face of the arroyo wall. He slid over the rim and twenty yards down its face in the shelter of boulders.

Hidden, he examined the bottom, made out the big boulders of the Ludlows' shelter. From his new position he spotted the only possible angle of attack. The rocks surrounded the Ludlows like a miniature stone wall. But there was an open space in that wall—the place through which they had entered. Directly across the gully bottom from that space between the rocks, a jumble of glacier-smoothed granite marked shelter. If he could reach that spot, the Ludlows would be in full sight.

But in order to reach it, a good fifty yards of open sandy arroyo had to be traversed—in full shooting view of the Ludlows.

The hooded man made his decision rapidly. The bend in the gully disguised whatever motions Kemp and Furbish were making to protect themselves. If he guessed correctly, both of them were now on his side of the arroyo, sneaking as close to the Ludlows as was safe. If anything happened to the Ludlows, there was still a chance to capture their prisoners. Kemp would want to try that....

There remained only one thing—to get at the Ludlows as soon as possible.

THE MASKED RIDER slid down the *barranca* in the shelter of rocks until he had reached the bottom. Fifty yards away now, across the open, sandy bottom, the smooth granite surface of the shelter he had picked stood out. If he could reach that—

The voices of the Ludlows reached him dimly. He did not wait to hear what they said but they seemed to be coming out of their hiding place.

There was no time to plan further actions. When they appeared around the rim of the biggest boulder, The Masked Rider would be in full view of them, an open shot.

He raised himself from his shelter, leaped over it and plunged straight for the hulking shapes of the giant rocks. In five fleeting seconds he had covered the space that separated his hiding place from the Ludlows.

A shoulder, then a head appeared around the rock corner. The Masked Rider whipped up one of the .45s, pulled the trigger. The shoulder was withdrawn abruptly when this bullet slugged into the rock.

In another second he had plunged in close to the great boulder, leaped, scrambled for a foothold on its eight-foot-high sides and poised there before he pulled the triggers of both guns.

On the other side of the rock the hatchet face of Art Ludlow had appeared, mouth open, an unspoken curse on his lips. There were three other shapes behind the rock, Lorie Rand's, Bucky's and Sam Ludlow's. Only Art Ludlow was standing apart, an open target.

He swooped up the ready gun in his hand when the towering, black clad figure of The Masked Rider appeared over the boulder's rim.

But his bullet was never fired. In the next second both slugs from the hooded figure's gun hit him full in the chest, knocked him sideways, writhing and spurting blood over the small stones that littered the bottom.

Lorie Rand screamed a shrill warning. At that second Sam Ludlow, whose body had been half-concealed by her shape from The Masked Rider, clamped his arm about her waist, dragged her in front of him.

His face was tight-set, cruel, as he whipped a revolver

from his belt and leveled it full on the broad-shouldered shape outlined against the sky above him.

"Take that," he snarled and pulled the trigger.

Lorie Rand screamed again. But before Ludlow's finger had tightened on the trigger, before the muffled explosion of his gun could shake the rocks about them, the seraped man disappeared.

It was as if he had been magically wafted from sight, so completely did his whole body vanish. But in reality when he saw the revolver in Sam Ludlow's hand coming up, saw the elder Ludlow had protected himself behind the slim body of Lorie Rand, The Masked Rider stepped backward, plummeted the eight feet to the sandy gully bottom.

The shot from Ludlow's gun knifed empty air.

But as quickly as the hooded man had acted, so did Sam Ludlow. With a straight-arm shove he sent Bucky Weldon head over heels into a niche of the rocks. Gripping the girl, he crab-stepped swiftly out of the shelter of the rocks and into the open of the gully bottom.

By that time, however, the masked man was concealed behind a convenient boulder, chest down on the earth, eyes glued on the bulky frame of Sam Ludlow, the loose-lipped cruel mouth, and in front of it the wide-eyed, terror-stricken features of Lorie Rand. Erosion had cut a niche at the base of his boulder and afforded him a sheltered eye-crack.

But there was no hope of downing Sam Ludlow. He held the girl tightly to his chest as he side-stepped across the gully bottom, gained the opposite side and made his way then up the arroyo. All this time his eyes were pinned on the boulder behind which he knew the hooded shape had moved. His gun jutted from under her arm-pit, every vital part of his body concealed by her small, lithe shape.

Softly, The Masked Rider swore, gathered his muscles ready to leap into action should Ludlow leave a shoulder or hip as enough target for lead. But he didn't. Before the flashing steel of the hooded eyes, Sam Ludlow moved towards the shelter of larger rocks and disappeared.

The Masked Rider slid out of the boulder barrier and into the open. On swift, silent feet he sped across the gully, gained the side up which Ludlow had disappeared.

A noise behind him made him wheel, gun coming up.

His first guess had been correct. Still intent on getting a portion of the gold, Furbish and Kemp had sneaked out of their hiding place and caught Weldon's gold-laden pony. But there were other things they wanted in that arroyo; one of them was a sure means of getting to the remainder of the caché.

They had led the pony down the gully towards the rocks behind which the Ludlows had concealed themselves, then tied the horse. Sneaking forward again, they had reached the Ludlows' shelter by the time The Masked Rider had made his attack.

With Art Ludlow dead, and Sam Ludlow side-stepping up the gully and out of range, Furbish and Kemp made a quick decision. They scaled the rocky wall, then moved forward until they were over the hiding place. Below, rubbing his head and staring at the gory shape of the dead Ludlow stood Bucky Weldon.

With a snarl Kemp jumped, landed with a solid thud beside the paralyzed younger Weldon. In another second Kemp had lunged forward, grappled at the invaluable bit of steel still clutched in Ludlow's hand.

THE YOUNGER WELDON let out a shout of warning. The Masked Rider, who had appeared at that moment in the open area of the sandy bottom, wheeled. His gun flipped up, exploded.

Kemp's newly acquired weapon did too at the same second. But Kemp's bullet sliced through the flapping cloth of The Masked Rider's cloak. The hooded figure's bullet sped swift and sure to its mark. Before Kemp's hulking thick-shouldered shape could pull the trigger again, he plunged forward, dug his face into the sand at the dead Ludlow's feet. He kicked once or twice in the final agonies of death and was silent. The side of his head, which had been blown open, began to leak blood into the all-absorbing sand.

The hooded man had to make his decisions fast. If he stopped, retrieved Bucky Weldon, there was a chance Ludlow would make a successful escape with Lorie Rand. Bucky would have to take care of himself.

He cast one look at the fallen Kemp, bent and raced up the gully bottom in the direction Ludlow and the girl had disappeared. A hundred yards up the arroyo he right-angled, moved silently, powerfully up the wall of the gully and out of sight.

His decision made, he had to act quickly to carry out his plan.

CHAPTER XIX

GUNS AND CACTUS

FOR A PASSING second Bucky Weldon stood regarding the two dead men almost at his feet. In the space of numbered heart heats he had seen death strike quick and sure at evil-doers. Momentarily it left him awed, silent. Then he, too, moved.

But it was not to run. He wheeled at a sound behind him, found himself facing a lanky, black-clothed figure catching his balance after dropping from the rocks above into the boulder-rimmed fortress.

Bucky's eyes widened; he made a move forward in the direction of the gun in Kemp's hand and stopped.

"How be you, son?" asked Furbish, a wide grin on his face. "Powerful lot of deadly action going on here. You better come with me, get outta this mess afore we git hurt."

"Who're you?"

"Me?" asked Furbish, the grin growing. He stepped in the direction of Kemp. "Me? I'm th' Reverend Furbish, son. A man o' God. A-workin' to git you outta this trouble soon as possible."

Bucky recalled seeing Furbish before. Then, as now, the preacherly tone of his voice, his long-tailed black coat, concealed Furbish's purposes well. Bucky relinquished the idea of dashing for the gun, decided it was best to put his trust in a preacher-man. After all he'd been taught that one should do so.

But the Godly-frocked one's actions were queer. Finding Bucky had not stopped him, Furbish grabbed the gun from Kemp's lifeless fingers and rose. He poked his small head over the boulder rim, found the coast outside clear. He grappled for Bucky's hand.

The younger Weldon sought to escape the clutch, but it was too late. Fingers of steel gripped his wrist.

"Yer comin' with me," snapped Furbish and led him around the rock and into the open.

In another moment Furbish had retrieved the pony idling in close to the wall of the *barranca*. Then gripping Bucky's wrist firmly in one hand, the pony's reins in the other, Furbish started down the arroyo away from the scene of Kemp's and Ludlow's deaths.

As they went more suspicions began to flash across Bucky's mind. As they passed out of sight of the dead men, conviction had grown to an eating worry in the breast of the younger Weldon.

WHEN HE GAINED the top of the gully rim, The Masked Rider moved swift and sure along it. Before him, he was positive now, Sam Ludlow had mounted the arroyo wall with the girl in an attempt to escape. With Art dead and his horses left behind, it was only natural that he try to do so.

The brush on that side of the ravine was thin, meager. Cactus grew more abundantly here in the serrated earth. Upjutting stands of eroded rock and large boulders concealed the path before him.

It was thus that he came on Sam Ludlow almost before he was aware of it.

Ludlow had taken refuge behind one of the exposed, stratified out-croppings that littered the rim. From behind it he had had a chance to see the hooded shape while still concealing himself. He whipped up his revolver, pulled the trigger. But at that same instant the approaching cloaked figure had spotted him and dropped from sight.

Now once again behind a wall of rock The Masked Rider had full reason to curse. He had hoped for a rapid and conclusive end to his search for Ludlow, a chance to shoot it out once and for all. As before, it was now a case of wits against wits in a constant battle to make the other show himself....

When the idea struck him, the hooded shape acted instantly. He removed the hood that concealed the features of Wayne Morgan, covered his head again with the cloak that shielded his shoulders and torso. The wide-brimmed black sombrero also he laid in the sand beside him.

There was a small *saguro* growing near the boulder behind which he had taken concealment. Staking everything on the belief that Ludlow's range of vision did not take in the cactus, the hooded shape moved to the edge of his shelter, reached for the cactus and jerked his hand back.

No shot came from the out-cropping of stone. He moved farther, exposing more of his body. In another second the hood had covered the *saguro*, the sombrero mounted on top of it—an almost perfect dummy of The Masked Rider's head—if Ludlow could not see too much of the plant.

With agile movements the shape that now wore á cloak about its features instead of a hood, slid snake-like into the shelter of the big boulder. But he did not stop. Silently he moved across' the dry, gravelly earth away from the boulder. In a few seconds he angled to the right, pointing towards the corner of the outcropping on the other side of which he knew Sam Ludlow and the girl were.

In this position, if Ludlow came around the outcropping he would see the hooded cactus plant and shoot.

It was ticklish work. The whole success of his plan depended on Ludlow's exposing mere inches of his body. If he did—

Noiselessly, The Masked Rider reached behind him, picked up a handful of loose small pebbles. He lifted one, flipped it over towards the hooded cactus. It clicked on stones, rolled noisily through them.

Back up against the stones on the other side of the out-cropping, Sam Ludlow heard that sound and swore softly. As before, he still held the girl's body before his, though now one hand was clamped across her mouth to prevent the scream he knew was sure to come if he loosed it.

The rattle of the pebble beyond sounded like footsteps of approaching doom. He clutched the revolver at the girl's side with steely grip, waited.

Lorie Band heard the sound too. She struggled vainly to wrench herself from the brutish, huge arms enwrapping her. But they quelled her movements instantly.

Another footstep sounded in the rocks around the corner of the outcropping. Sam Ludlow's heart began to pound in his throat. Another footstep. Then what sounded like two together.

Ludlow couldn't stand it any longer. He gripped the girl tighter, moved away from the shelter of the outcropping and aimed for the corner around which the footsteps seemed to come. The chances were ten to one on his side anyway. If he held the girl well up before him, there wasn't a portion of his anatomy anyone would dare shoot at.

Inch by inch he edged towards the rock corner. Gravel rattled once more around the corner of his shelter, only closer now.

With a muffled curse, Ludlow tensed his muscles, heaved himself and the girl out into the open. He landed with both feet set, his body pointed towards the source of the sound, Lorie Rand's struggling shape gripped to his chest.

And as he landed, his finger contracted on the trigger. He saw it then, saw the source of the footsteps. Beyond him, no longer concealed behind a boulder, the hated sombrero, the black hood of The Masked Rider appeared. His revolver exploded twice, belched flame in the direction of the hat, sent twin pellets of lead slicing through the empty hood.

At that second another explosion seemed to blanket his own. A red-hot little object that had all the force of an earth-bound satellite behind it, hit him in the left side, spinning him around helplessly, tearing at his vitals like an avenging sword.

He hit the earth with a stunning thump. Strange fires seemed to enwrap him, sear through his brain. They passed, gave way to a dark gray fog through which he seemed to be floating helplessly until merciful nothingness cast the blotter of black around him....

"BUT BUCKY?" THE girl was asking nervously as The Masked Rider led her down the gully wall on to the bottom. "What happened to *him?*"

The hooded man, once more attired in hood and black sombrero, shook his head, pressed forward. "I don't know. That's what we're going to find out."

The sinking within him grew as he approached the little fortress behind which the Ludlows had first taken shelter. The absence of sounds, of indications of Bucky, brought vague and eating premonitions to his mind.

Lorie Rand swallowed hard when they stopped at the hiding place. There were two dead men there but other than they, the place was empty, dismally empty. Not only that, but Dan Weldon's pony was no longer in sight. The hooded man cursed softly, wheeled on his heel. As he did a muffled gasp came from Lorie Rand.

She had turned too, faced up the ravine. Approaching them, not eighty yards away was a horse. Relief shot momentarily through The Masked Rider's mind. The pony was a sorrel, Blue Hawk's sorrel. And walking beside it was the shape of the Indian. But the figure with him was far more shocking. Dan Weldon sat in the saddle, but he was hunched forward, seemed scarcely able to keep his seat.

Before he reached them, Blue Hawk pretended to take fright at sight of The Masked Rider; but when the latter holstered guns and beckoned to him in a friendly fashion, Blue Hawk advanced again with a display of diminishing distrust. He began to talk.

"I found him, *senor*, saw the place where he had been shot a long time after somebody left there. You see, he had been making much trouble by doubling back on his tracks. There is a bullet wound in his shoulder, but in days he will be all right. I have bandaged it."

The hooded figure nodded, looked grimly up into Weldon's face. It was white-lined, tensed in pain. But in spite of that Dan Weldon opened his eyes, gazed down on them. Lights passed momentarily into his eyes, then faded.

"*Senor*," said the Indian, "I have found this too."

All eyes were turned as he pointed to the battered kyak that rode on the sorrel behind the form of Dan Weldon. On the scarred side of the kyak had been burned the letters "J R."

"You're all right, Mister," said Weldon slowly, laboring with his words. "This stranger here told me what he thought you were trying to do. He said he'd been watching you from a safe distance for a couple of hours. He'd been holding up here. Found me up in the ravine there, pretty well done up, I guess. That—that kyak there was Johnny R's—he—" Weldon indicated the Indian—"said he found it up above and that as near as he can figure it must belong to me. Guess it does for that matter. He's gonna have to share it with me."

But Blue Hawk shook his head slowly as he looked long into the eyes of the masked man. Both understood how Blue Hawk came to have that gold, for together they had salvaged it from the cliff's side and had held it awaiting return to its rightful owner.

"Bucky's up here somewhere," said the girl suddenly to Dan Weldon. "We can't find him. Something has to be done right away." She turned. "You leave Dan here with me. Bucky must be down the gully somewhere."

The hooded shape nodded grimly. "With Furbish," he said slowly and turned.

Blue Hawk had understood the look in the hooded eyes. Without a word he dropped the sorrel's reins, stepped to the hooded man's side.

"That tall one," he said. "Here are his tracks. The boy's and the pony's too, *senor.* It is only a matter of minutes—"

But he did not finish his sentence. The masked man grunted in surprise. Lorie Rand had seen too; one word broke from her lips.

"Bucky!"

A laden pony was making its way up the ravine towards them. Before it, with angry flashing eyes strode a lanky, raw-boned, black-clad shape. And behind it, pouter-pigeon chest thrown well forward stalked a miniature shape.

When the queer caravan came within shouting distance Bucky Weldon hailed the four figures near the rocks.

Moments later Furbish was sullenly gazing into the hooded eyes, listening to the high-pitched, excited voice of the youngster outlining the details of his downfall.

"Was a-tryin' to take off me an' Dan's gold," Bucky was stating. "When we passed close to a corner of th' gully, I pulled off a piece of rock an' lambasted th' rump of that cayuse so hard he jumped ten feet.

"Wall, that sorta threw mister Furbish off balance and quick-like I stuck out a foot. Shore he went down! Plumb kerflop, Dan. Yes sir, an' when he got up I done had this here .45 of the scarfaced dead *hombre* right next tuh his haid.

"Hey, Dan, you ain't listenin'. He makes a grab at me an' I blowed th' sand right out under him. Wuz he scared? Holy smoke—!"

But for some reason the older Weldon was looking at the girl and grinning in a way that made Bucky pause and look suspiciously at him.

CHAPTER XX

THE ROCK

AT THE BASE of a huge outjutting rock that over-hung a portion of the ravine two miles above the scene of the Ludlows' deaths, the five riders pulled up. Lorie Rand, Bucky and Furbish were once more mounted on the ponies that had bolted out of the range of the shooting and stopped to feed in an easily caught group not far off.

So too had the stallion joined the party when the hooded man's whistle sliced through the air. Blue Hawk was no longer with them. He had turned Dan Weldon over to the care of the group, and departed.

There was no doubt that this rock before which they now stood was the one Dan Weldon and they too had been searching for.

Outlined against the slate-colored side of the gully, the rock's face was dark, polished smooth by the passage of waters many ages before. Across that face, web-like lines, visible some distance off were traced in glittering net-work.

But what brought an exclamation from all of them was the shoulder-deep hole at the base of the rock.

At Dan Weldon's directions Bucky dismounted, descended into it and scraped manfully at the sandy debris littering its bottom. As he did, exclamations of delight broke from his lips.

The bottom of the caché resembled the inside of some long-buried Spanish galleon's treasure chest. Dully shining irregular objects peeped through the dark earth at its bottom. Weldon had worked at the rocky lips of the hole, widening it—but other picks had worked there too.

In ages past the gully had been the bed of a glacial stream, the rock worn smooth by the constant passage of waters over it. A whirl-pool at the base of the big black boulder had dug a basket-shaped hole directly into the solid rock.

Later, when the whirl-pool was gone and the waters moved slower over it, gold nuggets lifted by the current had rolled along the bed of the glacial stream, dropped one by one into the basket. Heavier than earth, the nuggets had stayed while the sediment of the river bottom was washed away. It was a *moulin*, a nugget *moulin*, the Utopian dream of every hard gold prospector.

Now, it was stuffed like a roast goose, with a fortune in nuggets. Its ages of rest hidden by shifting earth and sands had been disturbed.

"You see," Dan Weldon was saying, "I'd plenty of chance to think over every part of this trouble in jail. What Johnny R said kept coming back to my mind. 'It'll pull her off north,' he told Abe Rand. What he was trying to say was that the iron deposits in the rock would pull a compass off true north—steadily. In that way you could find it instantly from any part of the valley. Outside, the rock didn't affect a compass. I mean outside the valley.

"I thought of that," he went on. "Decided to have a try at it."

The man on the big stallion was smiling. Bucky Weldon clambered quickly out of the *moulin*, stared upward.

"Holy Smoke, you ain't going now, are you?" he said when the big black stallion was wheeled in the trailway. "Heck, they's this rat done gotta be strung up—" he pointed an accusing finger at Furbish, who grunted in surprise. "An' Dan's still all bunged up there. Maybe he'll be a-wantin'—"

The Masked Rider smiled grimly beneath his hood. "I was traveling south three days ago when I saw Johnny R almost murdered. It's a long trail—mine." He turned to Furbish. "Furbish," he said softly, "I imagine you're not going to drag me into this—that is, to hurt Dan's case. Are you?"

The fake cleric looked up sullenly. "Not me," he snapped. "No one ken hang a thing on me anyway. Shore, I know who killed Hess Rand."

The hooded man's head nodded. "You knew all the time! Kemp, of course. As I told Dan, Hess Rand was killed in the livery stable—and the man who shot Dan, shot from the same place. As for the rifle and the knife coming from the same place, that'll be the easiest thing to prove. What'll happen to you, though, Furbish, will be up to the judge."

Furbish muttered angrily.

The Masked Rider pressed his stallion's ribs.

"But you can ride part of the way back with us," Lorie Rand said suddenly, impulsively. "Why not? Dan—"

Weldon spoke up. "Mister, I hate to see you go. There was a time not so long ago that I had so many troubles I didn't know how I could possibly find a way out of them. And on top of them all I found I owed th' Rands a $8,000 mortgage on the Open A that I never heard of."

The girl looked deep into his eyes and what she saw there made her flush—happily.

"Be a sort of pleasure now, I guess, paying that off," Weldon said meaningfully. He turned to The Masked Rider. "Just think of the trouble I was in and you'll know how much I owe to you."

But the hooded head nodded slowly. *"Adios, amigos,"* he said. With another nudge and a wave of the hand he pressed the stallion into a lope. Farther down the ravine the rider turned sharply, mounted the gully wall. Then with another wave he disappeared.

And beyond that rise of land he joined Blue Hawk who had left the party to prevent their suspecting his and The Masked Rider's friendship.

SHUCKS!" SNAPPED THE younger Weldon. "I wuz thinkin' all th' time I'd shake hands with him. Holy Smoke, seein' The Masked Rider and I didn't even do that." Disgustedly he yanked at the reins of the little dun, mounted it. When he turned to Dan, who had pulled his own horse in close to Lorie Rand's, a half-muffled exclamation burst from Bucky's lips.

"Then he's gone," Lorie Rand was saying. "Who could he be?— Why should he try so hard to help us and then ride off—without even waiting for thanks? If—"

But the smile on Dan Weldon's face stopped her. "Maybe," he said grinning, "he didn't want to stay 'round with such high-powered competition as me, looking for favors."

The girl flushed when she realized that the tone of his voice was not humorous, but that in the rough, hard-bitten manner of his environment, Dan Weldon was seriously pleading for the love of the dark-eyed, wondrous creature on the pony next to him.

Bucky Weldon saw the glance that passed between them. A look of puzzlement moved across his face.

"Holy Smoke!" he snorted, again brandishing the .45. "Come on, you crooked, fake Preacher Furbish, let's get goin' outta here! We gotta get a *real* preacher—I need an aunt, an' you need a funeral orashun after they cut you down!"

BRAND OF THE QUANAHY CLAN
BY VAL MASTERSON

CHAPTER I

A DEAD MAN RIDES

THE NIGHT WAS cold, clear and sharp with the coming of fall on the high hills. Between the mute rows of cottonwoods, bright pools of silver moonlight lay glittering. Silence and its unworldly overtones chilled the little clearing. Eerie silence. Broken only by the soft moan of the wind and the weird far-off call of a night bird.

The setting was fit. For into it stalked the gruesome phantom of death itself. And as if withered by its grim apparition, the ghostly whistle of the night bird sank to silence....

Unguided by the loose reins on its neck, the little *palomina* paused for a second to munch the silvered gramma grass between its front hoofs. It raised its head once, snorted and rattled the bridle chains, totally unconscious of the mute figure in its saddle.

It was a man, booted, spurred, yet hatless. Gnarled hands lay gripping the saddle-bows before him stiffly; his feet, wide apart, were jammed into the *tapaderos* like those of a rider bracing himself against the abruptness of his mount's movements. But as the *palomina* moved forward in the grass, the figure swayed awkwardly in the saddle, bringing his features out of the shades into the cold, unnatural glare of the moon.

The face was set, colorless. The eyes were open yet saw

not. Over the face, not long before, the chill hands of death had flitted, setting the features in a grim mask, stiffening the muscles to iron stanchions.

The cause of his death was apparent. The flesh of his forehead was all but torn away by a terrible wound on whose blackened edges great clots of blood had congealed. But more ghastly still was the obvious story the wound told. For it was of regular pattern—two half-heart shaped indentations in his skull. The hoof mark perhaps of some violent, fear-crazed animal....

Oblivious of the horrible burden it bore, the little *palomina* jerked up its head, snorted again. Far off, beyond the blanket of nearby brush, came the rapid hammer of hoofs. Ears erect, stiffened, a whinny broke from the *palomina*. It

gathered its haunches, and with the instinct of ages, trotted off in the direction of two ponies, the gruesome thing on its back lurching....

OVER THE HUMP of a brushy knoll, the two riders, whose approach the *palomina* had heard, pulled their mounts up a treacherous shale embankment and halted.

Their flight had been precipitous, violent. For nearly three quarters of an hour, the big black stallion had raced at top speed, leading by never more than a length the smaller sorrel now idling beside it.

For a second the two riders were silent, heeding only the hard intake of their mounts' breathing. Finally, the rider of the sorrel spoke. His voice was low, tensed. Yet soft and guttural with rich accents of the south in it.

"Senor, it is not the thirty numbers of silver I have lost. Nor is it that this *cadrone* has cheated me of them. *Amigo,* it is—"

The shape of the Mexican Indian shrugged. The language of friendship need not be words. Wayne Morgan, the black's rider, knew that well.

Wayne Morgan's was not a youth's face; yet neither were the hard lines of his nose and chin a record of years. Rather, they spoke of trails hard ridden, of the sun blistered alkali deserts to the south, of snow gripped mountain passages with a knife wind of forty below etching its story into the thin tight lips, the rugged lines of the jaw.

About the eyes, crinkles of neither laughter nor hate softened the brittle candor of his greyish eyes. About Morgan there was something warm, yet curiously forbidding. Men, who had brushed acquaintance with him—and they a multitude—regarded him as an enigma. A curious combination of indomitable power and human sensibilities; a man who strode through his hard-bitten environment, but whose grey eyes could twinkle with sudden laughter and whose spirit knew no depths of charity and unstinting self sacrifice. Yet they knew him not by the name of Morgan—

His lean shoulders bore the accusations of a hundred crimes he had never committed. Doomed by them to forego the company of honest men, to flee the stern justice of an unjust law, he followed the ghost-ridden trail of men who can never come back—with buoyancy and courage.

In the troubled eyes of the Yaqui who rode beside him, Morgan was a leader and a friend. For it was neither force nor crime that placed Blue Hawk at Morgan's side. Rather a deeper friendship, an understanding that transended—as now—the power of words.

For nearly three quarters of an hour the rapid tattoo of his big black's hoofs had hammered a story of injustice in Morgan's ears. It showed in the glance he shot at Blue Hawk, in the cast of his thin hipped body in the saddle.

His words, though drawled, were meaningful, forceful. "He'll have to pay, Hawk! He took advantage of your race—a greaser trick if there ever was one. If he was the one that stole the money, he'll go back to face the Law if we have to draw him by the hair."

Blue Hawk's voice was tinged with sincerity. *"Senor,* I could not be wrong. Of course it was he who broke in the window. I tell you, *amigo,* I was walking in the alley—"

The Indian's sense of honesty was inbred, unbending. To him, the injustice, the mere accusation of theft rankled deep.

Not three hours before, Blue Hawk had entered the town of Long Stream to purchase supplies for Morgan and himself. In one of the unfrequented streets, he had come upon a man who had burst out of a second-story office window and escaped.

Later in a nearby bar, the same man had been apprehended by the town sheriff, a certain Beale Jones, and accused of stealing thirty dollars. Unfortunately, the thief, McTaggart, had seen Blue Hawk open a roll of bills to pay the bar keep Accosted by Jones, McTaggart had wheeled on the Indian, lied so capably that in less time than it took to tell, the sheriff had seized Blue Hawk, relieved him of the money and released McTaggart. Only a quick getaway on his way to jail had freed the Indian.

"But *senor,*" the Indian went on rapidly, "we did not

wait for me to tell more back on the mesa. There was one other man in the alley with me—walking ahead. He sees this McTaggart break the window and come out, too. He is closer and attacks this McTaggart bare handed. For a moment only. But this man was not in the bar—so I could prove nothing. But, *amigo,* I will know him next time. White hair—a tall man—"

Morgan nodded tersely, stopped the Indian. "You'll know McTaggart—without a chance of mistake!"

The Indian's nod was abrupt, sure.

"Good enough. The roadway's right below us," snapped Morgan. "You said McTaggart left town in a wagon. The short-cut we took should have brought us well ahead of him. When he comes up the grade— Wait—"

Through the thick brush below them came the heavy grate of a wagon, the rattle of shod hoofs on stones.

"Senor—"

Cat-like, the big stallion Morgan rode wheeled in its tracks, leaped into action. The Indian's sorrel gathered its haunches and followed, shoulder-deep in the tangled mesquite that blanketed the downhill slope.

But as they passed out of sight, on the bulging hillside above them appeared a small shape, the *palomina,* that paused, whinnied softly at the night-riding steeds below and began scrambling with its swaying, ghastly load down the slope.

NEITHER THE TRAIL-TRAINED Morgan nor the Indian noticed the light, unsteady hoofbeats of the following *palomina.* The big stallion moved easily in the brush, threaded rapidly through the low-growing pin oaks for nearly a quarter of a mile. Eyes and ears intent on the roadway below them, both men pushed their mounts forward to a twenty-foot embankment that dropped away sheer before them into the silvery ribbon of the dusty mountain road.

Plainly audible now came the sounds of the approaching wagon and team. Silently, the Indian slipped from his saddle, ground-reined the sorrel and moved to the lip of the brush.

Almost as he did so a team of bays and the clattering shape of a light buck-board rounded a corner in the moon-lit roadway before him.

"Amigo," the Indian whispered. "There are four of them! I did not know that. But that is he—McTaggart, the tall one driving."

In spite of the shades, Morgan's sharp eyes made out the figures. Two men rode in the driver's seat. At the buckboard's tail, their backs to him, were the hulking shapes of two others.

Blue Hawk bunched his lithe body for the twenty-foot leap.

"I will go first, *senor.* If they do not—"

But he got no further than those words. The buckboard was almost immediately below them by then. The rattle of the light rig filled the air, occasional sparks flew from the iron-rimmed wheels and ponies' hoofs. But Blue Hawk dodged back into the shelter of the brush, loosed the gun in his right holster with a quick upward movement.

Above the wagon's noise, another more formidable sound had broken on their ears. It was the heavy thunder of many hoofs, the sounds of a veritable tide of on coming riders.

The men in the wagon heard it at the same instant. The driver, McTaggart, pulled the team back on their haunches, skidded the buckboard to a crazy stop.

Uptrail, the thunder grew to a mighty roar. Out of the shadows that hid a rock-ribbed corner of the road, a phalanx of rushing shapes appeared. Five, then six riders burst into view, materializing with stunning suddenness of the gloom, their ponies' heads low, their jerking shapes pregnant with warning.

A wild shout broke from McTaggart's lips as with a single motion, all four men scrambled from their seats, braced themselves in the roadway. But in that second the oncoming horsemen were on them. In the dark, dust-clouded mêlée of horses and men, a gun flashed a rapier of flame.

CHAPTER II

OUTLAW'S LAW

BLUE HAWK HAD grappled at the sorrel's bridle, swung up into the saddle. Both he and Morgan sat, guns ready, eyes pinned to the scene below. Both recognized the fact that all of the horsemen wore masks. Yet for some reason, after the first shot, no other gun blared its message of death.

One of the wagonmen lunged in under a horse's belly, hurtled his body towards the shelter of nearby rocks as he drew his gun from its holster. But before two paces were behind him, a rider had wheeled, brought his gun barrel crashing down on the man's unprotected head.

A harsh, carrying voice blurted an order. Abruptly, the horsemen seemed to organize themselves in the gloom, back away from the buckboard. Then they swung about, moved their ponies headlong out of the roadway and into the downhill brush at right angles to the rearing team McTaggart had driven.

It had been a matter of seconds only. The riders had struck as quickly as they had come. One of the men from the wagon was grappling at the team's bridles. Beside him, arms and legs awry against the dust, stretched the second. The third stood, arms still aloft, his body turned towards the updrifting cloud of silvery dust that marked the spot in the brush through which the disappearing riders had burst.

"Amigo," Blue Hawk's words were tinged with perplexity. "Three of them only. McTaggart—he is no longer down there! They have taken him, *senor.* Those ponies I know—"

Morgan swung out of the saddle, pulled the big stallion's head around. With a backward glance at the men moving in the roadway, he snaked the horse uphill into the shelter of the brush. Out of sight from below, he paused.

Blue Hawk had done likewise. In the moon's rays, his bronzed face was cut in quizzical lines as he approached Morgan. Momentarily, he paused.

Then: *"Senor,* you have not been in the country long enough to realize. Those ponies' brands are well known in these parts. They ride the backs of thousands of cattle, of many hundreds of horses, too. Why should they want McTaggart? Why should those riders even disguise their faces, *Senor?* I do not understand. *Senor,* those are Quanahy riders, all of them. In this country when one says the name Quanahy, most men pause and listen.

Morgan slid into the saddle, turned to the Indian. Quanahy—he turned the name over in his mind. Yes, he'd heard that name.

"Quanahy—" he murmured. "Quanahy Curlicue—" he paused, frowned. "I know the name, but staying here doesn't find this McTaggart. We'll back-trail, cross the road and pick up those riders beyond!"

The black wheeled, but was pulled back on its haunches with a hand of steel. It snorted, reared, came back to earth with a solid thump. From the Indian, behind, came a hissing gasp.

Slightly above them, outlined against the farther stars, stood a *palomino,* pony, ears erect, eyes searching the outlines of the stallion and the sorrel. It rattled its bridle reins, whinnied softly.

Morgan's arm had moved with the speed of a striking snake. The .45 that peeped over the upright ears of the black was steady, ringing full the tall erect, hatless figure of the man on the *palomina* who sat staring steadily at them.

Yet the rider made no move, gave no indication that he had even taken note of Morgan's gun and the Indian.

Then, his words coming cold as steel, Blue Hawk broke the eerie silence.

"Amigo, it is him who was in the alley with me! The white haired one. Surely—"

THE WORD WAS clipped off, unbelieving.

For all his steady nerve, a chill crept along the tensed muscles of Morgan's gun arm, tickled the tips of his coiled finger as he lowered it. His eyes were glued to the set stern features of the *palomina's* rider.

The lone horse stood steady, regarding their approach with curious eyes. Twenty paces away, Morgan clucked to the stallion, stopped it. He could hear the soft, shrill intake of Blue Hawk's breath, the whisper of horror.

"Amigo, it is that one." He raised his voice in greeting. *"Dias, senor.* Why do you not say—"

Morgan's bitter voice cut him short. "No use. The man's dead. No one could be alive with that—" Morgan left the rest unsaid. "What's his name? Where did he come from?"

"*Quien sabe?* But he is the one—"

For a second, Morgan ran his eyes over the *palomina* and its rider. It was a sight to start horror in any man. The violent wound had certainly been the cause of the man's death. He had been trampled by a steer. Evidently rigor mortis had frozen him to the saddle.

The questions in his mind jerked Morgan into action. He pressed the black's haunches, reached out for the *palomina's* bridle. With a startled snort, the pony turned, trotted lightly up the hillside, away from them. On its back, the figure rolled unsteadily, yet did not fall.

Morgan whispered in the black's ear, sent it crashing up the hillside. But the *palomina* had taken the bit in its teeth. She was off up the hillside as fast as she could scramble and crossed the knoll.

Morgan pulled up, let the Indian's sorrel scamper to his side.

He could hear the *palomina* crashing aimlessly about in the brush beyond the knoll. The weird silence of the night-shaded slope, the thought of the horrible burden the pony bore, bulged the muscles of Morgan's cheek bones. What ghastly torture the man must have gone through. Dragging himself into the saddle—where now he rode, a bleeding shell, over the hillsides—into oblivion.

He lifted the black's reins, only to be halted by the quick whisper of Blue Hawk's warning.

"He is dead, *amigo*. There is nothing we can do now. The men below—if they hear us—"

Morgan's voice was terse. "Let them come. With this

man dead, your chance of proving McTaggart's guilt is small. That shouldn't stop us from going after your money. We'll stop the *palomina*, get him out of the saddle. After that we'll head off after these Quanahys and McTaggart. There's something almighty strange about their wanting McTaggart—"

The Indian nodded. With a word to the sorrel, he followed the big black up the hillside across the knoll. Outlined in the moonlight, they made out the shape of the *palomina*, standing as before, ears erect, watching them approach. This time she did not escape, but let Morgan's quick looping grasp clamp on to her bridle reins.

Morgan slid down from the saddle, stepped forward. For a second he paused, staring into that ghastly, set face, into the sightless filmed eyes. In spite of his determination, a certain chill of horror touched Morgan. He heard Blue Hawk alighting.

"We'll have to get his hands loose first," Morgan said. "Hold the pony—"

But Blue Hawk's interruption was quick. *"Amigo,* something else. This pony is Box B—*senor,* I was closer to McTaggart's team than you. They were Box B ponies also. *This man comes from McTaggart's ranch!"*

Morgan turned to the Indian. His eyes were hard cast, bitter; his words smooth velvet covering steel. "There are other brands here too! The brands of a murderer— Do you see his wrists?"

The moon's rays fell full on the knotted, gnarled hands clamped to the saddle bows. Blue Hawk hissed in surprise.

It was as though some one had circled the man's wrists with a knife, cutting deep into the flesh. Dried blood clotted the edges of the cuts, only half concealing the black and blue flesh—and the secret it told!

"Madre de Dios! They had tied his hands; someone had tied him down, *senor.* Someone who did not want him to *talk,* who then drove a steer over his body...."

Morgan turned and walked towards the black. The expression on his face the Indian knew, recognized well. Blue Hawk did not speak, but moved his lithe arms across the saddle's cantle and lifted the body of the dead man clear.

A second later, he had ground-reined the *palomina,* busied himself with the grim, awry limbs of the broken, lifeless puncher.

At the whisper of feet, Blue Hawk wheeled. The figure he faced now was far different from that which had approached the stallion. Delineations of grim meaning were written in it, meaning that had made it a name of terror to some, of hope to others.

From the top of his rabbit Stetson to the short length boots, the man was dressed in black. Boots, then trousers rose to a flowing ebony cape that swept downward from broad, capable shoulders. Above that, an inky hood, punctured with eye-slits only, masked the features and disappeared beneath the sweeping black rim of the sombrero Wayne Morgan had worn. The remainder of his dress had been folded flat beneath the black's saddle.

The voice that issued from the hood was bitter with implications.

"I lay this murder to McTaggart, Hawk. We're no longer a couple of saddle tramps riding through. The Masked Rider has a job. I want McTaggart first so we can collect your debt—then we both want to see some of that hanging that the law out here is always bragging about; but we want to see the rope around the right neck, for a change, and not around the wrong one—one that McTaggart will point out to the sheriff, and the sheriff will take in tow, like he did you!"

CHAPTER III

KING QUANAHY

THE BLACK STALLION set the trail through the underbrush. Like some monstrous avenging shadow, it shot through the glades, sliding with trip-hammer, mighty hoofs between the silent sentinels of cottonwoods and low growing pin oaks.

For some time they rode this way, across the treacherous terrain of occasional mesquite-dotted flats, or threaded through the shadowed reaches of winding gullies.

Once, when the Indian spoke, they turned and pushed across country until, coming along the sharp, rocky spine of a smaller hog's back, The Masked Rider suddenly made out lights and the distant configurations of houses in the valley below.

Only a matter of a quarter of a mile away, the shapes of several two story adobe ranch houses showed up, fences, corrals, several barns and a lantern-lit ranch yard.

"*Senor!* We have made good time. You see them in the road below!"

Out of the blanket of trees surrounding the *hacienda,* a little group of horsemen trotted. A moment later they turned in through the heavy gate, filed at a trot into the ranch yard before one of the lanterned porches.

"That's McTaggart riding in front—without a hat," snapped the masked outlaw. "We'll wait for an hour or so—"

The Indian shook his head. "*Si, amigo,* but as he goes in there I have feeling how he will perhaps never come out. These Quanahys stop at nothing—they are hard workers but bloody fighters also. If he rides for the Box B, perhaps we will all bid him goodbye, *adios.*"

"Wait!"

The hiss from the hooded man brought the Indian's sharp eyes back to the riders far below. McTaggart, because of his hatless head, was plainly visible. They could see his lanky, square shouldered shape swing out of the saddle and let another rider lead away his horse.

The remainder of the riders stayed mounted in a motionless circle about the bareheaded man.

The light of an open door was blotted out. A figure stepped out on the porch. A man who had something, a cane, in his hand, that supported the hulking bulk of his great body. The steps he took out to the edge of the porch were halting, awkward. He was quite lame.

A warning hiss from Blue Hawk tuned the hooded outlaw's ears.

"Look well, *senor.* That is he—King Quanahy. Everything on these hills, this land we walk on, those houses, listen well when he speaks. If McTaggart is to die, *senor,* he can thank King Quanahy—"

For all his former decision that McTaggart should pay for his ill deeds, the Indian bent his head, crossed himself.

When he looked up McTaggart had moved. He was walking towards the porch, straight for the looming bulk of King Quanahy. But for some reason, he did not hesitate.

A jarring exclamation broke from the hooded man. McTaggart's hand had come up, grasped that of the man in the doorway. From far below, a hearty grumbling laugh floated upward. Then King Quanahy reached forward, slapped McTaggart on the shoulder in greeting and led him through the lighted doorway.

Momentary silence clamped over the riders on the hillside. Then the first words broke from the Indian.

"Madre de Dios, senor. They are friends!"

"You're right, Hawk," snapped the man near the Indian. "And I'm riding back to the wagon!"

IT IS SAID that any organization is only the elongated shadow of one man. Of the Quanahy clan it was literally a fact.

King Quanahy had formulated a creed and upon its foundations he had built what, to him, when he considered it, was a magnificent and lasting tribute to his own energy and foresight.

There had been eight Quanahy brothers, sons of a father who had forged a small kingdom in this southland under the very noses of marauding Indians and in the face of the frightful odds. Nature, weather, drought and desolation can summon against all who attempt to carve a foothold in a barren, uninhabited wilderness.

But the older Quanahy was wrought of stern stuff. When at last he died, the Quanahy brand—the Curling Q—roamed a thousand square miles of land, and the Curlicue, as the ranch had come to be known, was a feudal kingdom.

But all this was but a foundation upon which King Quanahy, the youngest brother, had formulated a creed and a clan. Under his aggressive leadership, the vast Curlicue was broken into eight separate pieces. Over these each brother was an overseer. But as children grew, married and had other children, they grew not as separate families, but as a clan over which the eight brothers held virtually the power of life or death.

Quanahys did not marry without the consent of the counsel of brothers, for power of marriage was theirs too. Moreover, profits and earnings of each ranch were bulked with the others, lesser Quanahys receiving their remuneration as a salary. What one shared, all shared.

In a hostile land, profits were few. In spite of this, the Quanahy holdings grew. But not always was it through arduous work or wise investment.

In time the Quanahy Curlicue received a name for sharp and sometimes shady dealing, for acquisition of land and sometimes herds in a way far from lawful in even a lawless land. One by one, four of the brothers had dropped by the wayside, some with smoking guns in their hands, others when the long arm of the law caught them on alien soil in the midst of some bloody errand.

But three things had brought the other settlers in the territory to hate and fear the Curlicue more than anything else. A Quanahy was never known to argue with or raise his hand against another of his clan. Travelers across Curlicue land were met with suspicion and angry threats. And of the many who used the name, they paid homage to one law only, that of the clan council....

As before, when there was urgent need of a meeting of the family heads, a fire had been set burning on the topmost crown of Cobb Mountain which reared its lofty head above its surrounding neighbors behind King Quanahy's *hacienda*. Now, in the innermost sanctum of his home, the three remaining brothers had gathered....

King Quanahy entered first. There was something about the man that branded him instantly as a leader. In spite of his bad leg—caused by a wagon accident years before—his poise was commanding, purposeful.

Blue trousers, tucked inside his boots, rose into a matched store suit coat. In spite of its loose lines, the great wine-cask torso seemed to bulge it in every seam. Out of the collar of his grey shirt rose a channeled, wind tanned trunk of neck which supported the craggy bulk of his head.

But if his frame was commanding, his face was even more so. The nose was a hawk's, the chin jutting, the eyes predatory, sparkling, and cruel. His hair, though white, was trim and straight, brushed back from his forehead.

The room he entered was solidly panelled with hand-carved oak and one arching Spanish *ventana* opening on to the rear of the house. Other than that, doors were the only apertures to the room. In its middle, a massive, twenty-foot, oak table surrounded by equally massive chairs overshadowed every other piece of furniture.

As King entered, the three men now seated about it glanced up. Near the head sat Will Quanahy, white haired, almost toothless, and bent of back. He was the oldest. Next to him, Branch Quanahy, whose hair still showed the reddish tinges of former years, and Milt, whose eagle-eyed and hawk nose made him look a smaller replica of his brother, King....

Immediately after King Quanahy, Bill McTaggart strode into the room followed by another rider who carefully closed the heavy door leading to the remainder of the house and approached the table behind the two-head.

Despite Blue Hawk's condemnation of McTaggart, there was something about him that set him instantly apart from the type of men who were in the room. In the first place, he was younger, cleaner-cut. Standing at the end of the table, his somewhat lanky, broad-shouldered shape towered above the seated men.

His hatless head was covered by a scratchy mop of blond, unruly hair. His mouth, now hardened to a tight slit, was supported by a stubborn, rocky chin. The chin, the hair and the stubby nose above which a pair of light blue eyes sparkled, served to mark him as a young man not only of action but purpose.

"A hell of a way to get hold of me, that was. By this time that team of mine's spooked forty miles with grub scattered hell to breakfast. How'd I know you was going to bust in with six riders, hold me up, yank me off th' seat like a six-year-old stealing jam? Next time, King, we'll fix some sorta meeting place b'fore hand—"

The boss Quanahy settled himself into the chair at the head of the table, waved away McTaggart's words with a knotted, oak hued hand.

"Now, now," he said in his deep voice, "we don't want any of your friends suspecting who you are. I told young Dutch just what to do—and evidently he did," He paused, then fixed McTaggart with his dark, predatory eyes.

"I suppose," McTaggart was scornful, "no one recognized your ponies' brands."

KING SHRUGGED. "IT was a chance we had to take. If someone did, tell them we wanted to question you about our brother Fritz's death. Well, what happened in town?"

McTaggart looked up, glanced at the man to King Quanahy's right. Though his father, King, spoke of him as "young," Dutch Quanahy was at least five years older than McTaggart. He slouched over his father's chair, fixed McTaggart with dull, disinterested eyes. Little about this Quanahy marked him as has father's son. Dissolute and easy living had left puffy marks beneath the too-close eyes; a slouching bent shape and shuffling gait where his father's had always been purposeful, energetic. But in cruelty, he was known to be more than a match for his father.

"What about Moore?" King Quanahy reiterated.

McTaggart shrugged. "Just as you thought. This loan shark, Moore, was boasting out of his depth. Busting into his strong box was no trouble at all. I found two I.O.U.s for six hundred and eighty bucks and that was all. Personal notes signed with Sol Bascom's name—I left 'em behind an' took about thirty bucks, stuck 'em in my pocket to look like a robbery. I heard someone coming up the stairs and beat it just in time. But some Mex down in the street saw me. Whoever I heard, saw me going around a corner and called Beale Jones, the sheriff. I went in Hepple Frank's place to throw them off, but no soap. Beale comes in, starts to haul me off."

King Quanahy frowned, snapped. "And you shot him!"

McTaggart snorted. "That would of been swell, now wouldn't it! Nope, the same Mex, or maybe he was an Indian, was standing down the bar a ways. He had some money. All I did was just tell Beale Jones he'd find his money on the Mexican—and he did!"

King Quanahy slapped the table. "That's more like it!" He gave a humorless laugh. "The greaser is in jail and you're out. Son, you're a chip off the old block!"

McTaggart rose not to the praise. He scowled, squared his jaw. "Not till I find the Mex and give him his money back," he stated. "Do that maybe next trip—didn't have time this."

King Quanahy's chuckle died in his throat. "You'll do nothing of the kind." Momentarily, their gazes clashed, but Quanahy's turned on the other men seated about him.

His moving look gave McTaggart momentary respite. One fact gripped the tow-head inwardly. He had not said that old, white haired Abe Holt also had seen him coming out of the loan shark's window. Nor that Holt and he had grappled and McTaggart had broken away and run. He had no idea Abe Holt had been murdered.

Maybe, McTaggart thought, by that time Abe Holt would have spilled the story all over the Box B. Jumpin' catfish, he said inwardly, what would ole Sol say and—and Jane too! When he thought of Jane Bascom something inside him wrenched like a grappling hook in his conscience. It'd kill her if she knew where he was now, or heard what he was saying, or knew that with all his might and main he was seeking to destroy her father's life-time labor, to wipe the Box B off the range.

But the harsh grate of King Quanahy's voice brought the young tow-head back to his senses with a jerk.

"The last time we met," he was telling the others, "my plans had not yet been made. Since then, they've come to a definite head. I'm sure none of you know who this lad is—" he looked up.

FOR A MOMENT, silence gripped the others. Bill felt their eyes boring into him, searching his features. It was as though he stood before a jury waiting for an indictment. And he knew that some day soon this same indictment would be pronounced on him by other people under circumstances that now were beginning to attain nightmarish proportions in his mind—unless he could find some way out.

As if to confirm his bitterest thoughts, the cracked voice of old Will Quanahy, the elder, broke out.

"Thet ain't so hard," he rasped, quavering. "He's a Quanahy. He's brother Frank's boy."

CHAPTER IV

CURLICUE PLANS

KING QUANAHY CHUCKLED humorlessly. "You're getting old, Will," he said with a ripple of scorn in his voice. "You forget Frank was the oldest of us and the first of us to leave this world. Over twenty some years ago now. You remember—Frank was down in the Cross-Cut country. Got killed in a raid of some sort. It broke up his son, Bill, to think his father got killed stealing horses—I guess."

Quanahy looked at McTaggart. "He got mad a short time later, rode off one night without even saying by your leave. Quit the clan." His voice grew bitter, "Went south and set up ranching in the Hierba Verde country somewhere under the name of McTaggart. Died a short time back—it seems—broke. I heard about young Bill here, his son, some time ago when he was riding through. Had him up for a talk—and here he is. He's Frank's grandson."

As King Quanahy spoke, Bill McTaggart scrutinized the faces about the heavy oak table. Every word Quanahy spoke was truth, yet—could these men be relations of his?

King Quanahy leaned forward, his hawk-nosed face set, the dark eyes flashing vindictively.

"For the first time in fifteen years, Sol Bascom is where we can strike," he cracked the table with an iron fist—"and make it pay out. You remember I insisted—over everyone else's wishes—that that oldest kid of Hobart's be sent down into the Long Stream Bank to work eight years ago. I had a reason—now it's showing up."

Quanahy leaned back, eyes on the faces of his three brothers. Like men who had suddenly been animated by some inner springs, their faces tensed, hardened.

"And why?" snapped King Quanahy. "Year before last Sol Bascom outbid every cattle owner in the state for state pasture and grazing rights on the whole damn Rio Testa range and south of it. Three hundred thousand acres! His bid was eight cents an acre. And he paid in advance too—$24,000 in cold hard cash for the grazing rights on Rio Testa. And the only reason he got it was because that lunk-head son of yours, Will Quanahy, was afraid to go over seven and a quarter cents because he thought the land wasn't worth it!"

A shadow of a smile crossed the man's face, rippling the seamed flesh, and died as soon as it had come. His voice went on, terse, bitter.

"For years the Box B has literally ruined the production possibilities of half of the Curlicue holdings because Sol Bascom's land runs square between it and the home range here. Money? Bascom laughs at money, and why shouldn't he? He thinks we will eventually have to come up to his price—or else we'll have to give up the southern half because of competition and herding costs. Now we have an answer for him.

"During the past two years, by clever buying and a little pressure, we've increased our shares in Long Stream Bank to a controlling interest. Bascom doesn't know it—yet! He mortgaged the Box B and put a lien on this year's herd for the money to pay the government. I sent McTaggart down to Moore's office to see if there was any other outstanding indebtedness. There's none to involve settlement of these liens and mortgages!"

MILT QUANAHY HAD not spoken up to that time. He leaned forward, said: "Foreclosure—? You haven't said anything about that yet. How can we if the notes aren't due? Bascom's men have been chousing brush-poppers at least a month now. There's a big drive a-goin' on up—"

"Of course, you've been hearing a lot of things!" snapped his brother. *"But the bank's notes expire in a week!* Bascom stood to make a fortune out of his move. Twenty-four thousand dollars in mortgages? The Box B itself is worth ten times that. But here's the point. Those cattle have been roaming the Rio Testa country wild for two years! Thousands of them. Mavericks, strays from other ranges. Maybe fifty different brands of outlaw cattle dropping calves on the hills. Whose cattle are those? The Box B's—as soon as they leave their mothers. Besides, there were canyons full of wild strays in those hills when Bascom got the land.

"Was he smart? Of course he was! Eight cents was practically giving the land away. He let them run loose, get as wild as they liked. All he did was patrol the border fences and keep strangers out. Now at the end of two years, he's started to collect them in three or four different bands. He's bringing them all together to push them into Long Stream. Start shipping by the hundreds, because he sold them last year too.

"Them cattle are as wild as the hills they been raised on. It's been one hell of a job collecting them—I give him credit for that. Only there's one catch! If he doesn't get the cattle to Long Stream by the beginning of next week, the shippers won't start paying him on time and if the shipper's checks aren't ready to satisfy those liens when they come due—"

Quanahy shrugged his shoulders, let his voice drop away. Across his heavily seamed face a moving smile twisted the corners of his hard mouth.

"*Quien sabe?*" he said mockingly. "The bank will have to foreclose on such a large amount of indebtedness. They can't wait for their money even if Bascom *has* the Box B and cattle worth more. There'll be a sheriff's sale of the Box B. We will snap it up for a song—*a song!* After that, when the state grazing lease expires, we'll buy the lease and let him bring his cattle out. That is, only those with the Box B brand!"

"But—" queried Milt, "This all sounds mighty highfalutin'. You ain't said though how all this easy business of stopping Sol Bascom's going to be done."

Quanahy leaned back in his chair. He reached behind him, brought forth the cane without which he never moved. There was nothing particularly striking about the cane—which was of knotted though peculiarly straight manzanita wood—save its head. Instead of the usual heavily carved handle, the cane's head was a heavy-bulb-like padding of leather work. Though it appeared soft, when Quanahy struck the table rim with it, the sound was metallic, solid.

"What's the difference?" he said and shrugged. "The main herd up in Soldier Canyon is growing every day. Bascom is bringing the little herds out of the mountains steadily and pouring them into that location. Tonight, tomorrow night—the next—the herd will—" he made a gesture—"pouff—stampede!"

Bill shot a glance into the suddenly grim faces. In the years the older McTaggart, his father, had scratched a meager livelihood out of the barren ranch in the Hierba Verde, he had said little of the Quanahys, had never shown any of the traits that marked these men. And it was those traits that had driven him from them—to seek a home of his own in a grossly misnamed country, on a ranch that had first killed Bill's mother, then drained away the determination and strength of his slow-spoken father. Bill had been reduced to saddle-tramping and grabbed at King's offer.

It was almost before he was aware of it that Bill McTaggart had been drawn into the middle of this latest of King Quanahy's enterprises, and once embroiled, the late saddle-tramp had little chance to draw back, to retrace his steps.

So BILL HAD girded his conscience, decided to play along until the end was in sight, then make his break. But other events and unseen circumstances had complicated the picture.

"Whose gonna do all this?" asked Milt Quanahy. "You mean—him?"

A sort of chill crept up McTaggart's spine, spread down his biceps to his finger tips. Yes, he thought, he was pledged to go ahead—pledged by ties of blood and his own word. At one time the saddle-tramp, McTaggart, might have done it with clear and easy conscience. But that time was long past now. For all his youth and sureness, Bill McTaggart felt a river of doubt creep like slow-moving poison through his mind. Long after he had decided to follow King Quanahy, Jane—Jane Bascom—had entered his scheme of things.

"What's he gettin' out of it?" queried Will Quanahy's high old voice.

"None of us Quanahys could possibly do the job right," said King. "I had to get an outsider, someone the Bascoms didn't know. Yet a man we could trust. What does he get? Plenty. He'll come back into the clan again, get to use his right name—plus a full share in what the estate makes. Besides, a permanent half-interest in—"

King paused, his predatory black eyes brightening, a peculiar smile on his face as he looked up at McTaggart.

In what? raced through Bill's mind. In something he would never truly be able to think of as his own—in something that for the rest of his days would be haunted by a lithe, dark-eyed figure of a girl, whose features were right now being etched as with acid on his mind's eye.

"In the Box B!" finished King Quanahy.

CHAPTER V

THE RIDER STRIKES

FOR SOME MOMENTS after the Quanahy riders had left the wagon, Lobo Myers watched the uphill side of the road from whence the sounds of Morgan's and the Indian's moving mounts had come. In the moonlight, his wide, walrus mustache tips quivered a trifle, the scorching soft curses that had blued the atmosphere about him died to silence.

"Sufferin' kingsnakes," he blurted. "As if twenty of them riders ain't enough, they have to watch us tuh see we don't follow.

He wheeled from the grey road wall, approached the

figures of the man spread-eagled on the ground. As he did, the figure shook its head slowly, began to sit up.

Myers cursed once more, bent and scooped up the fallen man's hat, handed it to him. Rock French took it without a trace of a nod of thanks. The knock-out blow he had received left him a trifle groggy, shaken. But that did not dampen the swift anger that seared through him the next moment at the ignominy of being knocked out. He felt of the polished butts of the twin .45s at his side and wheeled on Lobo Myers.

Rock French was a killer—by profession and choice. In the wan moonlight his skin showed up jaundiced, oily, unhealthy. Everything about him—his cold grey eyes, the brutal bulging jowls—was ugly, reprehensible.

His paunch was bulging, misshapen with gross living. Heavy rolls of flesh masked the lines of his jawbone and sank away into the apoplectic trunk of his neck. His hands were puffy; beneath his queer little pig's eyes, rolls of loose skin sagged.

French was a killer. It read in every line of his disreputable appearance, in his glassy stare.

The grin with which old Lobo Myers had greeted French's arising, faded. He touched his waving mustaches, stroked the seamed, toughened hide of his ancient cheeks.

"Powerful unhealthy crack that rider give you, I admit," he drawled. "Stranger, I gotta little bottle uh liniment in my duds on the wagon. If she ain't spilt—"

His speech was broken into by a gust of laughter that rolled through the night like a burst of nearby thunder.

Lobo Myers grunted and wheeled. The team jerked up their heads, snorted in alarm. The figure holding their bridles moved into view. Once again came the bull-fellow guffaw. Rock French turned his head, stared with glassy, disinterested eyes.

The third member of the party might have been some illustration from a book of Arabian Nights—save for his costume. He was all of six four in height, which placed his eyes on a level with the team's ears. The moonlight fell across a massive expanse of chest and set in huge neolithic lines the jutting mountain of his torso. His head was bare, revealing a crinkled short-clipped poll of coal black hair, the low sloped forehead of a giant negro.

Jackson jerked down on the bridle irons, pacified the startled team with a throaty curse and strode toward Myers. With unleashed humor, he chortled, revealing a snowy patch of gleaming teeth, big as a horse's.

"Linuhment," he rumbled and cracked a mountainous knee with a paw as big as a ham, "white man, yo' sho' must figger dat medicine am pow'ful strong. D'yuh-all know who dat is?"

Inner mirth shook the craggy shape, stopped his words. Myers twitched his mustaches. As a matter of fact he knew who neither of these men were—other than that they were strangers to whom Bill McTaggart had offered a ride. Momentarily, he stared in disguised alarm at French, then at the negro.

French's words were icy, meaningful. "Shut up, Jackson."

BUT IT AFFECTED the negro's laughter not a whit. He gave a fresh bellow that shook the mesquite brush along the roadway.

"Linuhment fer dat man?" he blurted with mock scorn. "Yo' sho' he ain't split his'n little finger an' needs uh bandage too? Linuhment! Man, you-all should tell that tuh th' doctor-man in Dos Cuevos. Yes suh, he said tuh me, 'Boy, dat runnin' mate of your'n sho' gotta wrong name. Rock? He ain't rock, 'cause dat breaks when yuh shoot intuh it. Dis man jest sorta sucks 'em bullets up an' digesterates 'em like food!'"

French's stout body was stooping a little, faced towards the negro. His voice fell again like the cold driblets of icy water on stone.

"That'll be enough, Jackson," he said.

As before, the negro paid no attention, but faced Myers with his canyon grin, his huge body still shaking with laughter.

Lobo Myers let his eyes run over the man. Like most of his race, Jackson's hips were thin, almost out of proportion to the bulk of his mighty shoulders. A pair of tight, blue dungarees encased them. His shirt was a faded, skin-tight hickory garment that had long before seen its better days. It was unbuttoned at the neck revealing a shiny ebony expanse of bulging chest. When the negro moved, the corded muscles moved with the rippling sensuousness of big snakes beneath his skin.

"Don't pay no mind tuh him. Cast yo' eyes on dis, man! Mebbe you figger den they ain't no linuhment needed with dees parties."

So saying the negro brought a right arm as big and long as a railroad tie up before Myers' eyes.

A great rip in the sleeve revealed a corded trunk of muscles. And down the middle of it, a crimson channel of a wound dripped blood.

Myers' eyes bulged a little. The one bullet that had been fired during the past mêlée had indeed found a target. The slash, to Myers, seemed as deep and wide as a small river, and had already bathed the negro's arms in gore. Even French grunted in surprise.

But to this the negro paid little attention. Chuckling, he went to the wagon, jerked out an empty sack in its bottom and proceeded to wipe the exposed, bleeding flesh clean.

Myers shrugged and felt his mustache. He was not new in this country. An old-time puncher, he had long since given up the range and taken to the softer, less exacting life of the ranch kitchen. An unpleasantness having been the end of the cook at the Bascom Box B, Myers had just now taken his place on that job.

Bill McTaggart's journey to town for barbed wire and, sub-rosa, to Moore's office, had also been meant to afford Myers transportation out to the Box B. Hailed for a ride, McTaggart had picked up French and the negro a short distance out of town.

Other than a brief half-hour's ride together, Myers had never come in contact with the men before him. He turned busied himself with getting the team straightened out, the spilled boxes of grub back into the road. For a long time French watched him.

French's own pony at that moment was lying dead in a ravine outside of Long Stream where a sheriff's bullet, sunk into its neck many miles south, had at last done its deadly work. French was headed out of town towards the open range and a new mount, if he could buy or steal one. Jackson had sold the bare-back mule he'd been riding, in Long Stream for enough money to buy their week's grub… French's eyes were wandering to the team hitched to the buck-board.

Jackson would take care of Myers for him, he was thinking. Then a little work with the knife the negro carried would fashion hackamores for the time being, at least. Once beyond the first ridge, they would pick up or steal blankets, saddle, and better bridles. His puffy fingers drifted towards the polished pearl-handled guns at his side as he turned towards the working ex-puncher.

Whatever deadly intentions French had at that moment, were swept away in the next. He saw the big negro near him stiffen, his jaw flop agape. Something strange also was happening to Myers over near the buckboard's seat, for his eyes widened, turned into a pair of bulging moons pinned to something beyond French's shoulders.

Like a striking snake, French twisted his overweight body, stooping at the hips. As he did, a form materialized out of the brush on the downhill side of the road. A form that brought alarm and paralyzing recognition streaming across the killer's mind.

"The Masked Rider!" he hissed beneath his breath and froze to steel, his arm sweeping in the direction of his gun.

CHAPTER VI

THE KILLERS

THE FIGURE STEPPED out of the waist-deep brush into the moon bathed roadway. Behind it, its body hidden by the edge of the road, showed the great head of a black stallion. Detached from the shades, the man stood outlined against the moon. Everything about him blended with the color of the horse. The jet-colored, flowing hood; the cape that hung loosely about the broad shoulders.

Along its rim, French had made out the peeping, ugly

circles of steel that told him the snouts of two murderous .45s were pinned on the three of them.

A half gasp broke from the negro. "Lawd take me! De Masked Rider!" He swallowed, then showed his teeth in a breezy grin of welcome. "Where you come from? How come we ain't heered uh yuh, down thar? No suh, I ain't never think you wuz in dis country. I done heerd down in Roseville, they killt you up Painted Desert way. Seems—"

"They didn't," finished a steely voice from beneath the hood. "Get your paws up where they won't be tempted."

The outlaw in the mask watched the giant negro's ham-like paws arise, then those of the stout man to his right. At a nod of the head, he jerked the form of Myers into action. Momentarily, he surveyed them, taking in with practiced eye each man's story in a glance.

Then he said: "Heard shooting down this way. Thought I'd come down and see what's going on. And I'm glad I did—*Rock French.*"

A distinct tremor shot up the flabby muscles of the killer. The colorless, puffy features twitched a little, the lips tightened.

The negro, Jackson, burst out with a shout of laughter. "Lawdy me, how come you know dat name, man? We done travel five hundred miles 'spectin' tuh find people don't know it. How you like dat, Rock?"

There was no doubt about French's reaction. He spit out an oath, shot his bull head about. "Stay out of this and keep that big trap shut!" He turned back. "Just keep my name out of this," he hissed. "Now out with it, what do you want of us?"

Though his words were hot, the killer's mind moved clear and sharp. Here was a man before him who represented a cool fifteen thousand at least in reward for a dead or alive capture. How many more hundreds or even thousands, French did not know. One fact remained. Within reach was a small fortune protected only by a pair of .45s. Was it worth a chance at going for his gun? French weighed his chances in a fraction of a second—and decided no.

There was no hesitation, no lack of purpose in the hooded man's words. He passed over the negro's remark, shot rapid questions into Myers' bewildered face.

"McTaggart was driving, wasn't he?"

The ex-puncher nodded, gulped momentarily. "Sure. Bill McTaggart. He works for Sol Bascom up on the Box B spread. I wuz going up that way tuh cook fer him. He done stopped and give these *hombres* a ride up that way. They never said where they was going—" he glanced suspiciously at French. "Anyhow, six or eight riders done dry-gulched us 'bout half hour ago. Uh heard th' shooting. No harm— 'cept for some reason they musta wanted McTaggart. Drug him up on his saddle-horn, one of them did, and off they went. How—"

The man in the hood let his eyes drift off Myers' face to the brands on the nearby team. Blue Hawk had been right. They were Box B. He decided to make the ex-puncher talk.

"What spread were they riding for?" he caught Myers up short.

Myers colored, started to say something, stumbled to a halt. For a second his lean, seamed face was drawn in tight lines; his eyes questioning. Then he set his jaw.

"Never seen it before," he said.

But the man in the hood read his inner thoughts instantly.

"Don't lie," he snapped. "You know damn well where

those ponies came from, maybe why they were here. Out with it."

In his day, Myers had ridden the flanks of too many ranges, had brushed shoulders of too many of his hard-bitten brethren not to know that the tone in the hooded man's voice meant business, that he had met up with a will of steel and a determination to follow any set course to its bitterest end.

HE DECIDED AGAINST holding his tongue and let his angry, pent up thoughts loose with added venom.

"Shore I know," he blurted. "I don't give a damn if you're hooked up with 'em or not. Do what you want about it. Them riders were masked, but that didn't hide nothing. Them were Quanahy riders. Every man on 'em rode a Curlicue brand pony. Sure I seen it. Ain't they always tried everything, crooked 'er not, to wipe th' Bascoms offen this range? Ain't they done things tuh th' Box B that'd have old King Quanahy behind the bars fer th' rest of his life if it came out? Yes sir, that's why them riders got hold of us. They want something outta Bill McTaggart. An' that's why he ain't here now!"

The hooded man let the angry torrent of Myers' words end. Mentally, he reassembled Myers' torrid speech. McTaggart worked for the Box B all right, but Myers knew nothing of his being a friend of King Quanahy.

"Was another rider from your spread in town with McTaggart?"

Myers' angry face changed its expression. He shrugged. "How th' hell should I know? I ain't even been out there yet. But Bill didn't say-"

"He wouldn't have," snapped the steely voice from beneath the hood.

The grey eyes beneath the dark hood turned to French, took in the beady, smoldering eyes, the emotionless, heavy jowled face.

The man was a killer, capable of any crime. It was a good chance that he was linked with McTaggart, in some way. Perhaps had a hand in the horrible murder of the *palomina's* rider. Yet if that were true, why hadn't he been taken by the Curlicue riders? But questioning him would, in a sense, be futile. The masked man knew French by reputation as well as breed. And the same with the mountainous negro.

There was no time for pointless questions. Already McTaggart had been left at the Curlicue for precious minutes. And Blue Hawk was waiting there.

Decision showed abruptly in the movements of the hooded man. He surveyed the scene he had entered, made instant plans on the means of a rapid, safe withdrawal. The negro, he guessed—and rightly—concealed a knife. The killer wore two guns at his hips. Myers was unarmed. Three weapons stood ready to carry death in a single false move. Disarming them would take valuable time.

A shrill, sharp whistle from beneath the hood brought the black stallion crashing up through the brush into the roadway behind the masked man. With every sense alert, French watched him mount the horse, his muscles tensed, ready for instant action. But in spite of the lithe ease with which the hooded man swung aboard, the .45s never failed to center the men in the road.

"Face uptrail," he ordered tersely.

To a man they wheeled. The cold voice broke on Myers' ears with chill implications. "There's a dead Box B hand down here in the brush behind me. Judging from what he had in his pockets, his name's Holt—Abe Holt."

The sloppy lines of French's back seemed to shudder. The voice clicked.

"That's right—French. *Abe Holt.* A Box B rider but an old running mate of yours, if I remember, down Gila River way. Something happened to him."

The three men in the road heard only a swishing sound, then the crash of the big horse's body as it went off the road into the high brush.

French wheeled with an oath, sped both hands in the direction of his guns. But stopped them. It was too late. In a second they listened to the disappearing thump of the stallion's hoofs. Then a soft, humorless chuckle broke from the throat of the giant Jackson.

"Aby Holt's daid—you heerd what he said, Rock French. *Aby Holt!* He had plenty of money when he came dis way! But dis man don't say what happen to dat. *Where dat money go, Rock French?*"

CHAPTER VII

TRAPPED!

NOT MANY MOMENTS later, along a small shadow-hidden trail that wound along the side of the spiny hog's back that The Masked Rider and Blue Hawk had mounted, two figures moved on silent moccasins. Neither was tall enough to be a man. The light fowling pieces slung across their elbow's told of the reason for their late return to the Quanahy *hacienda.*

A soft hiss from the leading figure brought the lad behind him to an abrupt halt.

"Aw, you couldn't never find it in th' dark," said the latter in a whisper. "Yer crazy—"

Shhh!" the warning was sharp, commanding. "I tell ya you ken see their eyes in th' dark—old Milt says he shot one once, square in th' head that way. Listen—"

In the pause that followed, the long, lone wail of the mountain cat floated like the death cry of a lost soul through the brush. When its last shuddering, weird note sank to silence, the first speaker nodded.

"It's up there. Cummon, le's see—"

"Naw, too dark. Besides—"

But already the leading lad, who bore the name of his grandfather, Milt Quanahy, had slipped into the mesquite and greasewood, and with all the skill he could summon, began a silent ascent of the hillside. There was little for the other lad to do save follow, which he did as noiselessly as possible.

Moments later young Milt Quanahy parted the leaves of a manzanita bush and examined the knoll before him. Though accustomed to the darkness, it was only after examining every shadow that he finally shrugged and started to turn. At that second young Milt grunted, stared even harder into the dark. A hundred yards away, the magnificent head outlines of a huge black horse, first a vague shadow, then an ominous reality, could be made out. After a momentary silence, a muted, almost imperceptible hiss broke from his lips.

"See him—see the horse he's riding? We gotta do something quick. That's—it's The Masked Rider."

A shiver crept through the other's lean, small body. "You sure?" He leaned forward, stared, then pulled back with a jerk.

"Do something? We better get outta here fast as we kin run." He turned, but young Milt's hand gripped his biceps.

"You go tell King right away. I'll stay up here, watch him. If I'm not here, you remember where we saw him. I'll wait though. Now run!" He might have shot at the black target—but he was too young to learn to shoot at a human without warning, from ambush.

Like a frightened rabbit, the other boy wheeled and disappeared into the nearby brush.

THOUGH EVERY ONE of the hooded man's senses was trained to the sounds of the surrounding woods, he had not heard the movements of the boys a hundred yards away.

In order to prevent McTaggart from leaving the *hacienda* unseen, Blue Hawk had descended, crossed the valley bottom and was now posted on the opposite side where the rear of the big ranch house was visible. His cry, the repeat of the mountain cat's wails, had answered the masked man's.

Soon the hooded man saw four riderless ponies appear in the ranch yard below, only to be led out of sight by an unmounted man. When Blue Hawk's next floating cry came across the valley, the last lingering notes in it held a message for the masked sentinel on the hill.

He wheeled the big stallion, sent it at a quick trot down the mountain side in the direction of the *hacienda*....

YOUNG MILT DID just as he had told his running-mate and stuck to the shadowy tree trunks that were his post.

Long moments which to him seemed hours later—there was a scrambling movement in the brush below, followed by the sounds of ponies moving rapidly up the bad footing of the shale slops.

He came out of his cover, saw the black shadow of his

friend come running through the trees. Behind him first one, then four ponies in quick succession, trotted out of the brush into the clearing and made for him.

"There's Milt," someone's voice snapped at the sight of the approaching lad. "We must of scared the Rider away."

A motley of voices greeted this, but over them a commanding voice ordered silence. It was Milt Quanahy's.

The riders who had formed into a knot under the trees broke apart.

"Young Milt seen him," a voice broke out. "Guess it wuz the Masked Rider all right."

"Where'd he go!" questioned old Milt. "We got enough here to follow, him."

Young Milt's high voice cracked the gloom. "Yes sir, I swear it wuz him. He wuz standin' right there a way. Some-one come riding out of th' ranch yard and when he sees them, he started off. Looked to me like he was following the riders down in the canyon."

"Riders," snapped old Milt. "Dutch Quanahy, a couple of the boys and McTaggart, I'll bet! He wuz follow-ing them, huh? Well, by God, here's where we all make ourselves some reward money, boys! 'Cause I know where he's going—if he's heading for the same place Dutch an' McTaggart are! You boys got itchin' guns?"

A rattle of eager affirmatives crackled like rifle fire in the night.

"Come on, then," old Milt snapped. "We're heading for the Box B!"

Unbridled eagerness swept over the group as they spurred their mounts.

THE MASKED RIDER did not follow the exact trail Dutch Quanahy set through the hills in the direction of the Box B. Rather he skirted their flank, yet kept so close behind that only for short periods were they out of his sight or hearing.

The trail they took threaded along the bottoms of canyons, crossed a small range and dropped away into a valley whose level bed, bathed in the moonlight, glimmered between the occasional oaks rising out of stubble hay fields.

At the end of the valley, distant lights marked the riders' goal, the ranch house of the Box B. However, Dutch Quanahy did not enter the valley bottom, but with his riders, skirted the edge until the ranch house, now opposite him, was no more than a quarter of a mile away.

Pushing the big black forward as silently as possible, the hooded man was able to approach to within less than a hundred yards. He was alone still, for Blue Hawk's orders had been to precede if possible, rather than follow the riders.

Barely visible under the spreading branches of a big oak at the edge of the valley bottom, the form of McTaggart could be seen slipping out of the saddle. The three other men wheeled their ponies, leading McTaggart's mount, and with a brief *adios*, wheeled and galloped back into the brush from which they had come, in the direction of the Curlicue *hacienda*.

Well hidden in the trees, the masked man pushed forward. Under the oak, the lanky, square shouldered form of Bill McTaggart was turned in the direction of the disappearing riders. Momentarily, he seemed to pause waiting for the sounds of their leaving to die away. Then he moved slowly into the light towards the stubble field before him. But still he seemed to hesitate.

At last, with a shrug which the masked man in the shades of the nearby pin oaks could plainly see, McTaggart stepped off with long strides in the direction of the Box B.

But before he had taken three steps, a mesquite bush that grew in a moonlit spot immediately before him suddenly seemed to animate itself, to move and grow into a man.

CHAPTER VIII

EYE FOR AN EYE

MCTAGGART'S LANKY BODY jerked to a surprised halt. His right hand flipped downward, but paused there. The figure in the moonlit trail before him held a .45 lightly. Across the intervening space, the sound of Hawk's low and meaningful greeting drifted to The Masked Rider's ears. Momentarily, the thin, tight lips beneath the hood stretched in a grim smile. His plan was to let the tow-head, admit enough to Blue Hawk to make his arrest positive.

Before the smile had had a chance to die, the hooded man's senses were jerked to alert attention.

Instinct, perhaps the legendary sixth sense, warned him of the approach of other humans. Instantly on guard, he trained his ears on every creak of the mountain side behind him. Above the soft murmur of Blue Hawk's voice and the terse replies with which McTaggart greeted them, other sounds grew into meaning for the hooded man. Riders, men, were somewhere on the valley wall behind him.

A hundred, perhaps two hundred yards off in the *brasada*, a pony nickered softly, stamped the ground. Instantly, the hooded man wheeled, scanned the brush and low-growing oaks. No movement in their shadows gave him a hint as to the nearness of the approaching men.

He pivoted towards Blue Hawk. To all evidences the Indian had not heard the whinnying pony, for he was still in conversation with McTaggart. The hooded man weighed his chances. If he departed the scene now, it might leave the Indian at the mercy of McTaggart and the oncoming riders. He decided to allow Blue Hawk a moment more of conversation, then warn him—

He saw Blue Hawk's head jerk about as the pony's nicker floated down the soft wind to them again. Off to the masked man's right something moved abruptly in the brush, crumping dry leaves and branches under foot.

The big black stallion's ears flopped up to attention. That the seriousness of the situation was now acute, the hooded rider well knew. He started to move the black's bridle, then halted himself. If he broke for cover, McTaggart might recognize his shape and infer some relationship existed between Blue Hawk and himself. That would certainly not be safe.

The Masked Rider's hand gripped the bridle, held the stallion's head up and ready. He turned to the forms of Blue Hawk and McTaggart. Suddenly they parted; McTaggart to stalk in the direction of the ranch house. Blue Hawk to melt instantly into the shadows of the nearby oaks.

But no sooner had the men separated than a bull-like voice shattered the silence, breezing the rider's biceps to iron.

"He's up there somewhere, Milt. Now's your chance!"

Feet suddenly thundered through the crackling brush. Instantly the hooded outlaw knew that those sounds had not come from one side—but from three. Escape up the mountain was cut off; to his right and left came sounds of moving men. Straight ahead was the open field. But once out on it he was a clear target for rifles in the brush.

With a snort, the big black stallion wheeled in its tracks. At that second, out of the brush fifty yards to the hooded man's right, a stooping, racing shadow appeared. It gave a startled gasp, slid to a halt. A rifle, gripped in the figure's two hands, was slung abruptly up.

With no cry of warning, the intruder pulled the trigger almost point blank on the hulking figure of the man on the black stallion.

It was only the instinctive reaction of a life-time of danger that saved the black's rider. When the racing figure appeared, he had clinched the stallion's ribs, wheeled it, about-face. With a long leap, the stallion broke into the up-hill brush. As it did, the rifle's lead, followed by a rapier of flame that lit the night, sliced through the leaves and limbs.

THE ROAR OF the rifle had been an igniting spark. Instantly the whole mountain side seemed to come to life, to sprout men and guns. Like some sort of grim tide, they converged at a run on the spot the hooded man had left, drawn on by the noise of the stallion breaking through entangling branches.

The man in its saddle dodged a low-hung oak limb, guilding the mount's long up-hill leaps through the brush. It shot across a small clearing, broke headlong into the mesquite growth on the opposite side.

Almost under its nose, a man's shape popped out of the brush. Moonlight outlined the face of Milt Quanahy and the two .45s he held at arm's length full in the face of the oncoming black.

With a twist of his wrist, the rider brought the black to a rearing, sliding halt. It came back to earth with a hollow thump.

"Hoist 'em," crackled the triumphant voice of Milt Quanahy over that sound. "Hoist 'em. I got you now!"

For a fleeting second, the rider poised in the saddle. Square in the face of two guns that had appeared almost magically out of the thick *brasada*, there seemed no chance of immediate escape. If he had tried to run Milt down, the black would certainly have been killed.

Milt's face, fully visible in the moonlight, was writhing in an expression of bitter hatred.

"I got you," he snarled. "But you're too damn slippery a customer for me. By God, you don't get away this time, Mister Masked Rider. *You're through!*"

With that he shoved both .45s out, straight towards the breast of the hooded figure in the saddle before him and pulled both triggers.

The guns went off with roars like twin mortars that shattered the shadows of the whole canyon. Yet for all the certainty that Milt Quanahy felt at the instant he released the screaming lead, both bullets tore through empty space that had a fraction of a second before been filled by the fleeting black-caped shape.

And in the next second, almost under the very shoulders of the black horse, a flare of yellow flame burst. Throwing himself nearly out of the saddle in the instant that he had outguessed Milt Quanahy, the hooded shape had drawn, pulled the trigger square on the man in the trail.

Milt Quanahy went over backwards as though he had been hit in the face with a sledge hammer. The black reared, threw its massive body over the falling shape of the Quanahy and lunged headlong into the *brasada* and disguising branches of nearby oaks.

Milt Quanahy's dead body twitched once in the throes of death, then lay silent as the sounds of oncoming men and shouting voices surged like a wave up in the mountainside....

FAR BACK IN the hills, an hour later, the big stallion shook its head, waiting impatiently for the pony and rider the man on its back momentarily expected. Finally, the trotting hoof beats of the approaching sorrel were heard. A moment later, Blue Hawk's mount appeared out of the down-trail shadows.

"*Dias,*" the soft guttural voice of the Indian said when the sorrel had pulled up next to the towering black.

The man in the hood nodded.

"*Senor,* there is no other way now," Blue Hawk's words were restrained, but nonetheless filled with concern. "We must ride, *amigo.* This man you have killed is a Quanahy— Milt Quanahy. Even now the other riders bringing him to the *hacienda* are gathering a posse."

The jaw beneath the dark hood clicked. "I promise them a merry chase," he said grimly.

"*Si*—a merry chase—*senor.* But why? They will not give up like other posses. You were forced to kill a Quanahy. That death they will never forgive. An eye for an eye—it is worse than that, *senor.* Those who use the name of Quanahy have by now sworn to kill you on sight. That is their law. They will have men on the mountains waiting, watching the *brasada* gullies and the canyon sides. Behind a rock or a tree—in the *barranca* bottoms, will be a waiting rifle. Ready for enough sight of you to shoot. *Senor,* remember there are only two of us—many of them. Why take the risk?"

The big-hatted head shook. "Why—*quien sabe?* What did McTaggart have to say for himself?"

The Indian shrugged. "He was much surprised to see me. I asked him to return the stolen money. You warned me to say nothing if he claimed there was no money stolen and that it had been some sort of joke on this *Senor* Moore. But that was not his answer. He paid the thirty numbers, *amigo,* without question."

"And warned you he'd kill you if you told what you'd seen?"

"It seems, *amigo,* he is not that sort of man. Perhaps I have feeling we are mistaken in him—there is something perhaps we do not know about him. What? Who knows? He says to me, 'I'd have given this back before, but you weren't in jail when I looked.' That was all."

For a second the hooded man considered. His faith in Blue Hawk's ability to read the character of men was deep seated. Yet it seemed impossible to rid his mind of doubts. Some relentless, gigantic movement was on foot to crush the Box B, wipe it from the range, he knew. Abe Holt's murder. McTaggart's actions. Every indication pointed towards it, every fact they had met.

Time and time again he had by twists of fate been drawn into messes like this, and had had thrust upon him the task to ferret out just such unlawful machinations, bare them to the light, and bring, if possible, the wrong-doers to justice. Always he had somehow succeeded, by placing himself in the face of danger and ever-present death. Sometimes success came quickly—sometimes only after much bloodshed. The power and coldblooded nature of the Quanahys he had already felt. Though he did not know the Box B owner, the man in the hood abruptly understood the relentless crushing forces he faced. Besides, Rock French seemed mixed up in these. He was bad medicine. The Masked Rider's sympathies were quickened and, as always, followed by instant decision.

"Quanahys or not," he said sharply, "we're staying on this range, Blue Hawk, until we know more about McTaggart and what his aims are. It may happen we'll agree with them—but not in a thousand years with the Quanahys. And there is—someone else here!" He did not mention Rock French's name.

"If you stay, *senor,*" said the Indian quietly, "There is no other road I would wish to take. Something within you makes you take the danger trail now. You know not exactly why. Your blood, it is telling! Blue Hawk stays with you!"

THE MAN IN the hood nodded. "What about Abe Holt— the man on the *palomina?* Did you speak of him?"

For a second the Indian was silent. "*Senor,* that is why I think the McTaggart actions have perhaps misled us. *Si,* I said, 'Tonight I have found a dead man. You knew him—*Senor* McTaggart. Abe Holt. He was trampled to death—murdered.'"

The Indian paused.

"His answer!"

Blue Hawk nodded. "His answer?" The Indian's hand shot up, mimicking the absent McTaggart's actions, and grasped his own throat.

"In a terrible voice—'Who did it—tell me quick. *Who did it!*' But I did not have time to speak again, when the Quanahys came."

CHAPTER IX

JANE BASCOM

THE FIRST SOUND Bill McTaggart was aware of the next morning was the high pitched triumphant chortle of a rooster in the Box B corrals. He lifted his head off the roll of blankets he had rescued when Lobo Myers had brought the buckboard into the ranch, and he climbed out of his bunk. The rest of the bunkhouse was deserted, all Box B riders having been for weeks on the Rio Testa range with Sol.

McTaggart rolled himself into his clothes, stepped around in back and sloshed his face with cold water. With his eyes clearer, he returned to the bunk house, combed his gnarled mop of yellow hair and stalked out into the ranch yard.

It was quite early and, with one thought in mind, he made his way straight for the kitchen that ranged off the spreading, 'dobe structure under the nearby oaks. He stalked in through the screen door, caught a glimpse of Lobo Myers holding forth with a flap-jack griddle in the inner sanctums of the kitchen and slid onto one of the hard benches that graced the "grub-shack."

No word of greeting came from within, but several moments later, Lobo Myers, his face a series of ridged scowls and his overalls covered by a white apron, appeared with a stack of wheats, two fried eggs and a cup of steaming coffee. Their greeting was terse, to the point.

Moments later, McTaggart slid back in his seat, wiped the remains of egg yolk off his lips and pulled out the makings of a cigarette. At that moment, Lobo Myers appeared once more and leaned on the table facing the tow headed cowpuncher.

"Suppose you heard about Abe Holt when you reported last night."

McTaggart looked up, grunted. "Yeh. Went in an' took a look where you put him. Mighty queer all right. That cow track on his forehead's clean as a whistle. But them cuts on his wrists sure make it look bad as sin. What's tuh be done though?" he shrugged. "What th' hell does he go into town for when Sol tells him to stick around Soldier Canyon with them yearlings and Fred Stewart?"

Myers snorted. "*There's* a death that'll never be cleared up. Say, what time did you get in anyway?"

"Pretty late."

Myers considered a moment. His walrus mustaches wiggled. "I suppose," he said with fine scorn, "Bein' too much of a min-y-on of all labor 'round this workings, I ain't important enough to hear jest what th' hell happened tuh you last night an' why the Quanahys grabbed you offen that wagon."

McTaggart looked up, grinned almost owlishly. "Remember what old Soapy Smith says—'Cooks is cooks and ain't human long as they got a dirty towel around their middle. Take th' towel off an' they ain't even cooks.' Maybe that's why you been kept in th' dark."

Myers snorted in disgust.

"I'll tell you," said McTaggart, sobering. "King Quanahy wanted me to join th' clan. Asked me right out," he did.

Myers grunted in disbelief and wheeled on his heel. "You better get organized, cowboy. Sol will be ready to tear th' seat of yore pants off if you don't appear in Soldier Canyon with that barbwire *pronto.*"

McTaggart waved away the warning with a careless hand. "What happened to the saddle tramps we picked up last night—the colored lad and the other—what's his name—?"

"They wanted tuh stay in the bunk house, but I told them it was filled," the ranch cook laughed grimly. "No sir, they's something mighty unhealthy looking about that big negro. French didn't like it atall being shoved out into the cold night. I give 'em some grub an' told 'em to camp in the barn somewheres. They'll be around later. Th' white one's name is Rock French."

McTaggart looked up. *"Rock French?* Holy smoke, was that him? Ain't he wanted down south somewheres?"

MYERS NODDED. "HE sure'n hell is. But does that bother him? No sir, says he'll maybe play 'round these parts a while huntin' outlaws, long as—jumpin catfish!" the cook exclaimed. "I bet you ain't heard yet what happened after you left. We done got held up by Th' Masked Rider—"

A series of creases shot across McTaggart's normally smooth forehead.

"The Rider?" he questioned, pretending ignorance. "He in these parts too?"

Myers followed quickly with a graphic description of the scene on the mountain road.

McTaggart listened to little of this. Sure, he was thinking, he knew all about The Masked Rider. Hadn't he seen him kill Milt Quanahy? But the thought of that battle in the brush brought other, more painful thoughts into his mind. His jaw clenched and he stepped past Myers without saying a word and went out into the ranch yard.

Back in the grub-shack, Myers, a portion of his story still on his lips, looked after the disappearing cowpuncher. Momentarily his seamed face flushed in anger at the tow-headed puncher's lack of interest. But a moment later, his anger was supplanted by an expression of question and suspicion.

"Purty damn funny actin', if you ask me," he said aloud.

McTaggart walked straight for the bunk house, entered it and went to his bunk. The blankets he had used as a pillow were rolled in a tight canvased knot, strapped with a leather belt. He lifted it, took it outside to where the buckboard stood under a tree in the ranch yard. He dropped the blankets carefully in the bottom, away from the barbed wire, and went to the stable.

There was neither lightness nor decision in his actions as he hitched up the two ponies and led them forth. A slow, dull pain seemed to suffuse him inwardly. He approached the trip up the mountain filled with sadness which gripped his very soul. This perhaps, was his last ride for the Box B. And what was worse, he was on a mission which every sensibility he owned commanded him not to pursue. But in the manner of his breed, he set his chin, guided the shuffling team of bay ponies across the yard to the buckboard. As he did, a voice that cut like a knife into him, broke through the morning stillness.

" 'Morning, Bill."

But for all the dull pain, the premonitions that rode his lean shoulders, he turned with a grin.

OF ALL THE many favors which a gracious nature had seen fit to bestow upon Jane Bascom, by far the most striking was her smile. And with inner sinkings, Bill had turned to face it. The sight of the girl walking towards him through the brisk morning sunlight was like a palliative that swept away his fears.

Black lustrous hair fell in natural waviness about her forehead and face. It tended to soften the meaningful lines of mouth and eyebrows that Sol Bascom's parentage had put there. Her eyes were dark, deep pools. And like her father's, her features, though oval and finely chiselled, were those of an individual who thought and acted with independence of mind.

Stray fingers of premonition gripped Bill's heart, but he shook them away and summoned up every ounce of buoyancy he could gather.

He took in the flash of pearly small teeth, the lustrous, laughing eyes as she approached the wagon, and he asked archly, *"Dias. Tengo el gusto de la senorita de la Caga B?"*

The smile shifted to a throaty laugh. "You have the pleasure—and the thanks—of the whole ranch besides the *senorita* for getting out of that mess last night."

The laugh died, something sprang into her glance that clamped icy tentacles around Bill's vitals. She stepped towards him.

"Bill, what is it? Tell me. You weren't telling the truth when you came in last night—that they'd thought you were the puncher that killed Fritz Quanahy that night of the saloon brawl in Willard's City, I know it isn't true—I could tell by the way you said it. What was the truth? Did it have something to do with that shooting in the brush?"

McTaggart swallowed. A shadow of a smile flitted across his face.

"It was the truth," he said grimly, but knew the instant he said it that his voice did not ring right. It showed instantly in Jane Bascom's face as her high cheek bones suffused with color.

A small hand came out, touched the rude elbow of his hickory shirt.

"You're hiding something because you love me," she said softly. "Don't do it, Bill—the truth can't hurt me more than your attempting to lie can. What did happen?"

A tide of color swept up McTaggart's grim features. He looked down into the dark eyes before him. Over him, like a commanding tide, burst the desire to sweep the willowy, tender shape into his arms, to bare his whole heart in one impassioned outburst. She came closer. The sweet fragrance of her drifted up to him, demanding, unescapable.

He bit his lip. "You're right. I lied," he said abruptly. "But I can't tell you more, Jane. I can't! There's something— Well, I'm taking the best way out of a nasty mess, I think. Maybe the only way—you'll have to believe me, trust me long enough—"

He stumbled to a halt, staring at her with pained, anguished eyes. Was he lying to her now—or not? He hardly knew.

The girl nodded. "I trust you, Bill—I think I always will—"

To the youth before her, those words delivered the last crushing blow to his already anguished spirit. A flash of pain tore through him. He stepped forward, swept her into his arms, crushed her to him in a hard, long embrace.

A moment later, the arms that had crept about his neck slipped away. She stepped back.

"We shouldn't have done that, Bill. There are people around—even though it's early. If someone—"

"There's only Myers in the kitchen," McTaggart

answered, but he thought suddenly of the two men whom the ranch cook had stated had spent the night in the barn. Perhaps at that very moment they were staring out of one of the doors....

Bill turned, but the barn across the ranch yard showed no sign of the big negro, Jackson, nor of Rock French. A sigh of relief escaped from the tow-head....

BUT TWO MEN, out of hearing of the ranch yard, had watched the scene. One, far up on the valley wall behind McTaggart, had pulled his pinto pony to a halt when the two microscopic figures in the yard below had melted into one. It was Dutch Quanahy, King Quanahy's son, returning from an early morning reconnoiter of the spot where his uncle Milt was killed. As he watched, a bitter smile touched his lips.

"Jane Bascom, huh?" he said out loud. "By God, he'll have to be taught different!"

Almost opposite the spot where young Quanahy had stopped, Wayne Morgan, riding the big black stallion in the direction of the Box B, pulled up.

He saw, as Quanahy did, the tiny figure that he recognized as being McTaggart's lanky shape, talking to the woman in the ranch yard. A muted exclamation broke from Morgan as the ant-like shapes came together.

Adding one more unfathomable question to the already involved personality of Bill McTaggart, was the fact that besides being an evident traitor to the Box B, he was, it seemed, in love with the lithe and shapely woman below.

Morgan's thin lips stretched in a tight smile. He had intended going down into the Box B, posing as a saddle-free tramp looking for a job. The Bascom spread was running cattle in large numbers. The possibility of their needing another hand would give him an opportunity to observe McTaggart's activities at first hand.

But this last situation put other thoughts into the rider's mind. He decided to shun the Box B, contact McTaggart directly. With that decision made, Morgan wheeled the big black towards a nearby ridge top where Blue Hawk awaited him.

As he did so, the microscopic shape of McTaggart stepped into the hitched up buckboard, waved once at the shape of the girl standing near the ranch house gate, and sent the bays galloping recklessly out of the yard in the direction of Soldier Canyon Road and Sol Bascom.

CHAPTER X

McTAGGART TALKS

TEN MILES FROM the Box B, the buckboard McTaggart drove skidded and rattled up an almost impassable wagon road, threading along the bed of a brush-choked *barranca*. The morning sun beat with unrelieved intensity on the team of bays, and the addition of the bulky load they drew on the rig left them in a lather.

McTaggart, as an outlet to his wrought-up feeling, had driven them hard, seeking in that manner to escape the angry, self-condemnation that surged through him. He shoved his battered Stetson back on his head and picked a rising spot on the road ahead as a place to breathe the ponies.

The rig skidded crazily on the loose stones, but jumped ahead when he clucked at the bays. In another moment, the buckboard scraped through a close growth of mesquite, mounted a slight rise and stopped.

Far ahead, the rude road dropped over a terrace in the hills, skirted a sort of natural meadow and disappeared around the huge bulk of a spiny and abruptly rising wall of mountain.

The place at which the road disappeared was a natural gateway, a pass leading into the higher hills beyond. Around the bend, and some distance up the narrow canyon beyond, was the Soldier Canyon camp of the Box B—and Sol Bascom.

McTaggart frowned. Meeting Sol Bascom was a task he little enjoyed contemplating. Bascom was granite-eyed, hardbitten—a man who knew men and cows in every sense. McTaggart realized his explanation of his capture by King Quanahy would have to be well done not to strike a wrong note in Sol Bascom's frost-bitten ears.

One thing, however, was in McTaggart's favor. Bascom knew, sensed the relationship that had grown between the tow-headed puncher he had hired and his daughter. Verbally, he had neither condoned nor condemned it. But because he had said nothing, both Jane and Bill had interpreted his silence as a form of assent....

When McTaggart thought of that, his conscience, a rising, condemning inner voice, suddenly broke its bonds. He swore bitterly. The sea of doubt, uncertainty, on which he drifted, was racked by winds of cross-purpose and indecision. He had told himself, then Jane, that he was doing the best he could—he thought he was. *Was he?* A mute spectre rose in his mind—a spectre of the Box B without Jane, or Sol Bascom, or Myers—

McTaggart came back to his senses with a rude, freezing

jolt. His head jerked about, his tight mouth sagged agape, then snapped shut with a click of steel.

The mesquite bushes to his right parted and out of them, like some sort of ghostly materialization, rose the sweeping sombrero, the awesome black hood and square shoulders of The Masked Rider. He was on foot.

"What do you want?" snapped McTaggart, bravely.

The voice that issued from beneath the hood took the tow-head by surprise. He had expected a voice of warning, of steel—

"Just drop your gun on the rig-bottom," drawled the man in the hood. "I'd like to make *palabra* about where you came from, where you're heading for—and what game you have up your sleeve."

The tow-head's eyebrows raised, but he said nothing, pulled out the bone handled .45 at his side and dropped it with a clank on the rig floor-boards.

A wry smile twisted the tow-head's lips as he turned to the man in the brush.

"Powerful unhealthy 'round this country," he grunted acridly—"particularly for anyone wearing that black rig you got on. If I was you, I'd dust."

THE MAN IN the hood did not rise to the scorn in McTaggart's voice. "It's my own choosing," he said quietly. "Besides, my brand's in the open for anyone that wants to see it. Which is saying something that doesn't hold for other gents in this vicinity."

A flush colored McTaggart's grim cheeks. He chose his words carefully.

"Me? Is that it?" he snapped, and anger abruptly broke into his voice.

The cool gesture from beneath the hooded horseman stopped McTaggart. The Masked Rider had had opportunity to scan the other's features, to mark his movements. Coolly, he weighed appearances. Yes, he told himself, Blue Hawk had been right. The stubborn nosed tow-head in the rig before him was certainly not the type he had at first seemed. He looked clean, honest. And the anger now in his face was, in a sense, a righteous indignation. The wide-spaced blue eyes had no guile in them. McTaggart was just that: impulsive, outspoken, hard-headed.

"Before you go off half-cocked," the hooded outlaw interrupted, "let me tell you what I know and maybe what I'm going to do about it. I happened to see you a while back," he paused and added with meaning—"in the Box B yard."

The tow-head's blue eyes widened, he opened his mouth, but the other broke in.

"Also I saw you go into the Quanahy *hacienda* last night."

There was a pause. "So what?" said the tow-head scornfully.

"So putting things together," sharpness crept into the hooded man's voice, "I'd say you were on the way to doing something you better be damn' sure is the right move!"

"I'll be the judge of that," snapped McTaggart. "What interest have you got in anything I might do?"

"Just this," the hooded man said. "If you were on the wrong track, I'd hoped to help you find the right one. If there's something I can do to straighten things out, I'm willing." He shrugged. "It's sort of a wide open offer, I know—and it's up to you to judge what it might be worth to you."

"Thanks," snapped the tow-head, gracelessly, *"gracias!*

I'm doing what I think is th' best, the only way out of a situation you don't know anything about. I think maybe I'd best be left to work things out my own way. S'long."

He clucked to the ponies, but a steely voice brought them and him to a stop.

"I'm not so sure," said the man in the hood slowly. "I suppose Abe Holt is an example of how well you run things."

The tow-head's eyes widened. "You heard about that too," he said scornfully. "Well, I didn't have a thing to do with it. An' you can take that for what it's worth."

"And the jury can, too."

McTaggart's eyes sparkled, bitter rage tightened his lips, sharpened to a razor edge the tone of his voice.

"You talking about juries," he said acridly. "That's a laugh! I suppose you'll be at the court house as Witness Number One when they try me for murdering Abe Holt." He laughed.

"No," said the man in the hood slowly, "you already have enough rope to swing yourself with. As I said before, because I think you're just playing out another length of it, I'm taking the side of the—" he paused—*"the girl back there, in the Box B!"*

The man in the hood shrugged. He spoke sharply to the ponies. Taken by surprise McTaggart was jounced rudely as the ponies started up.

WHEN THE RIG disappeared, the hooded man turned, entered the brush and small trees that bordered the road. Some distance back from it, he found the black stallion nuzzling grass under an oak, and mounted.

For some moments he walked it slowly through the

aisleway of the thick woods, his fists clenched, his thoughts coming fast.

Soon, however, he pulled the stallion to a halt, searched the multiple small noises of the woods about him with sure-trained ears.

Decisively he turned the stallion, moved it across a barren patch of rock rising out of the dead leaves and grass, and doubled back on his tracks. Once in the disguise of the trees again, he moved into a welter of mesquite and pin oaks, dismounted and waited.

Blanketed by the surrounding woods, the faint sounds of a pony's hoofs on the dead growth came to him. Not many moments later, a form materialized in the trees and gave shape to a *palomina* pony. The hidden man's teeth clicked. The horse was Abe Holt's and the man who rode it, almost dwarfing the pony with his heavy, pot-bellied shape, was Rock French.

Perspiration was streaming down French's fat, pinkish jowls. But the small pig eyes showed no hint of the physical discomfort of the heat and his riding. They were cold, intent as they searched the humus bed of the woods for the signs of a big horse's hoofs. In his puffy right hand a drawn forty-five glinted light from its position resting on the pommel before French's bulging paunch.

The hooded man's hand rose and touched the nose of the stallion beside him. In this manner he had trained it against nickering at the approach of other ponies. The horse made no sound as the little *palomina* and the big shape that had bought it, wound through the trees and disappeared through the brush beyond.

But still the hooded man did not relax his watch from the brush, nor did he drop the gloved hand he held at the stallion's nose. For nearly five minutes he remained this way, silent, unmoving, the sharp gray eyes examining the surrounding trees through the slit hood.

Finally, the oak branches to the right and a hundred yards from the hooded man, shivered and parted. Stooping, a hulking mountainous shape slid into the open and moved on quiet feet between the tree boles in the direction French had taken.

Outlined against the farther brush, the man's shape was monstrous, a giant's. His hatless, close-clipped poll glinted like some sort of polished black marble, as the big negro, Jackson, stepped carefully through the trees and into French's trail.

For all his girth and weight, the black man moved almost, silently across the loose leaves. He bent, examined the ground, blinked and arose. A half smile touched the wide, heavy lips, then broke into a grin that revealed the gleaming, huge teeth.

He looked up at the sound of hoofs. The *palomina* came trotting into sight, the fat man on its back swaying heavily in the saddle.

The big negro nodded as Rock approached.

"Trail gives out down there a way," snapped French. "You seen anything?"

Jackson chuckled. "No more'n you, Rock. He sho' 'nough come dis way, 'cause when he left dat McTaggart man he was riding straight for dese woods. What yo' mean—de trail gives out?"

"Rocks," said the killer. "He crossed it down a ways."

A BURST OF laughter broke from the huge negro and rattled the branches throughout the little clearing.

"Shut up!" snapped French. "Are you crazy—maybe he's around here. And if he can't hear that bellow of yours...."

Jackson's laughter quieted to convulsive rumbles. He smote the tight dungaree that sheathed his huge leg.

"Fo' a suprostitious man like yo-all, dat sho' would be a bad sign then."

"Why?" snapped French impatiently.

"Why? 'Cause if he done crossed rock onct, we better gib up 'cause de next time he crosses rock, mebbe dat rock ain't stone atall."

"Stone—" snapped French. "What're you talking about?"

A renewed and muted blare of laughter came from Jackson. "Man, yo' sho' is hard tuh unnerstan' some things. But come on, le's go look where dem tracks gib out."

The *palomina* was wheeled and following the huge stalking shape of the negro, it disappeared into the overgrowth between the trees.

With that the hooded shape moved out of his hiding place, mounted the black stallion and moved quickly in the direction from which the two had come.

As he went, troubles rode heavily on the cloaked shoulders. He had tried the tow-head and found him unreasonable, as misguided as man could be. McTaggart had set his mind on hurting the woman he loved, it seemed. Yet what could be done to stop him? He couldn't be kidnapped and hidden in the brush.

Eventually he would have to be let loose, free to follow his bent at will. No one save himself knew what his next actions would be. But did even he know?

The man in the mask gritted his teeth. On top of all else, was now the constant threat of the killer, French, and his running mate, the giant negro. Vague premonitions touched the rider of the black stallion. He knew that sooner or later he would run face to face with French and the negro. He hoped it *would* be face to face—not *back* to face!

CHAPTER XI

DYNAMITE!

THOUGH SOLDIER CANYON was far from being a box canyon, Sol Bascom had made of it a nearly perfect natural corral in which to gather the swarms of cattle brought by the Box B punchers out of the Rio Testa range.

The wagon road along which McTaggart had driven passed across the pasture to the narrow canyon mouth and entered directly into the scene of Box B activities. The two barren, abrupt cliffs which formed this mouth were not more than one hundred and fifty yards apart. And, save for the wagon road, there was no break in the clutter of thick mesquite that choked it.

Beyond the mouth, the walls of the valley spread apart forming Soldier Canyon. Two miles above, the depression of the canyon disappeared into a rolling, uprising terrace of hills. Somewhere from the midst of the trees at this end, a small stream wound down into the canyon, moved off to the approacher's left into a marshy basin of low ground and rank grass where it disappeared into the earth.

Several hundred yards above this, Sol Bascom had strung a six-strand barbed-wire fence from one steep wall of the canyon to the other. Formed in something of a bottle neck, the fence led down to a gate so that cattle pushed forward from a wide area would converge gradually through it and into the natural corral.

Once inside, the cattle had only one means of escape—through the mouth of the canyon. Flanking them was the six-strand fence. To either side were rises in the canyon bottom which gave almost immediately into fifty foot shale cliffs. To keep the cattle from moving out of the mouth, Bascom stationed a patrol of punchers during the day and one or two riders at night.

Except for the marshy ground, the bottom of the canyon was cluttered with underbrush and small trees. But knowing the nature of his job, Bascom had left it so, for the cattle he brought down from the range were as wild as wolves and twice as man-shy.

THE AFTERNOON SUN had blistered the narrow canyon, for it was naturally sheltered from winds. But when finally the hot orb had disappeared behind the cliffs and shadows had begun to form under the canyon walls, the air became muggy, tepid.

In the sunset light, two riders pushed through the growth that rimmed the shale cliffs. One was Wayne Morgan, and Blue Hawk followed him, swinging easily to the motions of his sorrel.

Before them spread the canyon. Below, were the moving shapes of feeding cattle. Across the valley, a hooded chuck wagon, the flare of a camp fire and the distant shapes of moving figures, marked the Box B camp.

A muffled lowing floated up from the valley. Gathered in clumps in the dark mesquite, cattle were moving about, calling for lost calves, or nuzzling at the grass. For a long time Morgan sat quietly, taking in every detail of the scene. As he did so, a bluish haze slowly settled, misting the moving cattle, dimming the whole scene.

He turned to the Indian after a long silence and said: "Going to be a bad night."

Blue Hawk looked at the sky and paused as if smelling the dull, lifeless air.

"My people," he said finally, "call this *Uanato*—'don't know' weather. Further north—I would say we smell rain, if it gets colder, maybe snow. *Si*, much sky noise, and bad for the men below if the cattle get restless."

Morgan nodded, turned back to the canyon. Up from the mouth came a slow moving group of riders, aimed evidently for the camp and supper. They raised their hands and a faint hallo of greeting came from them as a rider on a pinto passed, heading towards the mouth.

"Night man," said Morgan quietly. "Taking the place of those other riders. Evidently that was the reason for McTaggart's barbed wire. Bascom didn't have time to fence up the mouth. We'll go around the other side of the valley, nearer the camp."

"*Si.*"

Once again the stallion's rider examined the inverted bowl of the sky. The atmosphere, the absence of stars, made him shake his head.

"A lightning storm," he said tersely. "I'll bet Bascom sleeps on an uncomfortable bed tonight—if he sleeps at all...."

IT WAS NEARLY midnight when the soft hissing voice of the Indian awakened Wayne Morgan. They had camped, after an iron-ration meal, on the cliffs overlooking the camp. Determined that McTaggart would have as little chance as possible to go ahead with doubtful plans, Morgan had placed Blue Hawk on watch for the first part of the night and decided to keep the morning vigil for himself.

He could hear the restless movements of the black stallion in the brush behind him when he opened his eyes. The hunched-over figure before him, that of the Indian, touched his shoulder once more.

"*Senor*, sky-flashes have started. But you must come. I think someone is down among the cattle!"

Soundlessly, Morgan reached for his gun belt, moved up on one knee. As he did, a brilliant streak of light shot before his eyes. Far off, a rumble of thunder rattled and silenced away.

By that time Morgan was on his feet stalking on long legs after the swift moving Indian.

Another flare of lightning guided them to the brink of the cliff!

"When the sky-flash goes off," whispered the Indian, "you may see better."

It was true. The shapes of cattle below in the mesquite gradually formed in Morgan's eyes. He sniffed the air. It was heavy with threat, ominous.

The Indian's hand went out, grasped Morgan's elbow.

"*Senor*, that was the sound I heard!"

In the silence that followed, somewhere off in the dark a cow lowed lonesomely. But beside that, Morgan made out the sounds of a pony's hoofs scrambling in the shaly dirt of the cliffs off to their right.

At that moment the skies were ripped by a cannonade of thunder followed immediately by lightning that for a second illuminated the small canyon with glaring intensity.

All at once, when it passed, a hoarse bellow broke from

below. The two men on the cliff could hear the rustle of the big herd as some animals heaved to their feet and others, already awake, began to move through the brush.

"The thunder's going to keep on coming down from the hills," Morgan snapped. "That means it'll always seem to be behind the cattle. If they get frightened any more, it'll drive them naturally down towards the mouth. But that's not where the rider we heard is heading."

He paused, trained his ears for sounds above the restless movements of the cattle.

As before, the sounds of a pony's hoofs broke with eerie, ominous import on Morgan's senses.

"He's going back now! Come, Hawk, we're heading towards the mouth. They have only one man down there—the fellow on the pinto. If those cattle start that way he'll be plenty thankful for any help we can give him!"

Both the sorrel and the black stallion were hobbled near at hand with their rigs ready for instant use. As Morgan pulled the black's *cincha* tight, a cannonade of a thousand guns broke over the valley, drenching it in lightning. He swore, swung into the saddle.

Far away came the murmur of voices, a shouted order or two from Bascom's camp.

"He'd better get organized faster than that," said Morgan. "If—"

But he got no farther than that. A deep rumble, then an ear-splitting jarring crash battered his ear drums and shook the very ground at his feet. The black stallion reared, only to be pulled back to earth by a powerful jerk.

The noise broke across the valley, reechoed twice before it died to silence. And over its thunder came the crash of falling rock and a second earth-jarring jolt.

For a moment Morgan stood in silence. Then he snapped one word that brought the Indian's head about with a jerk. "*Dynamite!*"

CHAPTER XII

STAMPEDE

CAT-LIKE, THE BLACK leaped towards the rim of the cliffs, slid to a halt on the very lip of the brush. Morgan's eyes were hard, glittering as he scanned the valley below. Small surging groups of the cattle could be seen running through the brush away from Morgan, away from the avalanche that clattered into the valley. He could hear Bascom's men shouting as they ran towards their remuda.

"McTaggart!" snapped from Morgan's lips. "It was his pony we heard. Another explosion like that and—"

A mighty vacuum seemed to form about Morgan's ears, deadening the air with pregnant warning. What followed it seemed like the crash of some ether-bound meteor striking the earth.

The stallion snorted and reared as the very earth beneath it heaved and moved. And as before, after the deafening explosion, came the grating sound of huge quantities of earth moving out into space and then crashing with all the terrible force of thousands of tons of solid matter.

Morgan shouted, wheeled the stallion. The valley below them, when it was lighted by a flare of lightning, showed a surging sea of backs swirling like the waves of some treacherous river.

There was no doubt about it now, the cattle had moved frantically away from the scene of this last explosion and in doing so, had formed a tight, compact, milling herd on the valley floor.

The thunder of hoofs on hard pan reechoed against the walls, beating back with ominous import to the men on the cliff.

Then, all at once the sea of backs below converged and moved forward with growing speed.

"He's done it!" shouted Morgan above the next burst of thunder. *"They're heading for the mouth!"*

His words were lost to the Indian in the thunder of the black stallion's hoofs. Sure-footed, it raced along the cliff rim while far below a dark river of beasts suddenly streamed out in the direction of the lips that formed the canyon mouth.

Behind Morgan and the Indian, as if to speed their mounts, came the muted hollow roll of thousands of hoofs, the sound of an army of cavalry breaking through a forest of mesquite.

In the quarter of a mile that the two riders covered, the rim of the valley looped in a wide arc. They followed it, but each knew from the roar below that the leading cattle were far ahead of them and would reach the mouth of the canyon first.

Yet Morgan kept up the distance-eating pace until at last the white outlines that marked the barren cliffs of the mouth loomed ahead. He pulled the black down to a quick trot, sent it out as far as was safe on the brushy, narrow hump.

The roar of the stampeding herd filled the air, drowning the words he shot to the Indian behind him. Then all at once the sky was lighted once more by the glare of a thousand brush fires lit at once.

In the illuminated moment the narrow passage below was plainly visible to Morgan. A surging river was streaming through it. Above the crush of frantic, terror-stricken bodies through the brush, the wild hammer of feet, he could hear distant shouts, then a crash of guns.

But the cattle below were beyond stopping now. In that second he had caught too the glimpse of bulging wild eyes, of blood-red nostrils.

Momentarily he considered retracing his steps until the black could find a foothold and descend to the little meadow into which the main body of the cattle seemed to be heading. But that too was useless; in the face of that mighty tide of terror-gripped, insane bodies, the strength of a mere man and horse would be like a fly's.

Morgan swung out of the saddle, swore tersely. To his left the river of bodies seemed to fade to illusive wraiths in the darkness. He knew that once in the meadow, they would linger not at all. If it had been daylight and Bascom's punchers were on that side, there might have been a chance. But once free, the herd, grown used to two years of unhampered freedom, would part and head for the brush, and work their way back into the open range. So, in a sense, here was the end of Bascom's hard work—months of labor gone to naught in a matter of moments.

OVER THE ROAR of hoofs below, Morgan heard the voice of Blue Hawk at his elbow.

"They will save some of them. Listen," he paused.

Off in the dark the sound of shouting voices and occasional shots were again distinguishable.

"He'll save a quarter of the herd," snapped Morgan, "if he can get them milling around on that side."

He leaned forward, piercing the black moving shadows

below. Yes, the rattle of their hoofs was already beginning to lessen.

He turned. "We'll go down the other side."

Moments later the two riders dropped over the shaly embankment and trotted their mounts down through the brush into the wagon road McTaggart had taken that morning.

Nearing the mouth of the canyon, Morgan pulled off to the right, into the shadows of the pin oaks. In the short time they had been making their way around, the stream of cattle had dropped off to less than two dozen laggards who lunged through the opening and disappeared after their fellows into the thick gloom. All at once the roar of the herd was gone, and the little meadow silent. Far away a thousand different noises indicated the separate passages of hoofs into the shelter of the hills.

Through the mouth of the canyon there floated to the riders the muted shouts of cowboys as they herded what remained of the cattle into a tight knot to prevent further stampede.

Morgan spoke first. "Well, that was the plan all right—and he went through with it. But why? Those cattle can be rounded up again, practically none of them got hurt. Why stampede them at all? In two weeks, three weeks, they'll all be back in the canyon again."

Blue Hawk shrugged. "Why, *senor!*"

After a short pause Morgan said thoughtfully, "It looks as if McTaggart and the Quanahys want to slow up the gathering of the Box B herd. During these next two or three weeks—*quien sabe?*—anything might happen to it."

"Perhaps you are right, *senor*," Blue Hawk admitted,

"but we have seen no Quanahy putting his hand into this trouble—"

He broke off short. Brush crackled and shook off in the shadowed woods to their left. There was a brief clatter of hoof beats and following them a pony came trotting out into a cleared place in the mesquite.

As it trotted, the empty *tapaderos* flapped loosely around its shoulders. Morgan spoke. Like a dart the sorrel Blue Hawk rode moved out of its tracks in the direction of the beast. Headed off, the riderless horse wheeled in its tracks seeking to escape the oncoming Indian. But the Indian's mount was sure footed, experienced. It changed its gait, headed about and ran shoulder to shoulder to the pinto.

A moment later, Blue Hawk rode back leading the shie-ing riderless mount.

Morgan nudged the black up next to the wild-eyed captive.

"A pinto—" he snapped. "If I'm not wrong, the same one that rider going out to guard the mouth of the canyon rode. No?"

Blue Hawk's mute nod was a compliment to Morgan's sharp eyes.

"You see well, *senor*. Even old *Senor Lobo,* the desert wolf, would bow to you."

The dark-hatted man's face was grim. "Look at the condition of its rig."

As if to cast further gruesome light on the wild eyed pinto's saddle, the moon broke through the clouds, bath-ing the little clearing in cool, silvery illumination. Blue Hawk saw then that across the seat of the pinto's saddle and down the stirrup aprons as if it had been sloshed there on purpose, was a wide, red ribbon of gore, of congealed blood.

For a second he was silent. Then the Indian said, "He who rode the pinto is somewhere in the woods, *senor.* Perhaps we shall find him, even in the dark."

Morgan shook his head slowly. "We'll try, Hawk. Do the best we can, but after he's lost that much blood, there's only a chance in a hundred he could live until we locate him."

And as if to punctuate this sentence with a last, grue-some note, a globule of thick, life's blood dropped from one trailing *tapadero* string into the dust....

CHAPTER XIII

BILL—!

BEFORE THE CATTLE were well started on their stam-pede out of the valley, Sol Bascom had had his riders out of their blankets and streaming towards the nearby remuda. By the time the herd leaders had reached the mouth, riders on bareback ponies were already racing towards the herd. Using their guns and every other means possible to break into the storming river of cattle, they had finally succeeded in cutting into it, and turning a part up the valley slope where it was finally stopped by the rising shale walls.

Though Sol Bascom had understood immediately what caused the stampede, his next activities were not aimed towards ferreting out and punishing whatever enemies there might be in the valley. Instead, he gathered his forces to retrieve what he could of the scattered herd, prepare for the many hectic days before him, and the job of getting the far-scattered brush-poppers back into Soldier Canyon.

The malefactors, he thought, were at least ten miles off by now. What he wanted was punchers, now, not gunmen. That the Quanahys were only tightening their grip on the Box B did not once enter his head.

He sought out a buck-toothed rangy puncher by the name of Sawyers, gave him the best horse he could find and sent him streaking in the direction of the Box B ranch house.

Nearly an hour later, Sawyers shot the pony across the stubbled fields outside the Box B, skirted recklessly close to the gate posts and into the ranch yard.

The high clatter of his mount's hoofs were a tocsin in the night that reëchoed against the silent barn and dark-windowed, rambling house.

Moving straight towards his goal, Sawyers sent the pony up to the picket fence that separated the house portico from the ranch yard and pulled up to a jerking halt.

"Miss Bascom."

He had only to repeat the name once again before a low voice issued from the darkened, shadowed window of the house next to Sawyer.

The buck-toothed rider's words were close clipped. "Sol says tuh tell you someone dynamited th' herd an' she stampeded hell-bent for breakfast. Wants you tuh bring some stuff and whoever yuh got around here up tuh Soldier Canyon in a hurry.

"Dynamite—" queried the husky voice. "But who could have—"

"He don't know. Just someone wanted tuh break up the herd. They shore did a good job. Sol says git Myers, a

wire-stretcher, the two extra rifles over the fire-place, an'
whatever loose hosses you got 'round here." He wheeled
his mount. "I'm gonna take one outta th' barn an' leave
mine. Jest about run out. Oh yeah, he says, bring some
more tarpaulins—gonna rain purty soon. You'll find 'em
in th' bunk house." With that he was off in the direction
of the silent barn.

Before Sawyers had left the ranch yard, Jane was dressed
and hammering at Lobo Myers' door. As the bucktoothed
puncher rammed his pony out of the yard with a barrage
of hoofs, the ranch cook stirred with a sleepy, "Yes'm—
comin'."

Not many minutes later, Myers had hitched the spare rig
out in the yard and roped the two spare ponies in the corral.
Leading them towards the buckboard, he saw Jane come
out of the ranch house with an armful of rifles. He hitched
the ponies to the rear of the wagon and went towards the
barn for the fence-making implement.

In the meantime, Jane hurried across to the empty bunk
house, entered and set a match to the low hanging kerosene
lamp over the door.

She moved across the rude floor, examining each bunk
for tarps that the punchers with her father had left behind.
Unusually enough, all of the bunks were made up—for
the punchers had been away for some time—save one.
That was Bill McTaggart's. A wry sort of smile touched
her serious eyes.

THE WORD SAWYERS brought had sent a cold streamer
of fear over her heart. She knew the extent of the gamble
her father was taking by leaving the delivery of the herd
until almost the moment the bank's notes would come
due. But in an operation the size Sol was in the midst of,

a mere matter of a day's feed off the Rio Testa was indeed a small fortune.

With this stampede and the work necessary to bring the herd back to its previous size, time would be at a premium. If anything happened—. She walked towards the bunk Bill McTaggart had but lately slept in. In her troubled eyes, she regarded it as a symbol that Bill was up in the canyon standing by her father. Her faith in him reassured her as she stood over the crumpled bedding, the loose awry mattress.

But she did not stand thus for long. Something white, rope-like, protruded from the spot where Bill's canvas-covered roll of blankets had been used as a pillow. She reached forward, pulled the thing out of its hiding place under the mattress. For a second she frowned. It looked like a six inch length of cotton rope. Yet all of a sudden her face paled and she steadied herself against the bunk.

Was this, shot through her whirling thoughts—was this the reason—could it be the reason for Bill's secrecy?

"Bill," she whispered in a tight, agonized voice. "It couldn't have been you with that—"

She lifted the rope-like thing in her hand. From either end a few black grains scattered out to the floor. What she held was a piece of fuse.

"With—*that!*" she repeated in a whisper.

CHAPTER XIV

HILLSIDE INDICTMENT

THE FIRST FINGERS of light found Sol Bascom stalking the border of the camp-fire under the looming cliffs of Soldier Canyon. His face was seamed, hard-jawed. Though he had ordered all of his punchers to turn in, except the night watch, he had kept a silent vigil over their sprawling blanket-wrapped shapes.

But it was not that he feared an attack. He needed time to think, to reconstruct out of the hectic violent scene of the night some clue that would name his attackers. Hours had gone by since the dynamiting and the salvaging of one-fourth the herd, but still he could not get at the solution.

He had accepted Bill's story of the Quanahy kidnapping as the truth. He was not even aware that Bill McTaggart had not been in camp at the time of the dynamiting. Too much had happened in those following, thundering moments.

At that very moment, though he did not know it, McTaggart was watching Bascom's every movement from the depths of his huddled up blankets. And his vigil was by a thousand times more painful.

Bascom paused in his stride, turned towards the flat bed of the valley. Already the moving shapes of cattle could be made out, nuzzling through the dew-wet grass, moving towards the swampy ground.

Bascom swore bitterly. Maybe a quarter of the herd, at the most. The square angle of his seamed, weatherbeaten jaw hardened, the dark eyes, so much like his daughter's, lighting with a fierce unrelenting hatred.

He had sent a puncher up to investigate the actual scene of the dynamiting, but other than confirmation that that was what had happened, the searcher brought back no clues.

If he could only wrap his hands around the neck of the yellow-livered, skulking rat who had done it, Bascom told

himself for the hundredth time— If it was them Quanahys again—

He was interrupted by a commotion down in the
brush of the valley mouth. A Box B rider appeared, then a
stranger at a quick gallop. Bascom swore with acrid venom.
For the second rider who had appeared, led a pinto pony
with wildly flapping empty stirrups.

"Vance's—" he snapped. "Vance's pinto."

Striding in the direction of the oncoming riders, Bascom
knew that his first guess had been correct. The night rider
he had stationed at the mouth of the canyon he had utterly
forgotten. Now, what the hell—

A second later the first rider pulled up with a jerk, his
mouth tight lipped, bitter.

"Listen to this!" he snapped.

By that time the second rider had drawn close. Bascom
saw that it was either a Mexican or an Indian and that his
eyes were a pair of flashing, hard beads.

"What is it?" snapped Bascom at the rider of the sorrel.

"*Senor,*" the Indian said in a quick voice, "I ride along
this way an' see this pony chewing the grass. He has no
rider. So," the Indian shrugged—"I want to take look, see
mebbe why he is loose with this saddle an' nobody there. I
see then, *senor,* there is blood on the saddle."

Bascom looked, the nut-brown surface of his cheeks
paling.

"I look around," said the Indian. "Pretty soon I find
him—you come?"

By that time the commotion had awakened the sleeping punchers. Like jumping jacks they had came out of
their beds and gathered wide-eyed and staring about the
bloody pinto.

"You're damn right I will," snarled Bascom. "Come on, you boys. Into th' leather and make it *pronto!*"

Soon, following the trotting shape of the sorrel Blue Hawk rode, Sol Bascom, a sullen eyed McTaggart, and four other punchers raced out of the camp across the valley bottom and out through its narrow mouth.

The place that the Indian took them to was little over a quarter of a mile from the canyon mouth off in the thick *brasada* and overgrowth of the hillsides.

WHEN THE INDIAN stopped, Bascom swung to the ground and stalked forward. Almost immediately behind him came Bill McTaggart. They halted abruptly over the thing the Indian pointed to on the ground.

The puncher, Vance, lay spread-eagled, his limbs crooked, just as he had fallen from his horse. His face, rather what remained of his face, was pointed straight up into the morning sky.

Bascom cursed softly, leaned forward and bit out one word.

"Trampled!"

"*Quien sabe?*" said the Indian's low voice.

Bascom straightened. "*Quien sabe* nothing! Look at that!"

To him the cause of Vance's death was obvious. Full across his forehead stretched a bloody gap, an indentation into the skull itself. And what was more, the mark of the frightful blow he had received was clean-cut as though it had been imprinted in dust. The triangular shaped print of a cow's front hoof.

"Trampled," said Bascom slowly, "Run down by them cows last night. Probably the dumb, honest kid jest couldn't see them cows get away an' tried to stand 'em off." He turned on McTaggart. "Shore he should of known better. How the hell did he think he could do anything with that hell-bent-for election tornado? He didn't have a chance of a fly in a hurricane, but he stuck. Lads," Bascom turned and looked through the hard-jawed, grim faces about him, "he stuck, and fer that I'm gonna give him everything he deserves, if I—"

The Indian's soft voice interrupted Bascom's words. "If the *senor* will look closer, there is something else. Perhaps you will open his vest a way—"

Bascom looked up, frowned. Then he bent, moved aside the mottled, calf's hide vest Vance had worn. A ripple seemed to run through the men about him and converge into the throaty curse that issued from deep in Bascom's throat.

Someone had pulled Vance's shirt out of his trousers so that with his vest up, the whole expanse of the right side of his bare chest was visible. Around his side, just under the fifth rib was an inch-long slit in the flesh. But the wound had been wiped clean of blood.

Bascom dropped the vest, stood up. His face was white, grim.

"Stillettoed," he gritted.

He reached down, loosened the gun holstered at Vance's belt, raised and spun the cylinder.

"Full," Bascom said slowly. "He didn't even get to draw it. By God I heard who was in these parts. There's nobody round here with reasons to do this. This is the doing of The Masked Rider, I'll lay money on that!"

"I think," came the soft voice of the Indian, "you would lose it too."

To a man, those gathered about the body turned. Over the knoll, a galloping team appeared drawing a light buck-board and two led horses. The driver was a girl, whose dark hair reflected the straying tendrils of light that had appeared in the east. In the seat with her, a grim, walrus-mustached shape gripped the rig's seat as the light wagon skidded and lurched.

The girl sighted the group of men outlined against the dark bank of trees a hundred yards off the road, and with utter disregard for the rocky terrain, shot the light buck-board straight into the mesquite in their direction.

McTaggart had turned with the others. His face brightened as he recognized the driver, but faded when she did not wave her hand in her usual light-hearted greeting. When she grew closer to the men standing in the brush, something in the face, the lack of color, its unsmiling lines, sent a cold river of foreboding sweeping through him.

A second later the buckboard jounced over the stones, drew to a jerking stop. Jane's figure sprang out lightly, came towards the silent men watching her. At her sides her fists were clenched tight.

When she caught sight of the body in the mesquite at their feet, her face paled even more, the lips tightened, but she did not falter.

"Honey," said Sol Bascom, "you'd better have not come up here. It ain't such a pleasant sight—"

TEN FEET FROM him the girl stopped. McTaggart could see that her face was working, that she was holding her chin firm in spite of the suspicious tremble of her lips. The thing that had swept through him became a strength-sucking sea.

"It's Vance," the girl's voice broke with chill implications about his ears. "If Vance's dead, that's just one more thing to be added up against the man that had this!"

One tight fist opened and was thrust out where all of the men could see it. They recognized what lay therein, to a man.

"Dynamite fuse," snapped Sol Bascom. "What you doin' with that— Where'd you get that thing!" he demanded.

There was no need to question further, for the girl's finger shot out, pointed square at the lanky, square-shouldered shape of the man at Bascom's side, at Bill McTaggart.

Bascom grunted, moved backward as though he had been shot.

"Bill?" he murmured unbelievingly. "He didn't give it to you. He was with us in the camp all the time. You sure you ain't mistaken, honey? Where'd you find it?"

The girl's voice was steady, her eyes staring straight into McTaggart's unhappy blue ones, yet for all that, not seeming to see him—

"In his bunk—at the Box B."

Bascom turned. "I don't believe it. Tell me. Bill, you wuz with us in camp an' these weren't yours at all. Now were they?"

McTaggart's stubborn jaw clinched, his lips became a tight line. The fabulous thing he had created was, as he stood there, crashing about his ears, shattering into a mess of broken hopes and crumpled faiths. Yet, for all his inner agony, he could not bring himself even to stoop to re-erect it for he knew that, as before, lies would only lead to more agony.

"It was mine," he said in a soft voice, "That dynamiting was mine, too."

"But, boy—" Bascom's hoarse, agonized voice broke

through the silent circle. "You've got no reason, you're loco crazy—"

"I did it," McTaggart turned a pair of hard blue eyes into Bascom's, "because I meant to."

Bascom's words came crisp and seering. "Whether you're crazy or not, you don't mean any such thing—"

Lobo Myers had followed the girl from the wagon. Now he stepped into the circle, lifted a horny finger at McTaggart's breast.

"He's been actin' funny," Myers stated. "There wuz that getting captured by th' Curlicue riders and bein' brought back. That got me to thinking about McTaggart. I'll lay twenty dollars to any man's one that ain't his name at all, Sol Bascom. Th' first time I ever heard of th' Quanahy Curlicue was down in th' Hierba Verde country. Was a man down there that quit th' Quanahy tribe an' changed his name. I don't know to what, but you ask McTaggart where he comes from. Hierba Verde, he'll say. Ask him— ask him!"

Bascom turned.

"A Quanahy," the name seered his lips. "You one of that sneaking, yellow-livered tribe—? You did that dynamiting for them, did you? What th' hell do they expect to get out of it?. I'll wrap my fingers 'round that yellow King's big throat and choke it outta him, boy, if you don't out with it." Bascom's voice raised. "What's their angle!"

McTaggart shrugged, the china-hard eyes he turned into the Box B owner's were steady, unflinching.

"Long Stream," he said slowly. "The bank."

Light broke across Bascom's seamed face. His jaw dropped momentarily, then snapped shut with a bony click.

"The bank," he repeated. "Them notes! I see—I damn

well see, McTaggart! By God, I could drill you where you stand, boy. But I'm not. They got a place to put people like you."

"Not only that," broke in Myers, "ask him about Abe Holt. We all know Abe Holt was murdered. How'd that happen?"

Bascom wheeled, his right hand flipped down and came up with a .45 gripped within its horny confines.

"Son, if you did that you've sure enough come tuh th' end of yore halter rope. Get yore hands in th' air—"

THERE WAS A rustle of the brush behind the men. But intent on Bascom's words, they did not sense it until the sharp indrawn hiss from the girl brought Sol Bascom up short.

Another voice, business-like, impersonal, broke about the Box B owner's ears.

"Drop the gun and turn around."

For a second Bascom was frozen to immobility. His thick fingers released their hold on the .45. It clanked noisily against the hard-pan.

When he turned, a hoarse gasp came from Bascom. Like an ebony statue poised against the background of the trees was a black horse and on it a black-cloaked shape whose grim lines Bascom knew only too well.

"The Rider!"

The big hatted shape on the stallion nodded. Words like whips crackled in the thin morning air.

"Get aboard your pony, McTaggart. You're coming with me!"

The tow-head shrugged. He had no desire to run from the well of trouble in which he had been plunged. But the menacing shapes of the twin .45s peeping over the stallion's erect ears left no room for argument. He turned, swung into the saddle of the bay pony ground-reined behind him. Then, at a nod from the hooded man, he turned its head and rode past him into the thick growth.

The man in the hood spoke brusquely in Mexican, ordering the Indian to remove the horses to a safer distance and to keep his hands away from his gun. The Indian shrugged, gathered up the reins of the remaining ponies and started trotting off in the direction of the Box B camp.

"Th' Law'll git you yet," snarled Sol Bascom. "An' if it don't, I will. You killed this here puncher of mine; you helped McTaggart dynamite my herd and now yer running away with him. But by God, it won't be for long—"

But by that time the great black stallion had been about-faced and, with a parting, watchful glance, the man in the hood had sent it leaping through the low trees.

For all his age, Bascom stooped with lightning speed, scooped up the forty-five in the dust. He wheeled, lifted it in the direction of the sounds of moving bodies in the blanket of trees.

He did not pull the trigger, but lowered the gun.

"A damn shame McTaggart had tuh he up there," he grunted. "I wouldn't want tuh hit him. Mebbe he weren't all tuh blame—"

Above the silence that followed his words came the shaking, repressed sobs of the girl behind him....

CHAPTER XV

ADIOS!

THE BIG NEGRO, Jackson, rubbed his eyes, opened his maw of a mouth in a yawn that would have done tribute to a hippopotamus. He rubbed his head with tremendous heaving movements, and sat up.

Near him the lumpy body of the killer, French, was still wrapped in sleep and the somewhat smelly blankets of the *palomina.* Jackson yawned again, examined the surroundings in which they had stopped. The impenetrable shadows of night had made impossible any further tracking of The Masked Rider.

With caution, French had insisted on breaking their way, the night before, through a welter of mesquite and pin oaks and picking out a bed in their midst. He wanted to take no chances in a surprise visit while they were asleep.

Off to his right, Jackson made out the shape of the little *palomina* nuzzling the grass before her hobbled feet. He grunted in accord with this state of things and bethought himself of the cavelike emptiness stealing through his midriff.

Heaving the mighty bulk of his torso forward, the Negro rose to one knee. Something amongst the leaves at his feet caught his eye, held it. In the dark, they could not possibly have seen it. And the fact that he had slept almost on top of it brought a roar of laughter bellowing out from his big throat.

French rolled over as though a quartet of cannon had gone off over him, scratching at the guns still buckled at his side. He rubbed his little pig eyes, opened them just enough to stare malevolently at Jackson's beaming, laughter contorted face.

"Wake up, man," rumbled Jackson. "Yo' sho' gonna see somethin' dat will make dem buttons you got fer eyes drop out on your cheeks. Lookee dat!"

Following a gigantic, horny finger, French's gaze dropped to the ground at Jackson's feet. There, indented in the soft earth among the leaves was what they had spent the whole afternoon searching vainly for—a huge round hoof mark.

There was no doubt about it. As soon as he saw it, French was out of his blankets kneeling over the mark.

"That's it," he snapped. "If I ever caught sight of that horse, I'll bet I'd know it in a thousand. Look at the size of it!"

French rose, grabbed the *palomina's* rig off the ground and swung it over his shoulder. While Jackson alternately watched him with questioning eyes and looked down at the hoof-print, French saddled the *palomina* and led it back.

"Bless de Lawd, Rock," grinned Jackson, "yo' sho' is powerful ambitious this mawnin'. Ain't dere gonna be no breakfas' fo' us folks atall?"

French shook his head, his eyes were squinting, intent. Visions of the reward money that would repay his diligence now sprang across his mind's eyes.

"An' why not?" the smile on Jackson's big face faded. "De Box B ain't so far away.' Sides, I don't see how we-all gonna get far dis mawnin'. Sho' 'nough, we wuz here yesterday an' didn't find him."

French looked up abruptly. "Here?" he questioned.

Jackson shrugged a pair of hulking shoulders, then pointed. "You-all see dat cottonwood over dere? You go along dat line of brush a little an' sho' nuff you'll come out square on dat piece of rock de Masked Rider crossed when we done lost his trail."

French followed the pointing hand, examining the trees and brush growth. In a second it developed familiar lines. The Negro was right; the preceding afternoon he and Jackson had come along not yards from the spot to which, unguided in the dark, they had returned.

A flush spread over French's pudgy, fat face, coloring the thick rolls of flesh beneath his chin, setting off in little red mounds the puffy spots under his eyes.

"You don't have to go on," he snarled. "This hoof print was here when we were here. In other words, the rider doubled back and hid in this brush, out of our sight when we came past!"

THE BIG NEGRO shrugged. "Dat's so, dat's exactly it, Rock."

Helpless fury touched French's words. "You blind fool! That's why I had you walking along behind me. If we met face to face with him, I'd shoot it out. But if we passed him and he hid, you were supposed to see him and yell. Did you yell? Hell no! You probably looked right in his face and walked past."

The wide smile fled from Jackson's features. The jutting neolithic angles of his jaw and monstrous lips suddenly hardened into coal black stone. French saw it and the muscles of his biceps twitched a little.

The Negro was a dangerous man when angered, which was seldom. French had seen him in action once. In a saloon across the border one night, four men had picked a fight with him. Single-handed, Jackson had cleaned them out. Not one by one either. When he had finished, one whose back had been broken died. Of the other three, two still limped from the vengeance Jackson had wrought.

But French's anger, backed by the thought of a pair of polished six-guns, flared up again.

"Did you see him or not? By God, I want to know."

Jackson shrugged. "Don' talk that way at me, you Rock. What I git outta dis when we do fin' him? You ain't said nuthin' about dat. I'se plumb tired out follering dat *palomina* on foot and mebbe I ain't so glad tuh keep on. What I git if I do?"

"That hasn't had a chance to come up yet with your messin' things."

Jackson laughed hollowly. "Mebbe I git bullets in de back. Why don' we do what I say an'-find out what happened tuh Aby Holt? When he left Doc LeMark's hide-out down El Paso way, he had money," the black man nodded, "Dat boy had money, I say. Saved it up, didn't he? After we hold up dat bank, does he spend it? No suh! I bet dat boy carry four or five thousand dollahs aroun' wid him when he leave. Up here, we fin' out he's daid. Where dat money go? Aby Holt don' spend it. He hide it! Why don' we look for dat?"

French shrugged his sloping, coat-hanger shoulders.

Jackson answered for him. " 'Cause you know in dis state a black man ain't got no rights tuh do nothin', nor hold office, an' dat law say too he ain't gonna git no reward neither for helpin' de Law run down murderers. Yo' is safe, but me—" a slow-growing grin spread across Jackson's features. "No suh, you is not plannin' on me gettin' nuthin'. Aby Holt mebbe got his money all caché when he dies. If we happen tuh find dat, bingo, you has tuh shoot me or else you gotta divide. Dat's why you jest as soon follow dis

Masked Rider instead; de law backs you up from payin' me."

Because they were true, the accusations Jackson shot jarred French to instant denial. He needed the Negro's help—for Jackson was as natural born to the woods as a wolf.

"No—" he started, but Jackson broke in.

"Yes suh, I see dat all clear." He opened his mouth and cracked the morning air with the rumble of laughter. "You an' me, Rock, we go different ways. I know all de time you is hard, but I don't like trabelling wid someone liable tuh pull out my eye an' eat it fer a grape when I ain't looking. Takes too much watchin'. *Adios*."

Before French could speak further, Jackson wheeled his massive body and stalked off up trail.

Fury spread across French's fat face. The little pig eyes grew hard, glassy. With a quick movement, he slid one .45 half-way out of its holster.

But he did not pull it farther. When the Negro's back disappeared, French holstered the gun and heaved himself on to the grunting *palomina*.

CHAPTER XVI

THE THICKNESS
OF BLOOD

T HE BAY PONY that McTaggart rode scrambled up a rocky hillside, mounted a brushy knoll top and trotted down through a tangle of brush into the little vale on the other side.

He could hear the movements of the hooded man's stallion behind him and knew that nothing he could do to escape would possibly be more than momentarily successful. When his bay moved into the cover of thick trees, McTaggart listened for the crisp order to halt. When it came, McTaggart pulled up the bay and turned in the saddle.

The outlaw in the hood stopped the stallion less than eight yards away. For a second, McTaggart stared at him with tight lips. Then he shifted sideways in the saddle.

"I'm not going to thank you," he broke out bitterly, "so don't think you can get me to do anything for you—for pulling me out. As far as—"

"You'd just as soon go back," the brittle voice from beneath the hood stopped him.

McTaggart swallowed, seeking words. His lips were tight with pain; a vast and cold sea of unhappiness was at that very moment sweeping over him, though he tried to mask it with reckless words.

"I'm a Quanahy," he blurted. "And what of it? You heard what I told Sol Bascom. I dynamited them cattle. Maybe I'd do it again—"

"Unless the law caught up with you and gave you twenty years to think it over!"

McTaggart looked up.

"Judging from what I heard," the hooded man went on, "last night's job for the Quanahys has left the Box B within their reach—if not worse than that."

McTaggart shrugged. "Didn't have enough dynamite fuses, or it sure in hell would. He saved a quarter of the herd. If pickings are good in the hills, he, may get more cows—enough to make a push into Long Stream."

"A fine mess," said the man in the hood. His voice rose. "Why don't you look a little closer? If the Quanahys take control, where do you get off? You think you'll be paid for this? Why are you lone wolf while King Quanahy sits back in the Curlicue and looks on? If you get into trouble with the law, is he going to help you?"

The hooded shape bent forward, his words snapping about the tow-head's ears.

"Why didn't King send Quanahy riders up here to help you? Would they be recognized in the dark? Man, it's as obvious as your face. Quanahy will let you pull rope until you snap it. Then—that's the thing to remember—then how far will he follow you?" The Rider's voice was brittle. "Not one inch!"

McTaggart's face was channelled with grim lines.

"That's my fight," he blurted. "Sol Bascom hasn't got me in jail yet. And he won't get me there. I'll tell you why I did it. Because if I didn't someone else would. While I had the whip hand, I had to use it. If it weren't me that did that dynamiting, maybe a couple of punchers or Sol would get killed. I figgered I could handle it. The Curlicue can wipe the Box B off the range with a twist of the wrist. They got a week to put the pinchers on Bascom, and do you suppose they'll stop even if I stop?" McTaggart's lean lips twisted acridly. "Stop? They'd shoot me quicker'n a six-foot sidewinder and go right ahead with their plans. I was doin' all I can to hang on to th' reins—they slipped now—Mebbe I'll go ahead with the Quanahys—"

The hooded man's movement stopped McTaggart.

"And break two hearts while you do it," he said slowly. "Your trouble, McTaggart, is that you're running two directions at once—both of them—" the man in the hood leaned forward—"both of them, McTaggart, away from your conscience. For instance—you say you'd done a complete job of it if you'd had more fuse; yet you left some behind."

THERE WAS SOMETHING in the words that stopped the tow-head. His anger died as his questioning gaze sought out the grey eyes visible beneath the hood.

"Quanahys are your flesh and blood," the masked man said. "Your father was a Quanahy. You're tied to them by bonds you don't even know exist. But they do exist. If they didn't, you'd never have gone an inch further along the Curlicue's trail. If they weren't Quanahys, if they were some other outfit, would you do it for them? You'd have rather tried to draw down on twenty of them at one time. One set of ties have to be cut—in a hurry. Which one's for you to decide. Just remember you were raised a McTaggart—not a Quanahy, when you do decide. And don't forget that if Quanahy blood were as good as McTaggart blood, none of this would happen."

The tow-head's eyes dropped. Like a surgeon's scalpel searching out a festering tumor, the hooded man's words had pierced McTaggart, and in his inner mind the tow-head knew that what he heard was true, only too painfully true. There had been a weak spot in his valiant armor. Obvious? It was obvious as white can make black visible. For him it was to decide, to cast all ties forever from him—then act. King Quanahy had hoodwinked him with stories of the wealth of the Curlicue clan, had played a symphony of family ties over a poor saddle tramp, so that when he should have fought them tooth and nail for Jane and the Box B, the Quanahy noose had pulled tight.

The tow-head raised his eyes. Sharply and briefly he

described what happened when he had faced the clan council.

"I didn't want to go ahead," he said bitterly, "but they promised me a half share. If I got that, there'd be a chance of my *saving* something out of the mess for Sol and Jane. If I didn't King or Dutch Quanahy would have all the say about the Box B. Understand? But the way Sol Bascom feels, I don't see what we can do now," he continued softly. "You're right, damn right. Thanks, stranger, for settin' me straight—I—I'm putting the shoes on the right feet an' King Quanahy's gonna know about it. I have a hunch though he won't wait. He gambled too much on wiping out the Box B. We got one hell of a fight coming. I better—"

The drowsing bay jerked alert at the tightenting of the bridle.

"Ride south," the hooded man said for him.

The tow-head grinned wrily, meaningfully. "Ride south," he snapped and sent the bay pony off at a quick canter through the trees. And the man in the hood knew it was not in the direction of the Curlicue, but of the Box B in which the tow-head moved.

He listened to the diminishing sound of McTaggart's horse's hoofs a moment, then kneed his mount gently.

CHAPTER XVII

DEATH'S TRAP

THE BLACK STALLION pivoted, heading for the knoll over which it had come moments before. Half way up the slippery hillside, it lunged to a sliding stop.

From somewhere in the trees behind them, a pistol shot

had cracked out. As with a single movement, the big horse about-faced. A spoken word and it leaped out down the hill.

For a fleeting second, the masked man had tested the direction from which the explosion had come and acted.

The big horse threaded at a quick trot through the thick growth, crossed an outcropping of shaly, soft earth and entered a little clearing.

The sight across the open space sent the hooded man swooping down out of the saddle and running, bent close to the earth, towards the opposite rim of the brush. Above the sprawled out shape of McTaggart, his riderless, quivering pony was standing, a pair of saucer-round eyes staring off into the brush. It shied at the oncoming dark-shaped shape and bolted.

By that time the man in the hood had reached McTaggart, and bent over him.

The tow-head's face was white, channelled with pain, his eyes closed.

The hooded man flipped erect. Out of the brush twenty-five yards beyond, a pair of pig eyes, in a fat, sweaty-jowled, smiling face appeared. But there was no smile of welcome in the eyes—they were dull, glassy.

"I seen you," snapped French, "talking up there. Figgered if I shot him you'd come—"

Below the pig eyes, the ugly little circle of a .45s snout ranged full on the dark cloaked shape above the fallen tow-head.

The killer shifted his body a little, another .45s dark eye appeared and centered.

The voice of the hooded man was brittle, cold. "You shot him so I'd come down?"

The oily smile drifted across the killer's fat jowls. He eyed with relish the dark sombrero, the slit hood beneath it and the long flowing cloak that reached down until the leather bottoms of two holsters peeped from its edge.

"That's what I said," replied French. "Don't move an inch—except tuh get yore hands up in the air."

The voice from the hood fell like chill driblets of water about the killer's ears.

"Don't move?"

French opened his mouth. A hollow roar shattered the still air of the clearing. It seemed to diverge from the cloaked shape like the release of a long confined thunder. A look of stunned surprise flashed across the oily face above the brush. A small hole magically appeared, square between the too-close, little eyes. Then with the crash of a felled ox, he went over backwards into the brush.

For all his wariness, French had played his last cards too quickly. He had disregarded the long rim of the cloak that dropped from the square lean shoulders. Too greedy, he had made his move when it still covered the gripped hands of the hooded man. The Masked Rider had weighed well his chances while running towards the fallen towhead—for in his tight right fist was the sheltered shape of a ready .45.

The masked man wheeled, stepped back towards McTaggart. He could hear the last twisting movements of the dead man in the brush. But he heeded them not, and bent forward.

As he did so, a far more ominous sound than that of the dead killer broke across his consciousness. Brush rattled and crashed under the oncoming feet of many horses.

THE MAN IN the hood wheeled, raced towards the bulky shape of the stallion. But it was too late.

Already beyond the black other sounds told of the approach of riders from that direction too.

Then suddenly they came into sight. Two men from his right. From French's direction, a pinto pony with a third. The man in the hood wheeled, faced them. Behind him other mounted men suddenly broke through the screen of brush. And all that he saw rode with guns appearing over the ears of their mounts. The hooded man knew he could kill one, perhaps two—but before they dropped, the other guns would have spoken—with instant death.

Startled by the noise, the black stallion flung up, its head and trotted off into the trees. But the oncoming men paid it no heed, their eyes were glued to the black cloaked, unmounted shape in the middle of the open space.

The rider of the pinto grunted and swore. It was Dutch Quanahy and the men with him, Curlicue riders.

He raised his voice, "Stay where you are, fellows! An' don't let this jasper make a move."

With that he slid out of the saddle, gave one passing glance at McTaggart and stalked, a crooked smile on his lips, towards the silent, black cloaked shape.

"I said," he snapped, "we'd do damn well to investigate that shot. Sure enough, look at what we got! Hoist yer hands, Mister Masked Rider. Git 'em way up!"

The man in the hood regarded the pair of drawn guns the Quanahy held out before him. From them, and from the others behind him, there was no possible escape. The lean shoulders shrugged and a pair of gloved, tight fists arose....

CHAPTER XVIII

HELL'S HACIENDA

KING QUANAHY'S SON slouched his stooping shape forward. The green eyes, usually dull, uninterested, had now brightened with cruel, hard lights. His puffy face, filled with its marks of dissolute and bad living, was writhed in an ugly sneer.

Running through his mind was the thought that here, for the first time in his life, was a chance to make his name a byword on the range. The outlaw before him, long sought, and long regarded—because of unfounded accusations—as a scourge of the land, had been trapped. Not only trapped, but caught in the full habiliments of his alleged crimes—as The Masked Rider.

The younger Quanahy's fingers fairly twitched with eagerness. But before he reached the hooded man, the other began to speak, and for all his violent intentions, Dutch Quanahy was forced to pause and to listen.

Here was no cringing figure, no halting, whining voice of the habitual criminal at last dragged to justice. Instead, the words which impinged on Quanahy's ears were drawled, slightly humorous. Of fear, there was none.

"I take it you're Curlicue riders," said the man in the hood so all of the group could hear. "If you are, I'd advise you to slow up, think a minute, before you've done something you'll be sorry for later."

Dutch Quanahy grunted, his eyes widened a little. "Slow up," he repeated. "I suppose you mean by that I'm not supposed to yank off that black hood you're wearing." His head went back and he laughed hoarsely, uproariously.

The laughter died. He turned, snapped: "Look and see whose over in the brush, Joe."

The puncher moved, rode towards the place in which Rock French had disappeared. While Quanahy's eyes were glued to the hooded shape, the cowboy pulled the inert, hulking flesh that had been the killer out into the open.

For a second the outlaw in the hood breathed easier. He had played for a moment of respite to stop Quanahy's approach and got it.

"Who is it?" snapped Dutch.

"Never seen him before."

"Watch this guy," said the Quanahy.

He turned on his heel, stalked in French's direction. For a second he stooped, examined the mutilated, fat features. Then arose and shrugged. He went over to McTaggart's limp shape, kicked it rudely.

A half-groan issuing from the tow-head shot a chill of relief through the hooded man. Quanahy grunted in surprise and bent over. When he rose, he turned to the others, said:

"A bad slash over his left ear. Gwan, Leo, you gotta canteen. Splash him a little. By God, I'm glad we caught up with that rannyhan finally. Yes, sir, he's agoin' back to King Quanahy in a hurry."

The man in the hood watched Dutch turn, come stalking forward.

"Now," he snapped, "we're going to get a good look at your face, Mister Who-Is-It."

Nearing the masked man, Quanahy's hand shot out towards the rim of the slit hood—and grappled at thin air.

His prey had stepped back so quickly, Quanahy was caught off balance. For a second an angry flush suffused his face; he had been made to look foolish in the eyes of his Comrades. Dutch's rage flared.

"I'd take it slower," said the cool, smiling voice beneath the hood.

"And why?" snapped Quanahy. "Stand where you are if you don't want to get split with lead!"

"I'm caught. I'll give you credit for being a smart man, Quanahy. I'm trying to protect you, and you ought to realize it. You want to unmask me, of course. Well, there's a time and a place for it—but not here."

Quanahy greeted the words with an angry laugh.

"I'm not joking," the cool voice went on. "You're letting your curiosity get the better of you. Take off this hood and this mask, and you'll ruin your chance of claiming any reward whatsoever. Why? With only these *Quanahy* men as witnesses, you wouldn't have a chance of convincing a jury that you had actually found me wearing them."

THAT THE DESPERATE man before him was playing on his emotions and fencing for time with his wits, Quanahy was not aware.

Dutch sneered. "A chance of convicting you," he grunted, then chuckled slyly, "with the man you murdered in the brush there we could string you up right now and be thanked by th' sheriffs in ten states! Collect rewards— You make me laugh! It would be like taking candy from—"

The drawling voice interrupted. "He wasn't murdered. If you'll look, you'll find an empty shell in his .45. The one he used on McTaggart.

Dutch Quanahy's cruel eyes narrowed, flared with cold

lights. "That's another thing," he hissed. "Why was McTaggart with you? By God, he'll have to answer to King for that!"

The puncher named Joe broke in. "Why not string him up right here? Pull off that hood—the rest of us boys are with you, Dutch. The jasper is killed ain't he? There ain't no answer to *that* question! I say, string him up!"

Affirmatives that crackled like pistol shots rattled the clearing.

"He's talking you out of it, Dutch."

"We want to see his face!"

That these other men were his real hazard, the hooded outlaw well knew. For that reason, he turned on the Quanahy.

"It seems to be my word against theirs," he said. "My advice is, take me to King Quanahy before you do another thing. How do you know he won't have better plans? And maybe he won't want *others* to see my face—eh?"

The mention of his father's name wrought a change in Quanahy. All of his life, no man of the clan had turned his hand without the confirmation of King Quanahy. For a second, young Dutch was torn one way by his desire to remove the mask, satisfy his curiosity and thirst for renown. The other way, by the thought that taking the initiative in so doing might end in bringing his father's rage crashing about his ears.

"Go on, Dutch, he don't dare move again!"

The younger Quanahy wheeled on the mounted speaker.

"Keep your big trap shut," he snarled. "I'm running this party an' by God I'll keep doing it! We're taking him this way down to King."

That the others were not in accord with this plan was

immediately apparent. But after a moment of angry grumbles, one puncher caught McTaggart's bay pony and another retrieved the *palomina* French had ground reined off in the trees. The big stallion had disappeared entirely.

"What'll we do about the dead one?" someone asked.

Quanahy's answer was brief. "Leave him here. Joe, you get McTaggart up into the saddle—use a little water on him. You, Mister Masked Rider, climb aboard that *palomina*— Wait—" his lips twitched, his face paled a little. "Forgot plumb about them guns—"

He walked around in back of the hooded man, reached in under the black cloak and one by one, brought forth two forty-fives.

The hooded man went forward and swung into the *palomina's* saddle while Quanahy tucked the forty-fives into his trouser front.

"Christmas," Quanahy was grunting, "if I'd of left them guns there—"

The lips beneath the hood were hard, grim, as the outlaw lifted his hands and moved out before the motioning Quanahy. He had played for a breathing spell and gotten it. The moments that it would take to get down to the Quanahy *hacienda* looked as though they would be the last during which he would ride as The Masked Rider. Vainly he weighed his chances for an escape, for the barest possibility of avoiding the riders behind. But there was none. They rode with ready, sure guns.

Stalling for time, he had advised young Dutch to take him to King Quanahy. The reasons he had invented to forestall his unmasking were, at their best, temporary. Blue Hawk was miles away; there was not the meagerest chance of his being able to effect even the most hazardous rescue.

The Quanahys rode with a grudge on their shoulders. He had had to kill Old Milt Quanahy, and for the Curli-cue riders, a lynching would seem no more than a just reward....

DURING THE HALF hour in which Dutch Quanahy moved his prizes rapidly out of the higher mountains and towards his father's *hacienda,* the puncher, Joe, had brought the jolt-ing, deadweight shape he held in the saddle before him to gradual consciousness. When McTaggart at last gained wits enough to stick in the saddle by himself, the puncher stopped and transferred him to his own mount. After that, McTaggart rode, like the hooded shape that led the proces-sion, with his guns gone and an armed man behind him.

A half mile from the *hacienda* the party rode out into the flat bathed in the midday sunlight. Ahead, the hooded man could make out the figures of children and women, standing on balconies or in the ranch yard wheeling toward the sound of distant horses.

The effect on those distant shapes was instantaneous. Colorful figures moved quickly against the background of the adobe walls. More children appeared magically in a gesticulating swarm.

Young Quanahy did not pause however. He sent the party straight towards the ranch yard at a fast trot. Before they reached it, a wild whoop broke out from the *hacienda.*

A moment later the masked figure, seated quietly on the *palomina,* was in the midst of an arm-waving, shout-ing crowd of children and men and women. Great, saucer-round eyes stared at him. Small boys scampered beneath the *palomina's* nose.

"*The Masked Rider!*"

It was a persistent, challenging clamor; a paean of primitive victory.

"Get out of the way! Let us in here!" Dutch Quanahy snapped and forced the *palomina* onward straight for the big, rambling porch.

The Curlicue riders slid out of their saddles, rimmed the man in the hood with menacing guns as he dismounted, and stalked at Dutch Quanahy's direction through the great open door.

A second later, with Dutch Quanahy's .45 touching his spine, the man in the hood moved through another door and into the council chamber of the Curlicue clan.

There was a girl whom the hooded man recognized instantly as Dutch Quanahy's sister, standing alone at the big table fronting the arched window which admitted the only light in the room.

For a second the hooded man stared. In feminine circles, the marks of King Quanahy's parentage that showed in his daughter's face and form, were not considered marks of perfection indeed. In body she was short and over-stout, almost gross. Her face was a round, shining moon upon which the signs of hastily applied cosmetics were most glaringly apparent under the sunlight streaming through the big window. Her hair was black, straight; her eyes shining with unrepressed interest. And in the way in which she regarded the man in the hood, it was plain that the men in Cassilda Quanahy's life, though few, had been eagerly welcomed....

Over the masked man's shoulder, Dutch Quanahy spotted his sister and grunted with rage.

"What're you doin' here? You know you ain't supposed to

come in this room. What's that stuff all over your face for anyhow? You look like a Piute war-dancer. Now get out!

A titter spread through Cassilda Quanahy's shape, converging in a fat, eager smile. To her brother's wrath she gave no heed.

"I heard you caught him," she said in a high, squeaky voice. "I just wanted to see." She straightened the over-tight bodice of her black dress nervously.

"Well, that's no reason for putting that stuff on your face," snapped her brother, still behind the hooded man. "I got my hands full without you. Where's King?"

"On the range somewheres. Ought to be back now."

"For Christmas sake!" Honest brotherly disgust cracked in Quanahy's voice, "Get out!"

HIS SISTER SHRUGGED and with another titter, a quick eager stare into the hooded man's eyes, she moved her fat shape through one of the heavy oak doors.

Dutch Quanahy swore, shoved the hooded man forward at the point of his .45, then moved him back against the wall facing the table. Standing in front of him, Quanahy ordered the men outside to enter.

The first man who came in was McTaggart, his hands aloft, his face a pale mask. Along the side of his head the ugly gash he had gotten from the killer's bullet still dripped blood.

With terse words, the younger Quanahy posted McTaggart beside the hooded man and leaned against the table, cuddling his .45. Behind him other armed men stationed themselves, awaiting the coming of the Quanahy boss.

The man in the hood did not speak to McTaggart. Why Dutch had treated him as another prisoner, he did not ask.

His own thoughts were coming hard and fast. The period of respite was drawing to a close. With the coming of King Quanahy, the final test of his wits and strength would come too. Grimly his lips tightened. Never had he been in a tighter spot, nor faced by more relentless enemies. But not for a moment did the steel of his courage weaken, even when the clatter of horses' hoofs and the high murmur of many voices broke against his ears.

The Masked Rider sent his glance quickly over the men in the room. He studied their faces and their positions. Dutch Quanahy seemed the most nervous. McTaggart was grim, but calm. He himself was under control.

In another moment there came the sound of the heavy man's footsteps with that ominous *clump, swish, clump....*

From Dutch Quanahy's relieved face, he knew that King Quanahy had arrived. In a moment more a heavy voice outside was saying:

"The Masked Rider! Where've you got him?"

Then King Quanahy entered the room.

CHAPTER XIX

A TOW-HEAD TALKS BACK

IN SPITE OF his game leg, King Quanahy fought, rode and worked with the best of his men. His hard-jawed, walnut face was streaming with perspiration; his clothes were stained with trail dust and the wind-driven lather of a hard pressed pony.

For a second he stood in the doorway staring at the forms of the two men standing arms aloft against the wall. Quanahy brought the heavy cane crashing down against the floor. A wry smile touched the corners of his rocky mouth, lit the predatory, dark eyes.

"Dutch, I wouldn't believe it! The Masked Rider—" he sneered triumphantly and clicked his hard jaw—"and McTaggart! I couldn't ask for more—possibly! How'd you do it, boy?"

The younger Quanahy shrugged, his triumphant eyes never once leaving the hooded man's shape. "I—" he gave the personal pronoun an accent—"found him in the *brasada*. Brought him back for you tuh unmask him."

"Good work!" King paid no attention to the obvious lead on in Dutch's words. He stepped out, went quickly to the head of the table. Then he turned on the dozen faces peering through the great door.

"Get Will and Branch," he snapped. "On the run!"

"They're already coming," said someone in the doorway.

King Quanahy set his jaw. "Joe," he said to the puncher who had ridden with his son. "I want you, Leo, Ben and Holt. That's four. You Dutch, stay where you are. The others—one in each corner."

One by one, the men he had spoken to filed to their stations at the four corners of the room. All were Quanahys and all wore on their moving hips polished, efficient Colts.

There was a movement in the doorway, a pushing of eager bodies. When they parted, the stooping form of Milt Quanahy appeared, and after him, the redheaded Branch.

King Quanahy's words rippled with triumph.

"Close the doors, all of them! We got enough men in here to take care of these two—and what goes on in here is going to be private."

There was a murmur of discontent, of a wolf-brood cheated of its kill. But the gleaming, predatory eyes of the

Quanahy boss brought quick action. In another second the heavy oak doors were slammed shut, locked from the inside.

When King wheeled, it was on his brothers and not the men against the wall.

"Here's where we settle one debt. There's the man that killed Milt." He turned towards the hooded shape, lifted a long, vengeful finger towards it.

"Fifteen thousand dollars reward," he snapped, "if not more. Dutch," he looked proudly at his son, "you've a head on you! The money's yours!" He turned slightly, faced the form of the grim-lipped, pale tow-head. "He'll make a fine example besides," he snapped with vicious clarity and meaning, "I want to show McTaggart what happens to a man who lifts his hand against the Curlicue brand!"

A perceptible tremor shot through the bodies of the other men. They had been taken by surprise at the venom in King's voice.

For all his steady nerves, the man in the hood tightened his lips, glanced sideways into the tow-head's features. They were pale, set, yet no fear showed in the steady eyes he lifted to the Quanahy leader's hawk-like features.

Quanahy was speaking straight to the tow-head.

"Well, finally, McTaggart, we caught up with you. It's a trifle queer," he sneered, "that you didn't tell us the other night that you were having an affair with the Bascom girl!"

The barest quiver of his eye-lashes were all that reflected the effect of the Quanahy's words on the tow-head.

"Jane—Bascom!" King wheeled to Will and Branch seated before him. "Do you hear that? That's why I've been out on the trail all day long alone trying to reconstruct something out of his mess But we'll make out!"

He smashed the oak table with a rocky, gnarled fist. "Sol Bascom, in spite of the way this fool did his work, is still in our hands—like this!"

HE RAISED THE fist, unclenched and squeezed it together slowly until the white balls of his knuckles stood out.

As he said this, the eyes of the man in the hood strayed from Quanahy's face to the arching, wide *ventana* at his back. The yard behind the house, due to King's "demands for privacy, was deserted. A hundred feet beyond the window, a great oak lifted its mighty trunk into sweeping branches, casting a shadow over the yard.

As he watched, an elderly, hunched-over Mexican plodded into sight leading a saddleless sorrel by an ancient rope hackamore. The Mexican, with only his back visible, tied the sorrel to a ring in the oak, produced a pair of pinchers and a hammer and set to work repairing the shoe on the sorrel's rear hoof. In a second two curious children, a boy and a little girl, came and stood by the sorrel watching the stooped peon at his work.

King Quanahy had wheeled again on McTaggart. "You had dynamite enough to blow the canyon to ten-cent pieces. What happened? You no more than spooked the cattle when you stopped the dynamite. The result is, only three quarters got away. Why?"

McTaggart opened his grim lips. "King, I don't give a hoot in hell whether you believe it or not 'cause it don't mean a thing to me which way. Some of the dynamite fuse got left behind."

"On purpose," Quanahy's face sneered.

McTaggart's lips tightened in a straight line. "Not on purpose when it happened. I don't know—but I think I meant to dynamite that herd right. I didn't—so that's that.

But if you want something to put in your pipe an' smoke—"
the tow-head took a step forward, a flush rising on his
face—"mebbe I didn't do it right. But if you try it now, I'll
shoot every damn Quanahy I set eyes on ridin' that range!"

King Quanahy's tanned features twisted. "So you're
figuring on pulling out," he sneered. "This love stuff—"

McTAGGART'S VOICE WAS tinged with bitter steel as he
blurted forth.

"It's this love stuff—!" he snapped. "I reckon so—if that's
the reason you want to put on it. I ain't palming cards. I say
I'm through with you and yore damn yellow-rotten Curlicue from now till hell freezes over. Savvy that? I'm quitting
cold and telling you to your face what's gonna happen. I'm
not a lousy murderin', crooked Quanahy—I'm a *McTaggart!* I'm on th' Box B side of the fence, King Quanahy, an'
if I find that horse-face of your on Box B or Rio Testa land,
I'm gonna shoot it right off your head. Them's words you
oughta be able to understand!"

For a second the Quanahy boss seemed to quiver in his
tracks.

Then like the crack of nearby thunder, his rage broke,
only to be stemmed abruptly after his curse. For a second
he was silent, the rapiers of his and the tow-head's glances
clashing.

When he spoke, his words were low, venomous. "You're
not through, McTaggart. You'll never be through. The Box
B is going to be Curlicue land before you see the light of
day again. *If I let you!*"

A shadow of a sneer crossed the tow-head's features. "I
don't scare, King. Not being one of your snivelin', crawl-
ing crew, I don't act like 'em. Get your men outta here an'
lend me a gun and I'll teach you why—face to face! You

won't? Because you're a dirty Quanahy, and a Quanahy is too yellow to stand up one against one, in an even fight!"

The eyes of the man in the hood had wandered again out to the sorrel beneath the big oak. The little stooping Mexican was still working steadily on the rear shoe; the children were gone. The outlaw's eyes lifted, examined the pony's flank. When they flicked back to the room, they were glittering with the mica-specks of polished granite. And they sensed that McTaggart was purposely stealing this show—to keep the Quanahy minds off The Masked Rider and give him time to think up some fast play?

To a man, those in the room had glued their eyes on King's hawk-like face. Immediately in front of the hooded man, Dutch Quanahy still stood, his captured .45s jutting from his waist band. At his back and seated were Branch and Will Quanahy. The men in the corners of the room had not moved.

King Quanahy picked up his heavy cane, and for all his size and age, moved like a tiger across the bit of room. For a second, his dark eyes glittered into the tow-head's set face.

"Men never talk that way to me," he snarled. "Never!"

It was no more than the flick of his wrist that moved King Quanahy's cane. And to the masked man the stick with its peculiar leather head no more than wafted the air near McTaggart's hair. But for all that, the bulb-like leather head did strike the tow-head on the temple—with incredible solidity.

McTaggart dropped like a felled ox, seemed to crumple at the knees, hips, and shoulders all at once. He struck the floor with a thud that shook the heavy table.

CHAPTER XX

EL ACEDERO

BOTH SEATED MEN had sprung to their feet, eyes on the fallen man.

For a fleeting second, King Quanahy stood over McTaggart. Then he wheeled. Will and Branch sat down.

"Joe, get him out of here fast as you can. Put him—" he stopped, turned to the hooded man—then back to the puncher—"you know where. With two men watching him. Let him come to by himself. Now, out with him!"

The puncher, Joe, shambled his long shape forward, grasped the limp McTaggart rudely by the shirt collar and snaked his body across the floor to the door. He heaved it open and disappeared with his burden.

King Quanahy wheeled, strode back to the table head.

"He bungled, but we can't afford to. When we're through here, I want thirty riders—with rifles. Dutch, that's up to you!"

The man in the hood had not missed one of King Quanahy's actions. The muscles along his shoulders tightened in spite of the cramped position in which he had been forced to hold them. In the next second, he knew his test would come. The test of a lifetime of danger and death.

King Quanahy's face seemed to smile as he turned.

"Now you," he gritted. "You've ridden a bloody trail—but your fatal mistake was shooting Milt—our brother. Quanahy blood never has flowed unrevenged. We Quanahys—"he struck the table—"swear that it never will. Why didn't I have you unmasked? Because we're goin' to make you unmask yourself—before you die!"

The hawk-like features twisted. He turned. "Dutch, you caught him. I'll let you have the pleasure of making him take off his hood. Show him what tricks you know, that make people take off masks!"

The eyes beneath the hood shifted to Dutch Quanahy's face. He saw it light with cruel, relentless lines. The younger Quanahy grunted, swung his hand down to his hip.

"Where?"

"Right here—Now!" gritted King.

A glittering, ugly shape of steel swung out of Dutch's holster. Its snout moved. The small, bitter eyes flicked up into the hooded man's. Then down to his feet.

There were seven Quanahy's in the room at that second. Each was armed; each bore in his heart a relentless hatred that only blood could quench. Did Dutch intend to shoot him repeatedly, painfully, in the knees, ankles, elbows?...

But at the second that Dutch Quanahy's gun moved lower, The Masked Rider struck. His hands flicked down, he went at Dutch Quanahy like a projectile from a mortar. A shout split the silence of the room.

The man in the hood hit the younger Quanahy full in the chest, with all his weight behind him. Both of their bodies went across the table top under the power of the charge and crashed with stunning force on the hard floor beyond.

But the shout had warned the hooded man. He twisted his body in the air so that he lit underneath the Quanahy and with the same movement yanked loose one of the guns at his belt.

Three men came hurtling in from the corners of the room.

"Let him have it!" the thundering voice of King Quanahy blasted the air.

In spite of young Dutch's entangling arms and legs, the hooded man flicked one arm out, knocked away the gun in his hand. Just above it and twenty feet away, loomed the mask-like face of a puncher whose hand was sweeping up a lightning fast .45.

THE HOODED MAN pulled the trigger almost in his face. Above the gun's flare, the contorted face seemed to change color, then drop forward full at the man on the floor.

Behind him was King Quanahy. Almost at his side, the seated older brothers were still locked with fright in their seats. That left two more men unaccounted for.

In the fleeting second that his gun had exploded, the masked man wrapped both arms about Dutch Quanahy and heaved himself over, bringing Dutch's stunned body with him, still as a shield.

The sound of scraping feet, of men stopping abruptly in their headlong approach broke against his ears. The voice of King Quanahy blurted:

"Watch out for Dutch."

Hardened by years on the trail, by the vicissitudes of a lifetime of perilous living, the muscles of the hooded man rippled and crackled under the strain next put on them.

But like a corpse rising from the dead, young Quanahy's head and shoulders, then his whole body moved up from the floor. His eyes stared, a muted shout writhed across his features. Behind the hulking shape, with one arm gripped about Quanahy's chest, came the hooded man.

Across the room, the punchers, their guns up and ready, let their jaws drop agape. For a second they were frozen to inaction. If they had pulled the triggers of their guns, it would have been full into the young Quanahy's face or body.

And in the second that their fingers paused on the triggers, the man in the hood propelled Quanahy's kicking body forward. Even King, standing at the head of the table, was taken by surprise. He moved, sought to heave his body out of the way. But before he could, both Dutch Quanahy and the hooded man were on him.

A fist shot out from underneath Dutch's armpit and yanked the cane from King's hand. King blurted something and let go, lunging backward.

"Shoot," he shouted at the two punchers. "Why're you waiting—"

But he had no chance to finish. Young Dutch, utterly unable to help himself, felt his body again rising in the air.

"Don't—" he blurted. "Don't shoot!"

The cane rose looping in the air, met the arching window with a shattering crash and went through it. Glass fell in a noisy rain.

A grasping hand slammed against the seat of Dutch's trousers, gripping it. Another hand grappled, then caught his shirt collar. Almost magically, his body seemed to rise and go hurtling through the air in the direction of the two punchers who had converged at the table.

Instinctively they side-stepped, dodging his oncoming shape. It went past them and met with a crash against the farther wall.

But their movement had given the hooded outlaw a precious allotment of seconds. His own body shot out in the direction of the shattered window, rising in a cat-like leap. His foot caught, held to the ledge of the big window.

"Shoot him!" roared the voice of King Quanahy. "Don't let him get that cane— The cane—he's taking it!"

In the fleeting second that he had been poised on the window ledge, the hooded man had surveyed the scene outside. There were no Quanahys in sight. The sorrel and the Mexican were still under the oak. Now, the hunched-over shape was turning—

THROWING HIS BODY into another vault the man in the mask left the ledge, hurtling straight towards the saddleless sorrel. He fired at the broken window, to keep men from it.

In the next second, the sorrel had reared away from the oak trunk, the ancient hackamore's line coming loose and by some magical means flipping over its hack. The old Mexican scrambled back from it as the running shape came for him.

Bunching his muscles, the hooded man jumped, caught at the sorrel's mane, lifted his body in a long jump. It was almost as if the sorrel had been moved with springs. For no sooner had the clinging, hooded shape clamped to its back that it wheeled out from under the branches.

Over the thunder of its hoofs came the soft voice of the Mexican.

"Around the next house, *senor*. Then the *brasada*."

The sorrel shot out like a bolt from the blue, dodged cat-like around the jutting corner of an adobe building twenty-five feet beyond.

As it did, a shot broke from the window, shattering the adobe wall and chewing out a six-inch gash.

Shouting men came pouring out of the window of the *hacienda*. And above the rattle of their feet came the hoarse bellow of King Quanahy:

"My cane—did he leave my cane behind?"

Far away came the crisp smashing sound of a heavy body breaking into high brush.

"Yes. Here it is!"

The little old Mexican moved away from the oak as the running Quanahys passed. He himself disappeared, with his stooping, halting gait, around a nearby corner. Moments later, well out of sight of the Quanahy *hacienda*, Blue Hawk straightened his back, sore from his long cramped position, discarded the ragged clothing he had worn into the *hacienda*.

"*El Acedero*—the sorrel one," he said softly to himself and smiled, "the wind is not as fleet if he wishes."

CHAPTER XXI

DEATH'S TRUMP

MOUNTING THE STEEP, brush-blanketed hillside that gave down into the Quanahy *hacienda*, the man in the hood trained his ears for the sound of pursuit. Moments later, when he stopped Blue Hawk's sorrel, it was on a vantage point overlooking the valley.

Below, the ant-like shapes of horsemen were gathering in the ranch yard. But though he examined the brush below, no signs of another group of riders could be seen. For a second he frowned. It was not like King Quanahy to give up a chase so readily. He should have had at least half a dozen men with mounts ready enough to give instant pursuit.

Blue Hawk would escape, well enough. He'd get away,

in his disguise, before the excited Quanahys would stop to think long enough to suspect him. Yet—

A second later, realization of King Quanahy's plans broke upon him.

Quanahy was too smart a leader to throw all of his men into a search of the hills for The Masked Rider. Even the brief hiatus between the hooded outlaw's escape and the gathering of men had given the sorrel ample leeway. Quanahy, he decided, had seen that.

The Curlicue boss had other plans which, to him, were as pressing and important as apprehending the hooded man. And that was a last and finishing blow to the Box B, while Sol Bascom's men were expected to be dispersed in rounding up the stampeded herd.

Confirming the hooded man's thoughts, the ant-like riders in the ranch yard below parted at the appearance of a bulky, quick moving man who made for a nearby pony and swung aboard. When he led the phalanx of riders at a hard gallop out of the *hacienda*, it was not in the direction of the hillside the hooded man had climbed, but towards Soldier Canyon—

HALF AN HOUR later, the saddleless sorrel idled hip-shot in the cover of thick mesquite. At its head, watching the terrain of a small clearing transversed by a trail, was the hooded man. Twice he had given the call of the mountain cat and waited with grim lips for its answer. When it finally floated with the afternoon wind into the brush cover, the hooded man had relaxed, waiting less anxiously.

The heavy hoofbeats of a big horse broke against his ears. The sorrel's ears flipped up. Out of the trees bordering the clearing came the massive shape of the big stallion. And the man on its back, whose shoulders supported a pony's rigging, was Blue Hawk.

In spite of the relief that shot through the hooded man at this sight, it died at the set, serious expression of the Indian. For all the violence of the scene in which they had but moments before taken part, their greeting was reserved, serious.

The Indian rode straight to the sorrel and dismounted. For a second he gazed into the hooded eyes of the man.

"I came at the last moment, *senor.* It was with much fear that I see you ride into the *hacienda* below. Then when King Quanahy's big voice blow through the window—"

"Hawk, I'll remember all my life what happened down in that ranch yard. Without the sorrel—" the hooded man paused.

"I was but a small nothing, *amigo.* It is you who faced them and gave them a taste of courage."

For a moment the hooded man regarded the set, bronzed face before him.

"What is it, Hawk?" You have something on your mind. You want to tell me something—yet you're not doing it. Why?"

THE INDIAN MOVED his shoulders. "I have said, *amigo,* old *Senor Lobo* can take lessons from you. You have but to look at my face and see there all secrets."

"What is it? McTaggart was killed?"

"No, *senor.* I see them drag him away into one house, then nothing more. I know from the way his arms drag he is not dead."

"King Quanahy then? His riders have headed for Soldier Canyon. How many of them left?"

"*Treinta*—thirty. But that is still not my secret, *amigo*. It is not that I would hide it from you—much sadness has fallen across these hills since last we saw each other. I do not like to tell you this—*Senor* Bascom is dead, *amigo*."

"Sol Bascom!"

"*Si.*"

"But—" like a cold hand, the thought gripped the outlaw's mind. Sol Bascom was no more. Momentarily a picture of the dark-haired girl shot across his mind. What her father's death meant to her stabbed with cruel import into his consciousness. That girl, left to match wits with the Curlicue riders! And with her father's death, she certainly had no chance of repulsing them—

"How did he die?"

The Indian moved his lithe shoulders. "The same as *Senor* Holt, and this puncher, Vance. The cow who walks with death, *amigo*. I know you wish to talk with McTaggart, so I stay in the camp, expecting the mountain cat's call. *Senor* Bascom goes into the woods alone, to see what the marks of the dynamite can show. An hour later, *amigo,* he does not come back. Soon I am worried, *senor,* and suggest to a caballero that we should look. It does not take long, *amigo*. He is in a rocky *barranca,* lying face down. When we turn him over, we see that the hoof print is there."

"The same one that killed Holt and Vance?"

"*Senor,* I would stake my life on it. I would know that cow's mark anywhere in the range country. It is the same one. And they have taken Bascom to the *ranchero*." The Indian paused. "When we look on the body, something catches my eye nearby. I do not say anything then, but on the way out, I pick up this."

He felt in amongst the saddle rigging slung over his shoulder, produced an object and held it forth.

It was a leather cuff, worn and battered with hard use. At one time it had been the choicest of tanned yellow leather. On either end, fancy work of rawhide stitching marked it as expensive workmanship. Now, adding to its disreputable appearance, dried mud and leaves clung to it. When the rider lifted it, he noted that one end was plugged solid with a tight handful of rags.

"And what do you gather from this?"

The Indian shrugged his shoulders. "One as blind as I, cannot say, *senor.* I only see what is there. That it had been covered by mud and leaves before it was found."

"Probably buried," snapped the man in the hood. He reached forward, tucked the leather cuff into one of the stallion's *alforjas.* "But that can wait, Hawk," the words came clipped out. "You said they took Bascom to the Box B. Then we ride to Soldier Canyon!"

There was much of deadly import that this whole set-up had suddenly taken on. This cuff had something to do with a killing. And an empty cuff would not be cause enough for a killing!

CHAPTER XXII

A SPECTRE VANISHES

THERE WAS A thick legged, oak table in the Box B livingroom, a ceiling-high book case, couch, and a crew of heavy, high backed Spanish chairs. In front of the eight foot maw of the fireplace, Jane Bascom was standing. For a long time she had been silent in the lonely, big room save for the quick inhalations that seemed to shake her entire body.

She had dried her eyes, done her best to make the cold, still shape that now lay in the sun-room off the living-room comfortable, even as she had in life.

The two punchers who had brought Sol Bascom home had been gone for some time. They had ridden back to Soldier Canyon with the news that there would be a gathering of the Box B hands back at the *ranchero* as soon as they could get there. Except for Sawyers and another puncher, Wilky, left at the canyon to guard what remained of the herd, all were right now riding in the Box B direction.

When Jane Bascom had at last been able to gain control of herself, waves of overwhelming sadness still washed over her. She drifted on an uncharted, merciless sea of despair.

With her father gone, nothing remained for her on the ranch. No ray of hope lightened the futile future for her. The Box B brand was to die along with her father. But one horrible question kept recurring to her mind. How had Sol Bascom, a man of few enemies, incurred the wrath of The Masked Rider? She did not hesitate to lay the crime at the hooded man's feet— As Vance had died, so had her father. It was the mark of the masked man.

The sun had set as she was standing in the living-room. When the long, blue shadows lengthened out across the little valley, she did not light the lamp on the big table. Finally, when even the barn was no longer visible in the shades outside the window, there came the sounds of hard-ridden horses from off in the dark. Moments later, the Box B punchers, fifteen strong, rode into the ranch yard.

HANSEN WAS LONG legged as a crane. His lean, spindly shape stooped as he leaned over the lighted table; his eyes took in the girl standing before the cold fireplace. Hansen had choused slick-ears more years than he would have told in the Rio Testa country. He couldn't remember the number of brands he had worked for. Of all the punchers in the room, he had been with Bascom the longest and had been the Box B owner's closest confidant.

For a long while he studied the girl. His grey, sparkling old eyes never relaxed to wander to the grim faces of the punchers grouped in the room. Hansen had brought all but two down with him, as were his orders, and in the manner of his breed, he had brought an ultimatum. Though Sol was dead, the fight would have to go on to the bitter, bloody end.

The girl's face lifted. She looked square into Hansen's old eyes. For a moment gratefulness showed in hers, but that died to bitter suffering. She glanced around the circle of faces.

"You must know how thankful I am to you," she said slowly. "But the Box B never grew by bullets or blood. It won't now. Work on the range is going to stop until the herd in Soldier Canyon can be brought down to Long Stream and shipped. Even if McTaggart and The Masked Rider have put their heads together to stop all further movements of cattle, I won't have bloodshed—"

Hansen cleared his throat, chose his words. "We all agree with you on one thing: begin moving what's left down into Long Stream. But th' Box B's got tuh fight Quanahy too, and we say, why not pay 'em back with their own *dinero?* Just figger that th' bank won't renew them liens and notes. You got a quarter of your herd. Using that as evidence of good faith, any gal as purty as you could raise th' extra money in no time further south. Meanwhile, us cow-chasers'll ride them mountain ragged until we kin locate enough to meet them loans. By God," he smote the table mightily, "the Box B kin go on in spite of McTaggart and The Masked Rider and King Quanahy. If they so much as shown nose in them hills, ain't a man here'd hold his hand…" He stopped.

At the mention of the tow-head's name, a change seemed to come over the girl's face. She bit her lips; but her chin was steady.

"There'll be no more bloodshed!"

There was a rattle of small stones dropped on the porch floor outside. The punchers in the big room wheeled. One went to the door, flung it open. Yet in the light that came from the lamps behind him, no one could be seen there. While their backs were turned, a window opening into the garden went up with a sharp crack. Some wheeled, went for their guns only to stop. Others let their jaws drop agape.

In the open window, outlined against the outer darkness, was a shape that had ridden with ominous portent in their minds all day. The hood and the cloak of the masked man. Resting on the window sill was a pair of polished .45 barrels whose snouts faced them, and whose hammers were drawn back ready.

"*Who—what d'you want?*" snarled Hansen.

The man in the hood spoke slowly, distinctly. And his words came like crisp, crackling flames to the punchers' ears.

"King Quanahy and thirty riders have moved in on Soldier Canyon. I rode out that way, saw you riders leave. Who ordered you out?"

HANSEN GRUNTED. "WHY do you care? If you get off of this ranch without being strung up higher'n a kite, you're going to be lucky without asking who's giving orders. As fer Quanahy—"

The girl's voice interrupted Hansen. Her lips were grim, her clear eyes sparkling.

"This is a trap, boys. He's lying for some reason—trying to draw us off of the Box B. No one is to move—"her voice became quiet and deadly earnest—"unless he forces us to at the point of those guns."

For a second there was silence. "You can't afford to take that attitude," said the man in the hood. "I was out at Soldier Canyon myself. I came back to tell you that your heard was scattered, stampeded again, the fences are down and you've already lost one rider. I don't know about the other one. I got out with this—" he lifted one skirt of the flowing cape.

There was a momentary pause. Every eye in the room saw in the lamp light the perforations hot lead had left.

"I don't believe you—" the girl began slowly.

"I'm not asking you to believe me—I'm asking you men in there to act, to find out for yourselves! Why keep on thinking I killed Vance? If I'd wanted to, do you suppose I'd knife him and try to hide it? The same with your father—every man in this room knows he was murdered. The thing now is to save the Box B while there's a chance. I'm asking for punchers who care enough about that to ride with me— If they do, I'm willing to take my chances riding with them!"

Hansen swallowed slowly. Disbelief crossed his mind, but he hesitated. One man—an outlaw—asking fifteen horny-handed, devil-may-care punchers to ride with him certainly had the earmarks of sincerity.

Jane Bascom's chin was firm. "Don't one of you move. It's a trap. You remember how McTaggart acted—"

"McTaggart's at the Curlicue—with an armed guard," snapped the hooded man. "Give me men and I'll prove to you that he wasn't responsible for Vance's death or for Abe Holt's. Whether the Box B stays on the range is a matter of minutes now. Minutes! You certainly care enough for the Box B—"

There was a rattle of far-off hoofs, the trip-hammer of a hard pressed pony crossing the stubble fields. The hooded man's voice sounded over them.

"Face the other way—towards the door all of you! And don't one of you make a false move."

Grumbling, the grouped punchers turned. As they did, the hoof beats grew stronger, suddenly hammering in the ranch yard. A rider slammed up to the porch, dropped from his mount and leaped across the porch. He spotted the punchers inside, slammed into the room.

It was the cowboy, Sawyers. Blood streamed from a gash across his forehead, his right arm hung limp and useless at his side.

"They got Wilky!" he blurted. "Th' canyon herd's stampeded and King Quanahy tore down every fence in it! Ain't a cow in—" he stopped, stared at the open window.

"*Jeepers!*" he heaved. "You here too! I seen you down at the mouth when Dutch went that way."

"Dutch Quanahy?" grunted Hansen.

Sawyers swallowed. "Shore. Th' Rider here took on about eight riders at the mouth. He got away, right after

Dutch got killed. By golly, what a fight! But it weren't no use, King brought his riders down from behind the cows with wire-cutters. Wilky and I were up at the gate and an' got out fast as we could— No sir, they ain't a brush-popper left."

Hansen interrupted. "He was just a-tellin' us he wants tuh—"

Jane's voice broke in. They turned to a man towards her, watching the hard lines of her mouth, her pale, agonized face.

"That makes four men who have died already for the Box B. No one is going to move—"

The man in the hood spoke, turning to Hansen. "You were boss next to Sol Bascom. Will these men follow you—do what you say?"

Hansen did not have time to answer. A low grumble, then fiery confirmations seered the air of the room. And in the hard-jawed, tanned faces, the hooded man knew there was hatred and courage enough to wipe the Quanahy brand off of the range itself.

But the girl's voice took the edge off their words. "Stop! Stop!" she said. "All of you! I said I wouldn't stand for it— and I won't. Not a man leaves this ranch nor even touches a gun except on my orders. You want to fight for the Box B—I'd rather turn the land papers over to the Quana- hys tonight than have another drop of blood spilled. I—" she paused. The high purpose in her words flowed away. Suddenly she was a woman, for all the steel of her courage. Her soft lips quivered, tears came fast and hard.

"Can't you understand?" she whispered through her tears. "My father wouldn't have let you, ever! He—he loved you boys like his own sons. And now Vance and Wilky have joined him. You—I can't let you…" Then her voice fled away altogether, became racking sobs that seemed to tear her thin shoulders.

Hansen swallowed. His eyes had been on the girl. Abruptly they came up, went to the window. A curse started from his lips. The hooded shape that had been outlined there before was gone—vanished in thin air….

Silence clamped over the room.

CHAPTER XXIII

MOONLIGHT SERENADE

MOONLIGHT LAY IN silvery, cool pools across the yard of the Quanahy *hacienda*. Here and there a bar of yellow light jutted forth from an open doorway into the silvered dust and the long, deep shadows.

In effect, the yard was a *patio* more than anything else. For on three sides were the adobe-walled living quarters of the Quanahy tribe. The fourth side opened to the winding roadway. Beyond the houses were the corrals and barns.

An hour later, Wayne Morgan moved his lean, thin hipped body around one of the adobe corners and paused. To his right rose the high wall of the main house, and almost directly before him was the great window staring with its unglassed, vacant eye into the night.

Through that window, a matter of hours before, The Masked Rider had escaped. Since that time, events of violent, bloody action had taken place. As the puncher, Sawyer, had witnessed, The Masked Rider had attempted to bottle up the mouth of the canyon against eight of the Curlicue men.

The move, though courageous, had been doomed to failure. After Dutch Quanahy had dropped, the riders had swept down on him like minions of a vengeful sky god.

It was only the powerful, quick-witted mount he rode that had saved his life. Blue Hawk, stationed out of sight over the valley, had been ordered to avoid being seen with the hooded man.

His reception at the Box B had been a blow. But in spite of his determination, he saw the situation clearly through the girl's eyes as well as his own. What she said was true. Sol Bascom would rather have lost the Box B than shed more blood. But in a hard-bitten environment, in a land where right rode always with might, blood and bullets were law.

The plan that had risen in the hooded man's head, however, was not premised entirely on the shedding of blood. And the longer he had stood in that window, the firmer he became convinced that the Box B might yet be saved. To the girl's determination he had, on the surface, bowed. But as Wayne Morgan moved through the shadowed Quanahy *hacienda*, he counted on one man who could convince her of the need for instant action—the tow-head.

The arrival at the *hacienda* had brought swarms of doubts and premonitions to harass Morgan. Though King and his thirty riders were still at large, the Curlicue ranch had the earmarks indeed of an armed camp.

As he stood at the adobe corner viewing the yard, men slowly filed into sight, walking across the pools of moonlight carrying rifles and twin pistols ready at their hips. With care they watched the shadows of the houses, the distant walls of the dark valley.

Morgan grunted quietly to himself. For a long time he had examined the houses, attempting to gain some hint as to McTaggart's hiding place. But though he searched every suspicious grouping of the armed men who patrolled the *hacienda,* he learned nothing.

He stepped into the shelter of the thick house walls. It looked suspiciously as though his search would be fruitless. It was neither healthy nor wise to stay in the *hacienda* too long. Eventually someone would spot him and question his being there. If he aroused suspicion, the search would be cut off short. His disguise was now discarded, so they would not connect him up, in the dark, with The Masked Rider.

MORGAN PRESSED AGAINST the wall, silenced his breathing. The slow footsteps of a man came toward him. He saw the shadow approaching and he pressed into the nearest doorway. The guard walked past so close Morgan could have touched him. When he was gone, Morgan moved with relief. As he did, heavier footsteps on the boards above him, evidently on the balcony right over his head, squeaked and groaned.

Morgan slunk further into the shadows. His foot struck something that rattled, then gave off a musical tinkle. Someone had left a guitar tucked away in the deep doorway.

Morgan cursed inwardly, reached down to silence the instrument and swore again when his groping fingers struck a noisy string.

A feminine voice from above spoke low:

"Who's there?"

Morgan clenched his teeth. Not only had his search been fruitless, but now he would have to make a break for the stallion, hidden in the high brush just beyond the adobe walls.

But, as he gathered his muscles, the voice came again, sharper.

"Answer me—who's there?"

The timbre of it struck a note in Morgan's memory. In another second he had moved out of the doorway, the musical instrument in his hand. Out in the moonlight he raised his eyes, regarded the speaker.

Twenty feet above him, leaning on the hand-hewn rails of the second story terrace was a round-faced, stumpy shape that he well knew.

"Well," Cassilda Quanahy eyed him questioningly, "what are you down there for? I don't seem to know you. Where—"

Morgan lifted the guitar, felt for the strings. The smile that touched his lean hard features lighted the gray eyes. The guitar gave off a soft, throaty minor chord.

"A donde ira," he sang softly to her, *"veloz y fatigada, La Golondrina que de aqui se va."*

Smiles brightened the moon face above him. A titter, then an eager tinkle of laughter floated down.

"Ah, excuse me," said the Quanahy's bright eyed daughter. "I—" She paused, flustered. "I didn't know you were serenading. Go on, do!"

Morgan laughed, let his voice die away. "For days have I searched the hills for you, *senorita.* Since I saw your beauty in Long Stream I have not been able to sleep. At last—" a lover's sigh escaped him. He smiled, raised the guitar once more.

"O si en el viento—" he started, and stopped. The eager titters from above had drowned out his words.

"Wait—wait," the animated butter-ball fairly hissed from above. "Not so loud. Maybe up on the balcony you won't be heard by so many people—"

The trip-hammer beats of King Quanahy's daughter's heart were nearly audible as the smiling, lean-hipped figure below, abruptly stretched his lithe shape, caught hold of a low hanging support and swung himself up onto the small balcony's railing. For a second he poised there on the woodwork, gazing at the now shrinking form. But the lights in the Quanahy girl's eyes were far from shrinking. In another second, she was slithering towards Morgan. He raised the guitar, brought another vibrant chord from it.

"I don't understand," she said. "I haven't been in Long Stream for a long, long time. I didn't see you when I was. But—" the conjunction came fast—"your singing is wonderful. Go on."

"When I can listen to the *senorita's* musical voice—? Never. I've come to talk."

MORGAN'S EYES STRAYED to the room off which the balcony gave. A tightening ran through his muscles, brought his jaw shut with a snap.

"So," he gritted his teeth, "while I've been searching for you, another man—. Whose is this?"

On long legs he strode into the room, grabbed an object off of the white-topped dressing table and brought it out. Accusingly he faced the girl with it. The object he held was a leather cuff—the mate to the one that had been found next to Sol Bascom's dead body!

At the anger that seemed to show from her new found cavalier's brim lips, Cassilda Quanahy's face went gray.

"That—" she stuttered. "Oh, an old leather cuff father gave me. He said there was another one like it somewhere around the *hacienda* and that I must find it—look for it wherever I go. But—" she shrugged a pair of overweight shoulders—"you should not be jealous." She tittered. "The owner won't mind your coming up here. He's gone!"

Morgan's eyes were still angrily surveying the puffy features before him.

"Gone! I'll bet not. I heard things on the range. The Masked Rider has come over here to see you at night— alone. Is that true?"

Cassilda Quanahy's coy eyes blinked shut. She shook her head, fairly bursting with suppressed laughter. "You are so jealous," she tittered. "Of course he was here. But he didn't come to see me and he wasn't alone."

"He was alone!" pressed her jealous swain.

"No—no—no!" she shook her round head rapidly. "There was another man."

"Who?"

"I could prove it," the moon-like face was triumphantly bright. "Except they won't let me go in the granary. I saw them take him in there."

A warm river of confidence swept along Morgan's backbone. In the midst of this mad escapade, like some form of manna from heaven, the information that he had all but despaired of getting from the girl had been thrust upon him. He almost cursed aloud, then stopped himself.

A wide smile touched his lean lips. "*Senorita,* I will believe you. I understand your father will be home in minutes. I must go, but tomorrow night I will be back—at ten."

Shadows swooped across the lunar expanse of face. "But no! You have to sing once more. You hardly finished—"

"Next time, *senorita,*" said the smiling man on the

balcony railing. "I wouldn't want your father's wrath this early. But tomorrow night, *quien sabe?* Perhaps I can stay longer. Until then, *senorita, adios.*"

A monstrous sigh shook the pudgy figure as Morgan slipped over the railing, dropped lightly to the ground. When the girl came forward to the rail, the lithe, thin-hipped figure was nowhere to be seen, and the disappointment that was written on Cassilda Quanahy's face would have touched the heart of Bluebeard.

CHAPTER XXIV

BLOOD IN A CELLAR

LIKE A TENUOUS shadow, a man moved across the brush-dotted flat immediately behind one wing of the adobe houses. Momentarily the moonlight caught the delineations of head and shoulders, covered by the flow-ing cloak and slitted hood. Behind him, well hidden in the brush, the giant stallion waited with a mate that Wayne Morgan had borrowed earlier from the corral of ponies on the hillside. By rare good fortune, Morgan had also found a saddle and bridle in a small hut near the unguarded corral.

Now, a bare few seconds after Morgan had left the girl, The Masked Rider moved with sure, silent steps towards a building somewhat set apart from the looming, rear walls of the *hacienda*. It was the granary. The hooded man had determined by allowing but seconds to elapse before he struck, that the Quanahy girl, rattle-brained as she was, would not possibly link him with the smiling cavalier of her balcony.

With both .45s out, he approached the building's

outlines until the door was in sight. For a second he examined its dark outlines, then heard the muted tone of voices
issuing through it. That the men were not immediately
beyond the door was apparent. Moving slowly, the hooded
man tried the door and a second later slipped through it.

The inside was heavy with the dry, earthy odor of wheat.
Huge bulky shadows marked the stacks of sacked grain. In
the middle of them, a shaft of light penetrated upwards,
casting a glare against the cobwebbed ceiling.

Moving forward, the outlaw in the mask saw that it
was a short stairway leading into the earth. At its bottom
showed the shape of a man's hatted head and beyond it, a
lantern. The man was talking low.

That there might be one or a dozen men in the granary's
cellar was a chance the hooded man knew he must take. He
bunched his muscles, then shot his body down the fifteen
foot staircase with all the power he could muster.

The man below wheeled with a blurted curse. But the
oncoming, hooded shape was on him at that second. One
.45 came down, crashed full on the battered sombrero. The
man dropped like an empty sack.

The hollow roar of a .45 blasted the small, earth-walled
place. Someone out of the hooded man's sight had heard
his approach, too. But the bullet, coming from behind,
splattered against a beam supporting the floor above. By
that time the man in the hood had shifted his moving body.

Over in one corner, arms spread-eagled and fettered to
the wall, was McTaggart. Standing over him was a hulking giant of a man, the Quanahy who had let fly the shot.
In his hand the smoking shape of his gun twisted, ready
to spout a second shot.

The thunder of The Masked Rider's gun seemed to

compress the walls of the tight room, then split it with sound. When his first bullet had missed its target, the man standing over McTaggart had sealed his own fate. His gun was still moving for a second shot when the hooded man's weapon spoke. The guard folded in the middle, fell to the floor.

Knowing that the sound of the shots would be like a tocsin to the men in the *hacienda,* The Masked Rider went forward like a bolt from the blue. He could see that McTaggart's wrists were shackled with baling wire and that it was cutting into his flesh. The tow-head's lips were grim; he said nothing.

It was the work of a passing second to release him, for the hooded man did not fight the wire, simply blew out the wall fastenings with two well directed shots. In another second, McTaggart was on his feet, leaping out after the moving shape of the hooded man.

THEY WENT UP the stairway, bolted through the outer door of the granary. Around a corner of the house came a running man who spotted them and raised his voice in a ripped-out command. But the man in the mask did not stop to silence him. He shoved McTaggart forward around the corner of the granary, and headed on fast moving feet towards the farther brush. In another second the hulking form of the black stallion loomed in the shadows.

McTaggart was in the saddle of the pony next to the black as soon as the hooded outlaw was in his seat. With a crisp order from The Masked Rider, they wheeled, sent their mounts crashing into the uptrail blanket of small trees.

But they did not pause, even after they knew that they had outdistanced pursuit from below. For half an hour the man in the hood pressed the two horses until at last they mounted a rise and dropped into the valley of the Box B. It was almost under the oak where McTaggart had met Blue Hawk that the masked man ordered a halt.

Across the fields the bright lights of the Box B glittered. McTaggart, his lips grim, had reined in his mount next to the hulking black. His words were low; but the hooded man broke them off abruptly.

"Sol Bascom is dead!" he snapped. "You've a job, boy, to do over on the Box B. A job of explaining yourself—I can't help you do that. I can only advise you to tell every-thing—*Adios*."

The man in the hood knew that those words spelled, in a sense, the depths of anguish to the tow-head. But he knew that if he explained further, precious time would be lost. The tow-head must be sent to the Box B immediately. He wheeled the black, shot it crashing into the brush at the rim of the valley. Once in it, he turned, saw McTaggart start at a slow trot across the fields.

Although Blue Hawk was stationed on the other side of the valley, the hooded man did not raise his voice in their signal greeting. Somewhere above him, on one of the ridges he and McTaggart had avoided, there should be a group of riders watching the Box B.

In a vantage spot, the hooded man paused, began to examine every looming shadow of the sky line above him. Somewhere— Finally, he spotted what he was search-ing for. On an untreed shoulder of land he made out the shapes of a dozen or more mounted men. No lights save that of the moon revealed them. Yet he knew that they sat their ponies watching every movement in the valley below. King Quanahy did not intend to attack! When he had brought his men back from Soldier Canyon, one thought had caused this move—if the Box B attacked the Curlicue *hacienda,* he would be more than ready for it.

The man in the mask was thinking hard and fast. He knew now that he had a plan that glimmered with hope. If he could bring the Box B and the Curlicue riders together without bloodshed—!

The stallion trotted across a clearing in the brush, moved shoulder deep in the growth on the other side.

As it did so, like some sort of mastodonic shadow sweeping upward from the earth, a giant shape leaped from its hiding place full at the outlaw on the black's saddle.

The stallion reared. But the uprising figure had judged his distance well. A pair of monstrous, octopus arms clamped about the hooded man's body, jamming his elbows to his side.

WITH HIS ARMS pinioned to his sides the hooded man's guns were useless. The big stallion came back to earth under the tremendous weight of the attack. With a lightning move, the octopus tentacles snapped downward. And as they came, the hooded man felt both .45s leave the holsters at his side.

In the moonlight, the neolithic, craggy features of the big negro, Jackson, had a triumphant smile as they flashed into the masked man's vision.

He threw his body out of the saddle so that, off balance, the big negro pulled both of them with a mighty crash off into the brush. But as they went, the quickly moving hands of the masked man had jolted the guns out of the negro's grasp. They slithered out in the moonlight and clumped solidly on the grassy floor of the clearing.

With a wrestler's heave, Jackson moved his big body,

tossing the hooded man from him. Then in another second, both of them were out of the entangling branches and in the clearing. To his right, not six feet away, the man in the hood could see his .45s glittering dully. And not four feet from them, crouched on one knee as he had dropped, was the giant negro.

The moonlight cast full on his face. His eyes were bright; the tight, bulging chest gleamed through his open-necked shirt. His lips were parted in a grin that showed the monstrous teeth.

Like trapped coyotes, both of them eyed the weapons on the ground. The negro sprang first, straight in their direction. But before his big body had moved inches, the masked man was on him. One fist caught Jackson a jolting upper cut. The other struck him alongside the cheek, knocking him off balance. But Jackson's reaction was immediate. He changed direction, swooped in on the smaller man with those great enwrapping arms.

"I got you dis time!"

CHAPTER XXV

THE RIDER
STRIKES TWICE

MOMENTARILY, THEIR MUSCLES crackled under the strain; then like felled oaks, they crashed to the ground locked in combat.

Doing so, they left the guns well out of reach of both. The black sombrero slipped away, the hooded man felt ham-like paws scrape along his shoulder, then grappled at his throat. But they missed their mark when the masked outlaw flipped his body backward.

Undismayed, a happy grunt slipped from the negro's lips. Fighting was second nature to him. He suddenly straightened, bringing up the hooded man's lean body as he would a child's. The Masked Rider could feel the tremendous strength in those mighty muscles then. He felt the negro's biceps tighten and realized that if the negro once caught the right hold, his back would be snapped like a pipe stem. The octopus hug cramped at his midriff; a wave of dizziness swept over his senses.

He brought up one fist, sent it smashing against the jutting jaw. The negro shook it off, grinning.

"You-all's caught now, Mister Masked Rider. You better gib up!"

The hooded man grunted. He knew the soft spot Jackson's race gave him. The negro's head and jaw were rocky as granite. Blows there he shook off and grinned. But when the hooded man sunk his fist into the negro's midriff, Jackson's tightening biceps weakened a little. Enough for the hooded man to jerk himself violently backward to loosen those ham-like paws. A second later he was free and backing away.

But this did not seem to bother the giant. He stood up. No more than eight feet separated the two men now. Beside him, the hooded man was dwarfed as a pigmy before Goliath.

Jackson was grinning again. "You-all gonna come with Jackson peaceful-like?"

The masked man said nothing. Jackson had not yet gone for his knife—that would come next. Without his guns, the hooded man had only his bare fists and his lightning fast brain to rely on. He clinched his jaw—doggedly watched the great body begin to come forward with outstretched arms—one step, two....

Once already the hooded outlaw had felt his strength seep away under the pressure of Jackson's octopus hug. He measured the negro's approach, judged the point of the jutting jaw.

The negro took another step. At the same instant the man in the mask came forward-threw all his weight behind his right fist. It struck Jackson's chin square. The grin disappeared. The arms flayed out but caught nothing—just out of reach now, the hooded figure stood. Jackson lunged.

It was no bull's rush. The negro was light on his feet as a giant cat. But his did not match the lightning speed of the other. The fleeting masked figure stood its ground momentarily, sent two crashing blows up under Jackson's guard. The negro's grinning face did not move a whit. He was willing to take blows on the chin.

His great arms swept inward, his body bent as he caught the lean shape full about the waist. With a heave, he lifted his opponent full off the ground.

A massive bear trap seemed to clamp on the outlaw's torso. His breath stopped, his lungs gasped for air. A paralyzing numbness shot up his spine. He knew that in the space of the next second, consciousness would leave him if he did not act.

He grappled at the mighty head, slipped a pair of gloved hands about the negro's forehead. Then with all the strength he could muster, he shoved outward. The negro had expected a rain of blows. The surprise move caught him off balance. He stumbled backward, bringing the two of them to the earth. They hit with a stunning smash.

Momentarily the bear hug around the cloaked chest loosened. And in the fleeting second the outlaw twisted and yanked himself free.

THE FIRST SIGNS of anger flared across the negro's face. He scrambled to his feet. Poised light-footed eight feet away was the shape that had avoided him. Jackson grunted like a wounded animal and charged.

The hooded man stepped backward. He was playing a desperate game. If it were his strength against the negro's, he could never hope to match that giant. Jackson up to this moment had been no more than playing with him. The negro had not struck a blow, seeking evidently to smother the hooded man under a bear trap hug....

Up to that moment a vast contentment had been growing in the negro's mighty body. He had fought all of his life. As French had witnessed, he had once vanquished four men in a hand-to-hand combat. To him, this battle seemed like the veriest child's play. He felt he could batter that hooded shape to a pulp at any second he wished. His plan was not to do that. He wanted his opponent alive and in good health. He wanted a secret out of the hooded outlaw and he couldn't get that out of an unconscious corpse. Yet the stinging blows ired him.

So he rushed, to put an end to the combat instantly— and met the surprise of his life.

The hooded man dug his foot into the ground, aimed at the point of the oncoming jaw. To him this was no game. Once captured by the giant, any fate, let alone his unmasking, might greet him. Desperately he steeled his muscles, shot his whole body's weight forward. He felt the impact of his fist clear down to the heel he had dug in the earth.

Momentarily fears grappled at him. He was hitting the

negro on an unprotected but scarcely vital spot. Already many times such blows had failed.

A paralyzing numbness sped along his right arm, cramping the muscles of his back, constricting, even the flat sinews across his solar plexus. But the desperate power he had thrown into that blow had taken the negro by surprise. The giant body paused in its rush, seemed to hover, a two hundred and seventy pound dead weight in mid air. Those giant arms grappled at thin air; across his features a look of stunned surprise shot.

Then a second later, Jackson, the giant, was sitting on the ground, his eyes still open but glazed. Across from him the masked outlaw was rubbing the muscles of his biceps. Jackson's eyes cleared. He rubbed his jaw, shook his craggy head. Then the wide chasm of his mouth abruptly parted in a grin.

The masked man glanced at his guns. He was now closer to them than the negro. He stalked forward, scooped them, then his hat, up. When he turned, the big negro had not moved.

"Lawdy me," grunted Jackson, unperturbed. "I sho' never been hit like dat before. Felt like a mule plumb kicked my chin off." He waggled it ruefully.

The man in the hood whistled. The stallion came at a trot, paused as the hooded man slid into the saddle.

"Where you-all goin'?" grunted Jackson. He lumbered to his feet. "Wait. Where you-all goin'?" he repeated. "I'se powerful respee'ful of a man got dat sorta kick. Mebbe I forget about de money!"

"Money?" snapped the hooded man.

"Sho'," grinned Jackson, "Aby Holt's money. You-all got dat, ain't you? Dat's why I'se after you."

"I found Holt," said the hooded man, "but I left everything on him as it was."

A perplexed look came across Jackson's face. "It sho' 'nuff wasn't in his pockets when I looked. Lawdy me, I think maybe you tell de truff." He paused, "You an me—we look fer it?"

The man in the hood spoke low. "I have a hunch where we can find it. Do you want to take a long chance?"

THERE WAS NO hesitation in the masked man's movements later as he sent the big black streaking across the stubble fields towards the Box B. Earlier he had made his approach carefully, taking advantage of every shadow. Now he drove the black straight for the gate, crossing the ranch yard with a thunder of hoofs. At the picket fence before the porch, he swung out of the saddle, examined rapidly the unsaddled ponies in the corral and stepped up the walk to the door. He went in without knocking.

Somebody had built a fire in the fireplace. Before it, turning at the sound of the footsteps, were Jane Bascom and McTaggart. For a second, astonishment swept across her eyes—only to die away. The tow-head's lips were grim, but in the face of each, the hooded man read a story that warmed him inwardly. That McTaggart had bared his heart indeed was obvious.

"You," the girl's voice was incredulous. "Bill has—" she paused. "Bill has told me what you've done. But you shouldn't come back here this way! There might be strangers who'd shoot you on sight."

The man in the mask stalked across the room.

"Before I left," he snapped, "I said you had a chance to save the Box B. You still have it. The Quanahys will be here before you can yell help—and there's no other way out."

McTaggart's eyes flashed. "Quanahys? After all they've done, why in hell should King make the case against him worse by—"

"By wiping out the ranch?" the hooded man snapped. "No. He's after me. I want fighters backing me up faster than you can get them. In here!"

"Bill!" Jane's voice was sharp with alarm.

But the tow-head had read in those hooded eyes the look he had seen before—it demanded action. He wheeled, went straight for the front door and was outside before the girl could say more.

They could hear the rasp of his voice out near the bunk house. But the girl had no chance to question. The hooded man went to the door that opened on the kitchen, closed and locked it against entrance. In rapid succession, he had locked the two others giving into the living room. Then he pulled down the shades.

There was a trample of boot heels on the porch. The sounds of running men eager for battle. A second later they swarmed in, pierced the hooded man with questioning glances. Following them came McTaggart.

McTaggart glanced around the circle of the hatless punchers, and saw in the grim jaws and the ready guns a sight that warmed his heart.

"The Quanahys seem to be coming down on us, boys. I think we all understand what's going on. Far as we're concerned, the Box B is ruined, washed up. There ain't a chance in hell of getting cattle enough to face the Quanahys' notes. But the Curlicue's on its way—they're after a man here that's stood with us since the word 'go'—and even before!"

The hooded man moved in next to the fireplace. Outside

there was a rattle of hard hoofs in the ranch yard, the harsh voices of men filled the air.

"He's right. All I ask is that you stand tight," snapped the man in the hood. "I just told them I was riding in to the Box B—and that they could catch me there!"

The piercing eyes behind the hood swept over the group of wind-and fight-hardened punchers, noting the grim jaws, the restless hands hovering over gun-belts.

CHAPTER XXVI

MURDER'S OUT

A STIFFENING RAN through the packed bodies. More sounds of riders surrounding the house were audible. A harsh, authoritative voice blared forth.

"Open up, Box B! We jest seen The Masked Rider come in here. He's in your house and, by God, we've come tuh drag him out by th' neck. You gonna fight or let us have him?"

The hooded man's directions to McTaggart came low.

"We got him in here, King Quanahy," McTaggart shot back to the unseen voice, masking his tone. "You gotta come in and get him."

There was a murmur of voices outside.

Then: "Remember," the Quanahy's boss shouted. "You asked for it. We're coming in."

For a second the hooded men's eyes shot through those about him. He had gambled heavily that they would play on his side. But he had placed even more of a risk on the

Quanahys' desire to lynch rather than shoot him. For to anyone entering the door, he was a sure target.

There was a grating rattle of feet on the porch. The Quanahys, ten strong, paraded in. At their head, showed the hard-lined face of King. In a small circle his men gathered about him. And in their midst was the white-haired head of Will Quanahy and near him, Branch.

King Quanahy's hard eyes surveyed the lean shape of the tow-head over near the fireplace. For a second, surprise moved across his face, but he blanketed it.

"Runaway maverick!" he snapped. "We'll take care of you later."

His gaze shifted, took in the hooded man near McTaggart. He raised a shaking, venomous finger.

"That's the man we want! He's killed Milt, my brother, and Dutch, my son. By God, he'll swing from the longest rope on the Curbeue—*tonight!*

"Yo're a fine example to be squawking about justice!" snapped McTaggart.

The voice of the hooded man broke in. "The Box B is backing me up, King Quanahy. If we don't hold our tempers, there's apt to be a lot of useless bloodshed—in a room small as this. I have an idea, though, maybe the Box B and the Curlicue ought to make *palabra.*"

The eyes of the Curlicue riders shifted to him. Surprise of a sort crept across their faces.

King Quanahy's eyes narrowed. Across his hawk-like face, a shadow of cruel laughter flitted. He leaned forward, throwing his weight on the big cane in his hand.

"You hear that, boys?" he gritted. "Talk— Do we want talk?"

The hooded man's voice brought him up short. There

was a steely note that King Quanahy had not often in his life heard used on him. A sneer darkened his predatory features.

"I had a purpose in getting this much of the Curlicue in this room!" snapped the hooded man. "You're here, Will Quanahy, and Branch too—for that purpose. As far as the Box B foreclosure is concerned, those cards are on the table—we all know about it. Here's something neither the Box B nor the Curlicue know about. Sol Bascom didn't only have large loans from the Long Stream bank, but also from the loan shark, Bartlett Moore. King Quanahy," he leaned forward, "it's a secret, is it not, that you *own* Bartlett Moore!"

A SLIGHT SHIVER shot through King Quanahy's hulking shape. He stuttered, then blurted out.

"A secret not even I know about!"

"How did Abe Holt know about it then?" snapped the hooded shape. He was not sure what he said was truth. But for him all clues had pointed in one direction. He played his hand—and waited for its effect.

For a second the glittering black eyes across the room darkened. Then Quanahy wheeled.

"If it's going to be a fight, men, let's get it over now!"

"Not yet," the steely voice shut him up. "McTaggart broke into Moore's to see how much indebtedness Bascom had with Moore. McTaggart found practically none. Moore hid the big notes. That false evidence was to throw the clan council off suspecting King. Abe Holt, one of the Box B hands, was a wanted man south of here and a smart man, too. Some way, we'll never know how, he caught wind of what King Quanahy was after. He suspected King's relations with Moore. That's why he left Soldier Canyon that night when McTaggart did and followed him. Caught him coming out of Moore's, and grabbed him to be sure it was the right man. It was. So he B-lined for the Curlicue and threatened to reveal. King, *that you and Moore had planned to double-cross the clan!*"

A shudder rippled through the Quanahy boss's big body. Behind him were what remained of the clan council and other clan riders. He could almost sense the tremor of surprise that shot through them. He opened his month, but the hooded man had already resumed his crisp, ominous words.

"You lured Holt into the granary and tied him down with wire. Abe Holt was found riding in a *palomina's* saddle where he had been held until death stiffened his body so much he couldn't fall off. The idea was that the *palomina* would wander back to where it belonged—to the Box B with him. Give the impression Holt had died in the saddle!

"Holt had quite a bit of money— To take care of it, he'd stuffed it in a leather cuff protected with cloth, and buried it. When McTaggart blew up Soldier Canyon wall, it uncovered Holt's money. Coming along the next morning, Sol Bascom found it. Someone saw him find it. *That someone knew it was Holt's!* He was afraid that the papers Bascom pulled out of the cuff held another secret of the relations between Moore and King Quanahy. So he rode up to Sol who, seeing that rider was unarmed, didn't go for his gun. But that rider *was* armed with a weapon that had already taken Vance's and Holt's lives. *So Bascom lost his!*"

The hooded outlaw glanced at Will Quanahy. The elder's old eyes were hardening slowly—yet with relentless bitterness—on his brother.

"That same man, because he knew McTaggart was in

love with Jane Bascom, had been at Soldier Canyon the night before to see that McTaggart did his work right. Vance was killed to be sure that if McTaggart slipped just a little, no one would be at the canyon mouth to stop the cows. All three," the outlaw clipped out the accusation, "were cold blooded, needless murders—*to help you double-cross the clan—King Quanahy!*"

CHAPTER XXVII

DEATH TAKES AN EXIT

THE DARK FACE of the Curlicue leader flared to instant rage. He gripped his cane, shot his glance around the circle of his punchers' faces.

The hooded man tightened his muscles. The climax had come. On what Quanahy did now, depended—in a manner—the masked outlaw's safety. He had gambled heavily on the clan council's reaction.

"Lies," King Quanahy snarled. "Unfounded lies to give a trapped man enough time to get out of here. You're slippery, Mister Masked Rider! If there were a connection between this Moore and me, what difference—"

"Enough to make you a rich man in your own name," snapped the hooded man. "You buffaloed the clan into thinking you'd promised McTaggart a half share of the Box B. No member of the clan owns anything in his own home. That's your own law, King. You never in your life would have let one of them own half of the Box B. *But you wanted it yourself!* Just after the clan foreclosed on the ranch, Moore would produce his own set of mortgage notes. The Curlicue would have to make a quiet adjustment in their holdings—by giving away McTaggart's share plus a few thousand dollars—to Moore. McTaggart, couldn't complain because by that time he would be a member of the clan! It was a double-cross against your own people, King Quanahy. *Not the Law, but they, are going to judge you for that!*"

For a second shadows flitted through Quanahy's glittering eyes. He glanced at Will, his brother, then at Branch. The grim lines of their mouths told King Quanahy that every word the hooded man spoke rang true to them.

"When Holt, Vance and Sol Bascom were found, they looked as though they had been trampled to death by a cow. But all three were murdered, King. Lay your cane on the table and I'll show these people how!"

"A crazy man!" snarled the Quanahy boss to the Box B punchers. "My men weren't brought here to listen to lies. That man killed Milt and Dutch." He turned to his men. "I'm leaving you to do the job of hanging him."

Like a whirling top, King Quanahy had moved, then slid towards the door, clutching the cane in an iron grip.

"Lies!" he snarled and stepped out.

"Wait!" rasped McTaggart. "He's not going to get away with that. Let's see that cane!"

The tow-head left the fireplace on surging, angry legs. The riders at the doorway abruptly gathered together and presented a solid, grim-faced front to him. In the horny, efficient paws of the men who now backed Will Quanahy were ready, meaningful guns.

"You can't get away with that," grated the tow-head. "If King Quanahy is the murderer, by God, he'll—"

WHITE HAIRED WILL QUANAHY'S old, cracked voice raised above the tow-head's.

"If he's done wrong," he said quietly, "the clan will soon get to the bottom of it."

"What can you do!" snarled the tow-head. "The clan's washed up on this range now. It's the clan of the damned, now!"

Outside there was a movement of horse's hoofs that sprang out in a quick gallop. The men in the packed room could hear it leave the porch front, cross the ranch yard and slow up at the gate. There the hoof beats faltered, came to a halt.

Suddenly a racking, fearful cry broke against the ears of the listeners. It rose, fell, then died away in shivering, quavering, ominous notes!

There was a scurry of feet on the porch. A gun went off on the porch with a blast like a mortar.

"He's got King!"

"Will—Oh Will!"

Horse's hoofs suddenly beat the earth out beyond the gate. Another shot blared forth. Like the quick patter of nearby rain, they rose, then died in the distance, slowly.

"Will, come quick! *Something's happened to King!*"

To a man, the Quanahys, frozen at first by that horrible cry, surged to the door, hammered out.

The cool voice of the hooded man stopped McTaggart in his tracks.

"Wait here!"

For long moments a silence, broken only by the hushed, bated breaths of the men, gripped the room. Finally, unsteady steps approached the porch, mounted it. It was

Will Quanahy. He entered. Walked to the middle of the room.

"Someone at the gate," he said in a halting low voice, "must have been waiting—pulled him off his horse, broke his back and escaped. His—his pants pockets were turned inside-out. The man they saw was big—very big—"

The hooded man moved his shoulders. "Somehow—I'd say—the murderer must have known that King had the money out of Holt's leather cuff." He looked at Will Quanahy, standing there holding the deadly cane, and he could not help but feel pity for this old man whose world had been shattered so suddenly. "You can just leave the cane on the table there. We'll attend to getting rid of it," he said almost kindly.

Old Will shrugged. It was as though a thousand years had fallen across his aged, bent shoulders. His seamed, ancient face was pale, grim.

"We'll keep it," he said softly. "Blood has been spilled a-plenty. The Quanahy clan's suffered more of a blow than you think. We'll meet you more than half way. Whoever made the cane had a steel head put under the leather—so it'd support weight. The leather head came off. The steel head was shaped just like you seen—like a cow's hoof—split so the leather padding wouldn't slip. We'll keep the cane—and them notes at the bank—they're good—for another year, if you want."

Then the oldest Quanahy shrugged, left the room....

FOR A LONG time the room had been silent. The Box B punchers were gone. Gone, too, were the Quanahy riders. In the living-room of the Box B, a tow-head, a girl, and the hooded man stood. The tow-head broke the silence first.

"You've hoed a powerful tough row for us, stranger. I

guess no one'll never see your face, but understand that you're mighty welcome on th' Box B no matter what circumstances bring you!"

The hooded man stalked towards the door. But the girl jumped up. Light glittered across her dark, soft hair, across the even lines of her oval face.

"But you can't go!" she said seriously. "You've done too much for us.... Go tomorrow or the next day. We'll see that you're safe—"

But the outlaw in the hood shook his head. Far above them, on the flanks of the mountain, Blue Hawk was waiting patiently. The outlaw knew that he should go, immediately. But long used to a lonesome existence, the presence of people, of friendly men and women, were like a comforting drug to his senses. But his must be the life of the open range, of nights and winds on the mesas.

"No," said The Masked Rider, "I'm afraid it's *adios*. I can only hope it's not forever." He paused. "The owl-hoot trail is a long one. Sometimes it winds back to pleasant ranges. But always it stretches out ahead farther than the eye can see. That's my trail. *Adios*."

Momentarily he regarded the girl. Inner sadness slid over him. For the grinning tow-head, she represented home, affection, warmth. For the masked outlaw, there would never be a trail's end like this. Almost wistfully, he glanced about the oak chairs, the cheery fireplace. This indeed was their home—while his was the cold flanks of the ranges, the mesquite, the primitive wilderness of hates and bloodshed in which he would forever roam.

"Adios," he said again, quietly.

There was a clump of high-heeled boots on the porch.

Later came the heavy, powerful hoof beats of the black stallion. When at last they had died away, the girl turned:

"Oh Bill, we are so awfully grateful to him. In spite of everything, we *could* have made him wait for our thanks...."

She turned, but it was straight toward the enfolding arms of the tow-head.

"He couldn't wait any more'n I can," said the tow-head owlishly.

Then he looked into the softly luminous eyes, the smiling, oval face. With a mighty sweep of his arms, the tow-head, McTaggart, gathered her to him.

Far, far away, sounded the faint call of the mountain cat, but the two in the room hardly heard it. To them, it meant nothing.

THE DEVIL'S
HENCHMEN
BY WILLIAM H STUEBER

CHAPTER I

ROPE

N OT EVEN BLACK night could blot out the hideousness of The Devil's Playground. Although no star shone and the full August moon was blanketed by sinister black clouds, still there was sufficient light to enable one to make out the rocks, the jagged cuts, the eroded slopes of the wasteland.

Here storms vented their spleen. In season, razor-edged northern gales shaved grit from mounds and flung it about like the biting particles that come from an airblast gun. Here summer cloudbursts hurled down their torrents to turn each dry wash into a muddy, roaring, short-lived river. Here noon's sun greedily sucked life from anything unfortunate enough to invade Satan's domain. And *here*—if anywhere on God's earth—the hunted man or beast could find his small portion of peace and rest, if he was staunch enough to endure life that was certainly worse than death.

Midnight. To complete the ghastly weirdness, there came the mournful cry of a mountain cat. Breaking strangling silence, it drifted over the tortuous land like the chilling wail of some dying thing. Then, as if to show the cat the nature of its whereabouts: as if to warn it to flee, the moon moved swiftly from behind its opaque curtain and doubled the grimness of the country by silver-washing the heights and intensifying the blackness of the depths.

Every stone, wash and atom of sand seemed to cry out, "Be on your way!" But had Satan and a thousand other demons gamboled in the hell-hole, the man who again uttered the cat cry would not have been frightened away.

His name was Blue Hawk. Now, gazing hopefully at the terrible panorama below him, there was something of ancient royalty upon his weather-beaten face and in his bearing. High-cheeked, long-haired, he sat his sorrel like some Yaqui chief, his every sense alert for sound or motion in The Devil's Playground.

But nothing stirred save shadows of the silver disk now

ready to dip again behind a cloud black as death. Truly, the hand of Satan was upon the wasteland tonight, and when the moon was hidden, the silence, the darkness gripped the Mexican Indian and held him taut.

Again the cold, fearful cry of the mountain cat came from Blue Hawk's lips. His sorrel, too, pricked up its ears as if also praying for a like response out there in the waste. Then it came!

Not the answer Blue Hawk hungered for! But the swish of a lariat slicing the night air; the swish that tells of an expert roper; a man whose eyes were keen enough to pierce the blackness where the Indian lurked.

Blue Hawk had ridden the range, the lonesome trail too long to try and escape the loop. Swift, accurately as a boa constrictor coils about prey, so rope fell over the Indian's head. A vicious jerk that all but unhorsed him, and the scout's arms were pinned down. He felt the tugs that meant a powerful man was keeping the lariat tight and working closer, hand over hand, as one hauling on a heavily weighed hawser.

THE INDIAN KNEW not what to expect. But he knew that nothing good was in store for him. Neither did fear strike at Blue Hawk—immediately. Yet, when a ghoulish laugh sounded closer to him, and he caught the ominous voice of another man, an icy finger traced the Indian's spine. Fear shook him now! Not fear for himself!

"Madre de Dios!" he moaned inwardly. "I am caught when I give the call. So, too, will *he* be caught by these devils, if he now answer or come."

In a split-second all of the Indian's mind, all his tense attention, went upon the badlands. Somewhere out there his master, The Masked Rider, was relying upon his scout's cry and surely he was coming on, phantom like, to perhaps become another prisoner of this laughing pair who threw true ropes in darkness.

Blue Hawk felt steel fingers grip his thigh, steal upward, probe a bit, then snatch away both his gun and his knife. Only by straining his eyes could he make out two blurred and smirking faces; the faces of killers born to their trade. Then he had other things to see—and feel.

The rope unbalanced Blue Hawk. He yielded to the tremendous pressure upon it. Tight-mouthed as both of the mystery men, he let one foot slip from stirrup. There came another swish; more deadly than the first. Even as colored lights flashed before his eyes, the Indian knew that a gun butt had cracked down upon his skull. He pitched into the chasm of unconsciousness.

A match in cupped hands threw flickering light upon the bronzed face of the prisoner. The man who held it until his fingers almost burned, straightened with a hyena's laugh.

"An Indian, Charley!" he said in a voice as ruthless as his face. "What you suppose he's snoopin' 'round here for?"

Charley grinned. "Reckon I shouldn't have hit him so hard. Looks like he ain't ever gonna answer any questions—on this earth."

"Sure he will. You can't kill his kind with a smash on the head. Indians are tough, *sabe?* An' this *hombre*—Well? What'll we do with him? He wasn't snoopin' 'round here for a good purpose, I'm bettin'. Mebbe—"

Charley took a half hitch around the prisoner's chest and under his arms. He caught the lines of Blue Hawk's sorrel. Although the loyal animal protested against it, Charley vaulted into the saddle. He threw a double hitch around the horn and laughed.

"Let's get goin', Art."

Art's chuckle was scarcely audible. "Ain't never heard of bringin' a gent out of unconscious land by draggin' him—face down over rocks an' gravel." It was not compassion that led Art to turn the prisoner over on his back. "Where to, Charley?"

"We'll let Garden say how this *hombre* cashes in—rope an' tree, his own knife or a bullet."

"You mean to drag this gent to the shack an'—"

"Three quarters of a mile ain't gonna hurt him—much."

"But Garden won't be there! Remember him say in' he'd

just get hisself another cup o' coffee, then light out for San Adella?"

CHARLEY GROWLED. HE remembered now. He twisted, in the saddle and looked at the prone thing on the rocky ground. "Then *I'll* be judge an' jury. An' I reckon safest thing to do is swing this galoot. If he did see or hear anything whilst snoopin', he mustn't ever tell about—"

He clipped the sentence and dismounted. Before the groaning Indian stirred again, Charley's dusty boots were an inch from the long black hair in the sand. He bent over, grabbed the black strands and hoisted the prisoner; hinged him at the waist and made him sit up. He slapped the bronzed face until Blue Hawk was thoroughly alive.

"What you snoopin' for?" rasped Charley.

Art dropped to his knees on the other side of the Indian. "You wasn't *spyin'* on somebody, mister?"

Blue Hawk rallied his wits. "I do nothing, *senors.* I—"

"You ride like a ghost; always keep where it's darkest an' make a noise like a mountain cat!"

"*Senors* make the big mistake," said the Indian quietly. "I—"

"You was workin' yore way *from* a shack, huh? You heard five gents palaverin', huh?"

"No, *senors!* I do not see a shack. I do not hear—"

"Then what in hell you doin' out here at midnight makin' mountain cat cries?"

Blue Hawk thought fast. He knew a good excuse would save his life. But they could tear him limb from limb and out of his mouth would never come the truth—that the cries were to enable The Masked Rider to locate him. For a few minutes the Indian prodded his brain in vain. Then a trace of a smile played around his thin-lipped mouth.

"*Si! Senors* make the big mistake, it is not I who makes the cry. It is the mountain cat. I only make the search for him. *Bounty, sabe?* That is how I earn my bread, *senors;* by killing the killers who plague all you cattlemen and—"

Charley guffawed. "Jest huntin' cats, huh?"

Art snarled, touched the keen knife to the Indian's throat. "Yo're a damned liar! An' I'll slit you ear to ear if you do it again. Now what were you doing?"

"I hunt—"

Charley's fist crammed the words back into the Indian's mouth. "There ain't been cat or bounty in these parts for all of five years!" He bounded to his feet. "He's a snooper sure, Art. Mebbe there's ways o' gettin' truth out of him!"

Blue Hawk realized how close he was to death. He said nothing; not even when the rope whistled up and over the stout limb of a tree that storm and Satan had not yet got around to destroying. He watched both killers take hold of the lariat, and out of the tails of his eyes he saw a blinking light nearby.

"Half a minute for truth, *hombre!*" clipped Charley.

Art put his weight on the rope. "The *truth* we know, Charley. Get his feet off the ground. Let him down again—an' make him prove the case against him by givin' that cat cry again."

FOR A SECOND Blue Hawk saw a loophole of escape. He would give the signal cry! The Masked Rider would come. Both gringoes would learn that sometimes what one insists upon is only that same one's death warrant.

"Heave!" snapped Art.

Rope choked the Indian. He felt that his lungs must burst; that blood must push through the very skin of his hot face. Until he trembled on the very brink of his grave, the killers held him swinging in the air.

"Down!" barked Charley. He ran forward, propped up the victim and shook him alive. "It was *you* makin' the cat call, wasn't it?"

Blue Hawk nodded. "*Si.*"

Art laughed. "Learns powerfully fast!" He rocked the helpless prisoner with a resounding smash on the jaw. "Let's hear you imitate the cat again, spic!"

Blue Hawk's hopes soared. He cleared his constricted throat. Few men could save their lives so easily. Only a cat call to be uttered and— The Indian's heart turned to a lead lump. Although he felt that the famous outlaw and master must be near at hand, he also remembered that *five* men had palavered in the nearby shack. To call was simplicity itself—to lure The Masked Rider; to subject him to grave danger and impossible odds, was less endurable than death.

"Cat call!" rasped Charley. "*Pronto!*"

The Indian's mouth froze in a grim, positive line of silence.

"Cat call, damn you!" barked Art. "You must have had a good reason for givin' it!"

"Sure he had good reason," said Charley. "An' that reason we'll get out of him if we have to hoist and lower him 'till dawn."

The rope squeaked over worn bark overhead. Blue Hawk snatched a breath and steeled himself for torture. Two questions kept flashing through his reeling mind. Had the outlaw heard that last cat cry? Would his sense of direction—he often owed his life to it—bring him to this tree *and death?*

CHAPTER II

THE BLACK APOSTLE

WHOSE EYES SO keen that they could discern another moving thing in The Devil's Playground? Yet it was there; a grotesque, sombre black splotch that moved as silently as a dark cloud drifts over the moon.

None could say whether it was man, beast or some mysterious, prehistoric hybrid. Perhaps an eagle, flying dangerously close as the black thing streaked across an unsheltered spot, might have recognized a combination of man and horse. Certainly not even that marvelously sighted bird of prey could have seen where man ended and animal began. For they moved as one; a symphony of blackness, silence and effortless motion.

The stallion, black, long-legged, sure-footed, moved as though upon wads of cotton to deaden hoof sounds. Seen once in a setting like this, so gallant, sleek and unusual an animal must live in memory forever. And yet the tense figure in the saddle was even more striking.

It was The Masked Rider; the outlaw whom countless reward hunters yearned to meet—*only* if by some miracle he would be unarmed and they unseen. The famous outlaw's trail began in Texas, more years ago than he cared to remember. Sometimes, getting news of additional money heaped upon his head, listening to accounts of fresh crimes charged against him, The Masked Rider laughed behind his mask; the bitter laugh of one unjustly accused and without opportunity for denial.

But tonight, not even a bitter smile was upon the outlaw's stern face. For he felt that Satan's red hand was upon the badlands; that *tonight* calamity would squeeze his heart and fate snatch away that without which he could not live. His fears were well grounded. Blue Hawk's cat call had thrice reached him—and now nothing broke the mausoleum silence.

In thick shadow of rock, the outlaw paused. His eyes, normally sincere, friendly for the deserving, were now the orbs of a man who knows that death lurks nearby. He waited perhaps a full minute; a black-hooded, black-cloaked, black-gloved statue upon a horse likewise still as the rock beside them. Then, grim mouthed and silent, the outlaw rode on—with the accuracy of a marksman's bullet; straight for the spot whence had come the last call of the Mexican Indian.

But fate jeered and as if Satan deliberately planned death for the hooded one, there came that for which the outlaw hungered. The cat call!

Instantly The Masked Rider realized two things; that he had been headed in the wrong direction and that this same call had never before been used by his scout. There was no trace of pleasure or welcome or even friendliness in it. That cry suspiciously said—but only in a manner comprehendible to the outlaw—"Beware, *Senor!* Enemies lurk. I am dooomed. *Adios. Madre de Dios* watch over you."

Again it drifted over the wasteland; weird, repulsive toned, loaded with the essence of death—and suddenly slipped by a strangling gasp.

THE OUTLAW'S BLOOD turned cold. Once he had mingled in the crowd at the base of a towering oak where vigilantes had unceremoniously swung up a cowardly killer. Even now, The Masked Rider recalled the killer's oaths choked off as the noose tightened. And in the next heart tick he knew that what had clipped the Indian's cat call was *rope around his throat!*

Had the outlaw been open to attacks by panic; had he been accustomed to losing his head and rushing in where angels fear to tread, he must have died long ago. Forever in his mind was the realization that one move of folly would probably be his last move of any sort! So, although that plaintive cat call spoke of bosom companion in gravest danger, the outlaw *thought* before he rushed. Then, eyes smouldering, teeth clenched and hands ready to fly for twin Colts, he rode on.

Had the moon's rays been white hot, the outlaw would scarcely have been singed, so swiftly did he traverse spots that offered no shield. A light flickering in the distance, made him pull up short. He looked, listened, his every sense and muscle rigid and alert. Borne on the first of fall's chilled winds, came the distance muffled voices of two men—and to drown them out, came again the warning cat call.

The Masked Rider turned south, let the stallion pick its own noiseless route up the steep side of a dry wash. He stopped; his eyes level with rock strewn flat land and his pulse leaping because of what he saw.

One leafless tree was in sight. Beneath its wide spread branches were two punchers—holding taut a rope from the noose of which Blue Hawk swung as if already dead.

"Coyotes!" gritted the outlaw.

He pressed boots gently against the stallion's side. No other command or act was needed to send the stalwart black into headlong flight. Yet, for all its speed, it raced practically without sound; the result of patient, endless hours of instruction to always gallop where grass was thickest or sand and clay softest.

BLUE HAWK LAY stretched beneath the tree that storm and Satan had overlooked. His neck was rubbed raw by rope; his breath came in quick, short and agonized gasps. And yet he was happy. The two gringoes could not distinguish one kind of cat call from the other! They did not know that the calls given at their insistence would steer the outlaw from this dangerous spot. They did not know that more cunning and less savagery *might* have resulted in two prisoners—the black one worth a small fortune, beefed or on the hoof!

Charley used the one match to light his own and Art's smoke. He slouched to the Indian and toed him in the ribs.

"Gonna tell us why you were cat callin', spic?"

"He ain't!" ventured Art. "Let's hoist him an' let him stay *up*. Sloan an' Dingwell oughta be comin' along soon an' we'll all go to—"

His mouth remained wide open. His eyes threatened to pop from their sockets. Few men ever gave such an exhibition of surprise and stark terror and frozen immobility.

CHARLEY JERKED AROUND. What he saw turned his blood to iced water and immediately he felt weak around the knees. Like Art, he stood rooted to the spot, his muscles refusing to respond to his desires to flee for his life.

The Masked Rider might have mowed down both killers. But a multitude of questions flashed through his mind as he tore down upon them. The answers he hoped to get from the Indian who even now was staggering to his feet with pain-choked exclamations of thanks and fears. The outlaw's hands were clear of Colt butts. He hoped they'd remain clear of blood. The last thing on earth he wanted was to kill—and yet, at any price, he meant to get the Indian out of harm's way and then decide what was to be done about the other pair.

Neither Charley nor Art could tell exactly what happened. Together they might have piecemealed a rational story—of a great black stallion whose hoofs never seemed to touch ground; of a rider so black he appeared to have leaped from a tar vat; of a great black mantilla, stiff in the breeze of his own making and worn that enemies' would never know whether their lead plowed into flesh or merely punched holes in black cloth. Two things Charley and Art would agree upon. That the phantom horseman came swift as death; that seconds after a dagger gleamed in moonlight, the Mexican was swept off the ground, snatched up like a sack of mail and borne off as if he weighed a pound.

Man doesn't fear the stampede—once thundering hoofs have passed him. Nor did Charley and Art fear death once the double-ladened stallion had plunged between them.

Art was first to snap alive. "Masked Rider!" he blurted as if there could possibly be any doubt in Charley's mind. "Throw down on him!"

Often it's easy to shoot a fleeing rider—if one has no scruples about lead in the back. Art whipped out his forty-five. Its barks were melded with those from Charley's gun. But where should one aim when the target is narrow and the black cloth billowing around it is several yards wide?

At the first roar of guns; the first tug of lead ripping through mantilla, the outlaw twisted in his saddle.

"You asked for it!" he said sharply. His Colt flamed twice. Only the burden in his other arm and the quick rise and fall of the leather beneath him compelled the outlaw to fire a third time.

He rushed on knowing that two corpses lay behind him. No tinge of pride coursed through him for either deed, daring or victory. Nor did regret sting him. He was in the emotionless position of a man who knows that he has merely obeyed the law of his kind; the law of the range and the trail—to shoot when shot at, to kill or be killed.

When distance and darkness made it safe, the outlaw pulled up and set the still dazed Indian upon his feet. Neither master nor devoted servant spoke for a few seconds, but looked at one another with eyes that expressed feelings better than gushed words.

"*Gracias, Senor,*" said Blue Hawk almost blankly. "But you take the big chance. The gringoes say I am to die because I listen to five *hombres'* palaver in shack. You see light? You do not think mebbe all five see you come?"

"Sometimes a man doesn't stop to count coyotes!" The black phantom's voice was grim. "What happened?"

BLUE HAWK SHRUGGED. "I try to find you, *senor.* Who looks for others in this hell-hole—at midnight? *Si,* I am the fool. I do not think mebbe eyes watch. They rope me. They say I snoop and listen to talk in shack. For that I am to die."

"*Important* talk, then!" clipped The Masked Rider. "And something here is not for others to see."

Curiosity did not grip the black Caballero. From the moment he hit the endless outlaw trail, he had cleansed his mind of it, knowing full well that even a nine-lived cat sometimes comes to grief because of interest in what does not concern it.

The Indian also knew that self-preservation was task enough—without going afield to satisfy a yearning for details of other men's business.

"I find *El Acedero, senor?* I get my knife, my gun? We leave this cursed land for—"

The outlaw shook his hooded head. "We don't go far!" he said solemnly. "I've told you about the Bunson family?"

The Indian nodded. New lights gleamed in his eyes; lights of gladness all too seldom there. *"Si!* Was it not they who once helped you?"

"To them I owe my life." The outlaw's voice was heavy with reminiscence. It might have been happening now; so clearly did he recall ill-fated days of long ago. So plainly did he see the five Bunsons helping him evade the law and the *justice* of hotheaded lynchers blinded to proof of his innocence. "*Si*, I'd have crossed my last river that night—if they hadn't believed in me."

Blue Hawk stood puzzled. "But they are in *Texas, senor.* They—"

"They are forty miles from San Adella. This morning— in Cemetery Junction—I heard that the old folks are in trouble; that Bob Bunson was coming to help them."

"But he is only a boy, *senor!*" The Indian smiled wisely. "Mebbe he does not help alone?"

"Maybe we camp in these parts," said the outlaw gravely.

Blue Hawk glanced back towards a tree, a rope—and two corpses. He had nothing to say, but looking at the sombre figure in black, he knew that the outlaw was also thinking that no wanted man could choose a more dangerous camp site.

"San Adella is bad town, *senor.* You have heard of Sheriff Lackey? Of Deputy Holtz! Of their posse that never comes back from the man-hunt without a prisoner—or a corpse?"

The outlaw nodded. It was his business to be forewarned of men and conditions before he made decisions. And although he'd heard the story of Lackey's swift justice more than once nicking the wrong men, he looked into the hazy distance and in a voice surcharged with determination, he said, "The Bunsons need help. I don't forget my debts. We ride."

"And the other three *hombres* in shack, *senor?*"

"The shack is empty—else the three would have run out to investigate the shots."

"But when they find two dead coyotes, *senor?*"

"Let *them* move. If towards us, then we'll give them some attention."

SOON THEY RODE off; skirting the badlands, heading for San Adella—not knowing that before them lay dangerous territory and men who'd stop at nothing to attain their ends. Silent as black ghosts, cautious as hunted and suspicious animals, they lurked in shadows and dashed across open stretches. The hooded outlaw rode two hundred yards or more in front of the Indian and the recovered sorrel ever mindful that to be seen together might well herald the crack of doom for both.

Neither master nor servant gave second thought to a long deserted punchers' line camp. Yet, on the lee side of the crumbling, sod-roofed structure, an unarmed man shrank in terror and gazed in awe. He saw *one* phantom-like rider;

a weird, black thing that closely resembled a huge bat just skimming the earth.

"Masked Rider!" the watcher told himself fearfully.

He bolted with the perspiration of fear beading his temples.

CHAPTER III

MOONLIGHT GRAVES

WIND HOWLED DOWN from the north and blew threatening clouds away from the moon. The outlaw didn't relish riding in the silver brilliance. But more than caution made him stop suddenly and peer down from the lip of an arroyo. For a few seconds, something below held him enthralled. Then, mindful of the fact that he was silhouetted against the moon, he swiftly moved away.

Afoot, crouched until he appeared running on both hands and feet, he made the arroyo edge again. Few things ever amazed the black caballero. What he saw now *did*. And more than mere curiosity made him attempt to fathom it.

A narrow ribbon of molten silver twisted on the bottom of the arroyo; the smallest of streams, either spring-fed or the last of a recent cloudburst. Two men worked in frantic haste beside the slow moving water. One of them broke a mud dam that had diverted the stream from the hole his comrade now filled as if his life depended upon speed. Not far to the south, where a shallow spot held water to make a miniature lake, two horses were ground-roped and standing still as statues.

How long he watched the strange affair, The Masked

Rider did not know. Nor did he shift his eyes at nearby sounds. That would be Blue Hawk! The outlaw saw the men in the arroyo glance critically at their completed task. The tall fellow drew a shovel lengthwise over the filled hole. The water ran into the channel thus made, readily ate away mud and broadened out until few human eyes could see that there had ever been any disturbance to check the stream's flow.

The two mud-splattered men walked water to reach the horses. On the wind came the jovial voice of the tall one.

"First rain'll damned near fill this cut, Ed. It'll wash things over so even we wouldn't be able to find the spot."

The runt grunted and swung into his saddle. "Nobody'll ever know what's buried there!"

They rode off; single file, tight-reined lest the horses step out of the water. Long before the plop-plop-plop of hoofs died in the distance, the tiny stream was again crystal clear.

A figure flitted to the outlaw's side. "Strange business, no, *senor?*"

The outlaw nodded.

"Road agents, mebbe? Caché gold, mebbe?"

"They didn't mark the spot and there's nothing to help them locate it. What's buried there is *never* to be dug up!"

"*Si!*" exclaimed Blue Hawk. "Then only *bodies* can be there. Mebbe they kill—"

"Yes," drawled The Masked Rider. "Maybe for being suspected of listening in on plans to do *this*, you were to be hung!"

The outlaw picked his way down the side of the cut. The Indian also stood near the mystery spot. Lack of tools did not long deter them. Blue Hawk used his hands to scoop mud into a solid pack that turned the water into a new channel cut by The Masked Rider. Then both of them went to work on the slippery slime of the grave's surface, their movements lighted only by the moon.

SUDDENLY THE MEXICAN drew away from the shallow hole. "Hair, *senor!*" he squeezed out.

The outlaw tensed. Seldom did fury so quickly grip him; seldom did wrath kindle such swift, hot fire in his narrowed eyes. The long muddy strands in the Indian's trembling fingers could mean only one thing—those coyotes had buried *a woman!*

"Dig!" clipped the outlaw. He set himself to cleanse the face about to be uncovered. Then fresh surges of rage snapped him to his feet.

"Two!" cried Blue Hawk again. "*Si, senor! Two!* A woman and a man!"

Water splashed. A match flickered in the Indian's hand. He glanced up at the hooded figure, suspicious of its tenseness and silence. The match dropped in mud that snuffed out the flame.

Behind the black hood, The Masked Rider's mouth was clamped in a dangerous line. The better to control himself and ease the steel fingers clutching his heart, he turned his back on the muddy hole and the kneeling Indian. Then through clenched teeth he managed, "Coyotes!"

Blue Hawk heard more than the single, sibilant word. He got up hopelessly. "Not friends, *senor?*" he gulped. "These old ones are not the Bunsons we came to help?"

The outlaw could only nod. Then he pried his lips apart and smothered anger with compassion. "And Bob Bunson also coming *too late.*"

For a while shock and bitterness rooted both outlaw and

scout to the spot. The Indian moved first—towards the side of the cut. Above highwater marks he knelt and began to scrape out a more fitting grave.

The masked man turned slowly. "Not yet!" he said solemnly. "Leave them as they were. It serves my purpose, *sabe?*"

"*Si, senor!*" Blue Hawk looked towards the sky. Almost reverently, he said, "I, to, do not rest until I take your friends out—and put in two coyotes!"

The outlaw stalked off. He shirked the task of covering the aged, agonized faces of friends with mud, and as he trudged to his stallion, he promised that some day, some-where, he'd face all the men connected with this damnable deed; face them with Colts ready to collect full pay.

Mounting, the black caballero needed little time to map a course. Blue Hawk to be executed for overhearing plans of five men. Two of them dead; two of them grave makers. Where number five might be was of little account. It was their rendezvous that held the outlaw's flaming attention. Unerringly he headed for it.

Blue Hawk gazed with misgiving up the tottering build-ing standing unprotected on a perfectly rounded mound. No light shone within, nothing stirred outside. Even the wind, whining across the wastes, shunned the structure as if fearing contamination by recent inhabitants.

"Bad place, *senor!* Better we—"

"Stand guard—some of the coyotes may return," cut in the outlaw determinedly. "Where men do business, they sometimes leave sign of *what* it is, *sabe?*"

HE RODE A few yards, then, dismounting, he pushed on afoot; silent as a prowling cat. Hesitating a moment in the black rectangle cast by the moon, he watched the closed door of the shack and regretted that it was silver washed. When he moved again, it was like a black cloth caught in a gale. Swift though he'd been, some one else was ready!

A gun barked. Lead chewed through the outlaw's black hood and whanged into the tinder dry door. Three split-second shots rang out; three leaden missiles whined short of their mark, for the outlaw had leaped for shelter.

A Colt bristled in his steady hand. He wasn't the man to waste ammunition on rock. Above it, he saw fast disappearing smoke rings. Let an inch of head show beyond it! Instead, came the scrape of boots and gravel, the squeak of weight in a stirrup, then the snort and clatter of a horse ruthlessly yanked and spurred into a gallop.

Few men would have held the outlaw's statuesque pose. But his was a mind never stampeded, and he realized the folly and danger of chase—that might well lead him into an inescapable ambush.

"We'll meet again, *hombre!*" he promised. "But you'll never get another chance to drill me—*from behind.*"

When fear or good sense silences a man's gun and makes him flee, safety might lie behind him. Alertly the outlaw waited, shifting in thick darkness with Colt ready. Tried to kill or drive him away? What else could it mean but that in this shack was something to be forever secret from spying eyes?

Black gloved hands inched up a sash. The black figure vaulted lightly into the room—eyes only for the table on which the moon drew a shadowed black cross. A piece of reddish stone touched black leather. The stone slid from a tilted palm and banged on the table top. Prom the outlaw's black hood came a half-laugh, half-oath. Then like some phantom thing blown by the draft through the open window, he was over the sill and swallowed by the night.

"Shale!" said the outlaw to Blue Hawk. "*Sabe?*"

"*Si!* Shale. *Oil!*" The Indian's face was puzzled. "But the five coyotes? Your poor friends?"

The Masked Rider never *guessed.* "All connected! Just *how* is what I mean to learn. And somebody pays whether the Bunsons were killed for oil bearing land—or mud!"

"You do not go—"

"To San Adella! Sheriff Lackey, his Deputy Holtz and his famous possemen will have their chance to uphold the reputations of the town, the law—and themselves."

"And I, *senor?*"

"Find a few camp sites. Caché grub, our clothes—*ammunition.* Ride to town. Find out about the Bunsons. And if you hear men moan over the loss of two partners, mark those men well!"

Scarcely distinguishable were the sounds of walking horses. Two things of inky blackness merged in the blackness of a sheer walled arroyo. Silence fell upon the wastelands and a new blanket of sombre clouds blotted out the star-gemmed heavens as if to drop a curtain over the handicraft of infamous men.

CHAPTER IV

WHERE LAW REIGNED

TWO MUD-SPLATTERED PUNCHERS rode into San Adella, split and went their separate ways. Their horses were stabled in different liveries—but the men met again at the rear door of the cowtown's only church, and the street out front lapsed again into wee hour silence and desertedness.

San Adella was no ordinary cowtown. She had things to brag about. When herd on herd of long horns were being driven north; when men schemed and killed for business for their strings of staunch freight wagons; when all America was gold mad and California bound, San Adella was in her prime. A riotous, ruthless, lawless town, she boasted that murder before breakfast was the rule and not the exception.

New faces appeared; the faces of men so lacking in dignity that they worked with pick, shovel and sledge. They were railroad bohunks; riff-raff shipped in from the east to sweat and slave and lay down ties and rails. Freighters laughed—until puffing things of coal and steam drove them out of business. And when they went and the railroad proved more than a crazy dream, San Adella hit the toboggan. She went down faster than she'd come up—to hit bottom, when she became a dusty, double-rowed line of deserted buildings that hurt the eyes and soured the soul.

Still, some old-timers remained loyal to the dead hole and kept alive two saloons, a general store and a bug infested hotel. What happened next was never definitely settled, but suddenly San Adella squirmed in her grave.

Some said the resurrection began when Bruce Garden drifted in. Others said that the coming of Big Steve McKay was the revival pill. The few women folks gave the credit to Reverend Procter Hill. The three newcomers fought each other for the honors; so valiantly that no one suspected that behind the scenes they composed as unholy a triumvirate as ever existed, and each of them gave different reasons for his prophecy that one day San Adella would be the recognized queen of the west.

Glowing pictures of the future brought in ambitious men. Business boomed. Buildings went up. And Sheriff Lackey and his "drill 'em first" deputy, spared no effort to keep the reborn town's reputation lily white. San Adella's revival was completed, her fame far flung, when the sixth lawbreaker met sudden justice in front of Lackey's ready guns—and when her first church doors opened.

"Church!" beamed Deputy Holtz. "By gee, that means law an' order's here, sure enough."

But The Masked Rider knew no barricades to any mission. San Adella might boast that no hunted man ever entered her streets and walked or rode out again; Deputy Holtz and his famous sharpshooting possemen might line each side of the long, dusty thoroughfare—yet the black outlaw determined to get through!

Now, bent double and close to flimsy rear walls, The Masked Rider wormed his way to midtown. He straightened with double vigilance, peered through stout bars and into a dimly lighted place. Withdrawing, he flitted down a driveway beside Sheriff Lackey's calaboose and office, glanced up and down the deserted street, then sped for the front door.

SHERIFF LACKEY HEARD no one enter. He went on reading a three day old newspaper. But at the first sound of a cold voice behind him, he swung chair and body in one startled, convulsive twist.

"Don't move, I said!" rapped the outlaw. He saw no reason to compliment the flabbergasted sheriff for being one of the few men who ever heard his commands the second time. "Sit down—as you were."

Lackey sat. Quickly he recovered from the stunning surprise. "Bucko," he began sharply. "This time you've picked—"

"Silence—and don't let the distance between that hand and that gun become much less, *sabe?*" Black boots made only the sounds of cat's pads as the outlaw moved forward. "You know two old people by the name of Bunson?"

Lackey looked hotly over his shoulder.

"I do—and damned glad to tell you that they're far beyond yore reach!"

The Masked Rider nodded bitterly. "Beyond reach of any human being!" he corrected frigidly. "Butchered! Buried!"

Lackey's recollection of his visitor's history made him turn carelessly. But he kept his hands full distance from the gun on his desk and the gun in his holster. Cheap life insurance! He knew the black phantom before him never fired until fired at.

"Dead?" blasted Lackey. "Yo're loco—or have you already *killed*—you mean to try an' pull some wool over my eyes? The Bunsons left town on the ten fifty-five. Plenty *dinero* with 'em, *hombre*. But you won't get yore paws on it, 'count the train doesn't even slow up 'till she—"

"The Bunsons are dead; buried in an arroyo eight miles from here."

"But—"

"We won't debate! Time's too short; your time—and mine." The black caballero backed up to the door. "Ride. Find them. Ask questions. Get answers, *sabe?*"

"You mean—"

"That if at this time tomorrow night you haven't got certain mangy coyotes, then *I'll* come and get 'em."

"You?" exploded Lackey. "Who—"

The sheriff clipped his hot words. It's useless to talk to a man who isn't in sight. Then, like a volcano erupts, Lackey snatched a gun, rushed through the doorway and boomed an alarm with all his lung power.

Other men took up the cry until all of San Adella seemed populated by maniacs shrieking, "Masked Rider!" Deputy Holtz came tearing out of a house. Possemen, armed, eager to avenge the insult to San Adella's reputation, galloped for liveries and driveways like minute men responding to battle's call.

"Split!" shouted Lackey. "Holtz! Take half the boys an' hit the north trail. Rest o'you follow me."

Fourteen horses soon thundered away in the night and San Adella returned to bed confident that again placards and tempting rewards would be hauled down to mark the passing of another outlaw foolhardy enough to cross swords with the law in this town.

IN THE REAR rooms beneath the white building topped by the cross of God, two mud-splattered punchers finished cleaning up. At ease in a comfortable chair, sprawled Big Steve McKay.

He was a bull-necked giant, well groomed, expensively dressed. His face, round and full, was perpetually lit by something closely akin to a wise smile. It was as if he never forgot to be amused by the fact that all San Adella thought he'd never even speak civilly to Reverend Proctor Hill— much less be a partner of the clergyman.

"You burned 'em right, Ed?" asked Big Steve with a chuckle. "Nobody's goin to fall over two skeletons later on?"

The door swung. Reverend Proctor Hill stormed in. A big man with too much soft meat on his bones, he was evidently hot, tired—and alarmed. No one in the stuffy room spoke as the Reverend ripped off and tossed aside his reversed collar. All eyes watched him snatch up a brown bottle and drink without benefit of a glass. All three men waited impatiently for the storm they sensed was brewing, while the Reverend bit off the end of a black cigar and puffed irately to get it burning.

Big Steve cracked. "Well? What'd the Jacksons have to say? Will they sell—or must we bury them, too?"

Smoke and a snort came from the Reverend's mouth. Ignoring the question, he faced the two punchers. Ed Sloan and Rip Dingwell grinned.

"Bunsons nicely planted, Rev," bragged Sloan. "Not a hitch!"

Hill peeled two ten dollar bills from a fat roll. He nodded towards the door. The punchers were spree-bound in a jiffy. Big Steve smiled. "What's up? Jackson's kick you out?"

"Bah! Having my own way, I'd use other methods than soft soap and this false front to get what we want—if it isn't too late."

Big Steve lacked time to reply. Bruce Garden entered, a jackal's smile wreathing his face. He took one look at Reverend and knew the false-fronted partner was badly frightened. Then Garden found greater annoyance.

"Where's Sloan and Dingwell and the other pair?"

Reverend Hill's cackle was sarcastic. "As planned, I took Mr. and Mrs. Bunson to the station. They *didn't* board the ten fifty-five train. Four masked men kidnapped them. They're buried, per your orders."

Garden frowned. "I told Sloan and—"

"To report here. Sloan and Dingwell *did*. Mescal and Quinn won't—*never*. They're dead."

Big Steve jumped out of the easy chair. Garden almost

jumped out of his shoes. "What?" they chorused. Both of them sensed the first real threat to carefully laid plans for getting control of vast acreage.

"Sloan and Dingwell went to dig the grave. Mescal and Quinn were supposed to wait for me at the shack. But when I got there to tell them to go use six-guns on the Jacksons, I found them stiff and cold."

McKay never relished the mysterious. A little alarmed, he began, "What the hell happened?"

"I don't know."

"They were all right when I left 'em," snapped Garden suspiciously. "Suppose they had an argument about splitting the pay they'll get later?"

"And ended it with bullets? When they were always closer than brothers?" Reverend's snort was insultingly bitter. "They had an argument with a *third man*."

"Sloan or—"

"The Masked Rider!" Hill got out the name like cracks of a rifle. "I doubled back expecting that by that time Sloan and Dingwell had finished the grave and would be coming along the trail. I saw the outlaw at the shack!"

"And you let him get away?" fired Big Steve.

Reverend Hill read the challenge to his courage in McKay's eyes. He let it pass. For a while he smirked at the other two who were trading puzzled glances. Through their three minds ran warning that The Masked Rider was a name to be reckoned with. All of them recalled the outlaw's history; recollections of *his* brand of justice. Reverend Hill found little comfort in his knowledge that the law pursued the outlaw even more relentlessly—and clumsily—than he pursued those who thought themselves above law.

"What's the outlaw doing in this neighborhood?" grated Hill. "I'll tell you. He saw the grave being dug or filled. He knows what's in it. He knows why they're there and he'll gun us like he gunned—"

Big Steve's eyes flamed. "Don't make the buzzard seem greater than God Almighty!" he blasted. "Right this minute, Lacey, Holtz and their posse are driving him out of the county—and he'll *stay* out."

Garden let his six foot, bony hulk slide into a chair. He smiled wisely. "No cause for alarm, Reverend. The outlaw's smart. He won't linger in these parts. Suppose he does? How many bullets needed to wipe out all he knows, everything he might intend to do—*and him?*"

But Hill found no assurance in the belligerence of his partners whom all San Adella considered his most bitter enemies. Even now he felt that piercing black eyes gleamed through the slots of a grim black hood—and centered directly upon him. A chill shook him.

"Smarter men than us have been finished by that black—"

"Forget him, Rev!" consoled Garden, "at least until he shows his hand. Then I'll show him mine—and it's the last thing he'll see." He swaggered to a chest of drawers. From the top one he picked a carefully folded paper. Spreading it on the table beneath the green shaded lamp, he studied it with Hill and Big Steve greedily glancing over his shoulders.

NEAR THE VERY center of the map, Garden, began to trace a section with a red crayon pencil. "Parcel number one," he gloated. He pencil-drummed on a section labelled "Jackson's." He looked his questions at Reverend Hill. "Parcel number two?"

"I can't swing the Bunson's daughter. Wish we'd got to Thad Jackson before he married her! If The Masked Rider—"

"Forget him, damn you!" snapped Garden. "He's an outlaw, *sabe?* There's plenty *dinero* on his head. He'll be plugged on sight by any law man—and hundreds of gents not wearing a badge. Now what about the Jacksons?"

"I think Loretta suspects I swung her parents towards selling because I profited. Anyhow, she hinted it was strange the deal went through so fast after her dad seemed set against selling."

"Suspicious?" growled Garden.

"Maybe—about what the old folks did with the cash you were supposed to have given them."

"And Thad Jackson?"

"Didn't have much to say—and those kind are *most* dangerous. He said he'd understand more about the quick deal after he'd heard from the old folks; said he'd give them time to get settled in the east and then begin to ask questions."

Garden laughed. "Get settled in the *east!*" He winked at Big Steve. Then to Reverend Hill. "Go see the Jacksons again. If they don't listen to reason, then Big Steve and Sloan and Dingwell will have to visit—with six guns poppin'."

McKay nodded. "Two more holes filled while Reverend spreads the news that the Jacksons have gone east to join Loretta's parents."

But all was not simplicity to Reverend Hill. He had nothing to say, although his sharp brown eyes were eloquent and his brain alive with one thought—The Masked Rider was in the vicinity; he'd had the audacity to issue an ulti-matum to the Sheriff.

Suddenly Ed Sloan barged in. He had made first direct contact with a posseman returned from Lackey's portion of the manhunters. Horse lamed, unable to keep up with the others, he had regretfully returned to town.

"You know why the outlaw visited the calaboose?" Sloan looked like a man being toasted on both sides simulta-neously. "He knows the Bunsons are buried. He's given Lackey twenty-four hours to dig up the bodies—*and the how-come!*"

Reverend Hill wilted like a starched collar plunged into boiling water. But Garden and Big Steve sneered.

"No harm done! Lackey can find the bodies and ask his damned questions. But *prove* something?"

Hill would not be consoled. "I've spread it far and wide that they boarded the ten fifty-five! Lackey—"

"Has great respect for that collar and church of yours!" cut in Garden like the mastermind he was. He got his snow white Stetson, crammed it on and stepped to the door. "Let's get ready to prove that The Masked Rider knew where the bodies were because *he* put 'em there."

"Lackey'll laugh at such stuff," whined Hill. "Who kills, buries—and comes to tell about the grave?"

"The Masked Rider does!" rapped Garden. "Ain't the whyfores plain? He sees himself get a coat of whitewash; another chance to pose as a caballero too good to be shot on sight, and also to blame the Bunson killings on *us*."

BIG STEVE LAUGHED. "Us poor innocents! But truth will out, *sabe*. Rev? And feelings against that black coyote will run high and wide. He'll get out of San Adella—and stay out. We'll be in sweet grass range."

Reverend Hill struggled to pull himself together. Gradually he forced himself to believe that the infamous deed—the opening gun in a campaign to make him and Big Steve and Garden fabulously wealthy—could be laid at the outlaw's door. Yet, even as he prepared to go with Garden to set the stage for the false, charge, he felt as if he was setting out for his grave.

"Lively!" commanded Garden. "Lackey'll question you sure as hell! You've got to be prepared to explain how people you see off on trains are found near home—buried."

CHAPTER V

FLAMING GUNS

I T WAS LATE afternoon when a solemn faced rider pulled up at the hitching rail of the flag bedecked Lonely Trail Saloon. Perhaps he chose that spot because four other black horses there would make his own less conspicuous; perhaps he chose it because every man not riding with Sheriff Lackey and Deputy Holtz, seemed participating in the grand opening of San Adella's newest business.

For a few minutes the rider stood beside the black stallion, his eyes roaming the holiday spirited street—and more particularly the men in sight. He judged unfavorably of both street and men. Then, turning like a man eternally on guard, he moved towards the half-doors of the drinking place.

Just over the threshold he paused again, to survey a beehive of activity and hilarity as if it held a threat against his life. The bar was lined three deep with bantering, shouting men; some in range rig, some in store clothes, but all of them sporting six guns. From the rear of the smoke-hazed place came the screech of three fiddles hopelessly out of tune and time. Flanking the sawing players, four women surviving earlier experience in cowtown dance halls, lent their squeaky voices to the discord that hurt the newcomer's ears.

He dropped into a chair at the lone unoccupied table. A white aproned man hustling drinks to the other seated patrons, stopped a moment, got his order, grunted and moved on. But even he was conscious of the fact that this customer was different from all the others. He was cleaner, better rigged, and had about him an air that said he wanted neither friend or foe.

His name was Wayne Morgan and he was entirely aware of the great risk he was exposing himself to—in a cause of two old friends buried in an arroyo. He knew that here he might encounter one of the extreme few who might have grounds for suspecting that Wayne Morgan and The Masked Rider were one; or even gain the perilous recognition of some one from the Rio Grande country who knew him as Morgan—on business bent!

He did not betray the fact that he studied face after face, listened tensely to singled-out voices—in deep rooted hopes of matching them with what he'd seen and heard in a moonlight washed arroyo. Nor did he give outward sign of knowing that a big, immaculately attired man was watching him like a cat at a mousehole. Least of all did Morgan display his feelings that in spite of song, music, jest and laugh, the very air seemed alive with a promise—of violent death.

Big Steve McKay shuffled over to the solemn stranger's

table. "Howd'y!" he grinned. Uninvited, openly not wanted, he nevertheless lowered his bulk into a chair that creaked under his two hundred and ten pounds of solid meat. "Ever see such an opening, stranger?"

MORGAN'S SMILE WAS cold—because somehow he could not shake the premonition that death and dead line were closer. "Once," he said neutrally, anxious eyes on the street doors. "Arizona."

"Reverend Proctor Hill's maybe tearing his hair out— damn him! He allowed San Adella didn't need another saloon. What's sky pilots know about what makes a town grow? He reckons—You just light in?"

"I did."

"Figger locating here steady like?"

"Depending."

Big Steve smiled—while his first suspicions grew. Who was this *hombre* who used words as if they cost a thousand dollars apiece; this *hombre* who made no bones about not giving a damn whether you are friendly or not?

"You look like a business man, stranger. You're no common cowpoke, I'll swear. If—"

He clipped that as a weasel-faced man shoved through the doors and blustered to the bar. Morgan, too, let his attention drift to the late comer—especially the badge on the dust coated vest.

"Drill-'em first Holtz," whispered Big Steve. "His equal in gun play ain't ever been—Hell! Won't be long before *he's* telling *everybody*."

True prophesy! The Deputy, long, snake-eyed and small-mouthed, burly, spun on a gnarled old man who had piped a question.

"*See* him? Wish to God I had! They'd print no more posters about that black coyote—and I'd be the happiest man alive. You got no idea how hungry I am to face that polecat who hides behind a black hood! I'll let him grip his Colt butts before my hands start for my holsters. And I'll wager to lay a neat row of lead straight across his middle."

Big Steve winked at Morgan. "He could! Fact! He's lightning fast. Fires with right hand smoke piece pointing left an' left hand one roaring to the right. You heard of Scissors Blane—who figgered to cut his man in half with lead? That's Holtz's style. He ain't ever come from the man hunt without somethin' to show for it. Well, sounds like *this* time he ain't got corpse or prisoner."

Morgan nodded. "It does."

The big fellow's smile hid an itch to choke the stranger who couldn't be drawn from his shell. McKay thought awhile, then with a bland grin, "What'd you say was your business in town?"

The outlaw meant to answer curtly. But to forestall even clipped response, a young fellow, clean-cut, agile as a timberwolf, shouldered into the saloon. Morgan judged him to be in the early twenties; the frontier youth who's a man before his time—and in whose eyes is the glint of one determined to tackle dangerous business that might result in life snuffed out.

Some one called, "Howd'y, Thad!" An old timer beamed and offered to "break the last Jackson's record for bein' teetotaler." But the young man pushed on as though deaf—until he reached the side of Deputy Holtz who was still wind-jamming as to The Masked Rider's fate if he showed face again in San Adella.

SUDDENLY THE DEPUTY felt hostile eyes upon him. He turned with a snort, to gimlet Thad Jaskson with narrowed orbs. Thad was immune. He glared back at the towering Deputy.

"You gonna ask Reverend Proctor Hill how come my in-laws are *buried* when he says he put 'em on the eastbound cars?"

"Sheriff Lackey'll hold the inquest, Thad."

"Lackey's chasin' a shadow. You're here—an' when Lackey ain't, you're sheriff. I mean to waltz along to the church with you. Hill's there now. Time needn't be wasted, *sabe?*"

"We'll wait for—"

"We'll *go*—or *I* will!"

Morgan watched tensely. His heart opened for the youth with courage enough to call the deputy in his own bivouac, and the outlaw instantly caught the murderous tension that always crackled when Holtz's dignity or badge was besmirched.

"Who's he?" inquired Morgan of smirking Big Steve.

"Thad Jackson."

"That I heard. I asked you who he is."

For a second there was promise of the storm brewing at the bar being duplicated at the outlaw's table. But Big Steve had never gazed into eyes such as were now before him. He took water gracefully, hoping the mysterious stranger's tone would modulate.

"Son-in-law of old John Bunson and missus. Reckon he's still feeling his wedding day oats. Ain't been married more'n a month, to Loretta."

The outlaw's face was blank with shammed indifference. Inside of him a blaze had been rekindled. Loretta Bunson!

Instantly Morgan saw himself ringed by Winchester-armed men, escape impossible for any legged man or creature larger than a chipmunk—until the girl's ruse broke the grim ring and held it open just long enough to let the hunted man slip through.

"Loretta," said the outlaw under his breath—his eyes on her husband, now wrathfully headed for the street.

Deputy Holtz snapped alive. "Hold on, you!" He took four quick strides—and the movements of his expert hands made other men scurry for cover. "Yo're startin' no ruckus in this town, *sabe?* Not with God's man! I'll put you under lock an' key first!"

The youth kept going. Holtz stiff legged behind. Venom of long standing differences between Thad and himself helped twist his ruthless mouth.

"You damned little squirt o' poison, I'll—"

The kid spun. His hooked fingers winged toward holster. He didn't know how or what happened. But in the next breath his wrist was gripped vise like. He jerked his face around. Eyes blazing with anger were squelched by the friendliness and good advice in other eyes beneath a black sombrero.

"I wouldn't, brother," said the outlaw quietly. "He's law, *sabe?*"

"But in front of this crowd he called me a—"

"Hurt as much as scissoring lead? Be smart. Let it slide."

"An' keep away from that church!" bellowed Holtz. "If you don't, brother-in-law or no, you'll cool off behind bars."

WHEN MORGAN LET the half door swing behind Thad's back, he turned to find Holtz with head thrown back and the dregs of a drink entering his mouth. The outlaw's brain teemed with questions—most of which gave birth to their own answers. He walked back to his table where Big Steve still sat, repeatedly asking himself how in the name of ninety holies, Stella Bunson, Loretta's sister, came to marry the windjammer who itched for fight only as an excuse to cut Thad down! For already he had learned that both Bunson girls were married—Loretta to Thad Jackson, and Stella to Deputy Holtz.

"Wasted energy—and damned dangerous," commented Big Steve gladly. "They'll shoot it out some day. That's in the cards." He chuckled. "Don't put your chips on Thad! Holtz'll kill him three times before the kid reaches a butt and— What'd you say was your business, stranger?"

Morgan got up. "Hardware, mister." There was a strained smile playing around the outlaw's mouth.

Big Steve wasn't adept at hearing unspoken words. He was glad to get the information; glad to learn the stranger wasn't the representative of big business—that might be interested in a new oil field.

"Hardware! Well, by God, San Adella would sure enough welcome you. She'll need hardware, mister. Big—"

"Lots of it—mebbe. *Adios.*"

The outlaw left the Lonely Trail fully cognizant of Deputy Holtz looking daggers into his back. He shrugged. "Bullets later? *Quien sabe?*"

Through swift gathering dusk, the outlaw rode cautiously out of town. Slow moving horsemen loomed ahead. Morgan astutely shed the weary, sullen stares of Lackey and his returning possemen. Other thoughts stirred in the outlaw's mind; grim thoughts that mostly converged upon himself.

Friends dead. One daughter, Deputy Holtz's wife; the

other, younger, recently wed to a youth destined to be Holtz's victim. Bob Bunson coming. Precious oil lands ripe for uncovering.

"Hell's due to pop!" Morgan told himself, wondering why Deputy Holtz showed so little interest in running down the killers of his wife's aged parents. "Hell's due to pop—but *no other Bunson gets hurt!*"

Grim resolution! Yet one thing quailed the outlaw. He felt that before long, he and Holtz would face each other, guns in hand. That seemed destined. Could he hurl lead at the Deputy; shoot the husband of a former benefactress, knowing that indirectly he was hurting *her?*

CHAPTER VI

IDEAS

BLUE HAWK HAD worked expeditiously. Black night found him hovering about the smallest of fires. Meat simmered in a skillet and even as he turned it, the Indian's every sense was on guard. The Law prowled the badlands! He'd seen fagged out possemen, all night, all day on the hunt. Fire, even so guardedly tended, might lure suspicious eyes—when The Masked Rider was there.

Suddenly the copper-skinned one stood tense. Only *his* ears could have caught that sound! He peered into inky night, turned to rigid steel and listened with bated breath.

It was closer now, plainer. The muffled sob that must be from a woman. Then, almost at his elbow, there was the slightest scrape of boot and stone. Blue Hawk spun around, going for his gun. His hand dropped; his eyes dilated.

"*Senor!* You—"

"Heard?" The Masked Rider's voice was hushed. "*Si!* We wait."

The Indian never debated the black Caballero's decisions. Yet he couldn't down his opinion. "Woman with cat's eyes no see this fire, *senor*—unless she trail me here before dark. Mebbe she wait? Mebbe now she see you, she come close?"

"Let the fire burn but keep out of sight." As the words flowed from under the black hood, the outlaw moved to meet the strange prowler.

At first he saw only a small white splotch. Then from the shadows of a deep and dark dry wash, stepped a figure so utterly out of place that the outlaw was gripped by suspicion.

He came from behind a boulder. As expected, the woman cried out and shrank. The Masked Rider glimpsed a panicky white face and terror widened eyes. But they alone could not have plunged him into such floundering amazement. Yet there was no danger of his revealing that he recognized Stella Bunson, Deputy Holtz's wife.

The Masked Rider soon knew that no matter what else had happened to her since their last meeting, Stella had lost none of her courage. Now she had shed the routing shock of his popping up in front of her, and she looked him square in the eye; almost mutely demanding that he clear out of her path or at least state his business.

"You walk a dangerous trail, ma'am," he opened gently. "Where to?"

"The—the border."

The outlaw felt no tinge of anger; no desire to comment caustically. Smoothly he said, "Four hundred miles. Afoot.

And now headed straight *west*. Still I have reason to believe you."

"I—I didn't leave San Adella afoot. My horse broke its leg. I had already started back to town. I—I—"

"*Sabe*. You're just plain lost? Likely enough, considering that you changed your mind about leaving these parts." A sharpness akin to accusation crept into the outlaw's tone. "I think you better tell me all about it—the truth."

The woman dared step closer to the black statue. "I don't generally share my troubles with strangers."

The Masked Rider smiled gently. "This time you *do!*"

MEN, HARD AND armed, seldom disobeyed the black Caballero's commands. Stella might have. But a gust of wind came ladened with the aroma of simmering meat and she felt that she stood at least half accused of having spied upon the outlaw's camp.

"I was running away from—from my husband. I just *happened* to come this way. I didn't—"

"And not many minutes ago you said you were headed back."

"Because I knew then that I couldn't go on without—without Buddy."

He didn't have to ask who Buddy might be. The answer was on Stella's face. "Most women folks think of their sons before they light out, ma'am!"

She turned squarely towards the full moon. Trembling fingers decorously bared her shoulder. The red welt of a quirt blow was as vivid as red string laid upon white flesh.

"He'd have killed me if I'd taken time to think."

"The Deputy?"

She nodded. "When he had to come home without

you—after months of bragging about how he'd finish you off—he was like a mad dog."

"Does he always let off steam by abusing you? And you'd go back for more—for the boy's sake?"

"I—I'd stay, get some money together and the next time—"

The outlaw turned his face. His shrill whistle ripped the night. The black stallion soon nudged the black cloak with silky nose. Mounting, The Masked Rider asked neither consent nor permission to pick up the fragile Stella and share his saddle.

"Maybe there won't be a *next time*, ma'am. If there is, maybe there'll be nothing for you to run from. *Sabe?*"

"You mean—"

"Ten feet separated the Deputy and me. He didn't have much to say. We'll meet again someday. Maybe sooner than he'd like—if he lifts a hand against you again!"

"And you'd dare?"

"I'm taking you close to town."

"But the risk!"

"*Close,* I said. Where I go, the risks are small."

They rode in strange silence. Twice Stella glanced up at the grim black hood and confessed to herself that only once before in all her life had she felt so strongly attracted by a man. The last time was in Texas, so long ago that she suddenly felt old. His face she saw now in her mind—and would never forget. His name she had never learned. Yet he left a scar upon her heart. Dead, they told her some months later; gunned down by a posse not unlike that from which her family had helped him escape.

And twice, the outlaw glanced down at his charge, nestling tight against him so that he could feel the thump of her heart. Texas! Years ago. A street ankle deep with dust. A girl. A dream of a modest spread, a proud brand, a ranch house shaded by cottonwoods. Shots—and dreams turned to cold, worthless ashes.

Now, behind the black hood that was the only brand he could ever hope to own, the outlaw dreamed his dream again—and to snap him back to earth, came the sudden clatter of frantic hoofs.

FOR A SPLIT-SECOND The Masked Rider's hand was poised to dart for Colt butt. Just as quick he realized that while those hoof beats had been born close at hand, they were those of a retreating horse. The outlaw checked the stallion's habitual bolt from contact with other riders in the night. He sat holding the alarmed Stella and wondering.

"W-what was that?"

The outlaw's laugh was short and lifeless. "That? The first *hombre* to pass up a chance to collect certain prizes! I'm wondering *why!*"

"You've got to turn back!" urged Stella. "Whoever it was may spread news that you're headed for town. The posse and Sheriff Lackey might ambush you."

But The Masked Rider nudged the stallion on. "Sometimes," he ventured drily, "A man sets his mind on doing something—and *does it*. Sometimes he also changes his mind about which trail he'll use—when eight or nine lead to the same town."

Then in swift, noiseless flight, the gallant black carried double across country.

Sheriff Lackey dropped the bay's lines over the Lonely Trail hitching rail and started up the saloon steps. Forty-three, grey and thin as a bean pole, he was one of those down-grade men who sometimes tap a reserve supply of energy and keep going. Almost twenty-four hours in saddle and badlands were wiped away by a drink and a sandwich. Then, tugging up hot chaps and settling his six-gun anew, he walked gingerly from the saloon—towards the Reverend Proctor Hill's church.

He knocked sedately on the rectory door. He knocked again, patently awed by the building and the man he expected to admit him. A bolt slid back. Lackey's "Howd'y, Reverend," ended in an astonished gape, for the Sheriff saw Thad Jackson pacing behind the sad-eyed clergyman.

"Come in, Sheriff," husked the Reverend. "I suppose you want to ask the same questions Thad asked?"

Lackey doffed his sombrero. His face apologized for his visit. "Yo're sure the old Bunsons got away on the ten fifty-five, Reverend!"

"Certainly! I've just explained to Thad that friends of mine were passing through San Adella on the same train. I put the Bunsons under their wing." Repetition made it easy for Will to adhere to Garden's cooked up story.

"You got no idea then how come they're buried here?"

"Oh yes! You see, when I first heard the sad news—even before Thad called here—I immediately started an investigation." Hill took a much folded yellow paper from his rectory coat pocket. "This is a telegram from my friends."

Lackey squinted at sprawled words. He looked up gravely. "Then chances are that the coyote who got 'em to leave the cars at the next stop—

"Was The Masked Rider!" appended Hill. "And so anxious to get his filthy hands on the Bunson money that he dropped his badge—the black hood."

THE SHERIFF THUMBED up his sombrero and scratched over one ear. "But why in the Lord's name did he fetch 'em all the way back here?"

"That," put in Thad Jackson quietly, "is what we'll get out of his own mouth—when we've a noose around his mangy neck!"

"Guilty as sin!" ejaculated Hill. "And the blackguard tries to have suspicion point elsewhere."

"Hadn't looked at it in that light," drawled Lackey. "Hadn't ought to—considerin' the *hombre's* history. Outlaw, I'll grant you. Rope or lead *is* his due. But *this* job was done by a coyote I wouldn't have tied behind a loco steer an' dragged to ribbons."

Reverend took out his faked telegram. "False-fronted buzzard! Reminds me of cancer beneath soft white skin. He'd kill his own mother for profit or—"

"But I ain't never heard of him killin' for *cash*," insisted Lackey.

"To get two birds with one stone?" Reverend snorted in disgust. Time to play the ace Garden had given him. "When you came in I was just about to tell Thad something that will make this hideous thing less of a mystery. A few days ago I spoke to old man Bunson. Our talk got around to outlaws. He said that four years ago—before he came to these parts—he'd crossed The Masked Rider's trail. He insisted that he *did* put several bullets into the outlaw, even if he didn't bring him to book."

Thad Jackson started. "You think that polecat came to square up? That only dumb luck brought him here when the old man's poke was heavy with cash?"

Reverend nodded. "More than likely! I know of a similar case; father and three sons butchered in cold blood by the *good* outlaw—because they happened to stumble on his camp site and tip off the local sheriff. Three years later the outlaw came to square up."

"Got nothin' to do with the Bunsons," said Lackey thickly. He reached for the doorknob. "Guess I'll—"

"It has plenty to do with *other* Bunsons," clipped Hill. "Perhaps the black coyote will try and make further collections for the old man's bullets!"

Thad's chin sagged. "You mean he'd dare come back—to get Loretta and Stella?"

"Wouldn't surprise me to find him gunning for *all* Bunsons. A blessing if the girls' brother Bob doesn't show up until the outlaw's planted."

Thad stared at Lackey. "What you goin' to do about it, Sheriff?"

Lackey straddled the threshold. "What can anybody do about a coyote who disappears like gun smoke when any one gets within a quarter mile o' him? This I swear—that 'till he is stretched out, effort to do such won't be spared."

THE DOOR CLOSED slowly behind the officer. Reverend Hill, inwardly purring with the ecstasy of successful lies, turned almost morosely to Thad.

"No intention of alarming you, son. But forewarned is fore-armed."

"If that black mongrel harms either Loretta or Stella, I'll burn out his eyes." Thad's fingers gripped the holster at his thigh. "I owe him plenty *now*. And when Bob pulls in, we'll team up, stay in the badlands 'till a black hood and mantilla goes into the same hole as the skunk who wears 'em!"

"Waste effort, son," counselled Hill. "Wiser, safer, easier—to get out of harm's way."

"You mean take up Bruce Garden's offer?"

Hill was at his double-front best tonight. He made a wry face. "I hate the man and all he represents—yet his offer is more than fair. I'd take it. I'd forget Loretta's poor parents. I'd get away from San Adella."

The youth looked sick. "Put my tail down an' run; advertise that I'm as yeller as *he* is rotten?" He looked up and straight into Hill's cold eyes. He had nothing to say. But the negative nod of his head was positive assurance that he wouldn't be driven out by anyone.

CHAPTER VII

VISITORS

B IG STEVE MCKAY gulped the last drink in the brown bottle, shoved back his chair, got up and stretched prodigiously. Beneath his feet sounded the mirth of excellent business in the Lonely Trail Saloon. In front of Big Steve, slouched down in a new chair, Bruce Garden drank in those pleasing sounds and smiled wisely.

In both their eyes was premature rapture over attained power, fame and colossal fortune; a dream of empire with San Adella their capital.

"We'll own both sides of Main Street from Corbin's Creek to a mile t'other side of the railroad," purred Garden. "We'll own every inch of oil land within ten miles of town. I'll make you Governor of the whole damned State or put you any place you want to be put."

"Unless," scowled Big Steve, "The Reverend puts us all in the soup—if not the noose."

Garden chuckled. "He's bedded down and I'm night-hawking him right careful. He won't stampede."

"Scared stiff of The Masked Rider. No telling—"

"Masked Rider be damned! I've got two irons in the fire. In time, I'll brand him, *sabe?* I'll plant him right at the Lonely Trail's doorsteps."

"Two irons?"

Garden nodded. "One I'm not talking about—yet. But when you see Matt Frost in town, you'll know the other one is plenty hot and ready for business."

"Frost?" exclaimed Steve. "*Killer* Frost?"

"Two reasons why I sent Eddie Sloan to fetch him! Mostly because he can't be tied when it comes to reading sign and finding what's to be found. *He'll* learn where the outlaw's ranging—and put holes in more than the black mantilla."

Big Steve was far from pleased. "Chameleon!" he snapped. "Frost ain't much interested in anybody but himself. He's your worst enemy—two minutes after he's been your best friend."

Garden lit a cigar. Smiling, he watched a smoke ring drift ceilingward. "He'll handle the outlaw. I'll handle *him*—and so keep Reverend in line. Rev's damned important to us, *sabe?*"

"Don't know about that! Six guns would get us as much as his soft soap will ever get us. We've gotten away with the Bunson thing."

"We couldn't get away with many more such killings! There's justice in Sheriff Lackey's eyes and Holtz is just rarin' to smoke somebody up. Better let Reverend handle the crowd that we want to buy out. He'll talk 'em into selling."

"Meanwhile—"

"Meanwhile take Dingwell and Sloan—soon's he comes back—and go settle the Jacksons. That'll be safe—if Reverend's obeyed orders. It'll be chalked up against The Masked Rider." Garden prepared to go out. "To see if iron *number two* is going to be any damned good," he volunteered.

"And watch Reverend! Hear?"

Garden laughed.

THE REVEREND PROCTOR HILL was bolstered by the visit of Thad Jackson and Sheriff Lackey. "Sure squirmed out of a bad corner that time," he complimented himself as he prepared for bed. "Garden sure knows how to smooth things over—and get the most birds per stone."

But in one corner of the Reverend's mind lurked fearful uneasiness. The Masked Rider. As if so insignificant a thing would somehow protect him, Reverend let a small lamp burn when he crawled beneath blankets.

For a while he feasted on glowing dreams of the future. What wouldn't he do with the wealth wrung out by six gun and smooth tongue? With millions at his command—

His dreams exploded. He bolted upright in bed, fingers clutching the blanket tight about his throat. For a second he dared hope he'd imagined things. But it came again; the slow, stealthy stride of some one in the church who must now be mighty close to the pulpit where candles flickered. Half a dozen more steps and that someone would be at the inside entrance to his rooms!

Hill flung blankets aside. With a wheeze of panic he flashed across the room, snatching up a robe as he passed a chair. Trembling hands inched open a drawer, groped in it, came out with a finger threaded through a Colt's trigger guard. On stockinged tiptoes, Hill moved to the church door.

He opened up an inch and peered out. On the wall was the flickering shadow of the crucifix at the pulpit. Hill's eyes furtively swept the row on row of empty pews and seats. Then he sucked in one great breath of heaven sent relief.

A bared, bowed head showed over the top of one bench. Hill smiled wanly. Some poor fool, harassed with trouble and chilly night, had come through always unlocked doors to seek comfort and guidance—at this blasphemous mockery of a shrine of God. Hill dropped the Colt into a pocket and tied the strings of the robe. Quickly he slid his feet into slippers. He went out to the praying man.

The man got up; a heavy-eyed, weary old man—at thirty odd. His face was that of a man who was not yet fully recovered from the shock of some devastating news.

Hill, hand raised and eyes skyward, cut the other's apologies for the intrusion. "The house of God knows no hour," he chanted. "I'm glad you came in—although I don't know who you are or what burdens you."

"Bob Bunson," announced the man as if ashamed of it. "I jest heard that my dad—"

"Bunson!" breathed Hill. Instantly he seized the opportunity to make an ally for himself and partners and an enemy for The Masked Rider. He rattled off his story, then, breathless, fished for a prompt decision as to what the grim, short-spoken arrival would do. "You're not staying in town—considering that the outlaw may have marked *all* Bunsons for slaughter? The safest course is often the wisest."

BUNSON'S HAND MOVED from his gun. It settled level with his shoulder—on the pulpit's massive bible. "He pays!" he squeezed out. "If he wasn't alone, *they* pay."

Hill understood the solemnity of the oath, the grimly clenched lips, the abrupt manner in which the visitor departed. The Reverend grinned. Men who say little about what they's going to do, most times *do it!*

"I've got a notion that The Masked Rider will find these parts entirely too damned hot for him," mused Hill, starting back for bed.

How long he lay wide awake, gloating over the promises of death for the outlaw, Hill did not know. But suddenly the breath was hammered out of him, his heart leaped up into his throat and every inch of him went clammy cold with stark panic—all brought about by a mere shadow on his bedroom wall.

For a second he dared not move even an eyelid. Then he screwed his eyes around in their sockets, looked out of their corners while his teeth chattered.

Beside the open window stood an apparition in black; terrifying aspects enhanced by statuesque pose—save for the black-gloved hand slowly, surely, reaching for the dimly burning lamp. The hand flattened out. It turned palm down. Like a jack knife drawbridge that weighed a thousand tons, it settled down on the lamp chimney. The wick smoked a moment. The light leaped, broke, caught again—like some live thing fighting for air that meant life. But the black glove sealed the chimney top and the light flickered out.

Moonlight centered its silver flood squarely on the Reverend's bed. He sat upright, a wheezing, wild-eyed marauder sensing a well-deserved disaster. He wanted to shout for help. His mouth was cotton dry; his vocal cords paralyzed.

From some doubtful spot in the darkness came the black Caballero's voice. "The law let the dead line pass—and did nothing. Now tell *me* why the old Bunsons are buried in an arroyo."

Hill took heart. Certainly nothing in those lifeless words warned of ruthlessness or denied him a fair hearing. He thawed his tongue.

"I saw them safely off from the station. They—"

"They were on the train—or in the hands of killers working under your orders?"

The Reverend rallied further courage. "You come into the house of God—"

"To stomp on a side-winding son of Satan? Yes! And I don't argue with him. *Sabe?* I asked you!"

"They—they were on the train. I *proved* that to Sheriff Lackey and Thad Jackson."

"By a telegram?"

"Y-yes."

"And after the operator in the switch tower obeyed your orders to write the *fake* message you ran a dagger into his back—so he wouldn't tell about writing *while a gun covered him.*"

"No! I didn't—"

"You didn't leave a black hood just outside the switch-tower door—*my brand.* You didn't leave the operator dead—and the switch for the Eastern Limited wide open?"

"I didn't—"

"Give a damn how many died as long as you lived and went on scheming? *That* we know. Now we want the names of the two coyotes who buried the Bunsons. *Pronto!*"

BEADS OF PERSPIRATION gathered on Hill's greyed temples. They ran together, then down his flabby cheeks in little shivering rivers. His eyes, those of a cornered rat, lacked even the rodent's courage born of death's fears. In a few fleeting seconds his spinning head was cleansed of every thought of vast power and wealth. All he yearned to possess now was life itself—and the threat to that, he read in the arm and hand that was shifting under the sombre black mantilla. He gulped twice, and so hard that his double chin shook like disturbed jelly. But he could not talk.

"The names!" rapped the outlaw. The nose of a Colt stared out from the cloak's folds. "Or do you die with them unsaid?"

"Y-you—you wouldn't drill an empty handed man?"

"Man?" gritted The Masked Rider. "Coyotes with three legs broken have deserved that name better than you. The names, *hombre*—before that clock ticks ten more times."

Few men could have issued so calm and smooth an ultimatum—knowing that just outside the open window had sounded the step of a prowler and spy! The outlaw, fully aware that either shot or shout would bring the entire town down upon him, shifted his position and split his mind between the window and the quaking man upon the bed.

Hill, nerve-wrecked, pulse sledge-hammering, licked thick lips arid by terror. "T-they forced me to—"

"Who? Why? Talk!"

"T-there's oil here, *sabe?* They found the sign first and asked me into a partnership. I didn't think—think there'd be any bloodshed or—"

"No lamenting! No excuses! Just *names!*"

The Reverend swallowed hard. His lips parted. He began

to speak a name. He clipped it at the first syllable. Eyes round as saucers were on the window—particularly the lower right hand corner where showed an inch of head and the business end of a sixgun.

Things happened even as Hill cried out in mortal terror. The gun boomed. A finger of flame lit the bedroom for a second. The Reverend's death cry was drowned by the frantic screams of a man outdoors.

"Masked Rider!" yelled Bruce Garden, tearing down along the north side of the church, firing shots in the air. "Masked Rider!"

San Adella came to life as if it had long awaited the alarm. From across the dusty street, Sheriff Lackey came on legs that moved like driving rods on a speeding locomotive. Men came from saloons both north and south as if carried forth by the crest of a flood.

The outlaw long since weighed his chances of successful flight. Scores of times his black mantilla had safely seen him through lead showers. But now he must run through a veritable cloudburst of metal. Nor long delay the start!

"The rectory!" shrilled Garden. He led the charge of men with weapons ready.

THE MASKED RIDER silently stepped into the church proper. Passively he listened to scurrying feet—bound for the exit he must use if he would reach the stallion ground-roped behind the church's long shed in the rear.

Flattened against the inner wall near the rectory door, the outlaw waited with a hymn book in each hand. Jabbering voices drifted in through Hill's open bedroom window. The Masked Rider's eyes were on the stained glass of the church window. A hymn book swished through the darkness. Colored glass crashed and showered down. The moon laughed in through the jagged hole.

"Side window!" harked a man. "South side window!"

The outlaw's mouth tilted with a bitter smile. Deputy Holtz was on the job! "South window!" gritted The Masked Rider. Then he cannonballed through the rectory and crossed the sill of Hill's bedroom window like a great black cloth viciously flung into the night.

In those few seconds before he struck full racing stride, the outlaw knew his ruse had partly failed—that three men were ready for him; that three guns were eager to spit lead and fire. In a fleeting glance stolen as he rushed pellmell, the outlaw recognized all three. Sheriff Lackey. Deputy Holtz. But the face that chilled The Masked Rider's blood, was the face of Bob Bunson!

Three guns barked as one. The outlaw distinctly felt the tug of three pieces of lead. But holes in his black cloak only served to make it stand less stiff in the breeze of his own making. He dashed on, knowing that already many other men were aware of trickery and rushing towards the rear of the church for a shot at the fleeting target.

Twice more The Masked Rider distinguished the rupture of cloth by lead. Then he was at the corner of the shed. He stopped as if a bullet had pierced heart or brain; not to fall, but to pivot with the suddenness that had more than once saved his life. There was nothing of haste in the parting of his riddled cloak; nothing of haste in the single shot he fired—at Deputy Holtz. Then swift as a black arrow, he bolted for his stallion.

Men hurled futile lead at the only target they could make out—the rapidly dying hoofbeats of a horse and rider they could not see streaking in the shadows of aspens bordering Corbin's winding creek.

Bedlam reigned at the rear of the church. For a few minutes, Deputy Holtz was shaken—and pained by a slight wound in his shoulder. Something persisted in telling him that had the black phantom so willed, that wound would have been in his *heart*. But Holtz was conscious of the strange stares of some of the crowd. He thought that at any moment someone might ask where was the often promised result of an outlaw-deputy lead debate?

"Horses!" snapped Holtz. "We're runnin' him down this time, so help me God!"

One man lurked in the shadows. His hard eyes were bright with wisdom and pleasure. His name was Bruce Garden. Abruptly he slunk off—like a man who knows whither he's bound and what he intends doing there while afforded splendid opportunity.

CHAPTER VIII

PROPOSITIONS

B RUCE GARDEN HAD happy thoughts while watching to make certain Deputy Holtz would lead hard-riding, straight-shooting men out of town in pursuit of the black phantom.

"Iron number two!" he mused, heading for the Deputy's house. "Reckon the deputy was in too big a rush to lock up behind him."

He tested the door, grinning as it gave way beneath his cautious pressure. At the head of narrow stairs glowed a tiny night lamp. Garden climbed with an oath for every creaking tread.

He peered into two rooms before he made out the labored breathing of a troubled sleeper. Lamp in steady hand, feeling safe to take his own good time, he walked casually to Stella Holtz's bedside. Setting the lamp on a chair, he smiled as he reached for the blankets bunched around the woman's slim shoulders.

Stella stirred. At the second tug she opened her eyes. She blinked as one seeing the impossible. Then, certain it was Garden, she shuddered and shrank from his touch.

"We'll get along fine—if you're as sensible as pretty," he grinned. "And no danger of the deputy interrupting us. He's lit out after The Masked Rider and—"

"Get out of here!"

"Yes ma'am! When you tell me where the outlaw's nest is!"

Stella seemed to fear for his sanity. "Tell you where—"

"Surprised I know you shared his saddle?" Garden's eyes narrowed. "I'd have drilled him *then*, if I hadn't been fool enough to dislike going heeled."

"It—it was *you* we heard?"

"Yes ma'am. But I'll keep it as secret as you'll keep the whole *affair, sabe?* I'm not the cuss who sees the deputy's wife gallivanting with the blackguard and tells about it—if she'll steer me to his nest."

"You think—"

"I *know* what Holtz'll do if he hears of such goings on."

Stella stared at the intruder; defiantly, although she did fear his tongue. "I was lost. He merely gave me a lift to town."

"Maybe so. But in San Adella, Garden's word is heavier

than the word of the accused woman. And in the telling, some yarns can be made to sound damned sour, *sabe?*"

"I won't listen to such swine as you!"

"For money then? Plenty to buy tickets for you and Buddy; plenty to set you up elsewhere?"

"Skunk!" Stella snapped. "Get out of here. Go peddle your lies—and perhaps people will be as anxious to hear that you were mighty set on finding the outlaw. *Why?*"

Garden tried to control the temper of frustration. "Because it's every man's duty to help lead that coyote down!" His hand lashed out for Stella's throat. "Maybe I can choke it out of you, you little wanton."

She pulled away with a shrill cry. But the long, thin fingers did not fall short of their mark the second time.

"Where's his nest, damn you?" snarled Garden. He squeezed until his knuckles cracked and the woman's face went ghastly blue. "Where's his nest, you little—"

HE JERKED HIS face around—too late to do anything about the man charging upon him. He let his victim drop, spun, tried to cover up, but a steel-like fist crashed into his face and he fell prone upon the bed across the woman's feet.

"Bob!" gasped Stella. She sank back upon her pillow in a dead faint.

Garden got up shaking cobwebs from his brain. Rallying his jarred wits, he rushed at Bob Bunson with a rabid oath. Bob side-stepped a blow that might have squashed his mouth. His fist cracked below Garden's ear. Bruce went down in a forward pitch. He didn't move again.

Shouldering the boney hulk as he would a dead dog, Bob packed him down the stairs and into the driveway beside the house. He dumped him without ceremony, dry washed his hands and went back to his sister.

"You know where that black coyote is camping?" he asked aghast.

She sobbed the story of the chance meeting. "I know where he picked me up."

"Get dressed. I'll wait downstairs. We're going there—now." He saw her wince. "You're not glad to help me square for dad an' ma!"

Stella shook her head. "I can't believe he'd do such things. I won't lead you to his camp—and your grave."

"*His* grave!" clipped Bob. "And even shootin' in the back's too good for him. I've heard—"

"You've heard everybody's side of the story except his. He didn't—couldn't—do the things Garden and the Reverend Hill accuse him of."

"Couldn't? Why, damn his rotten soul, he's just killed Hill—unarmed—in bed; without half a chance. Because he was afraid that more truth would out; afraid that Hill had the goods on him."

"But—"

"Why you sidin' with the buzzard? Was Garden right? You've met that mangy hound more'n once—behind the deputy's back? You *are* in love with him? You *would* shield the killer of dad an' ma?"

"I—"

"You'll get dressed for ridin'!" flared Bob. "I'll give you ten minutes—then take you as you are!"

He started out; a hurricane of fury and lust for justice as he saw it.

"Bob!" cried Stella. "Listen to me! I'll take you to the

spot where I met the outlaw once—if you promise to keep your hand away from your gun."

"An' let him add another notch to his? No, by God! I'll give him warning an' time to draw. Then I'm killin' him just like—"

"Then go find him on your own!"

Bob stared at her. In her determined eyes he read faith that would not be shaken—and a resolution that if he compelled her to ride with him now, she'd deliberately steer him away from any possible chance of meeting the man he sought.

"What good is promising to keep clear of guns?" he weakened. "What would you have me do? Ask him if he killed dad an' ma? You think he'd tell truth?"

"I know he would. I know he didn't—and I feel that he'll even convince you that all the things said about him are lies: with a purpose behind them."

HE SURRENDERED. "ALL right. We'll ride. I promise there won't be gunplay—unless he convicts hisself by startin' it."

Bob stormed from the room. Stella began to dress; fearfully, for a premonition of close pressing tragedy suddenly seized her. Why, she did not know, but she felt that death lurked at her elbow; dogged her every step prepared to strike without warning. Once she heard hurried footsteps in the driveway beside the house. She glanced timidly out of the window. A black shadow just disappearing around the rear corner of the house, tore at her nerves. She fled down the stairs.

Bellowing horses were glad of a respite and like possemen in the saddles, remained quiet and patiently awaited the rider coming down from the north.

Sheriff Lackey pulled away from the group on the knoll and went to meet the approaching one. "Ain't Holtz," drifted over Lackey's shoulder, "But mebbe he sighted the deputy."

The posseman shook his head when Lackey inquired. "Ain't seen him since we lit out, Sheriff."

Lackey frowned. "I saw his hoss kinda limpin'. I'm *hopin'* he turned back."

"Hopin'?" exclaimed the posseman. He didn't like the Sheriff's inflection. "You ain't hintin' that something might have happened to Holtz?"

"Of three men behind the church, that black buzzard elected to try an' plug *Holtz*." Lackey swept the wasteland with an insinuating glance. Somewhere in The Devil's Playground the outlaw was again safe and whole. "If the outlaw and Holtz happened to meet again, one of 'em got more than creased by lead. So I'm hopin' Holtz turned back. Somebody'd sure enough have sighted him if he hadn't."

"Nobody heard gunplay, Sheriff?"

"Nope!" Lackey shrugged. "Let's get the others an' hit for town."

Soon bitter, overworked riders were strung out behind the Sheriff, on every face the sourness of shattered records and reputations once proudly borne. Again the far famed San Adella law enforcers were returning from the hunt— empty-handed.

"Make us the best joke of the whole damned country if the outlaw's got Holtz, hey Sheriff!"

Lackey only snorted. But mutely he promised San Adella a festive day—when, and if, he had the black caballero ready for exhibition; stretched out cold and stiff or unmasked with a noose around his neck.

Deputy Holtz was not only safe as a bug in a rolled rug. He was extremely active—mentally especially—and equipped for business far beyond the scope of that covered by his badge. It was not accident that caused him to desert the posse when it had scarcely cleared the town; not accident that he went hell-bent back to the Reverend Proctor Hill's church. Two things seen there a few minutes previous greatly interested him.

"Garden gave the alarm," Holtz told himself elatedly. Then a sinister leer twisted his mouth. "An' I'm hellish sure I saw Bob Bunson in the half light behind the church."

FOR AWHILE HE was like an invisible sentry standing guard over the church, loitering in the shadows beside it. Occasionally he glanced across the street—at his home. And one of those glances resulted in his standing motionless and pop-eyed with galling suspicions. He saw Garden entering the Holtz house—and almost on his heels, Bob Bunson did likewise.

What transpired on the upper floor would have enraged any man. But it delighted Deputy Holtz and he ran from the kitchen exit in wild pleasure and catlike silence. Then, spurred by long latent dreams unexpectedly fanned into fires of reality, he mounted again and galloped out of San Adella—badlands bound.

He raked his mount with spur and quirt. "Get on, you half ton o' cussedness!" He laughed insanely. "They're due for a surprise when they find the outlaw's camp. Then I'll have plenty to say to *somebody else*."

CHAPTER IX

KILLER

TWO PIN POINTS of cherry red glowed in The Devil's Playground, and burning tobacco scented the crisp night breeze. A coyote strayed into the preyless waste, edged close to the fascinating glows before it discovered that two men were at ease beside a dead fire. The animal howled and dashed away in fright, stopped again, turned and snarled as if protesting against men so safely wrapped in darkness.

But the nimble footed killer went unnoticed by The Masked Rider and Blue Hawk. Other things occupied their minds.

"This *hombre* you hear with the woman, *senor,* he does not shoot at you?"

"That's what's got me stumped," said the outlaw smoothly. "I had already passed the spot. He could have emptied a gun into my back."

"The woman, *senor.* Mebbe she decoy? Bring you here killer waits? Mebbe his gun not works! Mebbe—"

"I've thought of a dozen maybes, *amigo.*" The outlaw's laugh was clipped and frigid. "It's plain hell, Blue Hawk— when you could take off a cloak and hood and be certain of friends and help, but you don't dare do it."

"*Si!*" said the Indian morosely. "Years touch you lightly, *senor.* Without the hood all Bunsons know you are Wayne Morgan—and their friend. But now they know you only as the outlaw and—and they also—"

"They also brand me the killer of the old folks; the killer of the switch and wire man in the tower; the butcher of Reverend Hill!"

"*Si, senor.* And like I say before, Bob Bunson is come—to join with Thad Jaskson. They make oath to track you down."

Seldom did prospects of his future worry The Masked Rider. But the irony of his present status nipped him hard and deep. To come to help them; to feel in honor bound to succeed or die trying—and to be in turn hunted by them! That, he thought, was fate and destiny's master stroke against him. And when he thought about the possibilities of meeting Thad and Bob—while they itched to draw and fire—he floundered in tempestuous seas of doubts as to *his* action. Would he cut and run—remembering that Bob Bunson was swift and deadly with a six-gun? Would he trade lead—with the Bunson most responsible for his being alive today? Would he rip of his hood, stand revealed as Wayne Morgan—risking the chance that such action would prevent bloodshed; although it might then become common knowledge that The Masked Rider and Wayne Morgan were *one?*

"You would not tell them that you are Morgan, *senor?*" asked Blue Hawk thickly.

"Can't! There may be a leak. When that's known by even a few, how long before it's known by everybody? And how much shorter the trail to lead or rope?"

"But if you meet?"

"Kill or be killed? Let 'em take what they once saved—my life? And leave the coyotes who killed the old folks behind me?" The outlaw ground out his after supper cigarette. "Shift camp, Blue Hawk. Two nights here is enough, *sabe?* Then head for San Adella and hear what's being said about the killing of that double-fronted sky-pilot. He was just going to name his partners, *sabe?*"

"*Si!* And one god hears and kills before the names come from the other's lips! Those partners I will find, *senor!*" Blue Hawk's eyes were unusually bright. "I have idea, *senor!* I go in Lonely Trail Saloon. I say to anybody who will listen, that I—"

OUTLAW AND SCOUT sighted them simultaneously; two riders visible only a few moments before they dipped out of view.

"Headed this way," said The Masked Rider calmly. He turned to Blue Hawk, who was ready to erase any sign of a camp fire. "Let it stay. They ride as if they know where they're going—and one of them is a woman."

"The Bunson you ride to town, *senor?* Then she *does* try to trap you—"

"Go! I wait. If they're looking for my camp, by God they'll find it!" He bent and blew an ember to flame against tinder dry wood. When the blaze grew beyond the chance of dying, the black caballero bounded away into the darkness beyond its dancing glow.

He had not long to wait. Crouched behind a great rock he watched the two riders stop far from the little fire. There came muffled voices. The pair dismounted. The woman sought the shelter of jagged stone, holding the lines of both horses. The man went forward afoot, hand upon gun butt, his every move that of a man who knows he invites death's caress. He walked a circle around the fire; an ever closing circle like a hunter beating up game. Then at last, patently puzzled, he stood disappointedly at the fireside. Suddenly Stella Holtz's scream ripped the cemetery silence.

Bob Bunson whirled—and the twist of his own body helped jerk the gun from his holster. Frankly amazed, he stared at the black spectre he had prayed to meet.

"Looking for some one?" asked The Masked Rider passively.

"For you—and expected you to be *behind* me. No *sabe* why you didn't shoot."

"Maybe I make allowances. A man's liable to believe anything he hears—when he finds both dad and mother butchered."

"Damned nice of you! I swear I wouldn't have been that way had I seen you before you got my smoke piece!"

"I know! You wouldn't have given me any choice as to whether I killed you or not. You'd have drawn—no questions asked. And another Bunson would have died—pleasing...."

"You know me, then?"

"A necessary helpful habit of mine, *amigo*—to *know, sabe?* Not to hear or think or guess; to *know*. Especially before I man-hunt. You wouldn't be here if you had such a habit."

"But I am here! Because I promised to ask you a question I don't expect you to answer four-square. Did you take off that hood and mantilla long enough to bamboozle my dad and ma into getting off a train?"

"No!"

"You didn't—"

"I answer no more questions, *amigo;* not for a man who insists I lie before I open my mouth." The outlaw backed up a dozen cautious strides. "I've nothing against you, Bunson. You and Thad Jackson will do what you *think* is right. I hope we don't meet again—with holsters heavy, *sabe?* There's bound to be more than palaver."

"Bank on that! Unless—"

"UNLESS I OPEN your eyes—probably save your life—by *proving* that I'm not the coyote you've branded me." The outlaw dropped Bob's gun in sand. "I ask few men for favors, *sabe?* Of you I ask *two*—don't touch your gun for three minutes. And don't cross my trail for two days!"

"I make no promises to a dirty—"

"Then make 'em *to the dead;* promises that you won't do anything to prevent my squaring their accounts. *Adios.*"

Swift as gun smoke on a windy night, the black phantom disappeared. Bunson swooped on his gun. But when he straightened, teeth clenched, trigger finger almost beyond control, there was not even a hint of a target. He spun on his heels and ran for Stella and the horses.

"Bob! Wait! Don't chase him. He'll—"

Her brother was in the leather and on his way. His Roman-nosed sorrel was at the fireside and not yet in full stride. Stella watched, fear cutting her breath to short snatches. Then to almost burst her ear drums although they were yards away, there came three shots spaced split-seconds apart.

Stella's heart leaped, to choke off her frantic scream. For a moment she stood clutching her throbbing throat, praying that Bob ride on. But he swayed again in the saddle and then tumbled and landed in a puff of dust, so obviously dead that Stella knew the futility of even scant hopes. And dust still rose over her brother's twisted form when a rider flashed by the fire; a rider blacker than the night, whose black hood and black mantilla flapped in the wind like the wings of some giant black bird. That was all Stella saw. Eyes closed, she leaned heavily against stone, on her lips a demand that God explain why He allowed such things as the outlaw to ride away unhampered.

How she reached San Adella, Stella Holtz did not know. There was a blank stretch, an empty, dark void between the moment when she saw her brother dead in a dust cloud and the moment when she sat clinging to saddle horn and staring at the blinking lights of the cowtown. Even then she could do nothing to guide her mount down the dangerous trail and into San Adella's main street. The first thing she thoroughly understood was that Bruce Garden had pulled up beside her.

"Hello!" he smirked. "The deputy's wife returning from another midnight tea with the blackguard?"

Stella snapped alive. She tried to ride around the tormentor. He laughed; a cutting laugh that unnerved her.

"Possemen all back—empty-handed. The Deputy ought to be along any minute. I'm waiting right here for him— with news that his wife wears two brands."

"I—I hope he closes your mouth with lead!"

"It'll surprise me none if he stops your gallivanting with a dose of it, ma'am! Holtz is damned proud of—"

Stella spurred, steered aside and went her way. But the nearer home, the greater her fears. Until, about to turn into the narrow driveway beside the house, she surrendered to complete panic. She rode aimlessly down the rear of San Adella's one street, Garden's threat ringing in her ears, Holtz's wrath-bloated face swimming before her swollen eyes like a mirage. An eternity, it seemed, she was lost in a labyrinth. Once before she had attempted to flee the deputy's menage and authority. She still remembered how absurd that had been. Whither turn? To her younger sister, Thad Jackson's wife? How long in hiding there before Holtz knew—and kindled a new blaze of mysterious hate for Thad; yes, even killed him for offering Stella refuge.

THEN WHEN SHE sank into deepest despair; when she saw no hope of closing Garden's evil mouth, she suddenly found the way. The only way! If only she could do it before Garden's lips had spewed their poison. Pear wrangling her, she dug in her heels, taking heart from the lights visible in a rambling house at the other end of town—Big Steve McKay's house.

The big fellow was alone, pacing the untidy kitchen. He stopped at the table to swill another drink—as if that would help him arrive at an important decision. He cursed a blue streak, dropped into a chair, hairy hands hanging between wide-spread knees and stooped over as if tons were on his broad back.

"First Mescal and Quinn," he growled. "Then he's got guts enough to come straight into town to get Reverend Hill! Who's *next?*"

The longer McKay thought about the black phantom's relentless work, the more certain he was that Garden's plans were destined to go up in the bluish smoke that came from outlaw guns.

Suddenly Big Steve bounded to his feet, the die cast. "Yes, by God! It's time to forget *dreams;* time to hightail. I'll grab what I can for helping him get hold of the old Bunson's land. I'll cut and run. Better alive with *dinero* in my jeans, than buried with the ashes of dreams."

Big Steve reached for his hat. His hand dropped, jerked upwards and closed on gun butt while his eyes went round with dismay. What rider so suddenly swoops down upon his house? The big fellow sprinted, bent to blow out the lamp. His pursed lips leveled as again a woman outside softly called his name.

Big Steve flung the door open. He gaped at Stella Holtz.

No good could come of the visit, he was certain, and gruffly he invited her in.

Stella groped for an opening. She knew there was nothing of finesse in her blunt, "Bruce Garden is waiting at the other end of town—to tell my husband untrue things about me."

McKay's face froze in ludicrous expression. As if he didn't have troubles enough of his own! Then light pierced his brain and he looked grave. So! She came to him for help, because like all of San Adella, she thought him Garden's most bitter enemy.

Big Steve put on a perfect show of knight about to defend fair lady. "The dirty skunk! I'll pound him to hell and gone if it's the last thing—What kind of lies, Mrs. Holtz?"

"He—he thinks I know all about The Masked Rider; that I meet him regularly."

"You don't?" Big Steve saw a spark of hope for the dreamed of fortune and power he had considered dead. If he could wipe away the black menace—

"I was lost. The outlaw rode me home. I do know where he camped." Sobs choked her. How could she ever forget the spot *now*—stained as it was with Bob's blood? "Yes, I know. And even if he's shifted, I'll search the badlands for his new nest. I'll kill him as I would a rattler. But Garden—"

MCKAY PUT AN arm across Stella's quaking shoulders. "Get on home, ma'am. You leave Garden to me, *sabe?* And come daybreak, you, me, and some straight shooting friends of mine will set out to bring that black buzzard down. And we'll *do it!*"

"You'll go see Garden *now?*"

Steve strapped on his gun belt. But even as he threaded the leather through the buckle, he heard other riders approaching. Instantly it popped into his mind that Deputy Holtz—*gun wizard*—might object to rumors of his wife in McKay's house.

"Get going, ma'am. The back door!"

Stella fled. McKay quickly sat at the table. He was nonchalantly pouring a drink when Bruce Garden and a stone-eyed man swaggered in.

McKay needed no introduction to the crooked-mouthed killer for hire. He knew Matt Frost; knew he was ready for business—and looked as if he'd already started it!

CHAPTER X

THE DERRINGER MAN

BIG STEVE SET up drinks for three. His own went untouched and his appraising eyes never shifted from the hired tracker and killer. Six years since Steve last saw Matt Frost. The face he would never forget, but the fellow's garb was beyond Steve's memory.

Frost, average sized, stood in brand new black boots. He wore a long black coat, white shirt with soft collar and white flowing tie. He was topped out by a black Stetson that looked five minutes out of the maker's box.

"But," mused McKay, "he looks more the tin-horn gambler than the killer. He looks—Hell! He ain't even packing a gun!"

Frost chased down his first drink with a second. He turned his snaky eyes upon McKay. "Come dawn, we're getting up a huntin' party. We're goin' after the black buzzard—scientifically and systematically. In forty-eight hours we'll have a corpse—nicely wrapped in a black mantilla."

"In forty-eight hours," said Big Steve skeptically.

"Yep—because Garden's payin' me a five hundred dollar bonus if I deliver the goods by then."

Big Steve smiled at the mastermind. "Too quick on the *dinero* trigger, Garden. I got a party that'll lead me to the outlaw's camp—and charge me nothing."

"Stella Holtz?" barked Garden.

"Yeah. She—"

Frost's laugh was hilarious. "Lucky you mentioned that! Hell knows what was in store for you—seein' as how she took her own brother to a spot where the outlaw could shoot him in the back."

"What?"

"I saw outlaw and female ten minutes apart—right after I found Bob Bunson; dead but still warm." Frost laughed again. "An' you was ridin' with her in the mornin'?"

McKay felt he was accused of being a fool. "You trying to tell me—"

"She's in love with the outlaw!" cut in Garden. "And lots of females do worse than have brothers butchered when love's at stake."

Big Steve's hopes died hard. As they breathed their last; as it seeped into his mind that the reputation of Matt Frost was more deadly than the man himself, so the plan side-tracked with the coming of Stella Holtz, was born again. All Steve wanted now was to get away. Might as well have a showdown with Garden *now*.

"Been doing some tall thinking," Steve began sourly. "The sum of which is that I itch for fresh pastures and—

Oh, you needn't boil over so *pronto! I'm* losing. Not you. The Bunson land'll be worth a few hundred thousand. I'm offering you my share of it—and of all our plans—for a measly five thousand cash."

Garden purpled with surprise and rage, mostly engendered by the manner in which Matt Frost pricked up his ears.

The killer whistled softly. "A few hundred thousand?" He glared at Garden. "So it was you who killed the Bunsons? *That's* why yo're scared of The Masked Rider; why you'd pay to' see him planted? *Not* like you said—that he's hurtin' business in San Adella by givin' the town a bad name!"

BIG STEVE KNEW he'd let cats out of bags. It didn't worry him. He was getting out! Nor was he alarmed by Garden's fury, mounting second by second.

"Five thousand cash," repeated Big Steve harshly. "By noon tomorrow."

Garden was speechless. For a while he made no effort to speak, but milled over the ultimatum. Five thousand was little enough—but as long as Big Steve lived, he could come back for more. Already Garden read threats in the eyes of both Steve and Frost.

The killer, silently probing the faces of the former partners, was not long in deciding which one he'd get behind— for most profit. Garden elected, he moved closer to him, aware of a big staked game and determined to know all about it.

"Garden, you didn't kill the Bunsons to get hold o' land that wouldn't feed two grasshoppers per acre. Why—"

"You and Garden argufy that later!" cut in Steve savagely, "I want to know where I stand."

The mastermind, certain and glad of an ally in Frost, looked contemptuously at McKay. "You made a bargain, Steve—a share of the profits *for a share of the risk.* You think you'll hole up safe—and blackmail me whenever you need cash? Not by a damned sight! Cut and run if you've a mind to. I'd as well play alone than with a yellow-livered—"

McKay whipped out his gun. Swift and totally unexpected as the move had been, he instantly learned that he'd erred in appraising Matt Frost. For the black coat parted as if a spring had snapped back each side. Frost's small left hand flashed up. In two eye winks—before his own six gun was fully clear of holster—Big Steve found himself looking into a derringer that leaped from Frost's shoulder holster.

Garden smirked. "You'll get your five thousand—"

"In time," purred Frost. He watched Big Steve sheathe his six gun and slid the derringer home. "You gents best shake hands—considerin' that when partners fall out, both of 'em most times land in plenty hell and hot water."

Truce did not appeal to Garden. "I got no use for a *hombre* who wants to bolt—"

"Why, McKay?" demanded Frost.

"Because you can't benefit by oil—when The Masked Rider's anchored you down with lead!" Steve stared at Garden. "You know that black son o'hell's rode into town—and killed Reverend Hill?"

Garden was momentarily stunned. Then he guffawed. "Well, I'll be— You got rattled over nothing at all, Steve. I plugged Hill. Didn't I tell you I'd ride close herd on him? I heard him about to mention names to the outlaw. I shut his mouth with lead, *sabe?*"

"You—"

"Sure! And tomorrow Frost sets out to do the same

doctoring to the outlaw. Hell! You and me—" He broke off and offered a friendly hand.

FROST WAS SCARCELY interested in the signed truce and the drink that sealed it. Oil! His head buzzed with possibilities. He glanced at Big Steve. Bargain buster; coward! But doubtlessly useful, else Garden would not have given him a partnership.

"Nicely patched up," thought Frost. "Reckon I'll let 'em show me the ropes; let 'em help get rid of the black outlaw—an' then take over their business *myself*. An' I'll want no partners; 'cept those in six foot holes."

Peace made and mind relieved, Big Steve yearned for progress. "What do we do, Garden?"

The Mastermind grinned. "Thad Jackson won't sell, huh?" He turned to Frost. "You want Steve to go along to *visit* the Jacksons?"

The killer padded to the door. "Does a man need help to eat two slabs of pie?"

Walking down the street with Frost, Bruce Garden thought of Steve McKay. Damn him! Letting Frost know the tempting nature of their business. Why in hell hadn't Frost plugged Steve?

"Would have saved me the trouble," thought Garden. "I don't need him—now that I've got Frost. And in time, I'll get rid of Frost, too. Why share what I can have alone!"

That an opportunity to eliminate Big Steve should come so suddenly into his eyes and mind, pleased Garden no end. He cut away from Frost, watching the hulk of Deputy Holtz who was just shouldering through the doors of the Lonely Trail Saloon.

"Both Jacksons before daybreak," promised Frost in hushed tones. "So long."

Garden did not hear. For in Holtz he saw the means to three ends—gain the deputy's closer friendship, have Steve taken care of, and rub out the possibility of any serious complications arising from his invasion of Stella's bedroom.

Only two men were in the saloon; Holtz, leaning heavily on the bar with his face that of a cat who's just eaten the canary, and a grim faced stranger seated at a table. Garden posted himself on Holtz's left, and now that he was at the tape, he scarcely knew how to start.

The deputy sensed something wrong with Garden. He almost feared that Garden had somehow become aware of recent events; that he knew Holtz had just dashed back from the badlands where he'd cachéd a black hood and cloak—and left Bob Bunson dead behind him!

"What's eatin' you?" Holtz demanded savagely. He looked prepared for the worst—and glad of it.

Garden looked about the saloon with uneasiness. He could not have more plainly said that he didn't think a reply should be made in public. He nodded toward the table far back at the rear door.

Holtz suspiciously started back. He dropped anxiously into a chair, watching Garden like a famished tiger watching a fat deer.

"Being a friend of mine," began Garden timidly, "I ain't standing by and seeing you hoodwinked, *sabe?*"

The deputy's smirk was caustic. "What you drivin' at?"

"I—I just saw your wife in Steve McKay's house—in his arms, in fact. Not being partial to such goings on, I spoke my mind to both. Steve—never a friend o' mine, you'll recollect—threatened to drill me if I didn't 'tend my own business."

HOLTZ'S FACE PUFFED and reddened. Not as an outraged husband's, but as a man whose long latent venom has at last a justified vent.

"The dirty tick-bitten—"

"Mrs. Holtz backed up Steve's plans to keep me quiet—by poisoning your mind against me with a poppy-cock tale o' me forcing my way into your house; *into her bedroom.*"

Holtz stared at the informer; a stare that told of cooling rage and indecision as to which course would be to his greatest advantage. For a few seconds he appeared ready to hurl the lie into Garden's nervous face. Then, reconsidering, he heaped a crackling oath on Big Steve's head. He thrust out a hand toward Garden.

"I'm obliged to you, Bruce," he said smoothly. "Damn fine of you to open my eyes. Some day—*pronto*—I'm hopin' to repay the favor."

Garden took the declaration at face value. Perhaps his apparent success in sealing Big Steve's doom, deafened him to the words Holtz left unspoken and yet sandwiched into his thanks. Holtz, brain afire and certain that Lady Luck was smiling upon him, shoved back his chair and got up.

"You'll not let on that *I* told you, Holtz?"

The deputy smiled. He shook his head. "I got my own ideas as to how to handle the whole shady business. You wait for me at my house."

Garden winced. "But—"

"You spoke truth? Then *be there!*"

Holtz started out, paused with the half door held open and looked back at Garden. In that part second glance and deadly grin, was a promise that much more than a wife's fidelity was to be settled before the sun again climbed over the eastern horizon.

Garden watched the door swing behind Holtz. He felt cheated and trapped, for suddenly he suspected that the deputy had left much unsaid that he wouldn't leave undone; that somehow the news had not been totally a surprise—and some sinister plans were in Holtz's mind.

Garden prodded himself out of the Lonely Trail Saloon. He couldn't down the feeling that every step he took towards the Deputy's home was another step toward disaster.

CHAPTER XI

ROADS TO HADES

H ALF A MILE from San Adella, under low sweeping branches of aspens and cottonwoods that fringed Corbin's Creek, The Masked Rider waited with patience remote from his emotions. He knew that shortly Blue Hawk would arrive—with startling news. Minutes ago, the Indian had signalled Morgan in town and in swift, hushed voices the rendezvous at the creek was arranged.

The scout arrived with the stealthiness of a mountain cat stalking prey through the brush. "News, *senor!* Much news. *Bad!* Bob Bunson. He is dead."

While well acquainted with unexpected death and calamity, the outlaw could not take this blow calmly. "Dead?" he gasped.

"*Si!* Worse! He dies—as you know—while hunting *you*. And the dog who shoots him in the back, makes his sister believe he is *you*. *Si!* The killer wears your black hood and mantilla!"

The outlaw stood with teeth clenched and blazing fires within him. But suddenly flames of hatred for the masquerading coyote were smothered by self condemnation and he felt in great part responsible for Bob Bunson's death.

"Wouldn't have happened—had I drilled the man who fired into the Reverend's bedroom," he gritted, sensing a connection between the two killings. "I should have forgotten myself and chased—"

"But all the town was alive, *senor*. To have chased him was only to bring death to yourself, no?"

"Yes—maybe. Next time—"

"But that is not all, *senor!* The girl goes to Sheriff Lackey. I hear her cry for her brother—and your life. Lackey say that tomorrow he round up men and comb the badlands inch by inch."

"That's why we shift tonight. We camp now in the hills north of San Adella."

Blue Hawk nodded gravely. Then as if he'd purposely held his worst news for the finale, he said ominously, "Matt Frost in town, *senor.*"

"*Killer* Frost?"

"*Si!* The derringer man."

The Masked Rider tensed. "Find out *why!*"

"It is he who backs up the girl's statement that The Masked Rider killed her brother, *senor!*"

"Watch him, Blue Hawk! Buzzards are only where there's something rotten, *sabe?* And buzzards fly *with buzzards.* I think Frost will lead us to the killers of the Bunsons and—"

"Madre de Dios! Then he meant— *Senor!* I go to see that *El Acedero* is fed and watered by the stableman. I come down driveway. I hear men walk alone in street. One is Frost. He say, 'Both Jacksons before daybreak!'"

The outlaw started. "And he rode out of town?"

"No, praise God! He stop first in eating place. Then he buy bottle in saloon and go to hotel. Mebbe now he drinks—to death? And then rides—with derringer ready!"

OFT TIMES MERE seconds had been precious to the outlaw. As if racing against time, he mounted. He recollected a previous meeting with the killer for hire. Few men were more evenly matched—hence both their guns had drawn blood, with death only staved off by the outlaw's hasty flight from on-rushing friends of Frost.

"The man you heard Frost speaking to?"

"His face I could not see, *senor.* But his *walk* I never forget. You think—"

"Birds of a feather!" clipped the outlaw. "Find him! Watch him! Maybe one of the men the Reverend was about to name."

"And you, *senor?*"

"I ride to warn the Jacksons. No fault of mine if Thad even talks to Frost—without keeping him covered with two guns."

Blue Hawk stood listening to the faint and dying sounds of the stallion; stood listening again to all the sinister stories he'd heard about Frost's derringer ability. For the first time since he'd joined the outlaw, the Indian felt the master was riding to face the crack of doom.

BIG STEVE MCKAY lived half an hour with galling regrets. Pacing his disordered rooms, he cursed himself for a double-dyed fool. Why in thunder had he lost his head? Why spill the beans to Matt Frost?

"He'll cut himself a slice—if not take *everything* in sight," moaned Steve. "He'll string along with me and Garden 'till he has everything in his own palm. Then?"

Already Steve could hear the derringer boom; already he could feel hot metal searing flesh, plowing into his heart. "Chameleon!" he said sibilantly. "When he learns we've got control of the best oil land in sight—"

Steve broke off with a shudder. He felt death stalking him now; felt sinister eyes already upon him. And more than imagination! For as his worried eyes shifted across the window, he saw a shadow that might be anything, quickly disappear from the lower corner as if a man had been peering in and had quickly withdrawn.

Hand clamped upon gun butt, Steve rallied the courage to glance outdoors. Then eager to shake the fears, the silence, the deaths that stalked in the night, he walked swiftly up the deserted street.

San Adella was wrapped in fog now. Only two small lights faintly pierced the shifting, opaque curtain—lights on posts in front of the Lonely Trail Saloon, still open on Garden's orders and in hopes of eventually gaining a reputation as an all-night carousing ground.

Steve entered the deserted saloon with a wheeze of relief. Lights! The smiling barkeep! Refuge here from death, he thought. Daybreak soon. There was law and order in San Adella. Not even Frost would kill openly and before witnesses. Tomorrow night? And the nights after that?

Steve husked an order across the bar and inwardly resolved to see Garden again.

"I'm getting out before—"

DOOR HINGES SQUEAKED behind him. Steve turned convulsively. His heart dropped back into place when he saw Deputy Holtz on the threshold, one half of the entrance held open by an extended elbow.

The longer Holtz looked at Steve, the narrower his eyes, until they were mere slits that matched the growing storm upon his ruddy face. He moved forward, murder in every stride, his mouth a crooked, lustful line that warned there would be no beating about the bush.

"What's my wife doin' in your house—in your arms—close to midnight?" croaked the deputy.

Steve was ready for anything but such a question. It tumbled him into a maelstrom of possible excuses from which he could pick nothing plausible. He backed up a pace, eyes rivetted to the deputy's hooked fingers primed to grab gun butts.

Self-preservation! Steve realized that he was slated to see the first actual demonstration of Holtz's gun craft. Yet he didn't hesitate making an attempt to have those twin weapons blazing in the right direction.

"She came to ask me to help her close Bruce Garden's mouth. He was set to tell you lies—"

"I've already palavered with Garden. He's proved it's *you* tryin' to make me the town fool, an' by God, nobody'd blame me for killin' you!"

Big Steve shrank in terror. His eyes furtively sought the nearest exit. In his reeling mind was one cherished hope—to get out; to face Garden again; to write finis to the mastermind's false peace making... with lead.

"Garden's a lying pole-cat!" whined Steve. Against almost any other man, he'd have drawn and banked on ability to save his hide. But he knew the futility of gun matching with Holtz. "Let's both find Garden. I'll make him back water, if—"

"He's had his say!" Holtz stood like a disappointed executionist. "I oughtn't give you chance to draw, you low-down, sneakin', yeller-livered buzzard!"

"But—"

"You won't pull an iron, will you? You'll take anything I dish up an' stand like a slobbering old coyote who—" Holtz broke off in disgust. He started away, to spin abruptly. "Clear out of town, you mangy mongrel. When dawn comes I'll be lookin' for you—to ventilate you proper!"

Holtz stomped out. Big Steve, perspiration on temples, flush of shame on his cheeks, gulped and tried to dilute the barkeep's acid leer.

"Ain't his wife nor reputation most in Holtz's mind," said Steve nervously. "I just got a hunch he's *got to* kill me—cause or no. He's sold out to Garden, that's what!"

The barkeep grinned as he would to taunt a coward. "You'd better shake San Adella, Steve! Holtz'll write his initials with lead—on your belly. Ever see his scissorin'—Hell! I saw him down Lank Nevins—in two pieces."

Steve stalked out. He'd get out of town—but damned if he wouldn't make it hot for somebody before he left.

BRUCE GARDEN FELT as if the walls of Deputy Holtz's parlor were the bars of a death cell. He waited, in a chair by the window where the westering moon painted a silver rectangle on the floor. An eternity, it seemed, he fried in fears like a condemned man awaiting the hangman.

Nerves frayed, he jumped up as feet crunched in the graveled path. Holtz came in smiling, puffing a cigarette.

"Within half an hour, one of your worries will he all over," snickered the deputy as he touched a match to a lamp.

"You—you mean—"

"Big Steve is goin' to *try* an' bolt."

"Try? Try to leave town?"

Holtz nodded. "He won't get far. Dead men let out no secrets before *we're* ready, *sabe?* I aim to smoke Steve to hell—fair fight or empty-handed."

Garden couldn't think straight. Before *we're* ready! His head buzzed with the dire possibilities of Holtz's strange emphasis. For a while the deputy gloated over the profound bewilderment into which his declaration had plunged Garden.

"What you blinkin' at?" demanded Holtz. "Still think you an' Steve and Reverend Hill pulled wool over the eyes of everybody in San Adella? Still think nobody knows you three *partners* were false-fronted enemies? You still think *I* don't know the stakes you were after?"

Hammer blows would have affected Garden less. Dazed, alarmed, he was totally speechless. Then, realizing the futility of panic, he thought he understood. He rapped out a scalding oath on Big Steve's head.

"He spilled the beans again?"

"Hell no! I've known for some time. There's oil—"

Garden held up a hand for silence. "Your wife! A woman can spread news quicker 'n—"

"My wife isn't upstairs. Reckon she's lit out for the Jackson's—after our little *set-to.*" Holtz laughed. "I ain't missed much tonight, Garden! I saw you an' her palaver. I saw her go to Steve's house. I saw Ed Sloan an' Matt Frost pull into town. I saw you an' Frost go to Steve's—and my wife high-tail out the back door. All in all, it looks like time to show my hand."

"You figure—"

"That you need a partner. *One.* I'm it. Steve cashes his chips *pronto.* Likewise Matt Frost. The Masked Rider's nothin' for either of us to fear. Sheriff Lackey'll cook his goose. Thanks to my wife, Lackey's sendin' no less'n seventy five men into the badlands at dawn. That'll leave just you an' me knowin' that hereabouts is black gold; more *dinero* than we could throw away with shovels."

INSTANTLY GARDEN KNEW the advantageousness of a badge man defending him and his dreamed of empire. Always a turn-coat, always ready to alter to suit current winds, he breathed easier while already he reasoned that after Holtz had pulled all the chestnuts out of the fire, he, too, would be eliminated.

"I'd have slept better these many nights—with *you* as partner," he frankly confessed. "Your badge'll cover a multitude of sins—and it can begin to do such *right now.*"

Holtz grinned. He had expected his proposal to bring forth much heat and white hot temper. Now, remembering Garden's false front, the deputy out-stared the mastermind.

"I'll play four-square, Garden," he said sharply. "No doctor'll be able to mend you if you don't! *Sabe?*"

"Yes. Of course! There's plenty for both of us. Work enough, too! Right now Matt Frost is riding to *visit* the Jacksons. Their land is the keynote to all my plans. You'd best hit for their spread. Let Frost get in his work. Then you settle him—*in the law's name.*" Garden chuckled. "Perfectly legal, what?"

Holtz did not comment. But his snakey eyes said he'd handle things without direction—after he settled with Big Steve McKay.

CHAPTER XII

PLANS OF DOOMED MICE

MATT FROST PULLED up on the edge of the mesa and frowned down on the scattered buildings of the Diamond R spread. Why was there light in the trim little house that so plainly spoke of hardworking folks painstakingly trying to make something out of nothing?

Like a wolf tempted by trap bait and yet wary of steel jaws, Frost spent a full ten minutes studying the place where he proposed to unchain death without compunction. He saw a shadow at a yellow rectangle that marked a window. It was motionless as the house itself and if judged by size alone, it was Thad Jackson.

Frost touched the derringer in his arm-pit holster. His hand slithered away. The large bore weapon wouldn't carry half the distance.

"Damn him! No hour for respectable folks to be up an' about. I figgered to be inside of the house before he'd know he had company. No sense riskin' lead whistlin' at me if I could catch him in bed or—"

He clipped the thought, turned his grey and went in search of an easy descent. A stone heaved against the door would doubtlessly move that stationary shadow from the window. Frost already visioned the door open and Thad

Jackson standing silhouetted against the front room lamp. What a target!

Frost's laugh was short and deep in his throat. "Soon's Garden an' Big Steve help me wipe out The Masked Rider, they'll savvy the feel of derringer slugs! I'll own the pick of all the oil range in these parts, an' Matt Frost'll be his own pardner!"

CLOSING IN ON the house, Frost felt contemptuous pity for McKay and Gardner. Fools! Should've known pardnerships never pan out. You never can tell what the other feller's thinkin'—smilin' at you while he schemes to cut your throat. Now take strangers! They don't—"

He checked himself, confessing that sometimes strangers couldn't be trusted much further than partners. He rolled off the names of several men he'd never have much faith in being able to trick or outsmart. Deputy Holtz! Snake-eyed badge toter who'd bottom-deck deal quick as a flea would hop. Masked Rider! Nemesis of wrong; fool who risked his neck to help the worthy.

"Next time we meet, he gets planted!" vowed Frost, turning the grey into the shadows of a lean-to.

Dismounting, he feasted his eyes on the shadow still at the side window. The derringer came slowly from its leather sheath. The stubby nose inched up. Frost's trigger finger stiffened. His lips stretched back in a wolfish snarl. But suddenly the tension went out of him and he blued the early traces of dawn with a vitriolic oath.

The shadow had moved away!

Few times since the law had branded him, did The Masked Rider loath his symbols more than during the time he was in the parlor of the Jackson house. He felt his very entrance, necessarily swift and sudden, to be extremely ill timed. For even as he crossed the threshold, Stella Holtz had collapsed in her sister's arms.

Thad Jackson, recovered in a split second from the shock of the unheralded intrusion of the black apparition, dived for the gun belt hanging over a chair.

"Steady!" snapped the outlaw. "My business here is friendly—if you want it that way." He skirted around Thad, snatched the tempting six gun. A flip of black-gloved hands and six shells spilled on the floor. "Help your wife with Stella. She's fainted."

Thad obeyed belligerently. His face went white with rage when he had time to note the bruises on her face and the welt of a quirt down one side of her pulsating throat. He gripped his tongue between his teeth until eyelids of a ghastly white face fluttered.

"The deputy?" he squeezed out.

STELLA NODDED. THEN she bolted upright on the settee, fury gradually coming into eyes that she was certain did not lie. That *was* The Masked Rider; standing trick against the door like an ebony statue.

"You!" she cried, voice rent by a still vivid vision of a brother slain in cold blood. Only Loretta's grip kept her from flying at the outlaw. "You dare to come here—"

"Knowing that you believe I shot your brother in the back?" The Masked Rider's tone was lifeless. "Glad I came, ma'am! You might be able to shed light on the buzzard who drilled Bob."

"*You* did! It wasn't even cleverly done. You warned him and rode away. But you dashed back and—"

"Let it stand that way, then! I can't prove otherwise. Nor have I the time."

"You can't deny what I saw. And because it's too late to do anything about it, I'm almost glad you did it. From end to end of this county, the news will spread. At dawn—"

"I know! Sheriff Lackey combs the badlands. Maybe I *have* crossed my last river. But I'll stay alive on *this side of it* at least until I do three things—give Deputy Holtz a chance to test his fists and quirt on me; find the coyote who killed Bob; and settle with the lobos who killed your parents."

Stella laughed hysterically. "Our champion!"

"Who's goin' to find me on his tail from now 'till he reaches the doorstep of hell!" swore Thad.

"Two things easier for you to do," said the outlaw quietly. "Move away from that window—before someone shoots *you* in the back. And when Matt Frost comes here—day or night—don't be without a gun *in your hand* as long as he's within derringer range."

Thad didn't know precisely why he *did* move from the window. "*Sabe!*" he said sarcastically. "*Another* masked rider killed Bob—and now you've laid the pipes to have blame for the next killin' laid at Killer Frost's door. But there won't be a killin' here! Not if I get a ghost of a chance to drill you first."

The outlaw reached for the knob behind his back. "I ride a dangerous trail to warn you," he said thickly, wishing it was sensible to rip off hood and cloak and so easily convince them he was their friend. "More I can't do. But like Bob, you'll have warning—not to cross my trail before...."

His mouth snapped closed. He never made mistakes— about stealthy footsteps outside shut doors. He bounded away from it, every sense taut, his heart in his throat for fear of the women's safety. A black-gloved hand ordered them into the next room. That they obeyed quickly, silently, earned the outlaw's mute thanks. The door burst open as he whirled.

Killer Frost turned to stone. He had heard muffled voices, but it was beyond the scope of his imagination to picture what he now saw—death ensheathed in death's own black. For a dozen heart ticks the killer for hire was hypnotized; the derringer hung in the limp hand at his side, and his saucer-round eyes were capable of recording one fact—that the outlaw's hands were in sight. And empty!

"We meet again," breathed The Masked Rider. "Beckon this time we'll *finish* our palaver without others of your breed sticking in their oars and—"

FROST'S HAND MOVED as if a minor explosion had driven it upwards. And even as the derringer leveled, so the trigger started back. Yet the killer knew he was too slow. He saw only one thing—a black gloved hand streaking for the folds of the black mantilla. A Colt boomed. It was the clutch of death that fired the derringer and as the large calibre bullet ripped into the ceiling, Frost pitched forward on his face, safe in Satan's embrace.

Thad Jackson's mouth was agape and he looked like a witness to the utterly impossible. His awed eyes shifted from the smoking derringer still in Frost's dead hand, to the chinked ceiling plaster and down again to The Masked Rider's hand—already empty.

"He—he *did* come!" Thad managed apologetically.

"And—by the grace of God—he *went. Adios.*"

But Thad reached the door first. "Wait! We've got to believe *now* that you didn't kill Bob. We've got to believe you'll try and find the coyote who did—and we want to help."

"Believing in me is all you can do. Sooner, later, maybe— I'll meet that skunk. With proof that I make no mistake when I send him to join Frost."

Stella Holtz ran tearfully to the outlaw's side. "I—I'm sorry for all I said. You've done us a great favor. Isn't there *anything* we can do—"

"For you own safety and peace of mind? Only be on guard until you see me again."

"You mean the deputy—"

"Yes! He strikes me as a *hombre* who'll do anything to hurt a woman. Your son is with you? Will your husband let you keep the boy—even if he doesn't want him?"

"I'm afraid—"

"Don't be! Just give me twenty four hours to take care of him. Meanwhile—for your good—don't do anything to correct the public opinion that *I* killed your brother."

"But Sheriff Lackey; the crowd that'll hunt you at dawn—mostly because of that!"

The outlaw's laugh was cold. "One gets used to hunters, ma'am. And don't let it throw you if this hunt ends differ- ent from the many others, for long after I'm gone—to boot hill or just somewhere out there in the dark—all three of you should be happy. Because no one can say how much oil is under these acres."

Three chins sagged; three pairs of eyes lit with aston- ishment.

"Oil!" sang Thad Jackson. "Lord! Then that's why they killed Loretta's dad an' ma!"

"*They,*" gritted the outlaw. "Reverend Hill and Matt

Frost. Two coyotes who died near a shack. *Part* of the brood. Others still live—and will carry on."

"Garden!" blurted Thad. "I see it now! He bought the old folks out, rushed the deal through, got a clear title—and killed them to get his money back."

"Garden, yes—but there are others. I want *every* man who had a finger in the pie."

Loretta shuddered. "The deputy! Do you suppose he aches for a gun fight with Thad—an excuse for killing him—because he knows we won't be bought out or...."

"Holtz—maybe. *Certainly* there were two buzzards in an arroyo—whom I'll meet *again,* somewhere, some how! And from those four—time being ripe—I'll learn the names of anybody else."

The black gloved hand groped behind the outlaw's back again. *"Adios,"* he said regretfully.

"Good luck!" called Thad.

The outlaw heard. Reward enough—that some one wish him well.

CHAPTER XIII

DEATH AT DAWN

S HERIFF LACKEY SEARCHED the eastern sky and growled against the lack of sign of dawn. He turned from the calaboose window like a thoroughbred at the barrier. Riders pulled up at the door. Lackey faintly smiled. Harbinger of a make-shift posse that should number seventy-five strong.

"Howd'y, boys," greeted Lackey, jovial now as his eyes

roamed north and south in the street and discerned many other horsemen converging upon the office.

"Promises fair weather, Sheriff," prophesied an old timer. "We'll get the makin's of a necktie party for certain. Where's that scissorin' deputy o'your'n?"

"Holtz? Reckon he'll be along *pronto*—an' die o'disappointment if a rope ain't stretched before dusk."

But Deputy Holtz's mind was profit inflamed, and he proposed to deal with one menace to rosy dreams at a time. In the crisp grey of dawn, he waited just north of Big Steve McKay's house, hand itching for the feel of booming steel, his snakey orbs on the light within the doomed man's house. It was a few minutes before the deadline he'd set.

Suddenly he stiffened, squinting at the rear door of McKay's. The corners of his mouth tilted. "Sneakin' rat!" he got out between gripped teeth. With slashing strides he started for his victim. "Glad he took the rear door— damn him. Dead men make poor witnesses an' I'll handle Holtz's story fine."

Big Steve was fifty yards from the split-rail fence of Jake's livery when he stopped short, spun and felt his blood turn to iced jelly.

Holtz closed to within non-miss distance. Then he stood flat-footed, legs wide apart, elbows out and hands at measured distances from gun butts and ready to clamp down.

Neither of them spoke; Holtz silently scowling and wishing his prey would make a move of any sort, and McKay's tongue thick, hot, paralyzed.

The deputy's patience snapped. "Draw!" he blasted.

But Big Steve knew crossed guns would cut him down before his own weapon cleared leather. Two routes of salvation opened in his panicky mind—plea and flight. The first seemed useless. But certainly Holtz wouldn't shoot a man in the back? Yet Steve primed himself to run for life even as he thawed his tongue.

"I am clearing out," he groaned. "I want no lead debate with—"

"Draw, you sneakin' wife-thief!"

Steve flashed about and broke for Jake's gate. For a dozen frantic paces his hopes mounted. They burst like a pricked soap bubble. He heard twin clicks. He sucked in a great breath as if he knew it to be his last. A gun barked. In the next eye wink Big Steve McKay was beyond terror and pain. Four bullets stabbed through his gun belt and into his back. He toppled like a wind snapped tree, not feeling the coup de gracé that crunched into the back of his head.

HOLTZ SWOOPED UPON the corpse, rolled it back down, snatched out McKay's gun and fired three shots skyward. He bent and swiftly laid the smoking weapon near McKay's outflung hand, to straighten convulsively as bald-headed Jake rushed from his stables and many feet came pounding up nearby driveways.

Sheriff Lackey was among the first arrivals. Bruce Garden was at his heels. Lackey stared sourly; first at the corpse, then at his deputy. And Bruce Garden also looked at both—not as another blemish on San Adella's reputation; but as a mighty fine piece of work.

"How come?" snapped Lackey. "Yo're the last man who ought to do such jobs. Yo're law, *sabe?* Yo're supposed to set examples—but the right kind. This—"

"I only asked the pole-cat to steer clear o' Mrs. Holtz. He cussed me—an' pulled a gun. I tried to pacify him. But when the third bullet fanned my cheek, I— What would *you* have done, Sheriff?"

Lackey scooped up McKay's iron. He broke it and counted three dented shells. Patently relieved, he shrugged. "Never had cause to believe Stella dealed 'em from top *an' bottom.*"

Garden crowded forward. "Holtz is right. I *saw* it. This comes under the heading—self-defense."

Lackey was glad to agree with the opinions of several other men. "Duly recorded that way, then." He turned abruptly. "Some of you tote him to the office an' let's get organized for more important business."

Deputy Holtz took charge as the crowd shifted. He beckoned to two surly-faced men. "Sloan. Dingwell. Lend a hand."

Three men responded. Holtz glanced at one. His confidence that he'd hoodwinked everybody was roughly jarred when he recognized the grim-faced stranger who ruined a shooting match in The Lonely Trail Saloon—and saved Thad Jackson's life.

"Two men will do," said Holtz sharply.

But Wayne Morgan casually knelt and lifted McKay's left shoulder. He let it sag down again. His eyes, steady and frankly hostile, bored into Holtz's.

"Good shooting," ventured Morgan. "This is the first loser in a fair fight that I ever saw shot *in the back.*"

The deputy's face was that of a wolf with fangs bared. "Second time you waltzed into my business, *hombre!* Why?"

"Maybe because this is the second time your business is too rotten to let slide?" said Morgan quietly as Lackey came to stand beside him. "The question is— Was it a fair fight?"

Outlaw, sheriff and killer were quickly aware of a change

in the attitude of the crowd. There was an ugly rumbling from the rear; the undertoned declarations of men who would countenance anything but the shooting in the back of anyone by anyone.

Lackey grabbed the bull by the horns lest there be serious trouble. "Nothin' to say, Holtz?"

"I said it! He cussed and fired—and started side-wisin' away. Reckon mebbe my first bullet kinda spun him around. I ain't countin' ten between shots when I'm faced by a killer. Three more bullets were on their way when he must've turned."

Someone laughed derisively. "It *might* be done!"

"It might!" agreed the outlaw. "So might a lot of other things."

LACKEY, FEELING HIS justice at stake even though he sought a loop hole to give his deputy a clean sheet, was hard pressed for a course that would satisfy everyone— mostly Holtz and himself. He found it!

"Yo're under arrest, Holtz!" he said solemnly.

The deputy started. "Under arrest? Why damn it all—"

Lackey worked in a comforting wink to Holtz. "Reckon a jury will have to settle this." He visioned hand-picked men, a swift, short trial and the *right* verdict. "If I have yore word not to hightail, I won't clamp you behind bars."

Holtz's rage knew no bounds. Technical arrest was easily endured. But to have it brought about by a stranger! "Just because a mealy-mouthed stranger poisons all your minds!" He glared at Morgan. "I ain't takin' this sittin' down, *hombre!* After a jury brands you a damned fool, I'll dust the court house steps with you. I'll—"

Lackey bristled. "Don't start another ruckus, Holtz!"

Abruptly he started for his office again, muttering against the high sun and his man hunters not yet at work.

But Lackey's fears of an eruption between Morgan and the deputy were baseless. As far as the outlaw was concerned, all the men, including Holtz, had disappeared. All Morgan saw or heard was centered about the corpse—in two men facing him squarely for the first time and ready to stoop and pick up Big Steve McKay.

The outlaw, tense, anxious, gave no outward sign that all of his attention was on the pair that had responded to Holtz's call for corpse shifters. They had answered to "Sloan. Dingwell." There was only fractional doubt in the outlaw's mind but that they were—grave diggers in a moonlight flooded arroyo! And because of that slight doubt, the outlaw easily dammed back the wrath that must otherwise have swept his eternal caution aside.

In a flash, Morgan decided what was to be done. He weighed the risks against the possible results, struck a balance in favor of the latter and with determined steps, he fell in between Sloan and Dingwell, who were clumsily carrying off the remains of Big Steve.

Bedlam reigned at Sheriff Lackey's office. Four score of men milled about, some impatiently forking horses, others circulating afoot in the crowd, all of them eager for the chase and armed as if they expected to encounter regimented foes.

Lackey stood on the top office step and bellowed a command for attention. He picked a round dozen experienced man-hunters; members of his original, celebrated posse.

"Divide the others amongst you. Scatter yoreselves in The Devil's Playground. Every man on his own hook, but none of you out of signallin' distance of somebody else. Raise hell at first sign of camp, hide or hair of the black buzzard an' every man will head to help you. Enough of us here to comb a hundred square miles before dark. Ride!"

MORGAN, ASTRIDE HIS black stallion now, hung close to Sloan and Dingwell. He found himself elected to ride with them, under the command of a red-thatched veteran with ferret eyes.

There was a brief conference between squad leaders, an allocation of territory. Then like crusaders, the distinct groups started out of town, as grim and determined a procession as any of the gaping townswomen had ever witnessed.

Morgan, deliberately sandwiched between Sloan and Dingwell, smarted less under the lash of the hunt's purpose, when he saw that Holtz had sullenly remained behind. Sheriff Lackey had so ordained. For appearances' sake! It didn't seem proper for a man half accused of back shooting to be out hunting an outlaw.

For a while Morgan contented himself with mutely riding beside the pair he suspected. Then, having tried to judge their shrewdness or gullibility, their sincerity, he pulled yet closer to them—determined to gain their good graces. Before he laid eyes on San Adella again, he meant to know much more about that arroyo grave.

"And the man or men who ordered it dug and filled," he vowed.

Suddenly Ed Sloan looked at Morgan and smiled. "Hadn't Lackey been there, Deputy Holtz might have showed *you* some fancy shootin'."

Morgan's pulse raced like storm waves dashing ashore. The voice—of the grave filler! Instant fires leaped to full blaze within the outlaw; an instant mirage floated before him and in the dirge of morning wind through bush and tree, was the old Bunson's plea for justice the law could not obtain.

"You heard me?" said Sloan. "I meant that Holtz would have cut you down, hadn't—"

"Not unless I *turned around!*" Morgan could not keep animosity out of his voice. "And there are buzzards worse than Holtz!"

He rode on, eyes narrowed, lips tightly closed.

CHAPTER XIV

PARTNERS

DEPUTY HOLTZ GRINNED as he swaggered into the sheriff's office and took his rifle from the rack near the pot-bellied stove.

"Plumb good fortune that Lackey ordered me to stay out of The Masked Rider hunt. Leaves me free to settle with Matt Frost—an' the whole damned Jackson-Bunson clan. Then it'll be just me an' Bruce Garden—an' oil."

Bruce couldn't last many days longer than necessary to gain control of precious acreage—and will it all to his good friend, Deputy Holtz.

Garden was standing in the office doorway a full minute before the deputy saw him. He entered nervous as a cat. "Why in hell did you shoot Steve *in the back?* You should've known—"

"It'll pan out all right! Frost is—"

"Dead! Pete Burlew was riding in to join Lackey's crowd. He found Frost in a wash. Measured between the eyes."

"By Thad Jackson?"

"Who knows? But why would Thad kill Frost? How would Thad know Matt was working for us?"

"You think—"

"The Masked Rider! What I don't understand is why Frost was moved from where he died—unless the outlaw also did that so's there'd be no chance of Thad running afoul of the law."

Holtz was far from worried or alarmed. "We needn't riddle it out. McKay's dead. Frost, ditto. I'm ridin' now to clean out the Jacksons.

"Not now! No telling who'll happen that way and sight you, what with the place so near the hunting grounds of Lackey's army. *Sabe?*"

Good counsel. Holtz felt small for not having reasoned so himself. "At dusk then."

Garden glanced at the stiff remains on the floor. With law behind him he no longer feared it or leaned towards silk-gloved methods to attain his ends.

"Ed Sloan and Russ Dingwell acted up in my house, shortly before your shots turned things upside down. They've suddenly got the idea that burying the old Bunsons is worth share and share alike, of everything I hope to gain—considering that The Masked Rider might get wind that *they* did the job."

Holtz frowned. "You got pardners enough—in *me*. An' I want no blackmailers knockin' at our doors, *sabe?*" Then he caught the significance of Garden's hand—pointing to Big Steve. Holtz grinned. "Yeah! We'll reserve room for Sloan an' Dingwell; right beside Steve."

"Then," smiled Garden, "with Lackey's crowd *sure* to smoke up the outlaw, we'll have clear sailing. I've got papers ready that'll give me title to the L.K. spread as soon as we get rid of the Borden brothers."

Taking his leave abruptly, Garden headed for home, his steps light and his future serene and bountiful. The one blemish to his mental picture of himself as lord and master of limitless wealth and power—Holtz—he considered as easily erased as a wrong figure in a sum of addition. Then sudden and dazzling as lightning striking close at hand, he realized that perhaps Holtz was also capable of erasing.

Garden walked slower; the meditative, fearful steps of genius awed and frightened by a monster of its own creation.

FEW MEN SUFFER uncertainty's sting as the Blue Hawk did when he fled from the partly opened side window of Sheriff Lackey's office. Flitting around the rear corner of the small building, he hurried down behind two other houses, then casually walked down a driveway and into San Adella's main street.

He saw Garden burdensomely walking south and Deputy Holtz strolling diagonally across the dusty thoroughfare towards the Lonely Trail Saloon. All the sinister things he'd heard through that window made his head reel—more so because he feared the master had left town as part of Lackey's army.

For a brief spell the Indian considered hastening to the badlands in hopes of meeting The Masked Rider. He cheeked himself.

"So many riders! One sees me with the master. News spreads. Never again are we safe together—or apart!"

How long would the outlaw be gone! Blue Hawk was as

much in the dark about that as he was as to why the master had so tempted fate by going.

"I wait! Mebbe soon he come. Holtz say he start for Jackson's come dusk. I watch him. Garden, too! *Madre de Dios,* do not have them change minds before I speak with the *senor.*"

San Adella had breakfasted by now and the few aged men left behind gathered in excited groups to discuss the day's one topic. Blue Hawk sauntered to Kilroy's General Store. He sank upon the bottom of four steps that led to the merchandise loaded platform. For a while he divided his attention between the Lonely Trail and Garden's smug house, occasionally glancing up the dusty street in vain hopes of sighting the outlaw.

The Indian began to roll a cigarette. It dropped unfinished from his fingers. A muffled shot had sounded in Garden's house! Blue Hawk got up, intensely interested and glad that the chattering old men nearby had not heard the report.

The Indian crossed the street aimlessly, a thousand questions flashing through his mind. He went down alongside of the Lonely Trail, doubled-back to Garden's and tip-toed to a window. Eyes leveled with the sill, he peered in scarcely knowing what to expect. The orderly kitchen was deserted; the doors to two adjoining rooms were tightly closed.

Fast in the clutch of curiosity, Blue Hawk picked a cautious way to the south window. He saw only a disheveled bed and a battered bureau.

"Cáscaras! Then in the other room *for certain!*" exclaimed Blue Hawk excitedly.

He was a yard from the north window when it happened. At the first brutal stab of the gun nose, he shot a glance over his shoulder. Garden! The Jackson death planner of the sheriff's office; the man to whom Matt Frost had said in hashed voice, "Both Jacksons before dawn."

"Inside!" rapped Garden, trigger of his forty-five half drawn. "Through the kitchen door. And I'll take *these!*" He ripped away the Indian's gun and knife. "Move, you greasy, snooping spic!"

Blue Hawk was not too amazed to resent the insult. Folly to battle a man with guns in both hands! "I walk to front street, *senor.* There is harm?"

"You lie! You sat on Kilroy's steps watching this house. I thought you would come over if you heard a shot. And you went from window to window like— Who are you? What'd you wan t?"

PRODDED BY GUNS, the Indian entered the kitchen. He watched hopelessly as Garden clicked two locks and one on the other door! Though he watched hawklike for an opportunity to jump his captor, none came.

"It is the beeg mistake, *senor.* True, I hear shot. I think mebbe you are hurt. I come to help. In my country a man helps the—"

Garden jerked up a trap door in the floor. A musty stench came up from the cobweb festooned cellar. He dropped the lid and, vigilance never relaxing, pulled stout rope from a closet drawer.

"Hands behind your back! I'll make you safe while I go find Deputy Holtz. You'll tell the truth—or the nearest you'll ever get to your country again is in a hole down that cellar."

The scout had no fears for himself. But he knew his importance to the outlaw; knew that all he'd learned about this nefarious pair *must* reach the *senor's* ears. Failure meant death for the Jacksons and for that, the black caballero would never forgive himself—or Blue Hawk. "Hands behind your back, damn you!" snarled Garden.

Blue Hawk obeyed—while he steeled himself for what was obviously his last chance to get out of this infamous house. He slowly put out both hands, inching them back with fingers ready to snap into a hard fist. He spun, set to lash out with both fists.

But Garden was ready. He stepped aside, weapon somersaulting in his hand. The butt sliced the air. It cracked on the Indian's bronzed forehead. He reeled backward. Garden followed up. He put everything he had behind a second blow that dropped the prisoner like a bleeding, poled ox.

"Now I *know* you was up to something," panted Garden, frantically throwing hitches around the Indian's wrists and ankles. Finished, he grabbed the scout by the ankle bonds, dragged him to the trap opening and without hesitation dumped him into space like a dead and useless calf.

He slammed the trap lid. Spent and breathless, he donned hat and coat and hurried in search of Holtz.

Blue Hawk opened his eyes and ground his teeth against the shooting pains in his head, his back and limbs. He thanked his lucky stars that the cellar had not been deep enough for him to suffer any broken bones.

"Fool!" he chided himself. "Mebbe now you die—and bring death to the *senor!*"

But not without every possible effort to avoid it! In darkness and stench that almost stifled him, Blue Hawk fought to free his hands. The knotted ropes were there to stay. He tried the cruelly tight bonds around his ankles. They gave so little that they seemed part of his flesh and bone. He rolled and turned and rolled again, until in four directions, clammy stone walls came under his fingers. But nowhere on the slimy, stinking floor could he feel anything except mildew crusted earth. Exhausted, he sank flat upon his back, striving to think—and finding it as useless as trying to see through the inky darkness.

"Lost," he confessed. *"Madre de Dios* help me—only that I may speak to the *senor* and save the Jacksons."

MINUTES DRAGGED LIKE weeks. When ten had gone into time's limbo, Blue Hawk's joints were chafed to bleeding by sawing ropes and stiff and sore by straining. Yet he kept a spark of hope alive-until heavy boots of two men thumped the floor above.

The trap lid dropped back. Holtz struck a match, touched it to crumpled paper and let the blazing torch flutter down. He laughed hideously as the prisoner pulled his hot face aside lest the firebrand light upon it.

"An Indian, sure as hell!" proclaimed the deputy. "Play safe. Just leave him down there. As is."

"Until?" asked Garden blankly.

" 'Till we find out how long he can go without grub an' water. Then we'll let him go on without 'em—for another week. Still livin' then, I reckon I'll *have* to waste a bullet on him."

Blue Hawk shuddered as darkness again blinded him. He wanted to know why God let such human animals live unchallenged—while The Masked Rider was priced and hunted like a coyote.

CHAPTER XV

THE DEVIL'S PLAYGROUND

NOT EVEN THE MASKED RIDER himself knew how he controlled himself so admirably while in the company of the wingless vultures—Sloan and Dingwell.

Times without number, the outlaw felt an urge to blurt his accusation that they had at least aided in the murder of the old Bunsons and positively did bury them. But he conquered the yearning and comforted himself with a promise that later there must come a better, safer opportunity. Once, deep in the wastelands forsaken even by repulsive reptiles, Morgan almost yielded to impatience. Disaster would have followed! For without warning, another outlaw hunter appeared on a barren ridge and hailed them.

It was high noon, blisteringly hot. From the southwest came a Satan's breath wind that parched both men and mounts. Morgan, never riding out of sight of Sloan and Dingwell, heard the latter's shrill whistle and aped Sloan's spurring to respond. Soon the parboiled trio gazed down into an arroyo that made the outlaw's heart pound beneath his ribs. He had looked into it before on a crisp night when a full moon painted the eastern wall with silver and left the western wall black. Here had run a narrow, twisting ribbon of molten silver; here had been a mud dam to turn the tiny stream away from a double grave. Morgan again saw two mud splattered punchers inspect their work;

saw them walk water to two horses patiently waiting in a miniature lake.

"I don't ride another yard away from home for a dozen outlaws," rasped Dingwell. "There's as cool a spot as I've waltzed on an' I'm restin' my bones good an' plenty."

Sloan recognized the spot. He grinned and winked at his pal. "I got a deck o' cards. An' I feel *dinero* comin' my way." He smiled at Morgan. "Set an' play a spell, stranger?"

The outlaw beat down hasty agreement. "Sheriff Lackey expects every man—"

"If all those other *hombres* can't scare up the black buzzard, then *we* can't. Come on down an' rest a while."

Morgan ground roped the stallion apart from the other two horses. He sat opposite the killers, a flat-topped stone in front of him and ready to serve as a table.

"Poker? Sky limit?" asked Sloan. He looked hopeful— because of Morgan's ready-money appearance. Certainly he was no forty-a-month-and-found cowpoke! "Suit you, stranger?"

Morgan nodded. He wondered if he could speak civilly to the coyotes; knew he *must* or put them on guard.

They played. They smoked. The outlaw knew his winning of the first three two-bit pots was the build-up for a higher ante. He lost a dollar opener; lost the next two straight, and lost a twenty dollar pot—although he held four aces that he didn't even show.

"Too bad," sympathized Sloan. He thought that *bottom* card had won for him and with his boot he signalled Dingwell to take the next pot, then give, the dumb stranger one to lure him on.

Dingwell slyly took his working capital from the stone. From now on he'd play only with the stranger's cash—in case something went wrong. "Open for ten dollars," he purred, greedy eyes on Morgan's roll.

The outlaw lost. He wished Dingwell had been a lot more clever in sliding out that bottom card. But more than that he wished either of the coyotes would give him half a chance to swing their talk to other than the game.

"Raise you five, stranger," said Sloan as if it hurt to be winning. "Yo're sure forkin' bad cayuses today, huh?"

Morgan's grin was frigid. "Easy come; easy lost."

SLOAN'S SAIL-BOAT EARS seemed to stand out more prominently. That roll? "*Easy* come?" He smiled. "Without riskin' the hangman's knot?" he asked with an apology between the words.

"Oil business," said Morgan curtly. "Grab up land before the other fellow knows what's under the surface and— Raise you ten, *partner.*"

The outlaw caught the startled glances that shot between the killers. As expected, they tried to pump more information out of him. He shied from guarded questions.

"You think there's oil about San Adella?" Sloan asked bluntly.

"Let's play poker now. Talk business later, *sabe?* You're due to clean me if I mix the two."

The sun moved on. The shadow of the improvised table doubled in length and swung around from Sloan to Morgan, and cigarette stubs dotted the ground. Horses whinnied as if to warn that day was rapidly dying and the last of Sheriff Lackey's disappointed man hunters had already turned wearily for home.

Greed knows no clock and is food in itself. So Dingwell promptly vetoed Sloan's hint that they adjourn.

"Not afraid of moonlight?" asked Morgan smoothly.

"Chilly. Hungry an'—"

"Loser's choice," cut in the outlaw. "We play until one of us is broke." He looked at the eastern horizon where silver brightness heralded a rising moon. "I'll open her—for twenty dollars."

Morgan lost, lost, and lost again. With feigned moroseness he stared at his all—forty dollars. He staked it all. Only twice before could he have lost as honestly as he went broke. He got up, stretched, yawned, smiled.

"Luckier in *oil*," he drawled. His narrowed eyes were on the silver-washed arroyo wall; on the spot where Blue Hawk had scooped away a few handsful of loose soil to dig a more fitting grave. Directly below that spot, shimmering silver now, mud and muddy water then, these coyotes had buried his truest friends. But it was not only *them* his blood boiled against. Small fry killers was on their faces, in their voices. And as they'd served masters, so they'd serve him, vowed Morgan. Out of their cowardly, ugly mouths would come the names of those higher up.

"Play again, sometime? In San Adella?" asked Sloan, Nice to have the immaculate stranger around—when they needed almost four hundred dollars again. He was easily taken.

Morgan shook his head. "San Adella has seen the last of me. Sold out last night—rather than risk a shot in the back. Thirty thousand cash cachéd hereabouts. We're heading south. *Adios.*"

Dingwell was tense as a well stretched fence wire. Thirty thousand cash! And six solid hours of poker, dangerous bottom dealing, for less than four hundred!

"Headin' south *now?*" asked Dingwell listlessly.

"Now!" Morgan turned to go. "*Adios,* gents."

Sloan bounded to his feet when hoof-beats sounded. Dingwell gripped his arm.

"Wait! Let him get started!" He trembled with anxiety. "Thirty thousand—cachéd hereabouts. Lord!"

THEY WAITED LIKE caged, starved animals at a gate about to be lifted. Then, hoofbeats threatening to fade completely, they bolted for their horses, swung to leather, turned the animals' heads—and sat petrified by fears. No sound broke the satanic silence of The Devil's Playground; no living thing stirred in the ghastly light of the moon. The stranger had disappeared as suddenly as if winged and flown away.

"Didn't go far!" guessed Sloan. He spurred his horse south. "You an' yore damned 'let him git started!'"

Big staked hopes die hard. When at last Sloan surrendered, he could cheerfully have cut out Dingwell's heart.

"Let's get back to the card table," suggested Dingwell. "If we haven't blotted out his sign, we'll get him yet."

"If!" exploded Sloan. He headed back dejectedly, a seething cauldron of bitterness.

Dingwell, a length to the fore, suddenly jerked up his mount. He sat still as death, leaning slightly, peering into the arroyo. Not at the card table! At a great rock not more than twenty yards further north. Then like a ghost he slid oat of leather, snatched out his six gun and stepped forth.

But Sloan also saw the top of the black sombrero! He dragged the Winchester from saddle sheath. It was his boast that at a hundred yards he wouldn't miss a target large enough to be seen with the naked eye. Now he measured the black top piece, striving to hit as close as possible to the bottom of distinct dents that could not be far above the sweatband—and skull was above that! He fired, holding his breath as he squeezed the trigger.

The hat dropped out of sight. Dingwell's squeal of delight echoed in the night. He scrambled down the arroyo bank with Sloan starting another avalanche of stone and sand six feet away.

"Slick, wasn't he?" growled Dingwell caustically. "Rides south, doubles back and starts to dig. He—"

"Steady!" boomed a deadly voice behind the killers.

Dingwell froze, six gun in hand hanging at his side. Sloan, already cursing the all but useless Winchester held across his chest, stood still as the rock that supported his recent target. Neither of them dared turn their heads, yet both knew the voice *wasn't* that of their card victim.

"Let that six gun drop—*straight down*," snapped The Masked Rider. He gave fifteen seconds' grace. His Colt roared. Dingwell's gun was kicked out of unscathed fingers. "I don't give orders twice, *sabe?*"

Sloan got time to digest that. When the command came, he promptly dropped the Winchester, unbuckled his six gun and joined Dingwell in six backward paces.

"Turn around," clipped the black phantom.

The bewildered pair seemed anxious to please or anxious to see the possessor of this buzz-saw voice. Empty hands voluntarily hoisted above their heads, they wheeled slow and steady as the pivot men of lines of soldiers. They saw only black; shapeless, immobile black that suddenly sprang to life and advanced upon them while it assumed the proportions of a hooded, cloaked man.

THE MASKED RIDER walked between his prisoners as if they did not exist. He stopped to hurl the Winchester as far as his stalwart arm could, scooped up both six guns and went on to the rock, from behind which he quickly emerged—punctured black sombrero on his head.

"That—that ain't the hat of the *hombre* who played cards with us right here; not more'n twenty minutes ago?" stammered Sloan.

A sound, deep, bitter, growled, came from the black mask. "You'll *answer* questions. Not ask 'em!" rapped the outlaw. His gloved hand flung out toward the spot. "Move *there*."

Dingwell's suspicions turned his feet to ton weights. He let Sloan stand closest to the ribbon of water, but not because he wanted the black caballero to see them precisely as they had been that night.

Sloan, courage ebbing but not yet run dry, tried to plug the leak by recalling things he'd heard about the black phantom—principally that he'd never been known to harm an unarmed man. But The Masked Rider ripped out Sloan's plug and hopes by going within ten feet and cautiously laying down both prisoners' guns. He backed away again; twenty careful yards with his hands empty and outside the mantilla.

"Ever stood *there* before?" he demanded.

"N-not me," managed Dingwell.

"Not me," said Sloan. Ten feet to two guns! The outlaw's daring was proven fact. Yet he must know that he couldn't climb out of the arroyo before Sloan could scoop up those weapons and plug him—front or back!

"Never dug a hole *there?*"

"N-not us." Dingwell squeezed out.

"You didn't fill a hole—and drag a shovel over the fill; to make a channel for the muddy water?"

"N-not us."

The Masked Rider backed up to the friendly darkness of the arroyo's west wall. "You're not a pair of sneaking, yellow streaked liars and killers whom a man can't properly cuss?"

Dingwell's lips parted.

"N-not us!" mimicked the outlaw. His disgust all but clogged the words in his mouth. "You're just two honest, hardworking *hombres* who'd shy from wrong like a mustang from a locomotive? And as such, it's my painful duty to leave you as I found you—but with these orders. When I turn my back and start up this wall, you start *south*. One step north will take you closer to those guns—and trouble. *Sabe?*"

Sloan's astonishment was too profound to permit him to reply. But Dingwell, his strained heart swollen with thanks, drew his first whole breath.

"Sure! Sure! We want no trouble with—"

The outlaw turned. He took three steps in sand and gravel. His boots skidded. He went partly to his knees. Recovering quickly, he turned face about—to see both killer's hands mere inches from sandy gum butts. Even when Dingwell and Sloan were erect with weapons whipping up, the outlaw stood motionless.

"Don't!" he fired. "I purposely gave you a chance for your lives!"

SLOAN'S TEETH WERE bared by a snarl. "You'll get the Bunson's chance!" he rasped. He slammed out two shots. Twice the mantilla was visibly rent. Then from the folds two Colts spoke as one although neither killer could have honestly sworn they'd seen black gloved hands move.

Sloan spun around with a scream. For a moment he

swayed like a pole balanced on end, to fall heavily against Dingwell as his comrade's gun belched fire.

Dingwell's lead plowed into the arroyo's wall. Long before he saw the fan-shaped flame leap from the outlaw's hand, he knew that missing his target because of Sloan's push, was his own death warrant. He felt hot metal bite into his chest. As his legs caved in and he would begin to spin crazily, he tried to hold himself erect and go on slobbering pleas for the quarter he'd never granted to anyone.

The Masked Rider darted forward. He'd witnessed death's harvest too often to give a second glance to Sloan. Dropping to his knees, he rolled Dingwell over on his back, raised a closed eyelid and saw the eye itself turned far up so that only white showed.

"Trail's end, *hombre*," he said, not ungently. "Cashing in with a back-shooting charge against you? Or are you writing something decent on your last page?"

A convulsive shudder ran the length of Dingwell's ungainly body. There came a sinister rattle in his throat as he tried to clutch his wound. He lacked the strength to bring up either hand.

Always humble and compassionate in the presence of the grim reaper, the outlaw bored heavily on the growing crimson stain. "Talking? Naming the bosses—or keeping mum and leaving them behind—*laughing at you?*"

Dingwell coughed. The outlaw wiped red bubbles from the quivering lips. "I—I had it comin'. I should've—should've known—"

"The bosses' names," reminded The Masked Rider softly.

"Reverend Hill. Big Steve. G-Gar-den. An'—an' that—that badge totin', scissorin' son of—"

"Holtz?"

Dingwell went under the wire.

The outlaw stood as still as Sloan's stiffening body. He knew he'd profit nothing by waiting—and profit possibly less by moving. He was as certain that someone was close behind him as he was that twice more the twin Colts in his holsters had rubbed out menaces to decency and justice.

"Dead?" gritted the man behind. "Move an' you join him!"

The Masked Rider had heard the voice of Sheriff Lackey twice before. He dared to turn his hooded head and look into the business end of a poised rifle. "Dead," he agreed. "Not all *fair fights* pan out the same, *sabe?*"

Lackey's face remained blank. "You heard about Holtz an' Big Steve? You—"

"A habit of mine—*to hear things;* especially things that are going to be whitewashed by what you call law and justice."

"Both of which you'll sample *pronto!*" clipped Lackey. He tightened his grip on the rifle and closed in on the outlaw as if treading on eggs. "An' first dose is takin' off that mantilla an' hood—so's I can get news spreading all east of the Missouri as to who you really are."

THE OUTLAW REALIZED that once uncovered, his life would be a short one. He hesitated.

Lackey drew a bead on the outlaw's heart. "Drop that mantilla, bucko—or I'll *roll* you out of it, *sabe?*"

The Masked Rider tugged at the strings under his chin. The black cloak parted and began to slip from his broad shoulders. Then like a gale catches a sail and hurls it out stiff, so the outlaw's body twist and supple arms filled out the black cloth and threw it shield-like over rifle and Sheriff's head.

Instantly Lackey felt as if a giant grizzly had dropped from the skies and caught him in steel pawed embrace. Kick and tug and wrench as he would, he couldn't break the bear hug. Nor did he struggle long before he was grounded, gagged and securely bound, with strands of his own shirt.

There was no elixir in triple triumph for The Masked Rider. "No quarrel with *you*, Sheriff!" he said blankly. "If you get loose, it'll be health insurance for you to give me plenty elbow room. *Adios.*"

Like a mythical bat, the outlaw put on his mantilla and faded into the night.

CHAPTER XVI

DEATH RIDES FAST

DUSK FOUND A pall of gloom hanging over San Adella. Old timers shook their heads with misgiving. Things had come to a pretty pass when the deputy sheriff was accused of back shooting—and almost four score of men failed to find a lone outlaw!

Women, recalling the cutting down of Reverend Proctor Hill, reasoned that anything could now be expected—to speed the cowtown down the infamous trail of old. Men accustomed to passing Lackey's office with due respect, now sneered openly and wondered when the gates of iniquity would be opened wide. The lone defenders of law and order, the only folks with any hopes that it would survive, were men who had ridden in pursuit of the black outlaw.

They gathered in groups to theorize on the day's failure and future conduct.

But the man who took the lack of prisoner or corpse hardest was Bruce Garden. Now, looking out of his front window, he felt prickly spasms of fear. Reverend dead! Mescal and Quinn dead! The outlaw very much alive—and desperately interested in the passing of the old Bunsons.

"If he ever gets wind of me—"

Garden clipped uneasy thoughts. That rider tearing down the street was not just another returning man hunter! Every man in the dusty street seemed of the same opinion, for they flocked to the arrival's side even before he began to bellow.

"Sheriff Lackey wants a dozen men at Ransom's Springs. *Pronto!*"

A red-thatched veteran elbowed through the crowd. "What's up?"

"I found Lackey tied like a calf for brandin'. The Masked Rider did it; threw down on the sheriff when caught red-handed at killin' Ed Sloan an' Dingwell. Lackey's hell bent on the outlaw's sign right now. He'll get him sure— with help."

No call ever brought more volunteers. But the redhead picked the experienced men who had often hunted with the Sheriff and the round dozen thundered out of town in churned dust.

Bruce Garden gripped the window frame. His pulse was galloping. "Sloan. Dingwell. Dead!" he mumbled. Small regrets for their deaths. But how in God's name did the outlaw know whom to strike—and with only one of the original clique surviving, how difficult was it to guess *who'd be next?* "M-me!"

Then Garden saw something that both amazed and angered him. He flung up the sash, thrust out his head and shouted at the man sauntering across the street.

"Deputy Holtz! Hi, Holtz!"

The badge wearer was soon in the parlor, smiling and smoking. He continued both although he quickly saw that Garden was all on edge.

"Why in hell haven't you started for the Jackson's?" asked Garden savagely.

"Got to be like a train? On time? What difference does half an hour or so make?" He laughed his deadly way. "Fact is I was just goin' for my horse—now that I think the crowds come home; now that I know Lackey an' that handful won't be anywhere's near the Jackson spread."

"Get going then! And get back here and get that damned Indian out of my cellar. Lackey knows Sloan and Dingwell did odd jobs for me. He might come here. I don't want the sheriff hearing things under the kitchen floor—and asking me questions."

HOLTZ LAUGHED AGAIN. He opened the bottom button of his vest and fingered black cloth. "Anything goes— as long as the hullabaloo lasts. Blame everything on The Masked Rider! If I hit a snag at Jackson's, I'll leave this trade mark when I hightail. If I don't use it there, I *will* when I beef your Indian behind Hilcox's barn."

"If The Masked Rider—"

"That black coyote don't worry me none! Knowin' some prayers, I'd say 'em and only ask that I could meet the skunk—gun play or just plain 'no holds barred.'"

Holtz stormed out. Garden tried to smile. He felt half fortunate in having even the temporary services of the deputy. He envied the fellow's nerve and courage—and went to bolster his own from a bottle in the kitchen cupboard.

Amber liquor gurgled into a short glass. It stopped abruptly. Garden was like a man instantly turned to stone. Then his eyes moved sidewise and a swift glance over his shoulder sat his every nerve to twitching. Quaking fingers put the bottle down. He turned around with trip hammers of fright pounding at his temples.

"You!" he gasped.

"Me!" cut through the black hood.

Something happened to Garden. Perhaps the voice, although razor-edged, broke the strangle hold the fearful black costume had gained; perhaps memory of the gun, handy on the cupboard shelf, opened courage's spigot within him. Garden only knew that suddenly the thing he had always dreaded—facing this black justice—had lost all its potency and he defied it.

"What do you want here?" Garden demanded angrily.

"Nothing—for myself. But others are entitled to everything you've got; including your life, and the pity of it is that none of it will do them any good."

"There's a court—"

"But your breed is too smart for that kind of justice!"

"So you appoint yourself the executioner of unarmed men, and without a shadow of *proof* that they're guilty of anything, you—"

Garden's eloquence died. His face went pasty white. For a second he was foolhardy enough to hope the outlaw had missed that muffled cry. But again it came—up through the floorboards.

"*Senor! Senor!* Blue Hawk. In cellar!"

The outlaw did not move. Fire flashed in the narrowed eyes behind the black hood. "Without a shadow of proof that they're guilty of *anything!*" he snapped.

"He—"

"Get him out!"

"A sneak thief I meant to turn over to Sheriff Lackey when—"

"Get him out!"

Blue Hawk was first up the weak wooden ladder, tortured flesh and bone forgotten, mud upon his skin and clothes ignored—but wide awake to the fact that a connection between him and the master must not even be suspected.

"Gracias, senor! This dog and Deputy Holtz would kill me for no true reason, *sabe?* Even now Holtz rides to Jackson ranch—to kill even *women, senor!"*

"He's mad!" shrilled Garden. "He doesn't know what he's talking about."

The Masked Rider's attention was on the scout. *"Si, senor,"* said the Indian in anguish. "Ten, mebbe fifteen minutes Holtz is gone. The women—the *Bunson* women…" He broke off, misinterpreting the outlaw's silence and lack of action as indecision. Then on a shelf beside the stove he saw his knife and gun. "Go, *senor! Madre de Dios* will get you there in time. I guard this dog with my life. He belongs to you later—unless I lose the grip and cut him to pieces before…."

Garden had not watched for opportunity and was not prepared to seize it. *Now,* with the Indian's back toward him and the black apparition reaching for the door, Garden darted for the cupboard. His hand flashed for the inch of gun butt in sight and he crowded an hour's prayer into one mumbled word.

Blue Hawk pivoted. He saw the gun snatched from the shelf. Never did he move swifter—to accomplish two things simultaneously. His boot crashed against the door. The stout wood would rob a bullet of velocity—if not stop it entirely. The master would not suffer the sting of lead. Nor would *he!* For as Garden frantically tried to pump bullets, the slender dagger swished from the Indian's hand, spun through space at bullet speed and struck Garden's chest true as an arrow.

"Dog!" snapped Blue Hawk. His six gun was ready now, but he held fire, knowing that Garden's single shot was the result of convulsive pain and not desire.

And Blue Hawk deemed it extremely wise to clear out of his erstwhile prison—and San Adella. He ran smiling in his cold way. It was good to know that the *senor* rode a black stallion whose speed and stamina had no equal. God grant he make the Jackson spread before Deputy Holtz, prayed Blue Hawk.

"Then? Puff! We are gone from this cursed place forever, our work it is finished and the *senor* much pleased that he owes less to the Bunson women."

The Indian reached the front street. Some men were running towards Garden's house; others stood and gaped. Two punchers accosted Blue Hawk.

"You hear a shot?"

The scout shook his head and looked surprised. "No, *senors*. I hear a dog's bark. Shot? No, *senors*. No shot."

CHAPTER XVII

HAND TO HAND

A S A MAN lives, so does he die. All his life Bruce
Garden had schemed to trick and cheat and injure.
He clung to his standard even when he knew that every
heart tick pumped away more of his life's fluid and brought
him that much closer to mortal's end.

There was an eight foot red trail behind him when he
flattened out on the floor, glad that men had burst into the
room. He felt himself being lifted, then stretched out on
the horsehair settee, and he tested his tongue and vocal
cords as if afraid they were already as useless as his eyes and
limbs. But he *could* talk; in whispers just loud enough—to
send somebody else to their grave! "Masked— Masked
Rider," he faltered.

"Knifed you?" asked a gnarled cowman. "Sure? It ain't
his style to *stick, sabe?* Why should he? Lightnin' fast with
Colts an'—"

"M-masked Rider," insisted Garden. "And—and now—
riding to—to clean out—the Jacksons. *All* of them."

"Woman killer?" The veteran's face flushed with angry
red.

Garden trembled. For him, it was getting darker and
colder. He thought of Holtz. Wanted part of the profits,
did he? Then he was certainly entitled to a share of the
losses. Bruce battled for another few breaths.

"Holtz. *Murdered* Big Steve. Holtz. In—in cahoots
with—with Masked Rider. They've—gone to Jackson's
together to...."

Satan's scissors clipped the mastermind's thread of life.

"Reckon we ought to ride an' find out whether he's just loco or not?" the veteran asked no one in particular.

A shout of assent went up. "Somebody ride to Ransom's Springs, find Sheriff Lackey an' fetch him to Jackson's," suggested one man. "Everything legal; no kick-back, that way."

The self-appointed leader stepped outside the front door and silenced the milling crowd. "Most of you rode all day lookin' for a black buzzard who couldn't be found. How many ridin' *now*—when we *know* where he's at?"

The answer came in a bolting for horses. The veteran smiled. "Get him this time—or he can't be got!"

Racing the clock as if his own existence depended on winning, The Masked Rider streaked through the night over dangerous trails where most riders would have hesitated to trot. He had been over this route before; to warn the Jacksons of Matt Frost's coming. He never took the longest way to any destination twice. Now he cut away from the beaten trail, plunged into such rock-strewn territory that had the stallion been any other animal, it must have slowed and faltered. But the sterling black galloped on undaunted; as if it knew that the lives of dear friends were at stake.

THE OUTLAW USED neither quirt, rowel nor voice. He knew the black would grind away the miles without being driven. Mile on mile went beneath the flying hoofs, the outlaw riding tight-mouthed, grim-eyed and hoping that when again their trails converged, he would sight the deputy.

Lights suddenly loomed ahead; distant lights no larger than the specks of fire-flies. The outlaw's jaws squared and he clenched teeth against the pricks of disappointing silence. Did it mean Holtz had already arrived, finished his job and retreated? The outlaw's heart stood still as he closed in on the snug house nestled in cottonwoods close to the side of the mesa. Then he saw what must ever remain as his most welcomed sight—a saddled horse standing wearily behind a wagon shed.

The outlaw risked riding to a stocked wood house. It was closer to the dwelling.

But there was no time to lose. The black caballero took only the few seconds required to set a pail of water before his stallion—for there was a freshly-filled pail resting on the ground. He reasoned that somebody had been in the act of carrying that water, but seeing the deputy coming on the prod, had set it down and made in all haste for the ranch house.

Apiece with the night itself, The Masked Rider eased silently through the darkness toward the house. Through a window he heard the low, full-throated voice of a woman:

"When Stella came in, Thad went out and got that whip. He was going to ride out to you and give you a dose of it— the same as you gave her!"

"Then why didn't he ride?" came the deputy's leering tone.

"We heard you coming—"

The reason why Thad Jackson was not at this moment brandishing the whip became instantly clear to The Masked Rider. A wisp of odor issued from the inside, on an eddying current. It was the acrid fumes of six-gun smoke. For a moment he feared that Thad had been killed in gunplay. But Holtz's next words proved otherwise.

"As for *you*, you've got more coming to yore hide," the

deputy snarled. This must have been directed at Stella. "An' what's more," the snap of a whip sounded, "yore Thad hero is goin' to stan' by an' watch you take it!"

The Masked Rider flew catlike to the front of the house. The sound of the opening of the door was drowned to the ears of those within by the commotion Holtz had started. There was a shriek, a crackling of a lash, and then the menace of a deadly voice over all.

"Hold it!"

At the same instant the muzzle of a gun jabbed cruelly into the spine of the deputy. The Masked Rider had flown across the narrow room, shouldered Thad Jackson aside, and with a free hand pulled Thad's frantic wife out of the way. Stella stood in a corner courageously and contemptuously facing the lustful deputy, who had already left several quickly delivered welts on her. The lash at this moment was coiled in mid-air. It stopped there, dead still.

WITH TWO FLICKS of his free wrist, the hooded spectre emptied the deputy's holsters and tossed the two guns on the nearby table. Holstering his own gun, he then reached up and tore the whip out of Holtz's grip.

For a moment it had seemed that heavily pent-up cries of relief were about to burst from the two women. But the grabbing of the whip stifled all prospects of sound, save that from the masked commander. Even Thad Jackson, nursing a bullet-torn and bleeding right hand, drew himself up along a wall and uttered not a word. All in the room sensed that swift, volcanic drama was on the instant of making, and in such tense moments there is neither time nor space for words.

The Masked Rider's eyes darted behind the slits of the hood. On the floor, kicked under a small shelf, lay Jackson's gun. Stella still held to her corner. More terror was now creeping into her eyes than had been there when the cruel lash was cutting into her.

The voice that issued from beneath the hood of black was stark cold and blade sharp, like the bluish steel edge of a razor slicing the air.

"There are two sides to an argument, and there are two ends to a whip," his words slashed sharply across the stone silence of the room. "You know only one, Holtz. You must get acquainted with both. When the other fellow holds the handle, the whip feels like this—"

The black-cloaked arm circled in a swift double arc, pivoting at shoulder and at elbow. A snaky mesh of plaited rawhide whined hissingly through the air. A fast forward snap of a dark wrist added a final burst of impetus, and then the heavy leather made momentary traction against human flesh at neck and cheek. There was a stinging, cruel crackle. And even as a whitened streak quickly grew red and sprouted blood, The Masked Rider once again pivoted separate arcs from shoulder and elbow and again cut flesh with cruel leather.

But fear had no place on the face of Deputy Holtz. The sting of the biting lash brought with its pain and blood, only white-hot rage to the face of the deputy.

"You white-livered, masked mange," be bit out between clenched teeth, "hiding behind yore two guns when you do a thing like that! Swingin' on a man who—"

"Not a *man*," corrected The Masked Rider. "There's no word made to fit what you are. Seems to me you were swinging this same thing on a woman—not more than ten seconds ago."

A third and a fourth time the lash drew blood, and one stroke tore the deputy's shirt at the shoulder.

"I'll tear you apart with my naked hands!" the deputy raged. "Throw yore guns away, you—"

"Don't worry about my guns," the hooded man cut in, throwing aside the bloody lash. "They'll stay where they are as long as you don't grab up a shooter."

A light of pleased amazement shot through the features of the burly Holtz. With the gleam of a near maniac in his eyes, he clenched his fists and bore down and into The Masked Rider.

There came the sound of crunched bone. The deputy's doubled fists came up, not out, and his head snapped back. When the black Caballero's right fist came away, Holtz's nose was plastered back against the deputy's face, a red, bloody, sickening blob of flesh and gristle.

SURPRISE AND PAIN wrote themselves on the big man's face, beside the ruined nose, and with a snarl of bubbling rage he tore once more into his cloaked antagonist. His body was bent forward at the waist, his weight was fairly off the floor as he flew at the hated outlaw. It might have been the pain, it might have been the red rage blinding him, but Holtz failed to keep his timing as the outlaw sidestepped, pivoted at the hip, and swung with the left.

Crackling, splintering, blistering sounds came, all wrapped in one. One tooth hung suspended through the upper lip. The remainder of the teeth from the fore part of his mouth, Deputy Holtz coughed and spat upon the floor while his knees wobbled, his head lolled, and he dropped in a heap face forward.

"Listen!"

It was Thad Jackson's alarmed voice. Faintly, from a great

distance, came the sound of thudding hoofs against hard rock. Many hoofs. They formed the sound-pattern of many drums that kept a rolling crescendo of rhythm that clacked with the menace of doom.

"You must ride!" Stella Holtz suddenly whirled in fright from her corner and shrieked to the outlaw. "Quick—the posse!"

The Masked Rider glared at the form on the floor. "Unfinished business, here," he pointed down.

He raced to a window and looked out, listened.

"They're almost here," he said. "I'd have to shoot some of them down, to get away. Look—Thad! You run out and grab your horse. Tell them I just made my getaway from here—steer them off. You, Mrs. Holtz, start attending to your husband. I'll hide some place—"

"Quick, follow me," cried Loretta Jackson.

The Masked Rider darted after her, to the rear as Thad Jackson retrieved his own gun, holstered it, and rushed outside, his bleeding right hand held rigid in the firm grip of the left. Loretta motioned the outlaw to a closet. A glance told the hooded man that here was no safety. He ran out the rear, looked up. One look was enough. He raised himself to a window sill, leaped, caught a sloping eave. Swinging two times, and then a third, he hurtled his body upward through space and caught a ledge with an instep. A mighty tug, and he rolled over, out of sight. Bent low, he soft-footed across the roof and padded himself tightly into an angled crevice that formed a gabled slope with a two-foot square of level footing.

The thunder of flying hoofs shook the Jackson ranch. Horses skidded to a halt as Thad Jackson came galloping up to meet the posse.

"Quick, get 'em!" came Thad's voice, forced with excitement.

The horsemen had already fanned side-wise, encircling the ranch house in their ring.

"Where is he?" Sheriff Lackey shot the question, skidding up to Thad, his horse lathering and rearing.

Thad motioned with the elbow of his left hand. "The sounds trailed off over that way. He came in, got the drop on us, and beat up Holtz. Yore deputy is *ruined!*"

"Beat up Holtz?" Half a dozen voices repeated it, with utter incredulity.

Sheriff Lackey knit his forehead and bored Thad Jackson through with keen, suspicious eyes. "Holtz ain't a man easily beaten up," he said, "an' fists ain't The Masked Rider's partic'lar style o' ruining folks. Guess I better take a look."

THAD'S THROAT LUMPED. The outlaw was not in sight, in the house, but if Deputy Holtz had already come to, he'd puncture Thad's plans. However, there was the chance that Holtz wasn't yet conscious, and if he was, that he couldn't do much talking through a mouth that looked like a wild bronc had been busted on it. The best thing was to brazen it through.

"Yo're wastin' time," shouted Thad, as the sheriff dismounted, "but go ahead an' grab a look. Make it snappy."

Several others dismounted and raced inside with the sheriff. Thad moved over toward the window and bent low to look in. Stella was seated on the floor, applying a damp cloth to her husband's face. Loretta was just coming in from the kitchen with a pan of water. The deputy was at the moment rolling over on an elbow. His eyes opened. Thad detected a momentary impulse to speak—but just then the deputy sank back, eyes closed, and he breathed heavily.

Thad smiled. He understood. Holtz had come to, fully, but seeing all these men around him he'd instantly decided that now was no time to speak. Later, he could make up a yarn to save his face—what there was left of it; now, there'd be only mortification.

Thad was about to cry out again, to call the men for the chase, but Loretta waved him to silence.

"How come?" Lackey asked, and the voice carried up to the outlaw on the roof.

"The Masked Rider," declared Loretta, firmly.

The Masked Rider wondered, pasted up there, silent, grim, in his nook of impending death. Loretta was speaking slowly. No attempt to rush them out for pursuit, on her part.

Lackey glanced at the guns on the table. "The outlaw chose *fists?*" Something strange seemed to creep into his voice. "And Thad, out there, is in a big rush to git 'im?" A moment of silence, and then, "Say—*who* pinked Thad's hand?"

"Fools, fools, all of you!" Loretta cried out, suddenly. "You think Thad wants you to catch The Masked Rider?" She stopped a moment, to laugh at them. "Thad would shoot his other hand off, first, himself! It was this slimy snake, here, who shot him. Look at Stella. Why don't you ask who did that? This slimy snake did! And look at *him*. His cheek, his neck. The Masked Rider did that—he pulled the whip out of your deputy's hand and gave him a dose of his own medicine. And when the snake came at him, he threw away the whip and finished him with his hands. He came here to murder us, all of us!"

The possemen made no answer. The outlaw held his

breath. What could Loretta have in mind, to save him? Again her voice reached the crevice in the roof.

"Thad's leading you away from The Masked Rider! And I—I'm keeping you here, till the outlaw gets a start on you that you couldn't make up on him. We'd see you in hell first, before we—any of us—would point out the way he went! He wanted to shoot it out with this snake, but your deputy was out cold. He wouldn't shoot at him there, on the floor; he wanted to wait till a fair gunfight could come off. But then we heard your posse. He rushed out of here, saying that if he didn't hurry he might have to shoot at some of you to get away—and he didn't want the blood of innocent men on his hands, even though they rode with blood in their eyes after him, to bring him back dead! That's the man *he* is—a *man, every inch a man!* Now go get him, if you can—he's got all the start he needs on you now."

More silence. Then, again Loretta's voice:

"WELL, WHY DON'T you go after him? No outlaw ever escapes San Adella justice, isn't that so? Or are you blind fools waiting around to get up courage to give three cheers for The Masked Rider and a length of rope for this henchman of the devil?"

"We heard Holtz was playin' in cahoots with The Masked Rider," came from Lackey. "Isn't that right, men?"

There came a momentary burst of harsh laughter from Stella, cut short by Loretta's imperious tones.

"Then what more do you need? If he's in with The Masked Rider, and you want The Masked Rider dead or alive, then you must have this one too, mustn't you? What are you waiting for? I'll get you a rope! We're only trying to bring him to, enough, so that he will know the feel of it around his neck!"

The small room had crowded with men. All the posse had entered, intent on a view of the incredible—Deputy Holtz disarmed and mashed to a pulp by a man's two hands. If the possemen had had more patience and investigated the grounds first, they might have discovered the strange black stallion and suspected the presence of their quarry. As it was, they were too late. For suddenly there came the clatter of flying hoofs making off on a diagonal from the direction of the woodshed.

Startled, the men looked up. At the window they saw Thad, a grim smile playing about his pained lips as he held his wounded hand. His grin, through the pain, seemed to mock them.

"The Masked Rider—" a posseman came to life. "He's gettin' away!"

"After '*im!*" shouted the sheriff.

Just then Holtz opened his eyes. "Quick," he said. "He was hidin' in the woodshed—he can't be far."

The room was already emptied of possemen, except for Sheriff Lackey. In his hands there appeared suddenly a pair of steel cuffs. "We'll have to make sure *you* don't get far," he said, clamping them on the deputy's wrists. "Guard him," he called at the window, to Thad. "We don't want *yore* help trailin' The Masked Rider!" He ran out of the room, and a minute later the hoofs under him pounded into distance after his posse.

From his perch on the roof, The Masked Rider had seen the play. Blue Hawk, once again, to the rescue. The Indian had padded softly to the shed, seen the stallion. Leaving it there, he had gone back to his sorrel and pounded noisily away into the night.

The outlaw allowed minutes to pass. From below came voices.

"Didn't you see him leave?" asked Stella.

"No," answered Thad. "He must've slipped off and sneaked around to the shed when he saw that all the posse was in the house."

The outlaw smiled. He wanted them to think just so. He waited more minutes, and while their voices were raised he noiselessly lowered himself to the ground. Then, once again, he was letting himself into the house.

"Look!" It was Loretta, staring unbelievingly at him.

"Easy, easy," the outlaw's tone was calm. "I shook them and circled back. There was some unfinished business, here." He threw slitted eyes at the manacled deputy.

UNCONCERNEDLY, THE OUTLAW stepped to Holtz and fingered the handcuffs.

"Just hold still," he said, softly. "We'll burn them off." He produced a six-gun. Holtz held his hands extended before him. The outlaw first padded rags under the steel, to soften the impact of steel dragging on flesh when the bullet would hit. Then he carefully furrowed three successive shots along each lock, each bullet plowing slightly deeper than the preceding. In that way the cuffs came off with no injury whatever to the deputy's wrists.

"Just hold that seat another minute," ordered the outlaw, proceeding to reload. "Come along with me," he added, dropping the deputy's guns into their holsters, after refilling an empty chamber in one of them. "This isn't for women's eyes."

"No!" shouted Stella, horrified. "He—he can get anybody, *that* way, with guns!"

The Masked Rider, stopping behind the deputy at the threshold, answered calmly over a shoulder. "That requires a bit more proof than he's given so far," he said.

Outside, proceeding to the gate, the outlaw offered the deputy the choice: "Name your paces. And scissor it, if you like. That seems your style. I'll try it, too."

"Ten," gritted the deputy, an unholy gleam lighting his eyes in the darkness.

Visibility was clear enough at ten paces.

"No count," declared the outlaw. "Make the first move."

Their hands were hip-high. The deputy did not answer. His nerve might have been shaken by the coolness of this hooded man who was inviting himself to slaughter. Holtz's hands shot down.

Six-guns flamed in darkness. Ten explosions, one on top of the other. Then The Masked Rider's six-guns were already sliding back into black holsters, as the unfired weapons of the deputy slithered to the ground.

Thad Jackson raced to head the outlaw off at the wood-shed, but The Masked Rider, fleet as wind, was already mounted.

"No—no—you can't go, like this!" Thad shouted. "Loretta, Stella—they want—"

"I want—too—" declared the outlaw, softly. "Good-bye and good luck—to you and to them."

Hours later came the cry of the mountain lion. The Masked Rider answered. He straightened his shoulders. For the first time in a long time they had drooped—riding away from the two girls, with not even a farewell. It had been easier, that way.

OBITUARY

H E WAS NOT feeling well. He was alone in his cabin,
working. He rose from his typewriter—perhaps to
get a drink of water, as the authorities later believed. That
was Saturday night. On Monday morning they broke
into the small cabin. All the lights still were lit. Half way
between his chair and the water he had risen for, they
found on the floor the dead body of William H. Stueber.

In the typewriter was page 126 of the Masked Rider
novel he was writing. Beside the typewriter was a pencilled
synopsis of the remainder of the story. This novel, to be
completed by strange hands, will appear next month in
the April issue of *The Masked Rider* magazine—the post-
humous work of one of the squarest men and straightest
characters it has ever been the privilege and honor of the
publisher to call a personal friend. Stueber was a man, a
hard man, with a heart of gold weakened by a great uphill
and bitter struggle against a swarm of handicaps crowded
into only thirty-seven years. His life earned him the admiration and the deep respect that his death brings at this
time to expression.

IN MEMORIAM:
A MAN'S MAN, A FRIEND

"I DON'T CARE what they do with my bones. I'll be dead then, when I can't take care of them myself." We once heard him make that remark.

His remains deserve a place of honor in the living memory of men of honor. He died before completing the novel under his name in this issue. That was finished for him. But his high place of honor he carved completely, himself. There he will rest, in the peace of the honorable dead.

WILLIAM H. STUEBER

www.ingramcontent.com/pod-product-compliance
Lightning Source LLC
Chambersburg PA
CBHW030926020726
47498CB00001B/131